Dear Reader,

Welcome to Montana. Our first stop is Big Sky, deep in the Gallatin Canyon, where my family had a cabin when I was a girl. I know the canyon well, so I'm happy to be your guide in *Cardwell Ranch Trespasser*. Watch out for the new guest at the ranch, though. There's just something about her I don't trust.

Our second stop is another part of Montana close to my heart. We'll be chasing rustlers with Hud Savage's cousin as we ride through the center of Montana and the wild country around it. What's a female stock detective doing breaking a charming cattle rustler out of prison, you ask? It's a *Big Sky Standoff*.

I hope you enjoy this trip through Montana. I'm so happy to be able to share with you a little of the state I love. Hope you'll want to come back soon.

B.J.

ABOUT THE AUTHOR

USA TODAY bestselling author B.J. Daniels wrote her first book after a career as an award-winning newspaper journalist and author of thirty-seven published short stories. That first book, *Odd Man Out,* received a four-and-a-half-star review from *RT Book Reviews* and went on to be nominated for Best Intrigue that year. Since then, she has won numerous awards, including a career achievement award for romantic suspense and many nominations and awards for best book.

Daniels lives in Montana with her husband, Parker, and two springer spaniels, Spot and Jem. When she isn't writing, she snowboards, camps, boats and plays tennis. Daniels is a member of Mystery Writers of America, Sisters in Crime, International Thriller Writers, Kiss of Death and Romance Writers of America.

To contact her, write to B.J. Daniels, P.O. Box 1173, Malta, MT 59538, or email her at bjdaniels@mtintouch.net. Check out her website, www.bjdaniels.com.

Books by B.J. Daniels

HARLEQUIN INTRIGUE

*Whitehorse, Montana
‡Whitehorse, Montana: The Corbetts
**Whitehorse, Montana: Winchester Ranch
‡‡Whitehorse, Montana: Winchester Ranch Reloaded
†Whitehorse, Montana: Chisholm Cattle Company

Other titles by this author available in ebook format.

USA TODAY Bestselling Author

B.J. Daniels

CARDWELL RANCH TRESPASSER
& BIG SKY STANDOFF

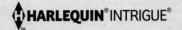

HARLEQUIN® INTRIGUE®

ISBN-13: 978-0-373-83793-9

CARDWELL RANCH TRESPASSER &
BIG SKY STANDOFF

Copyright © 2013 by Harlequin Books S.A.

The publisher acknowledges the
copyright holders of the individual works,
as follows:

CARDWELL RANCH TRESPASSER
Copyright © 2013 by Barbara Heinlein

BIG SKY STANDOFF
Copyright © 2007 by Barbara Heinlein

Recycling programs
for this product may
not exist in your area.

Printed in U.S.A.

HARLEQUIN®
www.Harlequin.com

CONTENTS

This book is dedicated to my editor, Denise Zaza, and all the readers who didn't want to leave the "canyon" and Cardwell Ranch. Thanks for talking me into this.

CARDWELL RANCH TRESPASSER

CHAPTER ONE

JUST INSIDE THE door, she stopped to take a look around the apartment to make sure she hadn't forgotten anything. This place, like all the others she'd lived in, held no special sentimental value for her. Neither would the next one, she thought. She'd learned a long time ago not to get too attached to anything.

The knock on the other side of the door startled her. She froze, careful not to make a sound. The building super, Mr. McNally, again, wanting the back rent? She should have left earlier.

Another knock. She thought about waiting him out, but her taxi was already downstairs. She would have to talk her way out of the building. It wasn't as if this was the first time she'd found herself in a spot like this.

She opened the door, ready to do whatever it took to reach her taxi.

It wasn't Mr. McNally.

A courier stood holding a manila envelope, a clipboard and a pen.

"Dee Anna Justice?" he asked.

She looked from him to the envelope in his hand. It looked legal. Maybe some rich uncle had died and left Dee Anna a fortune.

"Yes?"

He glanced past her into the empty apartment. She'd

sold all the furniture and anything else that wasn't nailed down. Seeing him judging her living conditions, she pulled the door closed behind her. He didn't know her. How dare he? He had no idea what kind of woman she was, and he certainly wasn't going to judge her by the mess she'd left in the apartment.

She cocked a brow at him, waiting.

"I need to see some identification," he said.

Of course he did. It was all she could do not to smile. Well, sneer, as she produced a driver's license in the name of Dee Anna Justice. She'd known where to get a fake ID since she was fourteen.

He shifted on his feet and finally held the pen out to her and showed her where to sign.

She wrote *Dee Anna Justice* the way she'd seen her former roommate do it dozens of times, and held out her hand impatiently for the envelope, hoping there was money inside. She was due for some good news. Otherwise the envelope and its contents would end up with the rest of the trash inside the apartment.

"Thanks a lot," she said sarcastically, as the courier finally handed it over. She was anxious to rip into it right there, but she really needed to get out of here.

It wasn't until she was in the backseat of the cab, headed for the train, that she finally tore open the envelope and pulled out the contents. At first she was a little disappointed. There was only a single one-page letter inside.

As she read the letter through, though, she began to laugh. No rich uncle had died. But it was almost as good. Apparently Dee Anna had a cousin who lived on a ranch in Montana. She ran her finger over the telephone number. According to the letter, all she had to do was call and she would be on her way to Montana. With a sob story, she figured she could get her "cousin" to foot most if not all of her expenses.

She had the cabdriver stop so she could buy a cell phone in the name of Dee Anna Justice. After she made her purchase she instructed the driver to take her to the airport, where she bought a first-class ticket. She couldn't wait to get to Montana and meet her cousin Dana Cardwell.

CHAPTER TWO

"You're never going to believe this."

Hilde Jacobson looked up from behind the counter at Needles and Pins, her sewing shop at Big Sky, Montana, and smiled as her best friend came rushing in, face flushed, dark eyes bright. Her dark hair was pulled back, and she even had on earrings and makeup.

"You escaped?" Hilde said. "I don't believe it." Dana didn't get out much since the birth of her twin boys last fall. Now she had her hands full with four children, all under the age of six.

Her friend dropped a packet of what appeared to be old letters on the counter. "I have family I didn't know I had," she said.

Hilde had to laugh. It wasn't that long ago that Dana was at odds with her siblings over the ranch. *Family* had been a word that had set her off in an entirely different direction than happy excitement.

Last year she'd reunited with her siblings. Her sister, Stacy, and baby daughter, Ella; and brother Jordan and his wife, Deputy Marshal Liza Turner Cardwell, were now all living here in Big Sky. Her other brother, Clay, was still in California helping make movies.

"A cousin is on her way to Montana," Dana announced. "We have to pick her up at the airport."

"We?" Hilde asked, looking out the window at the

Suburban parked at the curb. Normally the car seats were full and either Dana's husband, Hud, or Stacy would now be wrestling a stroller from the back.

"Tell me you'll go with me. I can't do this alone."

"Because you're so shy," Hilde joked.

"I'm serious. I'm meeting a cousin who is a complete stranger. I need you there for moral support and to kick me if I say something stupid."

"Why would you say something stupid?"

Dana leaned in closer and, although there was just the two of them in the shop, whispered, "This branch of the family comes with quite the sordid story."

"How sordid?" Hilde asked, intrigued but at the same time worried. Who had Dana invited to the ranch?

"I was going through some of my mother's things when I found these," Dana said, picking up the letters she'd plunked down on the counter and turning them in her fingers.

"That sounds positive," Hilde said, "you going through your mother's things." Mary Justice Cardwell had died nearly six years ago. Because it had been so unexpected and because it had hit Dana so hard, she hadn't been able to go through her mother's things— let alone get rid of anything. Not to mention the fact that her siblings had tried to force her to sell the ranch after their mother's death because Mary's most recent will had gone missing for a while.

"About time I dealt with her things, wouldn't you say?" Dana asked with a sad smile.

"So you found something in one of these letters?" Hilde asked, getting her friend back on track.

Dana brightened. "A family *secret!*"

Hilde laughed. "It must be on the Cardwell side of the family. Do tell."

"Actually, that is what's so shocking. It's on the *Justice* side." Climbing up on a stool at the counter, her friend pulled out one of the letters. "My mother had a brother named Walter who I knew nothing about. Apparently he left home at seventeen and married some woman of ill repute, and my grandparents disinherited him and refused to have his name spoken again."

"*Seriously?* That is so medieval," she said, stepping around the counter so she could read over Dana's shoulder.

"This is a letter from him asking for their forgiveness."

"Did they forgive him?"

"Apparently not. Otherwise, wouldn't I have known about him?"

"So you tracked him down on the internet and found out you have a cousin and now she is on her way to Montana."

"Walter died, but he left behind a family. I found one cousin, but there are apparently several others on that side of the family. Isn't that amazing?"

"Amazing that you were able to find this cousin you know nothing about." Hilde couldn't imagine doing such a thing—let alone inviting this stranger to come visit—and said as much.

"It's not like she's a *complete* stranger. She's my *cousin*. You know, since I had my own children, I realize how important family is. I want my kids to know all of their family."

"Right," Hilde said, thinking of the six years Dana had been at odds with her siblings. She'd missed them a lot more than she suspected they'd missed her. "I'm sure it will be fine."

Dana laughed. "If you're so worried, then you absolutely must come to the airport with me to pick her up."

"How did you get out alone?" Hilde asked, glancing toward the street and the empty Suburban again.

"Stacy is babysitting the twins, and Hud has Mary and Hank," Dana said, still sounding breathless. It was great to see her so happy.

"How are you holding up?" Hilde asked. "You must be worn out."

Hilde babysat occasionally, but with Stacy, Jordan and Liza around, and Hud with a flexible schedule, Dana had been able to recruit help—until lately. Jordan and Liza were building their house on the ranch and Stacy had a part-time job at Needles and Pins and another one working as a part-time nanny in Bozeman. Mary was almost five and Hank nearly six. The twins were seven months.

"I'm fine, but I am looking forward to some adult conversation," Dana admitted. "With Stacy spending more time in Bozeman, I hardly ever see her. Jordan and Liza are almost finished with their house, but Jordan has also been busy with the ranch, and Liza is still working as a deputy."

"And I haven't been around much," Hilde added, seeing where this was going. "I'm sorry."

"We knew expanding the shop was going to be time-consuming," Dana said. "I'm not blaming you. But it is one reason I'm so excited my cousin is coming. Her name is Dee Anna Justice. She's just a little younger than me—and guess what?" Dana didn't give Hilde a chance to guess. "She didn't know about us, either.

I can't wait to find out what my uncle Walter and the woman he married were like. You know there is more to the story."

"I'm sure there is, but let's not ask her as she gets off the plane, all right?"

Dana laughed. "You know me so well. That's why you have to come along. Dee Anna is in between jobs, so that's good. There was no reason she couldn't come and stay for a while. I offered to help pay her way since she is out of work. I couldn't ask her to come all the way from New York City to the wilds of Montana without helping her."

"Of course not," Hilde said, trying to tamp down her concern. She was a natural worrier, though—unlike Dana. It was amazing that they'd become such close friends. Hilde thought things out before she acted. Dana, who wasn't afraid of anything, jumped right in feetfirst without a second thought. Not to mention her insatiable curiosity. Both her impulsiveness and her curiosity had gotten Dana into trouble, so it was good her husband was the local marshal.

For so long Dana had had the entire responsibility of running Cardwell Ranch on her shoulders. Not that she couldn't handle it and two kids. But now with the twins, it was good that Jordan was taking over more of the actual day-to-day operations. Dana could really start to enjoy her family.

"I'll get Ronnie to come in," Hilde said. "She won't mind watching the shop while I'm gone with you to pick up your cousin."

"I have another favor," Dana said, and looked sheepish. "Please say you'll help show my cousin a good time while she's here. Being from New York City, she'll be bored to tears hanging around the ranch with me and four little kids."

"How long is she staying?" Hilde asked.

Dana shrugged. "As long as she wants to, I guess."

Hilde wondered if it was wise to leave something like this open-ended, but she kept her concerns to herself. It was good to see Dana so excited and getting a break from the kids that she said, "Don't worry, you can count on me, but I'm sure your cousin will love being on the ranch. Did she say whether or not she rides?"

"She's a true city girl, but Hud can teach anyone to ride if she's up for it."

"I'm sure she will be. Did she tell you anything about her family?"

Dana shook her head. "I still can't believe my grandparents had a son they never mentioned. Or, for that matter, that my mother kept it a secret. It all seems very odd."

"I'm sure you'll get to the bottom of it. When is she arriving?" Hilde asked, as she picked up the phone to call Ronnie.

"In an hour. I thought we could have lunch in Bozeman, after we pick her up."

Fortunately, Ronnie didn't mind coming in with only a few minutes' notice, Hilde thought as she hung up. Hilde suddenly couldn't wait to meet this mysterious Justice cousin.

DEPUTY MARSHAL COLT DAWSON watched Hilde Jacobson and Dana Savage come out of the sewing shop from his spot by the window of the deli across the street. Hilde, he noticed, was dressed in tan khakis and a coral print top she'd probably sewn herself. Her long golden hair was bound up in some kind of twist. Silver shone at her throat and ears.

Colt couldn't have put into words what it was about the woman that had him sitting in the coffee shop across the street, just hoping to get a glimpse of her. Most of the time, it made him angry with himself to be this besotted with the darned woman since the feeling was far from mutual.

As she glanced in his direction, he quickly pretended more interest in his untouched coffee. He'd begun taking his breaks and even having lunch at the new deli across from Needles and Pins. It was something he was going to have to stop doing since Hilde had apparently started to notice.

"She's going to think you're stalking her," he said under his breath, and took a sip of his coffee. When he looked again she and Dana had driven away.

"I figured I'd find you here," Marshal Hud Savage said, as he joined him. Colt saw Hud glance across the street and then try to hide a grin as he pulled up a chair and sat down.

He realized it was no secret that he'd asked Hilde out—and that she'd turned him down. Of course Hilde told her best friend, Dana, and Dana told her husband. Great—by now everyone in the canyon probably knew.

The "canyon," as it was known, ran from the mouth just south of Gallatin Gateway almost to West Yellowstone, miles of winding road along the Gallatin River that cut deep through the mountains.

Forty miles from Bozeman was the relatively new town of Big Sky. It had sprung up when Chet Huntley and a group of men started Big Sky Ski Resort up on Lone Mountain.

Hud ordered coffee, then seemed to study him. Colt bristled at the thought of his boss feeling sorry for him, even though he was definitely pitiful. He just hoped the marshal didn't bring up Hilde. Or mention the word *crush*.

Hilde had laughed when he'd asked her out as if she thought he was joking. Realizing that he wasn't, she'd said, "Colt, I'm flattered, but I'm not your type."

"What type is that?" he'd asked, even though he had a feeling he knew.

She'd studied him for a moment as if again trying to decide if he was serious. "Let's just say I'm a little too old, too serious, too...not fun for you."

He knew he had a reputation around the canyon because when he'd taken the job, he'd found there were a lot of young women who were definitely looking for a good time. He'd been blessed with his Native American father's black hair and his Irish mother's blue eyes. Also, he'd sowed more than a few oats after his divorce. But he was tired of that lifestyle. More than that, he was tired of the kind of women he'd been dating.

Not to mention the fact that he'd become fascinated with Hilde.

Hilde was different, no doubt about it. He'd run into her a few times at gatherings at Hud and Dana's house. She *was* serious. Serious about her business, serious about the life she'd made for herself. He'd heard that she had been in corporate America for a while, then her father had died and she'd realized she wasn't happy. That was when she'd opened her small sewing shop in Big Sky, Montana.

Other than that, he knew little about her. She was Dana's best friend, and they had started out as partners in the shop. Now Dana was a silent investor. Hilde also had her own house. Not one of the ostentatious ones dotting the mountainsides, but a small two-bedroom with a view of Lone Mountain. She'd dated some in the area, but had never been serious about anyone. At least that's what he'd heard.

Some people talked behind her back, saying that she thought she was too good for most of the men around the area. Colt would agree she probably *was* too good for most of them.

"Maybe I've changed," he'd suggested the day he'd asked her out.

Hilde had smiled at that.

It had been three weeks since she'd turned him down. He'd had numerous opportunities to date other women, but he hadn't. He was starting to worry about himself. He figured Hud probably was, too, since the canyon was such a small community, everyone knew everyone else's business.

"I thought I'd let you know I might be taking off some more time," Hud said after the waitress brought him a cup of coffee. Neither of them had gotten into the fancy coffees that so many places served now in Big Sky. Hud had taken off some time when the twins were born and a few days now and then to help Dana.

"Things are still plenty slow," Colt said, glad his boss wanted to talk about work. He and Hud had gotten close since he took the job last fall, but they weren't so close that they could talk about anything as personal as women.

"Dana discovered she has a cousin she's never met. She and Hilde have gone to pick her up. Stacy's babysitting all the kids right now, so I have to get back. I'll be in and out of the office, but available if needed. Dana wants me to teach her cousin to ride a horse. She's going to try to talk Hilde into taking her cousin on one of the river raft trips down through the Mad Mile. I told her I'd do whatever she wants. As long as Dana is happy, I'm happy to go along with it," he added with a grin.

"Wait, Hilde is going on a raft trip?" Colt couldn't help but laugh. "Good luck with that."

"I think there's a side to Hilde you haven't seen yet. You might be surprised." Hud finished his coffee and stood. "Might be a good idea for you to go along on that raft trip," he added with a grin.

As THE PLANE flew over the mountains surrounding the Gallatin Valley, the now Dee Anna Justice prepared herself for when she met her cousin.

She'd been repeating the name in her head, the same way she used to get into character in the many high school plays she'd performed in. She'd always loved being anyone but herself.

"Dee Anna Justice," she repeated silently as the plane made its descent. The moment the plane touched down, she took out her compact, studying herself in the mirror.

She'd always been a good student despite her lack of interest in school. So she knew how to do her homework. It hadn't taken much research on her laptop to find out everything she could about her "cousin" Dana Cardwell Savage.

The photos she'd found on Facebook had been very enlightening. Surprisingly, she and her "cuz" shared a startling resemblance, which she'd made a point of capitalizing on by tying back her dark hair in the plane bathroom.

"Dee Anna Justice," she had said into the mirror. "Just call me Dee."

The man in the seat beside her in first class had tried to make conversation on the flight, but after a few pleasantries, she'd dissuaded him by pretending to read the book she'd picked up at the airport. He was nice-looking and clearly had money, and she could tell he was interested.

But she'd needed to go over her story a few more times, to get into her role, because once she stepped off this plane, she had to be Dee.

"Hope you enjoy your stay at your cousin's ranch," he said, as the plane taxied toward the incredibly small terminal. Everything out the window seemed small—except for the snowcapped mountain ranges that rose into a blinding blue sky.

"I'm sure I will," she said, and refreshed her lipstick, going with a pale pink. Her cousin Dana, she'd noticed, didn't wear much—if any—makeup. Imitation was the best form of flattery, she'd learned.

"Is this your first time in Montana?"

She nodded as she put her compact away.

"Staying long?" he asked.

"I'm not sure. How about you?" He'd already told her he was flying in for a fly-fishing trip on the Yellowstone River.

"A short visit, unfortunately."

"Dee Anna Justice," she said extending her hand, trying out the name on him. "My friends call me Dee."

"Lance Allen," he said, his gaze meeting hers approvingly.

Any other time, she would have taken advantage of this handsome business executive. She recognized his expensive suit as well as the watch on his wrist. He'd spent most of the flight on his computer, working—his nails, she noted, recently manicured.

She'd known her share of men like him and hated passing this one up. It didn't slip her mind that she could be spending the week with him on the Yellowstone rather than visiting some no-doubt-boring cousin on a ranch miles from town. But the payoff might be greater with the cousin, she reminded herself.

The plane taxied to a stop. "You don't happen to have a business card where I could reach you if I can't take any more of home on the range?" she asked with a breathy laugh.

He smiled, clearly pleased, dug out his card and wrote his cell phone number on the back. "I hope you get bored soon."

Pocketing his card, she stood to get down her carry-on, giving him one final smile before she sashayed off the plane to see if her luck had changed.

HILDE WASN'T SURPRISED that Dana was questioning her impulsive invitation as the plane landed. "What if she doesn't like us? What if we don't like her?"

"I'm sure it will be fine," Hilde said, not for the first time, even though she was feeling as anxious as her friend.

"Oh, my gosh," Dana exclaimed, as her cousin came off the plane. "She looks like me!"

Hilde was equally shocked when she saw the young woman. The resemblance between Dana and her cousin was startling at a distance. Both had dark hair and eyes. The ever-casual ranch woman, Dana had her long hair pulled up in a ponytail. Her cousin had hers pulled back, as well, though in a clip.

All doubts apparently forgotten, Dana couldn't contain her excitement. She rushed forward. "Dee Anna?"

The woman looked startled but only for a moment, then began to laugh as if she, too, saw the resemblance. Dana hugged her cousin.

Hilde had warned her friend that Easterners were often less demonstrative and that it might be a good idea not to come on too strong. So much for that advice, she thought with a smile. Dana didn't do subtle well, and that was one of the many things she loved about her friend.

"This is my best friend in the world, Hilde Jacobson," Dana said, motioning Hilde closer. "She and I started a sewing shop, even though I don't sew, but now I'm a silent partner and Hilde does all the work. She always did all the real work since she's the one with the business degrees."

"Hi," Hilde said, and shook the woman's hand. Dana took a breath. The woman's hand was cold as ice. She must be nervous about meeting a cousin she didn't know existed. It made Hilde wonder if Dee Anna Justice was ready for Cardwell Ranch and the rest of this boisterous family.

"Let's get some lunch," Hilde suggested. "Give Dee Anna a chance to get acclimated before we go to the ranch."

"Good idea," Dana chimed in. "But first we need to pick up Dee Anna's bags."

"Please call me Dee, and this is my only bag. I travel light."

The three of them walked outside and across the street to where Dana had left the Suburban parked.

"So how far is the ranch?" Dee asked after they'd finished lunch at a small café near the airport.

"Not that far," Dana said. "Just forty miles."

Dee lifted a brow. "*Just* forty miles?"

"We're used to driving long distances in Montana," Dana said. "Forty miles is nothing to us."

"I already feel as if I'm in the middle of nowhere," Dee said with a laugh. "Where are all the people?"

"Bozeman is getting too big for most people," Dana said, laughing as well. "You should see the eastern part of the state. There's only .03 people per square mile in a lot of it. Less in other parts."

Dee shook her head. "I can't imagine living in such an isolated place."

Dana shot Hilde a worried look. "I think you'll enjoy the ride to the ranch, though. It's beautiful this time of year, and we have all kinds of fun things planned for you to do while you're here. Isn't that right, Hilde?"

Hilde smiled, wondering what Dana was getting her into. "Yes, all kinds of fun things."

DEE STARED OUT the window as they left civilization behind and headed toward the mountains to the south. They passed some huge, beautiful homes owned by people who obviously had money.

She tried to relax, telling herself that fate had gotten her here. The timing of the letter was too perfect. But luck had never been on her side, so this made her a little nervous. Not to mention the thought of being trapped on a ranch in the middle of nowhere. She fingered the business card in her pocket. At least she had other options if this didn't pan out.

She considered her cousin. Dana, while dressed in jeans, boots and a Western shirt, didn't look as if she had money, but she drove a nice new vehicle. And was a partner in a sewing shop—as well as owned a ranch. Maybe her prospects were good, Dee thought, as Dana drove across a bridge spanning a blue-green river, then slipped through an opening in the mountains into a narrow canyon. Dee had never liked narrow roads, let alone one through the mountains with a river next to it.

"That's the Gallatin River," Dana said, pointing to the rushing, clear green water. Dana had been giving a running commentary about the area since lunch. Dee had done her best to tune out most of it while nodding and appearing to show interest.

The canyon narrowed even more, the road winding through towering rock faces on both sides of the river and highway. Dee was getting claustrophobic, but fortunately the land opened a little farther down the road, and she again saw more promising homes and businesses.

"That's Big Sky," Dana said finally, pointing at a cluster of buildings. "And that is Lone Mountain." A snowcapped peak came into view. "Isn't it beautiful?"

Dee agreed, although she felt once she'd seen one mountain, she'd seen them all—and she'd seen more than her fair share today.

"Is the ranch far?" She was tiring of the tour and the drive and anxious to find out if this had been a complete waste of time. Lance Allen was looking awfully good right now.

"Almost there," Dana said, and turned off the highway to cross the river on a narrow bridge.

The land opened up, and for a moment she had great expectations. Then she saw an old two-story house and groaned inwardly.

So much for fate and her luck finally changing. She wondered how quickly she would escape. Maybe she would have to use the sick-sister or even the dying-mother excuse, if it came to that.

Just then a man rode up on a horse. She did a double take and tried to remember the last time she'd seen anyone as handsome as this cowboy astride the horse.

"That's Hud, my husband," Dana said with obvious pride in her voice.

Hello, Hud Savage, Dee said to herself. Things were beginning to look up considerably.

CHAPTER THREE

DEPUTY MARSHAL COLT Dawson got the call as he was driving down from Big Sky's Mountain Village.

"Black bear problem up Antler Ridge Road," the dispatcher told him. "The Collins place."

"I'll take care of it." He swung off Lone Mountain Trail onto Antler Ridge Road and drove along until he saw the massive house set against the side of the mountain. Like many of the large homes around Big Sky, this one was only used for a week or so at Christmas and a month or so in the summer at most.

George Collins was some computer component magnate who'd become a millionaire by the time he was thirty.

Colt swung his patrol SUV onto the paved drive that led him through the timber to the circular driveway.

He'd barely stopped and gotten out before the nanny came running out to tell him that the bear was behind the house on the deck.

Colt took out his can of pepper spray, attached it to his belt and then unsnapped his shotgun. The maid led the way, before quickly disappearing back into the house.

The small yearling black bear was just finishing a huge bowl of dog food when Colt came around the corner.

It saw him and took off, stopping ten yards away in the pines. Colt lifted the shotgun and fired into the air. The bear hightailed it up the mountain and over a rise.

After replacing the shotgun and bear spray in his vehicle, he went to the front door and knocked. The nanny answered the door and he asked to see Mr. or Mrs. Collins. As she disappeared back into the cool darkness of the house, Colt looked around.

Living in Big Sky, he was used to extravagance: heated driveways, gold-finished fixtures, massive homes with lots of rock and wood and antlers. The Collins home was much like the others that had sprouted up around Big Sky.

"Yes?" The woman who appeared was young and pretty except for the frown on her face. "Is there a problem?"

"You called about a bear on your back deck," he reminded her.

"Yes, but I heard you shoot it."

"I didn't *shoot* it. I scared it off. We don't shoot them, but we may have to if you keep feeding them. You need to make sure you don't leave dog food on the deck. Or birdseed in your feeders. Or garbage where the bears can get to it." Montana residents were warned of this—but to little avail. "You can be fined if you continue to disregard these safety measures."

The woman bristled. "I'll tell my housekeeper to feed the dog inside. But you can't be serious about the birdseed."

"It's the bears that are serious about birdseed," Colt said. "They'll tear down your feeders to get to it and keep coming back as long as there is something to eat."

"Fine. I'll tell my husband."

He tipped his Stetson and left, annoyed that people often moved to Montana for the scenery and wildlife. But they wanted both at a distance so they didn't have to deal with it.

As he drove back toward Meadow Village, the lower part of Big Sky, he thought about what Hud had said about a raft trip down the river. No way would Hilde go. Would she?

HILDE HAD BEEN watching Dee Anna Justice on the ride from the airport to Cardwell Ranch and fighting a nagging feeling.

What was it about the woman that was bothering her? She couldn't put her finger on it even now that she was back in the sewing shop—her favorite place to be.

"So what is she like?" Ronnie asked. The thirty-something Veronica "Ronnie" Tate was an employee and a friend. Hilde loved that she could always depend on Ronnie to hold down the fort while she was away from the shop.

"Dee Anna Justice? It's eerie. She looks like Dana. But she doesn't act like her."

Ronnie seemed to be waiting for Hilde to continue.

Hilde weighed her words. Dana was her best friend. She didn't want to talk about Dana's cousin behind Dana's back.

"More subdued than Dana, but then who isn't? She's from New York City and all this is new to her."

Ronnie laughed. "Okay, what is wrong with her? I can tell you don't like her."

"No, that's not true. I don't *know* her."

"But?"

What *was* bothering her about the woman? Something. "I just hope she doesn't take advantage of Dana's hospitality, that's all." Dana had flown her out here and was paying all her expenses, and Dee was letting her. That seemed wrong.

Ronnie was still waiting.

"I don't want her to be a hardship. Dana is stretched thin as it is with four kids, two still in diapers."

"How long is she staying?" Ronnie asked.

"That's just it—Dana doesn't know." Hilde had always thought visitors were like fish: three days and it was time for them to go. But then again, she enjoyed being alone to read or sew or just look out the window and daydream. Dana was more social, even though she'd deny it.

"I'm sure Dana will show her a good time," Ronnie said.

"I'm sure she will since she has already drafted me to help."

After Ronnie left, she was still wondering what it was about Dee Anna Justice that bothered her. She started to lock up for the day when she recalled Dee's reaction to Hud as he'd ridden up on his horse.

Dee had suddenly come alive—after showing little interest in Montana, the canyon or the ranch before that moment.

DEE MOVED RESTLESSLY around the living room of the old ranch house this morning, running her finger along the horns of some kind of dead animal hanging on the wall. Hud had told her, but she'd forgotten what kind.

Last night, while Dana had seen to the kids, Hud had shown her around the ranch. Dee hadn't been impressed with the corrals, barn, outbuildings or even the view. But Hud, who was drop-dead gorgeous and so wonderfully manly, was very impressive. She'd never met a real live cowboy before. It made him all the more interesting because he was also the marshal.

When the tour of the ranch ended, Hud had excused himself and she'd been forced to stay up late talking with her "cousin." Dana had shared stories of growing up here on the ranch.

Dee had made up a sad childhood of being raised by nannies, attending boarding schools and hardly ever seeing either of her wealthy parents. The stories had evoked the kind of sympathy she'd hoped to get from Dana. By the time they'd gone to bed, Dana had been apologizing for not knowing about Dee and saving her from that lonely childhood.

"Ready?"

Dee turned to smile at Hud. He had offered to teach her to ride a horse this morning. Her first instinct had been to decline. She'd never been on a horse in her life and she really didn't want to now. But she loved the idea of Hud teaching her anything.

"Ready," she said past the lump in her throat.

Hud must have seen her reluctance. "I'm going to put you on one of the kids' horses. Very gentle. There is nothing to worry about."

"If you say so," she said with a laugh. "Let's do it."

Hud led the way outside. He had two horses tied up to the porch railing. She felt as if she was in Dodge City. This was all so…Western.

"Just grab the saddle horn and put your foot in my hands and I'll help you up," Hud said. She did as he instructed, wobbled a little and fell back. He caught her, just as she knew he would. The man was as strong as he looked.

"Let's try that again," he said with a laugh. Behind them, she heard Dana come out on the porch with the two oldest of their children. Dee had forgotten their names.

"Is she going to ride my horse, Mommy?" the little girl asked.

"Yes, Mary, she needs a nice horse since she has never ridden before," Dana answered.

"Really?" The kid sounded shocked that anyone could reach Dee's age and have never ridden a horse.

This time Dee let Hud lift her up and onto the horse. She gripped the saddle horn as the horse seemed to shiver and stomp its feet. "I don't think it likes me," she said.

"Star likes everyone," the girl said.

Dee was glad when they rode away from the house. She'd always found children annoying. It was beyond her why anyone would want four of them.

Once she got used to the horse's movement, she began to relax. The day was beautiful, not a cloud in the sky. A cool breeze blew through the pine trees, bringing with it a scent like none she'd ever smelled before.

"So this is what fresh air smells like," she joked.

"A little different from New York City?"

She laughed at that. "It's so…quiet."

"You'll get used to it. Did you have trouble getting to sleep last night? People often complain it's too quiet to sleep."

She hadn't been able to sleep last night, but she doubted it was from the quiet. Dana had put her in a large bedroom upstairs at the front of the house. When she'd tested the bed, she found it to be like lying down on a cloud. It was covered with what appeared to be a handmade patchwork quilt, the mattress on a white iron frame that forced her to actually climb up to get into it.

The sheets had smelled like sunshine and were soft. There was no reason she shouldn't have drifted right off to sleep. Except for one.

She found herself reviewing the day in small snapshots, weighing each thing that happened, evaluating how she'd done as Dee Anna Justice. She was much more critical of herself than anyone else could possibly be. But she'd learned the hard way that any little slipup could give her away.

"Dana tells me you grew up back East?" Hud asked, clearly just making conversation as their horses walked down a narrow dirt road side by side.

The real Dee Anna Justice had never been exactly forthcoming about her life growing up. But she'd always gotten the feeling that something had happened, some secret that made Dee Anna not want to talk about her life.

She'd found that amusing, since she would put her childhood secrets up against the real Dee Anna Justice's any day—and win hands down, she was sure.

"It wasn't like *this,*" Dee said now in answer to his question. Then she quickly asked, "Did you grow up here? I get the feeling that you and Dana have always known each other."

"My father was the marshal," Hud said. "I grew up just down the road from here. Dana and I go way back." Something in his tone told her that there had been some problem before they'd gotten together. Another woman? Or another man?

Dee made a mental note to see what she could find

out from the sister, Stacy. She'd only seen her for a few minutes, but Dee could tell at once that Stacy and Dana were nothing alike. And while the two seemed close, she got the feeling there was some sort of old friction there.

She'd spent her life reading people to survive. Some people were literally an open book. If they didn't tell you their life story, you could pretty well guess it.

Glancing over at the cowboy beside her, she knew he was honorable, loyal and trustworthy. She considered what it would take to corrupt a man like that.

HILDE PUT THE Open sign in her shop window. As she did, she glanced at the deli across the street. She'd gotten used to seeing Deputy Marshal Colt Dawson sitting in that front window and was a little surprised to find someone else sitting there this morning.

It surprised her also that she was disappointed.

She shook it off, chastising herself.

"Colt has a crush on you," Dana had said a few days before. "Hud says he hasn't dated a single woman since he asked you out and you turned him down."

"I'm sure he'll snap out of it soon," Hilde had said. Colt Dawson could have any woman he wanted—and had. The man was too handsome for his own good. He'd gotten his straight, thick black hair from his father, who was Native American, and his startling blue eyes from his Irish mother. On top of that, he was tall, broad-shouldered with slim hips and long legs, and he had this grin that…

Hilde shook herself again, shocked that she'd let her thoughts go down that particular trail. It was flattering that Colt had asked her out, but she was his age, and he hadn't dated a woman his own age since he'd come to

Big Sky, let alone one who was looking for something more than a good time.

As she started to turn away from the front window of her store, she saw the man at the deli's front table get up and leave. Colt Dawson quickly took his place, his blue-eyed gaze coming up suddenly as if he knew she would be standing there.

Hilde quickly stepped back, but she couldn't help smiling as she hurried to the counter at the back of the store.

A moment later the bell jangled as someone came in the front door. Her heart took off like a shot as she turned, half expecting to see Colt.

"Just need some black thread," said one of her older patrons. "It's amazing how hard it is to keep black thread in the house."

Hilde hurried to help the woman. When she looked out the window again, the front table at the deli was empty, Colt long gone.

"Why didn't you go out with him?" Dana had asked her. "What would it have hurt?"

She hadn't had an answer at that moment. But she did now. A man like Colt Dawson was capable of breaking her heart.

DEE HATED IT when the horseback ride ended, even though she could definitely feel her muscles rebelling. She'd insisted on helping as Hud unsaddled the horses and put them in the corral. *Helping* might have been inaccurate. She'd stood around, asked questions without listening to the answers and studied the man, considering.

Back at the house, Dana announced that Hud was

going to take care of the kids while she and her cousin went for a hike and picnic at the falls. That is, if Dee wasn't too tired.

She would much rather have taken a nap than go on a hike since she hadn't gotten much sleep last night, but she couldn't disappoint Dana, especially in front of Hud. So she'd helped pack the lunch to the pickup and the two of them had driven out of the ranch and toward what Dana called Lone Mountain.

"So this is the town of Big Sky?" Dee asked a few minutes later. "I thought it would be bigger."

"It's spread out. There is the upper mountain where the ski lifts are, and the lower mountain where the golf course is. Plus a bunch of houses you can't see from the road," Dana told her. "We'll have to take the gondola to Lone Mountain, if you're here long enough. I think you'll like that—the view is nice. And tomorrow I've set up a rafting trip for the three of us."

"Oh, Hud is going?" Dee asked.

"No, he's taking care of the kids. Hilde is going with us. In fact, she's joining us for the picnic today." She turned onto a narrow road that went past a cluster of houses and businesses before climbing up through the pines. "Yep, there's Hilde's SUV already parked at the trailhead. Hilde is so punctual." Dana laughed. "It's amazing we're best friends since we are opposites on so many things."

Hilde. The best friend. Dee recalled yesterday feeling Hilde watching her a little too closely. Dana was so trusting, so open. Hilde was more reserved and definitely not trusting, Dee thought. Dana parked next to Hilde's SUV, and Dee glimpsed the woman behind the wheel, her brown eyes so watchful.

DANA CHATTERED AWAY on the hike up to Ousel Falls. Hilde dropped behind her friend and Dee. She hadn't been up to the falls in several years and was enjoying the gentle hike through the pines. She could hear the roar of the creek. It was early in the year, so snow was still melting in the shade and the creek was running fast and high.

The cool air felt good. Hilde was wondering why Dana had insisted she come along. She felt like a third wheel. Not that Dee and Dana seemed to be hitting it off. Dee was quiet, nodding and speaking only to say, "Really?" "Oh, that's interesting." And "Huh." Clearly she wasn't finding anything all that interesting in the information Dana was imparting about the area and its history.

Dana stopped to wait for her in a sunny spot not too far from the falls.

At the falls, Dana opened the cooler she'd brought, and they sat on rocks overlooking the falls to drink iced tea and eat roasted elk sandwiches.

"It's…interesting," Dee said of the sandwich. "I thought you raised beef?"

Dana laughed. "Wild meat will grow on you," she promised. "Hud always gets an elk and a deer each year. We both really like it."

"I'm not sure I'll be here long enough for it to grow on *me,*" Dee said.

This gave Hilde an opening. "So how long *will* you be staying?" she asked.

"I'm not sure," Dee said, and looked to Dana, who appeared shocked that Hilde would ask such a thing.

"As long as she wants to," Dana said.

Dee smiled. "That could definitely wear out my welcome. The more I see of this place, the more I love it here and never want to leave."

"Montana does that to people," Dana said.

"At least this time of year," Hilde said. "You might not find it as hospitable come winter."

"Oh, I don't know." Dee stretched out on the ground and stared up at the blue sky. "I can see myself sitting in front of that huge rock fireplace at the house with a mug of spiked cider, being pretty content."

"A woman after my own heart," Dana said.

Hilde began to clean up the picnic, putting everything back in the cooler before she got up and wandered over to the edge of the falls.

"What has gotten into you?" Dana whispered next to her a few moments later.

"Sorry. I was just curious how long she's planning to stay," she whispered back. "I didn't mean to be rude." When Dana said nothing more, she glanced over at her. *"What?"*

"You're jealous of my cousin."

"No, that's not it at all." But Hilde could tell there was no convincing her friend otherwise. "Fine, I'm jealous."

"Don't be," Dana said with a laugh. "You're my *best* friend and always will be." She lowered her voice. "Not only that, Dee has had a really rough life."

"She told you that?" Hilde asked, unable to keep the skepticism out of her voice.

"She didn't have to," Dana said. "I could tell. So be nice to her for me. Please?" Hilde could only nod. "I'm going to get my camera and take a photo."

Hilde turned back to the falls, thinking maybe Dana was right. Maybe she *was* jealous, and that was all it was. The roar of the water was so loud she didn't hear Dee come up behind her. She barely felt the hand on her back before she felt the shove.

She flailed wildly as she felt herself falling forward toward the edge of the roaring falls, nothing between her and the raging water but air and mist.

Dee grabbed her arm and pulled her back at the last second.

"I found my camera," Dana called from over in the trees, and turned in their direction. "Look this way so I can get a picture of the two of you." A beat, then: "Is everything all right?"

"Hilde got a little too close to the edge," Dee said. "You really should be careful, Hilde. Dana was just saying earlier how dangerous it can be around here." She put her arm around Hilde's shoulders. "Say cheese."

Dana snapped the photo.

CHAPTER FOUR

"I DON'T THINK your friend likes me," Dee said once they were in the pickup and headed back to the ranch.

"Hilde likes you," Dana said, not sounding all that convinced. "But I think she might be a little jealous."

"I suppose that's it," Dee agreed. "Well, I hope she accepts me. I feel so close to you. It's almost like we're sisters instead of cousins, you know what I mean?"

Dana readily agreed, just as Dee had known she would. "Hilde is just a little protective."

"A *little?*" Dee said with a laugh. "I think she's worried I will take advantage of you, stay too long."

"Put that right out of your mind," Dana said, as she parked in front of the house. "You're family. You can stay as long as you'd like."

"Hilde has nothing to be jealous of me about," Dee said. "She's beautiful and smart and self-assured and has her own business. She's what I always wanted to be."

"Me, too," Dana said with a laugh.

"Oh, you have even more going on for you," Dee said. "You have Hud. And the kids," she added a little belatedly, but Dana didn't seem to notice. "And the ranch. I bet you were practically born on a horse."

"I have been riding since the time I could walk,"

Dana said, then fell silent for a moment. "Do you want to talk about your childhood? I don't mean to pry."

Dee realized that she'd sounded jealous of both Dana and Hilde. The truth had a way of coming out sometimes, didn't it? She would have to be more careful about that around both women.

"There isn't much more to tell." Only because the real Dee Anna Justice hadn't been forthcoming about her family. There had definitely been something in her background she hadn't wanted to talk about. But it could have just been that some wealthy people didn't like talking about themselves or their wealthy families.

So now Dee had to wing it, hoping to give Dana enough to make her feel even more sorry for her. "As I told you last night, when I wasn't away at school, my parents were never around. My father traveled a lot. My mother was involved in a lot of charity and social events. I grew up feeling alone and unloved, yearning for what everyone else had." At least the last part was true.

"I'm sorry, Dee. I wish I had known about you. Maybe you wouldn't have felt so alone," Dana said, as she parked in front of the house. "I would have shared the ranch with you."

Dee watched Hud come out onto the porch and thought about Dana's generous offer to share what she had. "Hud mentioned some high country back behind the ranch that has a great view. I'd love to see it. But this is probably a bad time."

As Dana got out, she suggested it to Hud, who said the kids were napping and he'd be happy to take her if that was what she wanted to do.

"You sure it's not an inconvenience," Dee said.

"Not at all," he said.

She watched as he gave his wife a kiss and felt that small ache in her stomach at the sight.

"I'll help with dinner when I get back," he said to Dana.

"I'll help, too," Dee said, even though she'd never cooked in her life. In New York City it was too easy to get takeout.

She followed Hud to the four-wheeler parked by the barn and climbed on behind him, putting her arms around his waist. He started the motor and they were off. It didn't take long before the house disappeared behind them and they were completely alone.

Dee watched dark pines blur past. The air got cooler as they climbed, the road twisting and turning as it wound farther and farther back into the mountains. She laid her cheek against the soft fabric of his jean jacket and breathed in the scent of him and the mountains.

There were few times in her life that she'd ever felt safe. It surprised her that now was one of them. Hud was the kind of man she'd always dreamed would come along and sweep her off her feet. How could she still believe in happy ever after after what she'd lived through?

Her parents had hated each other to the point where they'd tried to kill each other. Her father... She didn't even want to think about the role model he'd been to his daughter.

And the men she'd met since then? She let out a choked laugh, muffling it against Hud's jacket. They'd hurt her in ways she'd thought she could never be hurt.

She'd been waiting her whole life for a hero to come along. When she'd seen Hud Savage come riding up, her heart had filled with helium at the sight of him. He looked bigger than life, strong, brave, the first real man she'd ever known.

She held on a little tighter, wishing Hud was hers.

When they reached the summit, Hud stopped the four-wheeler and shut off the engine.

Dee let go of his waist, stretched and climbed off to look out across the tops of the mountains. "This is amazing," she said, actually meaning it. "You can see forever."

"It is pretty spectacular up here, isn't it?"

She tried to imagine living in country like this. It seemed so far away from the noise and filth of the big cities she'd wandered through so far in her life. What must it be like to wake up to this every morning?

Hud began to point out the mountain peaks, calling each by name with an intimacy that plucked at her heartstrings. She could hear his love for this land in his voice. There was nothing sexier than a man who loved something with such passion.

It took all her self-control not to touch him.

"So what are those mountains over there?" she asked, wanting this moment to last forever. She didn't listen to his answer. She just liked the sound of his deep and melodious voice. Desire spiked through her, making her weak with a need like none she'd known. She wanted this man.

"You have a wonderful life here," she said, realizing she'd never been so jealous of anyone as she was Dana Savage. "It's so peaceful. I can't imagine having the tie to the land that you do. I've moved around a lot. I've never felt at home anywhere." *Until now,* she thought, but she didn't dare voice it.

Like Hilde, she was sure Hud was wondering how

long she was going to stay. But she'd never met a man she couldn't charm. Hud Savage would be no exception.

She moved to the edge of the mountaintop and breathed in the day. She'd been telling the truth about her family moving around a lot. Her father couldn't bear to stay long in any one place—even if he wasn't forced to flee town before the law caught up to him. A small-time con man, he worked harder at not working than he would have had he just gotten an honest job.

"I feel as if I could just fly out over the tops of all these mountains," she said, as she freed her hair to let it blow back in the wind. She stuck out her arms, laughing as she laid her head back. The wind felt good. She felt alive. Free.

"I wouldn't get too close to the edge," Hud said, stepping to her. "I don't want to have to explain to Dana how I lost her cousin."

"No, we don't want that," she agreed, as she met his gaze.

"We should get back. The kids will be waking up and Dana will need help with dinner," he said.

Disappointed, she pulled her hair up again and turned to walk back to the four-wheeler. For a moment, she had felt as if he was responding to her.

She hadn't gone but a few feet when she stepped on a rock, twisting her ankle as she fell. Hud rushed to her as she dropped to the ground with a groan.

"How bad is it hurt?" he asked, frowning with concern.

"I think I just twisted it, but I can't seem to put any pressure on it," Dee said, wincing in pain as she held her ankle. "I've spent my life walking on sidewalks. I don't know how to walk on anything that isn't flat. I'm sorry."

"Don't be sorry. It happens. Can you get to the four-wheeler?"

She made an attempt to put weight on her ankle and cried out in pain. "I don't mean to be such a big baby."

"I'm just sorry you hurt yourself. Here, I can carry you over to the four-wheeler. If it's still hurting when we reach the ranch, Dana will take you over to the medical center."

"Are you sure you can carry me?" she asked. "I'm so embarrassed."

"Don't be. I can certainly carry someone as light as you," he said, lifting her into his arms.

She was quite a bit slimmer than Dana since her *cousin* had delivered twin sons not that long ago. Nice that he'd noticed, she thought. She put her arms around his neck, and he carried her with little effort over to the four-wheeler. She hated to let go when he set her down on the seat.

"How's that?" he asked.

She lifted her leg over the side, wincing again in pain but being incredibly brave. "Fine. Thank you."

"No problem." He got on and started the motor. "Dana is going to have my hide, though."

"I'm sure it will be fine by the time we reach the house. I don't want to upset Dana or get you into trouble with her. It's already starting to feel better."

Dee wrapped her arms around Hud's waist, leaning against him again as they descended the mountain. She breathed in the scent of him. She would have him. One way or the other.

AFTER THE HIKE to the falls, Hilde was still trembling an hour later back at the shop. The worst part was that there was no one she could tell. The shove had happened so quickly, even now she couldn't be sure she'd actually felt it. And yet, she knew that Dee had pushed her. Was she trying to scare her?

Or to warn her to back off? The shove had come right after Hilde had asked how long Dee would be staying.

The shop phone rang, making her jump. She really was getting paranoid, she thought as she answered. "Needles and Pins."

"Hi," Dana said. "I just wanted to call and tell you what time we're floating the Gallatin tomorrow."

"Dana, I—"

"Do. Not. Try. To. Get. Out. Of. This."

"You don't need me," Hilde said, and realized she *was* sounding jealous. "I really should work."

"I know business is slow right now. Remember? I'm your silent partner. So don't tell me you have to work. Come on. When was the last time you floated the river?"

"I've never floated it."

"*What?* You've never been down the Mad Mile?"

"No, and I really don't think I want to do it now when the river is so high. Dana, are you sure this is a good idea?"

"I've already talked to Dee. She's excited. She was trying to get Hud to go with us. Stacy said she'd watch the kids, since Hud said he had something he had to do. Dee was excited to hear you were going with us."

I'll just bet she was.

"Come on. It's going to be fun. You need a thrill or two in your life."

"Don't I, though." What could she say? That there was something not quite right about Dee Anna Justice?

That the woman had shoved her at the top of the falls?
But then grabbed her to "save" her?

"Great," Dana was saying. "We'll pick you up tomorrow at your place so we can all ride together."

"Great," Hilde said. By the time she hung up, she'd
almost convinced herself that Dee hadn't pushed her.
That there was nothing to worry about. That she was
just jealous. Or crazy.

More likely crazy, she thought, glancing out the front
window of the shop hoping to see Colt Dawson. His
usual table was empty.

COLT WAS AT the marshal's office filling out paperwork
when Hud walked in.

"I would really appreciate it if you would go on this
rafting trip with Dana and her cousin this afternoon,"
Hud said. "Dana's cousin is a little clumsy. Hell, a whole
lot clumsy. I don't want her falling off the raft and taking Dana with her."

Colt looked at his boss. "You aren't really asking
me to babysit your wife and her cousin, are you? Why
don't you go?"

"I have to take care of a few things at the station. Oh,
and I did mention Hilde is going, right?"

Colt swore under his breath. "You think that's going
to make me change my mind?"

Hud grinned. "I could make it an order if that would
make you feel better."

"You should be worried about Hilde drowning *me*."

His boss laughed. "You'll grow on her over time.
Look how you've grown on all of us around here."

"Yeah. What time do I have to be there?"

"You probably better go change." He told him the

name of the raft company and where they would be loading in about an hour. "Good luck."

Colt ignored him as he left to head to his cabin. When he'd taken the job, he'd lucked out and gotten a five-year lease on a small cabin in the woods outside of Big Sky. One of the biggest problems with working in the area was finding a reasonable place to live.

At the cabin, he changed into shorts, a T-shirt and river sandals. As he did he wondered what Hilde would have to say when she saw him. He'd never been tongue-tied around women—until Hilde. What was it about her? She seemed unfazed by him. He really didn't know what to do when he was around her.

He knew what he wanted to do. Carry her off and make mad passionate love to her. Just the thought stirred the banked fire inside him.

Colt shook his head, realizing how inappropriate his thoughts were under the circumstances. Hilde hadn't looked twice at him. His chances of getting her to go out on a date with him didn't even look good.

Well, he'd make this float with her and Dana and Dana's cousin because Hud had asked him to keep an eye on them. But he would give Hilde a wide berth. She'd made it clear she wasn't interested. The best thing he could do was move on. Maybe there'd be some young woman on the raft who'd want to go out to dinner later tonight. Best advice he had was to get back on that horse that had thrown him.

With that in mind, he drove down the canyon to where the rafting company was loading the rafts. Dana waved him over as he got out of his pickup. Her cousin stood next to her. He did a double take. The two looked a lot like each other, especially since they were both wearing their hair back. Her cousin was a little slimmer and not as pretty as Dana. There was a hardness to the woman that Dana lacked.

Hilde was standing off to the side, her arms crossed over her chest. He got the feeling she didn't want to be here any more than he did. She wore white shorts and a bright blue print sleeveless top. Her honey-colored hair was pulled up in a way that made her look even more uptight.

He gave her a nod and turned his attention to Dana and her cousin.

"This is my cousin Dee Anna Justice," Dana said.

"Just call me Dee." The woman shook his hand, her gaze locking with his, clearly flirting with him.

"Colt Dawson."

"Colt is a deputy marshal. He works with Hud."

"How interesting," Dee said, still holding his hand.

He didn't pull away. He knew Hilde was probably watching him. Impulsively, he said, "Maybe you'd like to hear more about crime in the canyon at dinner tonight."

"Maybe I would," Dee agreed and looked to Dana.

"Oh, remember? My family is coming tonight for dinner at the ranch so they can meet you," Dana said. "Colt, why don't you come?"

"No, I couldn't. I—"

"I know you don't have other plans," Dana pointed out.

She had him there.

"Hilde's coming, too," Dana said.

He glanced at Hilde. She was studying the ground at her feet, poking one sandaled foot almost angrily at the dirt.

Minutes later, they were all dressed in wet suits and life jackets provided by the rafting company. Dee latched onto his arm as they started to load the rafts, riders sitting three across.

Their guide, though, had him move to a spot on the outside next to an older woman and her husband. In the row directly in front of him, Dee was forced to sit in the middle with Dana on one side and Hilde on the other. Both Hilde and Dana were given paddles.

From where he sat, he could catch only glimpses of Hilde. As their guide shoved the raft off from the shore, everyone on the sides paddled as they'd been instructed. The raft went around in circles for a few minutes before everyone got the hang of it.

Hilde took to paddling as if she'd done it before. The woman was right about one thing. She was serious in most everything she did. He liked that about her and felt like a jackass for having asked Dee out in front of her.

Now they would all be at some family dinner tonight at Cardwell Ranch. He couldn't imagine anything more uncomfortable—unless it was this raft ride.

THE RIVER SWEPT them slowly downstream past huge, round boulders and through glistening, clear green water. A cool breeze stirred the trees along the bank. Overhead, white puffy clouds bobbed along. It was the perfect day for a raft trip.

Hilde tried to relax and enjoy herself, but the memory of what had happened up at the falls made her edgy. She was only too aware of Dee in the seat next to her. She could feel the woman watching her as if measuring her for a coffin. Who was Dee Anna Justice? Not the woman Dana thought she was, that much was clear.

But how was Hilde going to convince Dana of that? Maybe it was better to keep it to herself; after all, Dee would be leaving soon and probably never come back.

Out of the corner of her eye, she could hear Dana and Dee talking and laughing as the raft picked up speed. Behind her, she was aware of Colt. She'd heard him ask Dee out. Not very subtle, she thought, realizing that she'd hurt him when she'd turned him down for a date. That surprised her.

She tried to concentrate on the river and her paddling. But it was hard with Dee so close and Colt probably watching everything she did. He probably hoped she'd end up in the river.

The Gallatin was known as one of the premiere rafting rivers in the West. The river wound through the narrow canyon with both leisurely waters as well as white-water rapids.

Most of the raft trip so far had been through fairly calm waters, the navigation easy. They'd passed through a few sets of rapids here and there that had had most everyone on the raft screaming as they'd roared through them, water splashing over the raft, Hilde and the other paddlers paddling furiously to keep the raft from turning or capsizing.

But Hilde knew that the rough part was ahead, where they would have to run technical rapids past House Rock for the Mad Mile in the lower canyon.

The Mad Mile was a mile of continuous rapids. The cold water ran fast with huge waves, holes and a lot of adrenaline paddling in the Class IV water. That stretch of river required more precise maneuvering, especially this time of year when the river was higher, and she wasn't looking forward to that.

Hilde noticed that Dee and Dana seemed to be having a great time. She was glad she'd decided not to say anything to Dana. She could almost talk herself into believing that Dee hadn't pushed her at the falls. Almost.

She didn't dare sneak a look back at Colt. She concentrated on her paddling. Not telling Dana was the right thing. It wasn't like Dee was…dangerous.

That thought hit her as the raft made the curve in the river just before the Mad Mile. She could hear Dana explaining about the next stretch of river ahead. Dee actually seemed interested.

They made it through the first few rapids, and the raft passed under the bridge. House Rock was ahead, a huge rock that sat in the middle of the river, forcing the fast water to go around it on each side.

The ride became rougher and wetter with spray coming up and over the raft. There were shrieks and screams and laughter as the raft dipped down into a deep hole and shot up again.

Hilde could see House Rock ahead. It was the other rocks they had to maneuver through that were the problem. The guide picked a line down through the rocks and shouted instructions to the paddlers.

The standing waves were huge. The raft went into the first one, buckling under them. The front of the raft shot down into the huge swell, then quickly upward, stalling for a moment.

Hilde reached with her paddle to grab the top of the wave and help the raft slip over it when suddenly her side of the raft swamped. She tried to lean to the middle of the boat, but Dee was pushing against her. Before she knew what was happening, she was in the water, the top of the wave crashing down on her, the current pulling her under.

As she struggled to reach the surface, Hilde realized she wasn't alone. Dee had fallen out of the raft as well—and she had ahold of Hilde's life jacket. She was dragging her under.

She fought to get away, but something was wrong. She couldn't see light above her. Was she trapped against House Rock? She'd heard about kayakers getting caught against the rock and almost drowning.

But she wasn't against a rock. She was rushing downriver through the huge rapids—trapped under the raft. Somehow, her life jacket had gotten hooked onto a line under the raft. As she struggled to get it off, she realized Dee still had hold of her. She kicked out at the woman, struck something hard, then worked again to free herself.

She couldn't hold her breath any longer. The weight of the raft was holding her down. If she didn't breathe soon—

Arms grabbed her from behind. She flailed at them, trying to free herself from the life jacket and Dee's grip on her. The life jacket finally came off. She had to free herself from Dee's hold and swim out from under the raft before she drowned.

The darkness began to close in. She could no longer go without air. She felt her body give in to the strong grip on her.

CHAPTER FIVE

HILDE CAME TO lying on a large flat rock with Colt Dawson kissing her. At least that was her first impression as she felt his mouth on hers. She coughed and had to sit up, gasping for breath.

She could see where the raft had pulled over downstream. The guide was leaning over Dee, who was lying on the side of the raft. "Dee." It was all she could get out before she started coughing again.

"Dee's all right," he said.

Hilde shook her head and let out a snort. "She tried to drown me." Her voice sounded hoarse and hurt like the devil.

Colt looked at her for a full minute before he said, "She tried to save you and almost drowned."

She shook her head more adamantly. "She was the one who hooked my life jacket on the rope under the raft." Hilde could see he didn't believe her. "It's not the first time she's tried to hurt me. When we were up at the falls, she pushed me."

He seemed to be waiting.

"Then she grabbed me just before I fell."

Colt nodded and she realized how crazy she must sound. But if he had been under that raft with her...

"Is Dana all right?" she asked, looking downriver.

"She's just worried about you."

"And *Dee,*" Hilde said, seeing how her friend was clutching Dee's hand.

"She's probably worried about Dee because her cousin almost drowned, and this raft trip was her idea," Colt said. "You apparently kicked Dee in the face."

"Because she was trying to hold me down while she hooked my life jacket to that rope." She could see that he didn't believe her and felt her eyes burn hot with tears. "Colt, you have to believe me—there is something wrong with her cousin. I was under that raft with her. She wouldn't let go of me. She hooked my life jacket onto that rope. If you find my jacket…" She was trying to get to her feet.

"Hilde, I'm not sure what you think happened under the raft—"

"I don't know why I expected you to believe me," she said angrily. "Especially about someone you have a date with tonight." He reached for her as she stumbled to her feet, but she brushed off his hand. Stepping down through the rocks, she found a place to cross that wasn't too swift. She could hear him behind her.

All she could think about was getting to Dana, telling her the truth about Dee. Dee was dangerous. Dana had to be warned.

She still felt woozy and should have known better, but she made her way downstream toward the raft. Dana was still holding Dee's hand as she approached. The sight angered her even more.

Hilde remembered right before she'd gone into the river. She'd tried to lean back, but Dee was pushing on her, pushing her out of the boat and going with her.

There was no doubt in her mind that the woman had tried to drown her.

"She tried to kill me," Hilde cried, pointing a trembling finger at Dee, who lay on the edge of the raft clearly enjoying all the attention she was getting.

"Are you all right?" the guide asked, sounding scared.

"Did you hear what I said?" she demanded of Dana. "Your cousin tried to kill me."

Everyone on the raft went deathly quiet. "She pushed me off the raft, then she pulled me under and hooked my life jacket on the rope underneath the boat. If Colt hadn't pulled me out of there…" Hilde realized she was crying and near hysteria. Everyone was looking at her as if she was out of her mind.

"I tried to help you," Dee said in a small, tearful voice. She touched her cheek, which Hilde saw was black-and-blue. "If you hadn't kicked me I would have gotten you free from under the raft."

"She almost drowned trying to save you," Dana said.

Hilde let out a lunatic's laugh. "*Save* me? I'm telling you she tried to kill me, and it wasn't the first time." She felt someone touch her arm and turned her head to see Colt standing beside her.

"Let me get you off the river and into some dry clothes," he said, his gaze locking with hers. She saw the pleading in his eyes. He thought she was making a fool of herself. No one believed her. Everyone believed Dee. "I'll take care of Hilde," Colt said to Dana. "You make sure your cousin is okay."

Crying harder, she looked at Dana, saw the shock and disbelief and pity in her eyes. Through the haze of tears she saw all the others staring at her with a mixture of pity and gratitude that it hadn't been them under the raft.

Her gaze settled on Dee. A whisper of a smile touched her lips, before she, too, began to cry. As Dana tried to assure her cousin that Hilde was just upset, that she hadn't meant what she'd said, Colt urged Hilde toward the edge of the river and the vehicles waiting on the highway above it. The guide had apparently called for EMTs and a rescue crew.

"I don't need a doctor," she said to Colt, as he drew her away from the raft. She could feel everyone watching her and tried to stem the flow of her tears. "I don't need you to take care of me."

"But you do need to get into some dry clothes," he said. "My place is close by."

She looked over at him, ready to tell him she had no intention of going to his house with him.

"You can tell me again what happened under the raft," he said.

"What would be the point? You don't believe me." She stumbled on one of the rocks. He caught her arm to keep her from falling. His hand felt warm and strong on her skin.

"How about this? I believe you more than I believe Dee."

She stopped, having reached the edge of the highway, and glared at him. "Then why didn't you speak up back there?"

"Because it's your word against hers, and as upset as you are, she is more believable right now. That's why I stopped you from telling them about what happened at the falls. Come on, I know this EMT. He'll give us a ride."

"I AM SO SORRY," Dana said for the hundredth time since the raft trip.

Dee planned to milk the incident for all it was worth but was getting tired of hearing Dana apologize. Almost drowning had gotten her out of helping with the huge family meal Dana had cooked. It also had Hud hovering protectively over her.

Dana had told all the family members about the mishap on the river as each arrived. Dee noticed that she'd left out the part about her best friend accusing her cousin of trying to kill her.

It would have been amusing except for the fact that Hilde had almost drowned *her*. Hilde had kicked her hard. For a moment, she'd seen stars. She really could have drowned under that raft. She was lucky she hadn't died today.

She'd had to meet all the family before dinner. There was the sister, Stacy, a smaller version of Dana, whom she'd met only briefly before. She had a pretty, green-eyed baby girl named Ella. Dee remembered that because she got the feeling Stacy might be a good resource—even an ally in the future.

Jordan and his wife, Deputy Marshal Liza Cardwell, were nice enough, but both were wrapped up in each other. Newlyweds, Dana had said. Then there was their father, Angus, and their uncle, Harlan. The talk at that end of the table was about the house Jordan and Liza were building somewhere on the ranch. Far enough away that they hadn't been a problem, Dee thought.

Apparently Dana had another brother, Clay. He worked in the movies in Hollywood and seldom came up to the ranch. Another positive. Hud's father, Brick, wasn't well. He lived in West Yellowstone and seldom got down the canyon. That was also good since he was an ex-marshal.

At the sound of a knock at the front door, Dee looked through the open dining room door into the living room. She could make out a dark shadow through the window.

Probably not Hilde or Deputy Colt Dawson, she thought with no small amount of relief. Hilde had come off as crazy on the river earlier. Dana had been shocked by her friend's accusations and torn in her loyalties. Dee had pretended to be hurt, which only made Dana more protective of her.

Hopefully that would be the last they saw of the woman, she thought, rubbing her jaw. It didn't surprise her that Hilde was turning out to be a problem. That first day Hilde had asked too many questions and was too protective of Dana. Not only that, she paid too much attention.

She suspects something is wrong.

Dee had run across a few intuitive people in her life. Best thing to do was get them out of your life as quickly as possible. After what happened on the river today, she didn't think she would have to worry about Hilde again.

She'd seen the moment when Hilde had realized there was nothing she could say to convince Dana that cousin Dee had been responsible for her almost drowning. Blood was thicker than water—didn't Hilde know that? Dee almost laughed at the thought since she and Dana shared none in common. But it didn't matter as long as Dana believed they did.

All the others on the raft had felt sorry for Dee. Everyone agreed Hilde was just upset and confused. They had tried to comfort Dee, telling her she shouldn't feel bad. The bruise on her cheek from where Hilde had kicked her was now like a badge of honor. She'd tried to save the woman—but there was no saving Hilde from Hilde, she thought now with a silent chuckle.

But apparently Deputy Marshal Colt Dawson was determined to try. Nice that he forgot he'd asked her for a dinner date tonight. She hoped she wasn't wrong about him not being at the door. No, he was probably home taking care of poor Hilde.

She'd seen Dana on the phone earlier. No doubt checking on her friend. Dana was so sure that once Hilde calmed down she would realize that Dee hadn't tried to drown her. So far Dana hadn't seemed to have any doubts to the contrary. Dee had to make sure she stayed that way.

Hud got up from the table to go answer the second knock at the door. Dee got the impression that most anyone who stopped by just walked in and didn't bother knocking.

As the door swung open, she felt her heart drop. She stumbled out of her chair and into the living room. "Rick?"

He saw her and smiled. Anyone watching would have thought everything was fine. Dee knew better.

"Rick, what a surprise." She hurried to the door, belatedly remembering to limp only the last few steps. She'd managed to hurt herself again in the river—at least that was her story. It would get her out of helping Dana with the dishes and the kids.

"I had to come after I got your phone call," he said smoothly. "Are you all right?"

"It's just a sprain," she said, and realized Hud was watching and waiting for an introduction. Before Dee could, Dana joined them.

"Rick, this is my cousin Dana I told you about and her husband, Hud. Rick…Cameron, a friend of mine from back East." She gave Rick a warning look. "We were just sitting down to a family dinner. Tell me where you're staying and I'll—"

"We always have room for one more," Dana said quickly. "Please join us. Any friend of Dee's is welcome."

Rick stepped in, letting the door close behind him as he looked around, amused at her discomfort. "*Dee,* are you sure you're all right? I've been worried about you."

"I'm fine. You really didn't need to come all this way just to check on me." She bit the words off, angry with him for showing up here and even angrier that he didn't take the hint and leave. She hung back with him as Hud and Dana returned to the large family dining room, where everyone else was waiting.

"What are you doing here?" she demanded under her breath so no one else could hear.

"Is that any way to greet an old friend, *Dee?*"

Her mind whirled. How had he found her? Then with a curse, she realized what she'd done. She'd left a change of address so she could get Dee Anna Justice's mail in care of the ranch. That way she'd know quickly if her cover was blown—as well as collect at least one of Dee Anna's trust fund checks.

In retrospect that had been a mistake. She should have known Rick would come looking for her once he realized she'd bailed on him and the apartment. He'd know the real Dee Anna hadn't gone to a ranch in Montana.

"You can't stay," she whispered. "You'll mess up everything."

He smiled at her. "I can't tell you how good it is to see you, *Dee*."

"Stop doing that."

"I set another place for you, Rick," Dana called from the dining room doorway. "Come join us and I'll introduce you to everyone."

Dee had indigestion by the time the meal wound down. Dana had introduced Rick, and he'd seemed to be enjoying himself, which made it worse. She couldn't wait until dinner was over so she could get him out of here. The trick would be getting him out of town.

Rick could smell a con a mile off. The fact that she was going by Dee Anna Justice had been a dead giveaway. He knew she was up to something. He would want something out of this.

She couldn't have been more relieved when dinner was finally over. Fortunately, because of her re-"sprained" ankle, she didn't have to help with the dishes. Rick helped clear the table. She heard him chatting in the kitchen with Hud and Dana.

She was going to kill him.

Finally, Rick said he was leaving and asked Dee if she felt up to walking him out to his rental car. She wouldn't have missed it for the world.

"You have to leave," she told him outside.

He glanced at the stars sparkling in the velvet canopy overhead and took a deep breath. "This is nice here. A little too hick for me, but the food was good," he said, finally looking at her. "I've missed you. I thought you would have at least left me a note."

"What do you want?"

"You always were good at cutting right to the heart of it. Isn't it possible I really did miss you?"

"No." He hadn't come here for a reunion. If anything, he'd come to blackmail her.

"Look," she said. "I will cut you in, but I need time. I don't even know what there is here yet."

He laughed. "You can call yourself Dee or anything else you like, but remember, I *know* you. You've staked out something here or you would be gone by now. Is it the land? Is it worth something? Or is there family money I'm just not seeing?"

"There isn't any hidden wealth," she said. "I'm just spending a few days here like a tourist while my cousin shows me a good time. She's picking up my little vacation. That's it."

"You're such a good liar. Usually. But I don't get what you could possibly be thinking here. Does Hud have a rich brother I haven't met yet?"

"Rick—"

"You'd better get back into the house," he said, glancing past her. "You really shouldn't be on that bad ankle too long." He chuckled. "Don't forget to limp or you're going to be doing dishes with the women in the kitchen the rest of your little vacation."

With that, he climbed into his rental car and slammed the door. She slapped the window, trying to get him to roll it down, but he merely made a face at her, started the engine and drove off.

She stood in the faint moonlight mentally kicking herself. Rick was going to ruin everything.

"ARE YOU FEELING BETTER?" Colt asked, as Hilde came out of his bathroom dressed in the sweatpants and T-shirt he'd given her.

She nodded. He'd changed into jeans and a T-shirt

that molded his muscled body. She'd never seen him in anything but his uniform before. No wonder he was so popular with women.

He handed her a mug of hot chocolate with tiny marshmallows floating in it. He must have seen her surprise.

"My mother used to always make me hot chocolate when I had a hard day in school," Colt said, and grinned shyly. "I thought it might help."

She curled her fingers around the mug, soaking in the warmth, and took a sip. She couldn't help smiling. "It's perfect." She was touched at his thoughtfulness. "I don't believe I thanked you for saving my life earlier."

He waved her apology away. "I'm just glad you're okay. Would you like to sit down?" he asked, motioning to his couch.

She glanced around his cabin. It was simply but comfortably furnished. He'd made a fire in the small fireplace. This time of year it cooled down quickly in the canyon.

The fire crackled invitingly as she took a seat at one end of the couch, curling her feet under her. She'd finally quit shaking. Now she just felt scared. Scared that she was right about Dee. Even more scared that she wasn't. Had she wrongly accused the woman?

Colt seemed to relax as he joined her at the opposite end of the couch. "Why don't you tell me about Dee?"

She hesitated, upset with herself for the scene she'd made earlier. It was so unlike her. No wonder Dana had looked so shocked. She shouldn't have confronted Dee in front of everyone, but she'd been so upset, so scared. She'd almost drowned. If Colt hadn't pulled her out when he had...

"You can tell me how you really feel," he said quietly.

She took a breath. "I don't know anymore."

"Sure you do," he said and smiled. "Follow your instincts. I have a feeling your instincts are pretty good."

Hilde laughed. "After seeing that hysterical woman on the river a while ago?"

"Almost drowning does that to a person."

She studied him for a moment. He was way too handsome, but he was also very nice. He'd saved her life and now he was willing to listen to her side of it. "What if my instincts are wrong?"

"You know they aren't."

Did she? She took another sip of the hot chocolate. It *did* help. Bracing herself, she said, "There's something…off about Dee."

He nodded, urging her to continue.

"I admit I was worried when Dana told me that she'd asked a cousin she'd never met to come visit. She's paying for all Dee's expenses. That seemed odd to me. But according to Dana, Dee recently quit her job. Add to that, no one knows how long she plans to stay."

"So you thought right away she might be taking advantage of your friend."

Hilde nodded. "After we picked her up at the airport, Dana was telling her all about this area. I noticed that she didn't seem interested. It wasn't until we reached the ranch and she met Hud that Dee perked up."

He nodded but said nothing.

"I know this all sounds so…small and petty."

"Tell me about the day at the falls."

She finished the hot chocolate and put her mug on the table next to her elbow, noticing the bestseller lying open, his place marked halfway through the book. It was one she'd been wanting to read, and she was momentarily distracted to know that Colt was a reader.

"I didn't want to go on the hike, but Dana insisted. I was probably rude. I asked how long Dee planned to stay. Shortly after that I was standing at the edge of the falls. Dana had gone over to the picnic spot to look for her camera, and all of a sudden I felt a hand on my back and a hard shove. Then Dee grabbed me and warned me to be careful, that it was dangerous around here."

"You believed it was a threat."

"I did."

"But you didn't say anything to Dana."

"I was too shocked and—"

"You talked yourself out of believing it."

She nodded. "Also, Dana was enjoying her cousin so much, I didn't have the heart to tell her."

"You feared she wouldn't believe you."

Hilde let out a laugh. "With good reason. She didn't believe that Dee tried to drown me today."

"But you do."

She swallowed, then slowly nodded. "She wasn't trying to save me. I know you find that hard to believe because I tried to fight you off moments later, when you were only trying to save me."

"Why do you think she pushed you at the falls and yet saved you, then today tried to drown you and maybe really did try to save you?"

"I don't know. It makes one of us seem crazy, doesn't it?"

He smiled. "What is it you think she wants? Dana and Hud don't have a lot money. She can't possibly think she can get her hands on the ranch. She's going to wear out her welcome within a week or so."

"That's just it, I don't know. I just can't get over the feeling that she wants something from Dana. But the more I think about it, the more I feel I must be wrong. What if I'm overreacting? Maybe she *was* trying to save me in the river today."

"Maybe she didn't push you at the falls?"

She looked away. "Dana thinks I'm jealous." She turned to meet his gaze. "Maybe I am." She got to her feet. "I should go home."

Colt rose, too. "What are you going to do?"

"Stay away from Dee," she said with a laugh. "Like you said, she'll wear out her welcome and leave."

"Hud called while you were changing clothes. He's taking Dee up to Elkhorn Lake on a horseback ride tomorrow. Dana's idea. I think we should go."

"*What?* And give her another chance at me?"

He grinned. "That's what I thought. You don't think you imagined any of this. Dee's dangerous, isn't she?"

"Yes. But you're the only person who believes me. Dee always comes away looking like a hero."

"Almost as if she planned it that way. If you really think Hud and Dana are in danger, then I think we need to keep an eye on Dee. Meanwhile, I'll be keeping an eye on you."

Hilde couldn't help but feel a small thrill at the last part. She liked the idea of Colt keeping an eye on her. She told herself not to make anything of it.

"The last thing I want to do is go on a long horseback ride with Dee Anna Justice. What makes you so sure she won't try to kill me again?"

"I can't promise that. But it will look more than a little odd if you meet with yet another accident. I have a plan. But you probably won't like it."

She didn't, but she was so thankful that Colt believed her, she would have gone along with anything he asked.

"Right now, she's won," he said. "You need to throw her off balance and stay close to Dana. There's only one way to do that."

"HE'S A BOYFRIEND, isn't he?" Dana said excitedly when Dee returned to the house after walking Rick out. Hud had apparently gone up to bed. Everyone else had left as she was coming back into the house.

"No, he's…" She saw the sympathy in Dana's expression. Her "cousin" was waiting for some heartbreaking love story. How could she disappoint her with so much at stake?

"Your ex, isn't he." Her cousin drew her over to the couch and patted the cushion, indicating she should sit and spill all. Dee was thankful she had only Dana to deal with now. Dana saw what she wanted to and clearly loved finding a cousin she'd never known she had. Hilde wouldn't have been fooled by her relationship with Rick.

"I can tell he still cares about you," Dana was saying. "He followed you all the way to Montana to make sure you were all right."

Maybe it would be better for everyone to think Rick was a boyfriend, then when she broke up with him and sent him packing, it would play well with the family. It could buy her more time here. She wouldn't want to go back East right away after such a traumatic breakup.

"That's why you quit your job," Dana said. "Did you work with him?"

Why not give her what she wanted and then some? "He was my boss."

"Oh, those kinds of things are so…sticky."

"I knew better, but he was unrelenting."

"I can see that in him. To fly all the way out here."

"I should never have called him and told him where I was. But I knew he'd worry and I certainly shouldn't have mentioned that I sprained my ankle."

"You couldn't know that he'd follow you," Dana said. "He seems nice, though. Is there no chance for the two of you?"

No chance in hell. "He's married," she lied.

Dana looked worried. "Children?"

Dee shook her head. "He and his wife are separated. He's always wanted children, but his wife didn't. She says she doesn't like kids."

Her cousin looked shocked. "Oh, how awful for him."

"Yes. I feel sorry for him, but he needs to try to work things out with his wife."

Dana agreed.

Dee realized she was painting too sympathetic a picture of Rick. "He's been so despondent since I broke it off and…" She lowered her voice. "He's been taking… pills. I'm worried sick he might do something…crazy, between the depression and the drugs. Still I shouldn't have called him to check on him." Like she would have ever called him, but she was grateful that Rick was quick on his feet when it came to lying.

"You did the right thing. Just imagine how you would have felt if you hadn't called and something had happened to him."

"Hmm," she said. "You're right. But maybe I should go back home. I hate bringing my problems to your door."

"Don't be silly." Dana reached out and squeezed her hand. "That's what family is for."

She'd always wondered what family was for. A part of her felt sorry for Dana. The woman was so caring. It must be exhausting.

"You're tired and you've had such an emotional day," her cousin said, glancing at her watch. The fact that Dana still wore a watch and didn't always carry a cell phone told Dee how far from civilization she now was.

"I hope Hilde is all right." She watched Dana's expression out of the corner of her eye, trying to calculate whether or not Dana would call her friend to patch things up or not.

"It's just a good thing Colt was there," Dana said. "He'll take care of her. I'll give her a call later to make sure."

"I feel badly about what she said."

"Don't let it bother you. She was just talking crazy because she was scared. Still, it wasn't like the Hilde I know at all."

She could tell Dana was worried about her friend. "Almost drowning would do that to anyone. I just don't want to come between the two of you."

"You won't. I shouldn't have insisted Hilde come on the raft trip. It really isn't her thing. And anyone would have panicked if they'd been trapped under the raft like that."

"It was just such a freak accident," she agreed.

"I'm sure Hilde realized that, once she had a chance to calm down. I wouldn't be surprised if she shows up tomorrow to apologize."

Don't hold your breath on that one. "I hate to even ask what you have planned for tomorrow," Dee said with a small laugh. She hoped Dana would come up with something away from the ranch with Hud and as far away as possible from Big Sky and Hilde and Rick. "You really are showing me such a great time. How will I ever be able to repay you?"

"It's my pleasure. I thought you'd like to ride up to Elkhorn Lake."

"So you'll be able to go?" she asked.

"No, I have to stay here. Hud is going to take you by horseback, if you're up to it. The lake is beautiful and the trip is really wonderful."

Oh, yes. She couldn't wait.

"I think his deputy Colt is going along."

Dee swore silently. Colt? The man who'd saved Hilde.

"It sounds like fun," she said, although it had sounded much more fun when it was just going to be her and Hud. "I just wish you could go. Maybe next time?"

Dana nodded. "You must come back every year."

Or never leave. "Oh, I would love that."

"Well, sleep tight and don't worry about Rick."

Easy for Dana to say.

CHAPTER SIX

THE NEXT MORNING, Dee got up early and borrowed Dana's pickup to drive into Meadow Village. She still didn't get the town of Big Sky. Everything was so spread out, but it was all close enough that it didn't take her long to find Rick's rental car parked in front of an older motor court motel.

Rick had always been cheap, usually out of necessity because he was broke. She could only guess that that was the case this time.

She had to knock three times before he finally opened the door wearing nothing but a towel wrapped around his waist.

"I wondered when you'd show up," he said with a grin.

She shoved past him into the room. It was pretty much what she expected: bed, television, bathroom. A discount-store piece of so-called art of a mountain from some other state hung on the wall over the unmade bed. Rick's clothes were strewn on the floor and there were a half-dozen empty beer cans next to the bed.

"You always were a slob," she said, turning to look at him. "You have to leave. Now."

"I wish I could, but I spent every dime I had just to get here·to see you."

How had she known that was the case? She reached

into her shoulder bag. "Here's enough to get you back home and a little extra so you won't starve on the way. The next flight is this afternoon. Be on it." With that she started to leave. "And Rick. No drugs."

"Come on, you know I'm clean. Anyway, you need my help."

She stopped next to him. "No, I don't. I know what I'm doing."

"You and I used to make a pretty good team, as I recall. I'm probably the only person you can truly trust."

"Unless you get drunk or high and shoot your mouth off."

"I've kept your secrets all these years, drunk or sober. Come on, there's a bond between us that not even you can deny." He touched her shoulder.

She pulled away. "I mean it. Don't buy drugs with that money."

"Don't try to kill that blonde woman again."

"I don't know what you're talking about."

"Remember when you and I were little more than kids and I almost drowned? I know you, remember?"

"Then you know to stay out of my business, don't you."

By the time she returned to the ranch, Hud was busy saddling horses. She drove into the yard, but didn't get out of the truck right away. She liked watching him, watching the muscles in his arms and back, imagining being in those arms. Desire hit her like a sucker punch. She wanted him, and she'd always made a habit of getting what she wanted, any way she had to.

"Best get dressed," Hud called to her, as she climbed out of the truck. "Dana's put out some clothes for you to wear in your room."

She smiled. "Thanks." Inside she went right to her upstairs room. She could hear Dana in the kitchen with the kids. How could the woman stand that noise all the time?

She quickly dressed in the Western attire her cousin had so thoughtfully put out for her, right down to the cowboy boots. Fortunately or unfortunately they were close enough in size that all the clothes fit.

"They're my prebaby clothes," Dana said when Dee came downstairs in them. "I knew they would fit you."

They did, she thought, as she caught a glimpse of herself in the front window reflection. At a glance, she could pass for Dana. A slightly skinnier version, but still...

Dana had made her a breakfast sandwich since she'd apparently missed the usual ranch breakfast. She couldn't believe how these people ate. It was no wonder Dana hadn't gotten back to her pretwins weight.

Breakfast often consisted of pounded and floured fried deer steaks, hash browns, milk gravy, biscuits and eggs. She'd never seen anything like it in her life. There would be changes if she were running this house.

There would have to be a lot of changes. She realized with a start that she hadn't thought this through. Getting Hud would be hard enough. But what to do with Dana and the kids? Dana would have to go. So would the kids. She wasn't interested in having them even come visit on weekends or summers.

She thought of Rick. Maybe he could be helpful after all. She was debating calling him to tell him they should talk, when she looked out and saw with a groan that Hud was saddling *five* horses.

"I see Hud has saddled a bunch of horses," she said

nonchalantly to her cousin over the screaming of the children. "Did you decide you could go on the ride with us after all?"

Dana smiled but shook her head. "I need to spend some time with my babies."

"Then Mary and Hank are going?" She was amazed that she finally remembered their names. They were cute kids. If you liked kids.

"No," Dana said with a laugh. "They're too young for this ride."

Just then the front door opened. She turned and was unable to hide her shock as Hilde came in duded out in Western attire. "Hilde?"

"Dee," the young woman said. She hurried to Dee and took both her hands. "I am so sorry about yesterday. Can you ever forgive me?"

Even if she hadn't been good at reading people, she would have seen through *this* apology. But out of the corner of her eye, she saw that Dana was smiling, buying into every word of it. The only gracious thing to do was pretend it was real.

"Hilde, you don't need to apologize, really. I was so scared for you. I'm just glad you're all right. It was such a freak accident."

"Wasn't it, though?" Hilde agreed. "Thank you for being so understanding. I told Dana I couldn't wait until I saw you to tell you how sorry I was for thinking you had anything to do with my almost drowning."

I'll just bet. "Well, it's good to see you looking so well today. Thanks for coming by."

"Hilde's going on the ride up to the lake with all of you," Dana said.

It took all her effort not to show how that news really made her feel. Hilde was smiling as if she knew exactly what Dee was feeling right now. Apparently such a close call with death hadn't taught Hilde anything.

"That's great," Dee said. "But I would think you'd want to stay home and rest today after what you've been through."

"That's what I told her," Dana said. "But Hilde is tougher than she looks." She smiled and gave Hilde's arm a squeeze.

"I'm not so tough," Hilde said to her friend. "Look at your cousin. She almost drowned yesterday, too, and look how *she's* bounced back." Hilde turned back to her. "Oh, Dee, that bruise on your cheek looks like it hurts. Did I do that?"

"I know you didn't mean to," Dana said quickly.

Ha, Dee thought. "So who else is going with us?" she asked just an instant before Hud came in the door with Colt Dawson right behind him and Rick bringing up the tail end. "Is anyone protecting Big Sky?" Dee asked. "It seems the entire force is right here."

"The other two deputies are holding down the fort," Colt said. "So don't worry about the canyon being safe while we're here with you."

Dee swore silently as Hud asked if they were ready to go. "I can't wait," she said. Rick was more of a dude than she was. She hoped he got saddle sores.

As they all filed out to the saddled horses, she wondered what the trail was like to this Elkhorn Lake. Hopefully it wasn't too dangerous. She would hate to see anything happen to Hilde. Let alone Rick. Horses were so unpredictable.

Before she mounted her horse, she surreptitiously picked up several nice-sized rocks and stuck them in her pocket.

COLT MADE SURE that he and Hilde stayed behind the others as they rode away from the ranch. He liked riding next to her. It was a beautiful Montana spring day. The air smelled of new green grass, sunshine and water as they followed the creek up into the mountains. Sun dappled the ground as it fingered through the pine branches.

"So tell me about Hilde Jacobson," he said, as their horses ambled along. The others had ridden on ahead, but Colt kept them in sight in case anything happened.

"There isn't much to tell," she said. Then, as if realizing he really was interested, she added, "I grew up in Chicago. My father was a janitor, my mother worked as a housekeeper. I was an only child. My father was determined that I would be the first in his family to go to college."

"And you were?"

She nodded. "I went into business. My father had worked around corporate America and decided that would be the world that I should conquer. I gave it my best shot at least for a while."

"How did you end up in Big Sky owning a fabric store?"

"My father died. My mother told me to follow my heart. I hated big business. I came up here skiing, met Dana and Hud, and the rest is history."

"You and Dana are close, aren't you?"

"We *were*."

He heard the catch in her throat.

"Your turn," she said after a moment. "Tell me your life story."

"I grew up north of here. I married young. It didn't work out. I went into law enforcement and got the job here."

"You like Big Sky?"

He looked back at the country they'd just left behind and nodded. "It's not as open as I'm used to—the mountains are so much larger—but it grows on you living in the canyon."

"Doesn't it?" she said. "Some people think it's paradise and hate to leave."

He saw that she was looking at the two riders ahead of them. Dee was in a deep conversation with Hud. Rick was nowhere to be seen.

DEE WAS LEANING toward Hud and pretending to be fascinated by the different types of rock faces ahead when Hilde and Colt came riding up. Colt cut Hud away from her as slick as the ranch cow dog she'd seen herding calves in the pasture.

A few moments later she found herself riding next to Hilde, also not a coincidence.

"Where's Rick?" Hilde asked, looking behind her. "We seem to have lost him."

"I think he needed to see a tree about a dog. Isn't that what you locals say out here?"

"I'm not a local," Hilde said. "I'm actually from Chicago, and I think it's a dog about a tree."

"Really? I just assumed you were like Hud and Dana, born and raised out West."

"So is Rick from New York City, too? Is that where the two of you met?"

Dee smiled over at her to let her know she knew what she was doing and it wasn't going to work. "I'm still surprised you were up for this ride today after your near-death experience yesterday." She touched the bruise on her cheek. "I know I was still feeling the aftereffects this morning. I didn't realize Montana was such a dangerous place."

"It sure *is*—when you're around." With that, Hilde spurred her horse and rode on up to join Colt and Hud.

So much for that earlier apology, Dee thought with a curse.

She hadn't planned to actually drown Hilde yesterday, but at some point it hadn't seemed like such a bad idea. Dana would have eventually gotten over losing her friend. In fact, she would have needed her cousin even more.

But Dana would have had to lean even more on her husband. Dee had hoped to avoid all of that and just get Hilde to keep her distance. Apparently her plan hadn't worked after the incident at the waterfalls or on the raft trip.

Hilde needed stronger encouragement to get out of her way. Dee stuck her hand into her pocket, closed her fingers around one of the rocks, hefting it in her hand. Ahead, the trail narrowed as it cut across the side of a rocky mountain face. The horses with Hud, Colt and Hilde fell into single file as they started across the narrow trail.

Dee looked down at the drop-off. Nothing but large boulders all the way down to the creek far below. She let Hilde and her horse get a little farther ahead. She didn't want to be nearby when things went awry.

Poor Hilde. She was having such a bad week. First almost falling off Ousel Falls, then almost drowning in the Gallatin River. Clearly she shouldn't have come along on this ride after what had happened yesterday. She really wasn't up to it.

Dee lifted the rock, measuring the distance. The trail was narrow. If a horse bucked off its rider right now, the rider could be badly hurt—if not killed.

She told herself she had no choice. Hilde had managed to get back in Dana's good graces. Dana was more apt to believe whatever Hilde came up with now. And there was no doubt Hilde would be trying to find out everything she could about cousin Dee.

Reining in her horse at the edge of the pines, she pulled back her arm to throw the rock. All she had to do was hit the back of Hilde's horse. If it spooked even a little, it might buck or lose its footing, and both woman and horse could fall.

Just as she was about to hurl the stone, a hand grabbed her arm and twisted the rock from her grip. She let out a cry of both surprise and pain. Turning in her saddle, she swore when she saw it was Rick.

"Don't be a fool," he said under his breath. "If she has another accident this early, it will only make everyone more suspicious."

"I have to stop her. She's onto me."

Rick shook his head. "I'll help you, but not here. Not today. Be nice to her but watch yourself." He dug into her pocket to pull out the other rocks. "Just in case you get another smart idea while looking at *my* horse's backside," he said, and rode on up the trail to catch up with Hilde.

HILDE KEPT HER eye on Dee during the ride to the lake. But the woman seemed almost subdued after their little talk.

Rick spent most of the time talking with Hud on the last part of the ride up and even when they'd reached Elkhorn Lake. Hilde saw Dee watching the two of them. She got the impression Dee didn't like her boyfriend talking with Hud.

When Hud broke out the lunch Dana had packed, Colt brought her over a sandwich and sat down with her on the rocks at the edge of the lake away from the others.

"Have you noticed the way she is with Hud?" she asked quietly before taking a bite of her sandwich. They'd both been watching Dee.

"Yep."

Hilde locked gazes with him. "I think I know what she's after. She wants Hud."

Colt let out a laugh. *"Hud?"*

"I've been trying to figure out what she wants other than a Montana vacation, all expenses paid."

"She likes to flirt."

"Did she flirt with you?"

He admitted she hadn't except for a few minutes at the river before the raft trip and he suspected that little bit of flirting with him had been for Dana's benefit only. "If Hud's what she's after, then she's wasting her time. He's crazy in love with Dana, not to mention they have four kids together. Hud would never be interested in Dee."

"She wouldn't be the first woman who went after another woman's man."

"Or vice versa," Colt said.

Hilde glanced at him. She knew Colt was divorced. Earlier he'd said he'd married young and that it hadn't worked out. Had another man come after his wife? Or had Colt been seduced away from his marriage?

"But I don't believe any woman can get a man to leave his marriage unless he's willing," Colt added, keeping her from asking him about his marriage. "As they say, it takes two to tango."

"I agree," she said. "Hud would never jeopardize his marriage for a fling with someone like Dee." But had Colt?

"So what's Dee's plan, do you think?" Colt asked quietly. They both watched Dee, who was sitting in a tight circle with Hud and Rick. She was taking tiny bites of her sandwich, clearly not interested in food. Rick had Hud talking, and Dee appeared to be hanging on Hud's every word.

"I wish I knew," Hilde said, feeling a growing desperation as she watched the woman. Dee had wormed her way into Dana's and Hud's lives and she wasn't finished yet. "Now that I know what she's capable of, if I'm right and she is after Hud and she can't get him through seduction, then she will do something more drastic. That's what has me scared."

COLT LOOKED UP from his lunch to study Hilde. She was breathtaking: the sun on her face, her hair as golden as autumn leaves. He was surprised when he'd first come to Big Sky and learned that Hilde and Dana were best friends. They were so different.

Dana was all tomboy. She could ride and rope and shoot as well as any man. Being a mother had toned her down some, but she was a ranch girl born and bred, and she was at home in the great outdoors.

Hilde was all girl, from the clothes she wore to the

way she presented herself. He didn't doubt for a moment that she was smart or that she was strong. She could get tough, too, if she had to. He'd seen that the way she'd gone after Dee on the river, but there was something so wonderfully feminine about her. Clearly she enjoyed being a woman.

The combination of smart, strong and ultra-feminine was more powerful than she knew. He suspected it scared away most men.

Dana had told him that Hilde didn't date much. "She must know the kind of man she wants. I just hope she finds him. Hilde deserves someone special."

Colt looked away. He was far from anyone special, but he did wonder what kind of man she was looking for. Or if she was even looking. He thought of his short marriage and the heartbreak it had caused. He'd told himself he would never marry again. But that was before he met Hilde.

They had just finished their sandwiches when there was a splash followed instantly by a scream. He and Hilde turned to look across the lake in the direction the sound had come from and there was Dee swimming in the clear, cold water.

She was laughing and shrieking, but clearly enjoying herself.

Colt noticed that even Hud was smiling at the crazy Easterner.

When it became apparent that she was nude, the men turned around and let her rush out of the water without them watching.

"Did you see that?" Hilde asked.

"I didn't peek."

"Not Dee. Did you see that even Rick turned around?

Doesn't that seem odd if the two were boyfriend and girlfriend?"

Colt shrugged. Everything about Rick Cameron seemed odd to him. Add Dee to the mix and you had a rodeo. "She does like attention," he said.

"And she's getting it. Hud isn't completely immune to her. If for some reason Dana wasn't around…"

Colt frowned as Dee came out of the trees dressed again, her hair wet, her face aglow from her swim.

Hud laughed and shook his head when Dee suggested he should have come into the water. No man was completely immune to a woman's attention, especially one who, on the surface, seemed so much like his wife.

Colt had learned that the hard way.

CHAPTER SEVEN

AFTER THE HORSEBACK ride up to the lake, Hilde couldn't wait to get home, shower and curl up in her bed. She hadn't gotten much sleep last night. Add to that everything that had happened to her in the past forty-eight hours and she knew she had good reason to be exhausted.

"Are you sure you don't want to stay and have dinner with us?" Dana had asked. "Hud is going to broil some steaks. I'm making a big salad."

"I would love to, really, but the ride took a lot out of me," Hilde said. She could see that her friend was disappointed, but Hilde had had all the Dee she could take for one day.

She gave Dana a hug, hugging her more tightly than she normally did, afraid for her friend. "Thank you for the offer, though," she said when she let go.

"Once you get to know Dee you'll see how vulnerable and sweet she…" Dana's words died off as she must have seen something in her friend's expression that stopped her.

"Be careful," Hilde said. "I don't want anything to happen to you."

Dana gave her a sympathetic look, and Hilde sensed that things had changed between them. It made her sad, but she couldn't blame her friend. Dee was like a slow but deadly poison.

"Oh, Hilde, aren't you staying for dinner?" Dee said all cheery, as she came down the stairs. She'd showered and now wore a sundress that accentuated all her assets—which were no small thing. "I know Dana has missed you. I'm afraid she's getting bored with me. I'm not much fun."

"You are plenty fun," Dana said to her cousin. "I could never get bored with you."

"Am I the luckiest woman in the world to have such an amazing cousin?" Dee asked with a too-bright smile. "I'm so glad she found me and invited me to Montana. I'm having a terrific time. I've missed having family so much."

"I know that feeling, so I'm glad," Dana said to her cousin, then turned to Hilde. "Change your mind about dinner."

"Another time." Hilde held Dana's gaze. "Take care of yourself." And she was out the door and headed for her SUV. It was all she could do not to run. She saw Colt glance up from where he and Hud were talking by the corrals. Concern crossed his expression, then his gaze went to the porch where Dee was standing, backlit by the light coming from inside the house.

Dee said something to the two men. Hud laughed and Dee started to come off the porch toward them. Dana called from the kitchen for her cousin. Dee hesitated, clearly disappointed, but went back inside to help Dana.

On the drive to her house, Hilde felt sick to her stomach. She'd never been violent. She was a forget-and-forgive kind of person. At least she thought she was. But for a few moments back there at the house, she'd wanted to walk back to the porch and punch Dee in the face.

"I really need some rest," she told herself, as she parked in front of her house. Once inside, she showered and changed into her favorite silk robe before padding into the kitchen for a glass of warm milk. She knew she couldn't eat anything the way she felt right now.

Back in the bedroom, she finished the milk and crawled into bed with a book she'd been wanting to read—the same one Colt was reading. A book would be the only thing that could get her mind off Dee and her fears for Dana and her family.

She'd read only a few pages, though, when she must have fallen asleep. When the ringing of the phone woke her, she was lying on the open pages of the book, her cheek creased and damp. It took her a moment to realize what had awakened her.

"Hello?" she said, snatching up the phone. Her first thought was that something had happened out at the ranch. Her heart took off like a shot.

"I was afraid you were out with your boyfriend."

She didn't recognize the voice, but her heart was still pounding. "I beg your pardon? I think you have the wrong number." She recognized the laugh, though, and sat up in the bed, trying to shake off sleep. "Rick?"

"One and the same," he said with another laugh. "I've been sitting here having a few drinks, thinking about you."

Hilde groaned inwardly, afraid where this was headed.

"I know your type," he continued. "You like nice things but you try to hide the fact that you come from money."

She was momentarily surprised by his insight.

"I like nice things, too, but I'm afraid I don't come from money. Far from it." Another laugh. "I'll make you a deal. You want to know the scoop on *Dee?* If you can get your hands on ten thousand dollars, which I have a feeling you can without much trouble, then I will tell you things about dear *Dee* that will make your hair stand on end."

"You sound drunk."

"Not yet."

"Why should I believe you?"

"Because I know she tried to kill you on the river. I'm betting it wasn't the first time she put a scare into you."

"You would sell out your own girlfriend?"

He chuckled. "That's the other thing. *Dee* and I have a complicated relationship. I'll tell you all about it when you get here. How she sold my soul to the devil a long time ago. You'd better hurry before I get too drunk, though. I'm starting to feel the effects of this whiskey." With that he hung up.

COLT WAS AT the marshal's office when the call came in. He saw the dispatcher look in his direction then said she would put the call through to Deputy Marshal Colt Dawson.

The woman on the other end of the line sounded hysterical, and for a moment he didn't recognize Hilde's voice. "Where are you?" he broke in, hoping she would take a breath.

"At the Lazy T Motel, room 9. It's Rick Cameron. He's dead. She killed him, Colt. She killed him because she knew I was coming here tonight."

Colt wondered why Hilde was going to Rick's motel

room, but he didn't dare ask right now. "Step outside the room. Take some deep breaths. I'm on my way." The moment he put down the phone he called Marshal Hud Savage, then he headed for the Lazy T, siren blaring and lights flashing.

Hilde was standing outside, just as he'd told her to. She wore a pair of jeans, a blue-and-tan-print blouse and nice sandals. Her hair was piled on top of her head. Had this been a date?

Jealousy bit into him like the bite of a rattlesnake, filling him with its venom. "What are you doing here, Hilde?" he asked the moment he reached her.

"Rick called. He said he'd tell me about Dee for ten thousand dollars. She killed him. You know she did." The words came flying out, tumbling all over each other.

"Easy," he said and drew her to the side, away from the motel room doors. They had opened, and guests were looking out to see what was going on. "You were going to pay him ten thousand dollars?"

She nodded. "I was asleep when he called. I dressed as quickly as I could."

He had to smile. Only Hilde would grab a matching outfit to come pay off a con man. She'd even taken the time to pull up her long hair into a do that made her look like a model on a runway.

"Stay here, okay?" he said, holding her at arm's length to look into her face. She'd been crying, but she still looked great. As he stepped to the door of the motel, he heard Hud's patrol pickup siren in the distance.

Several more guests stuck their heads out to see what was going on.

"Please go back inside," Colt told them. Inside the

motel room he found Rick Cameron sprawled on the
bed. There was an empty bottle of whiskey on the floor
and an empty bottle of prescription pills under the edge
of the bedspread.

He checked for a pulse. Hilde was right. The man
was dead. Still when the EMTs arrived seconds later,
they attempted to revive him without any luck.

"Looks like an overdose," one of the EMTs told Hud
as he came in the door.

Colt stepped out to Hilde, but she'd already heard.
"No," she cried, trying to get past him to talk to Hud.
"This wasn't an accident. He knew I was on my way
over."

The EMTs brought out the body and loaded it into
the ambulance. Hud came out after them and walked
over to Hilde, clearly unhappy to see her there.

"Dee killed him," Hilde said before the marshal
could speak.

Hud raised a brow but didn't respond to the accusation. "I'm going to have to ask you a few questions.
Why don't we go down to the office?" He turned to
Colt. "Stay here and talk to the motel owner when he
gets here."

Colt nodded and didn't look at Hilde as she and the
marshal left. The lines had been clearly drawn now.
Hud had made that point by telling him to stay there
and wait for the motel owner.

He and Hilde were alone on their side of that line,
and from Hud's disappointed look as he left, they were
on the *wrong* side.

HILDE FOLLOWED HUD in her SUV the few blocks to the
marshal's office, her mind racing.

Rick had been ready to tell her the truth about Dee. Surely Hud would realize it was too much of a coincidence for him to overdose right before she got there. She said as much as she followed him into his office.

"I've seen enough of these where the victim mixed alcohol and heavy-duty pain pills. It looks to me like an accidental drug overdose," Hud told her.

"Well, you're wrong." She hated the way her voice broke. Even to her own ears, she sounded close to hysteria. Why wouldn't he believe her?

"Hilde, you're upset. You've been under a lot of strain lately—"

Of course Dana would have told him about her breakdown on the river. "Are you telling me you can't see that people have a lot of accidents around Dee?" she snapped.

"Why don't you tell me how it is that you're the one who found the victim," Hud said, as he settled into his chair behind his desk.

She'd known Hud for years, ever since she'd moved to Big Sky and met Dana. He was like a brother to her. But when he'd sat down behind his desk just then, she saw him become the marshal, all business. She felt the wall come up between them and had to fight tears of frustration and regret.

Taking a breath, she tried to calm down. But she was at war with herself. She knew he wasn't going to believe her, but at the same time she had to try to make him see the truth.

"I was asleep. Rick called me." She told him about the conversation, recalling as much as she could of it.

Hud nodded when she finished. "You said he sounded

as if he'd been drinking. He said he would give you 'the scoop' on Dee. His words?"

"Yes and the way he said 'Dee,' I got the impression she might not really be Dee Anna Justice." She instantly saw skepticism in Hud's expression. No doubt Dana had also told him that she thought Hilde was jealous of her cousin. "There is something wrong with Dee. I feel it."

She quickly regretted blurting it out when Hud said "Hilde" in a tone that made it clear she was too biased against the woman to be credible.

Thank goodness Colt believed her.

"Hud, you have to admit it's suspicious that he calls, ready to tell me about her, and ends up dead."

"You said he sounded drunk. He might have already taken enough drugs to kill him. Which would explain why by the time you got there, he was already dead. Also, you have no idea what 'the scoop' on her might have been. He was a disgruntled ex-boyfriend."

"Was he?" she asked. "All we have is Dee's word on that. I assume she has an alibi?"

"She was at the house. Hilde, she was there all evening."

She knew Dee was behind it. Maybe she'd put something in the bottle of bourbon that was beside the bed. Or hired someone to kill him. But there was no doubt in Hilde's mind that she'd killed him.

"Rick was addicted to prescription drugs," Hud said with a sigh. "Dee said it was one reason she'd broken up with him. She was also worried that he might hurt himself because of the breakup. Apparently she told him after the horseback ride to the lake that they wouldn't be getting back together."

Hilde smiled, not surprised that Dee had covered her

bases. Again. "She set that up nicely, didn't she?" she asked, unable to keep the amusement out of her tone.

"Hilde." His voice reeked with impatience.

She got to her feet, giving up. She'd cried wolf too many times without any proof to back it up. No one believed her. Except Colt. If he was telling the truth. She groaned inwardly at the thought that he might just be indulging her because he liked her. Liked her? Or just wanted to get her into his bed because she was a challenge?

"If those are all your questions..."

"Did you see anyone leaving the motel when you drove up?" Hud asked with a sigh.

She shook her head.

"The motel room door was unlocked?"

She nodded.

"Did you hear anyone going out the back as you entered?"

Why was he doing this? He believed it was an accidental overdose. Was he just trying to get her to see that she was wrong? "I didn't see anyone. I really can't tell you any more."

Hud gave her a regretful look. He knew she was angry that he didn't believe her, but there was nothing she could do about that.

"She's after you, Hud."

"Who?" he asked, frowning.

"Dee. She wants *you*."

He got to his feet, angrier now. "Hilde, I don't know what's gotten into you. You of all people know how I feel about Dana, about our family." He shook his head. "Go home and get some rest."

She nodded, seeing that there was nothing more she

could say. "If you have any more questions, you know where I live." With that she left.

COLT HAD A pretty good idea how things had gone the moment Hilde answered the door. He'd thought about waiting until morning, but he was worried about her. If things had gone as he suspected they had, she would be upset and might welcome company.

"I just wanted to be sure you were all right."

She shook her head and motioned him inside. "Dee had an alibi. Not that she needs it. No one believes me anyway. She set this up so perfectly, telling Hud and Dana about Rick's drug problem and that she was worried he would do something terrible to himself."

"I'm sorry," he said. "*I* believe you."

"Do you?" She met his gaze with a fiery one of her own. She was good and mad, and she'd never looked more beautiful. He'd only glimpsed this kind of passion in her before tonight. "Or are you just trying to get into my pants?"

He laughed. "As tempting as that offer is, I like to think I have a shot without being forced to lie to you. I believe you, Hilde. It's too much of a coincidence that he should overdose when you're on the way to his motel room. She got to him. I'm not sure how, but she got to him."

Tears filled her eyes. "Why can't Hud see that?"

"Because Dee's good at hiding her true self and Hud operates on proof."

"Colt, I don't even think she *is* Dee Anna Justice."

He raised a brow.

"It's the way Rick called her 'Dee.' I heard him do it

on the horseback ride up to the lake. Is there any way to find out if she's even the woman she says she is?"

Colt gave that some thought. He wasn't sure he believed Dee was pretending to be Dana's cousin. He wasn't sure how she could have pulled that off, but he was willing to put Hilde's mind at rest and his own.

"I'll see if I can get her fingerprints. I might need your help."

"You know you have it," she said. "Would you like something to drink? I have some wine."

"You're tired. I should go."

"I could use the company. Just one drink."

He smiled. "If you had a beer…"

"I do."

He followed her through the house to the kitchen. Her house was neat as a pin and nicely furnished. But not overdone. He realized they had that in common: a minimalistic view of the world.

She handed him a beer, poured herself a glass of wine and led him into the living room.

"Dee already told Dana that Rick had been depressed and she was worried about him, since she told him it was over after the horseback ride," Hilde said. "I swear she must have been planning to drug him right from the moment he showed up."

"It's proving it that's the problem," he said. Sitting here in Hilde's house seemed the most natural thing in the world. "I want you to stay away from her unless I am there to make sure she doesn't try to kill you again."

Hilde looked up in surprise. "You can't believe she would try again. She couldn't get away with *another* murder."

"Rick's death will probably be ruled an accidental

overdose," he reminded her. "Consider how it would look if something happened to you now. You've been having a streak of bad luck. Plus you've been…overwrought." She started to object, but he held up his hand. "I'm just saying how Dee would spin it. You got careless, you haven't been yourself. You get the idea. That's why I want you to give the woman a wide berth until she leaves."

"She's not leaving."

"Well, she can't stay forever."

"She can if she finds a way to get Hud all to herself," Hilde said. "I told Hud that Dee was after him."

Colt groaned. "I can imagine how he took that."

"He needed to be warned."

Colt couldn't argue that. He just hoped it wouldn't have the opposite effect and make Hud more sympathetic to Dee.

"She knows we're onto her." Hilde drained her wineglass. "What scares me is what she'll do next. I'm afraid for Dana and her family. If she makes a play for Hud… I have a feeling Dee doesn't take rejection well."

Colt agreed that the whole family could be in danger. "I wish there was some way to get her out of that house."

"I doubt dynamite would work, even if Dana would let you blast her out. Dee has completely snowed Dana."

He could hear her disappointment. "I know it's frustrating seeing Dana and even Hud taken in like this. But you have to admit, Dee is good."

"She's playing this perfectly, too perfectly," Hilde said. "Which makes me think this isn't her first time she's done this."

"Whatever *this* is," Colt said. "I'll see what I can find out about her. Meanwhile, I'll see what we can do about getting her fingerprints." He'd have to be careful. He couldn't let Hud find out that he was investigating his wife's cousin. If Dana wasn't so happy having found a cousin she never knew she had, then Colt was sure Hud would be suspicious of Dee by now.

"I want to help."

"You are going to stay clear of the ranch unless I'm with you. Promise me."

She promised, but he could tell her concern for her friend was weighing heavily on her. What worried him was that if Dee decided to make a move against her, she would use that concern and Hilde would fall right into the trap.

He finished his beer, saw how late it was and got up to leave. Hilde walked him to the door. As he opened it, a cool breeze blew in, ruffling her hair. He reached to tuck an errant golden strand behind her ear like he'd seen her do the few times she'd worn her hair down.

But the moment he did, his hand slid around to the back of her slim neck. His eyes locked with hers. Her skin felt cool to his touch as he drew her to him.

THE KISS WAS gentle and sweet and so unexpected. Just the touch of his lips sent a jolt through her. Colt must have felt her tremble because he pulled her closer. She could feel his heart hammering under the hard muscles of his chest.

Her lips parted and she felt a rush of heat as he enclosed her in his arms and deepened the kiss.

She felt light-headed. No one had ever kissed her like this. She leaned into him, into the kiss. For the first time in days, Dee Anna Justice was the last thing on her mind.

Colt pressed her against the wall. She could feel the passion in his kiss, in his body. She wouldn't have been surprised if they had made love right there.

Headlights washed over them. Dana pulled in behind Hilde's SUV. They both drew back as if the lights were ice water thrown on them.

"I should go," Colt said. He touched her hand, his gaze locking with hers for a moment. Then he sauntered out to his patrol pickup and drove off.

"Are you all right?" Dana cried. "Hud told me what happened." She turned to look after Colt. "Did I interrupt something?"

"No, it…" She waved a hand through the air. "I'm just glad to see you. Did you want to come in?"

"Just for a moment. I know it's late, but we were out of milk and I couldn't sleep without making sure you were all right," Dana said as she stepped inside. "You've been through so much lately."

"Haven't I," Hilde said.

"You found his body? That must have been horrible."

"You have no idea." She realized she couldn't confide in her once best friend.

"Dee is a basket case."

Hilde tried to hide a smile. "I'm sure she is," she said.

But Dana knew her too well. "Hilde, the man was her *boyfriend.*"

"Was he? Or is that just what she told you? Dana, the only thing you know about her is what she's told you. How can you be sure any of it is true?"

Dana stood in the middle of the living room, suddenly looking uncomfortable. "I know you don't like her, but to be this suspicious about everything she says or does—"

"She's playing you, Dana. You told her about the past six years that you didn't have your family because of the fight over the ranch, didn't you?" She saw the answer in her friend's face. "You are so desperate to have family that you're blinded by this woman."

"I don't understand why you're acting like this," Dana said, sounding close to tears.

Hilde tried to stop herself, but she couldn't. She had to tell Dana everything, had to try to reason with her, to warn her.

"She tried to kill me, Dana. At the falls? She pushed me while you were getting your camera, only grabbing me at the last second before I fell."

"Why would she—"

"Because she doesn't want me around you."

"That's crazy," Dana said.

"Yes, it is. And she's living with you and your husband and your children."

They stood only inches apart staring at each other, but Hilde felt as if there was a mountain range between them, one neither of them might be able to climb.

"I'm worried about you, Hilde."

"Really? Because I'm scared to death for you. She killed Rick to keep him from telling me the truth tonight. He'd called me and said he'd tell me Dee's secrets, but I got there too late."

Dana was shaking her head and Hilde saw that her friend was never going to believe her. Until it was too late. "I should go."

Hilde nodded. "Watch her, Dana. I think she's after Hud."

Dana gave her a disbelieving look as if Hilde had finally lost her mind, then she turned and left.

Hilde closed the door behind her and leaned against it. She hadn't even realized she was crying until she tasted the salty tears.

CHAPTER EIGHT

"YOU CAN'T BLAME yourself for Rick's overdose," Dana said the next morning at breakfast. Hud had left early, called in on some new case. Her "cousin" had been trying to console her. "There are just some people who can't be helped no matter how hard we try."

Dee heard something in Dana's voice. "Like Hilde? I feel responsible for this rift between the two of you as much as I do for what Rick did."

"Don't. Hilde has just been under a lot of strain lately. I didn't realize how much. Then to find Rick like that…"

"So Hilde was the one who found him?" Dee felt her blood pressure rise like a rocket. That bastard. After their horseback ride, he'd threatened to blow her plans out of the water if she didn't include him. "Why would she go over to Rick's?"

Dana looked away to tend to one of the kids. "Apparently he was upset after you broke things off with him again. He called Hilde, wanted ten thousand dollars to tell her things about you."

If she could have killed him again, she would have made this time much more painful. "Why would he do that?" she wailed. "It must have been the drugs talking."

"I'm sure it was."

"So what did he say when she got to his motel room?" Dee asked, trying hard not to let her fear show.

"He was already dead."

Dee tried not to breathe a sigh of relief. "I'm sure he just wanted a shoulder to cry on."

"But to ask her for ten thousand dollars for information about you…" Dana said, and looked at her.

Dee saw the doubt beginning to bloom and knew she had to nip it in the bud and quickly. "I told you Rick had turned to pills," she said, and began to cry again. She'd learned to cry on cue so this was the easy part. "Well, the truth is…Rick had a drug habit. I'm so ashamed."

"You have nothing to be ashamed of," Dana said, quickly coming to her side.

"How could I have fallen in love with a man like him? I didn't know for a long time. Once I realized…I tried to help him. But it was too late. He'd blown all his savings on his habit. It wasn't love that brought him all the way to Montana or me. I was too ashamed to tell you this, but the real reason was to ask me for money. When I turned him down, both for money and his feeble attempt to get me back, I guess he was desperate. He knew Hilde didn't like me.… She was probably ready to give him the money for any kind of dirt on me she could dig up. Oh, Dana, I'm sorry. I know she's your best friend.… See why I feel so badly about all this?"

"But you shouldn't. You haven't done anything. We can't control the way other people react." Dana sounded sad.

"We need to do something to cheer us both up. I would love to go into Bozeman. We could have lunch, maybe do some shopping. What do you say?" She held her breath. She'd seen Hud go off to work this morning and had a pretty good idea that Dana didn't have anyone to take care of the kids. Couldn't really call Hilde, could she? Also, she'd heard Dana promise to make pies with the kids today.

"That sounds wonderful," Dana said. "But I'm afraid it will have to wait." Mary and Hank came running into the room, as if on cue.

"We're making pies with Mommy today," Mary announced.

Dee smiled, but did her best to look disappointed. "As fun as that sounds, Dana, would you mind if I borrowed your truck and went into Bozeman? You probably could use some time alone, and I need to do some shopping."

"Of course. The keys are in the truck. Please help yourself. And when you come back, there will be pie!" Dana laughed as the kids began to cheer noisily.

Dee couldn't wait to leave. "I might take the whole day, then," she said, as she hurried upstairs to get her purse.

COLT CALLED THE shop the next morning right after Hilde opened. "How are you doing?"

She glanced across the street to the deli, half expecting to see him sitting in his usual place. She was disappointed to see that the table was empty. "I'm okay."

"Did you get some sleep?"

"Yes. The wine and you stopping by helped," she admitted.

"Good, I'm glad to hear that. I wanted you to know that I have to go up to West Yellowstone today on a burglary case."

She could hear the smile in his voice and laughed.

"And you thought you'd better remind me that I'm not to go near Dee?"

"Yeah," he said. "Too subtle?"

"I appreciate you thinking of me."

He was silent for a moment before he said, "I've been thinking of you for a long while."

She didn't know what to say, especially since a lump had formed in her throat.

"I wish that kiss hadn't gotten interrupted."

"Me, too."

"How did things go with Dana, or shouldn't I ask?"

"Not well. I know I should have kept my mouth shut, but Colt, I had to warn her. If I put even a little doubt in her mind…"

"You did what you had to. Listen, I probably shouldn't be telling you this. Hell, I *know* I shouldn't. I meant to tell you last night. When we searched Rick, we found three different forms of identification in three different names. We sent his fingerprints to the crime lab in Missoula and we're waiting to see if we get a hit. Right now, we don't know who the guy is."

Hilde felt her heart take off at a gallop. "So there is more to the story. Just like there has got to be with Dee."

"It sure looks that way."

"We have to get her fingerprints."

"Hilde, promise me you won't do anything while I'm in West. You know how dangerous she is. Also…"

She heard him hesitate. "What?"

"She's gone into Bozeman today to do some shopping. She stopped by the office to ask Hud where there was a good place to have lunch. When she heard he's going to be testifying in a trial down there this afternoon, she talked him into having lunch with her."

Hilde never swore so she was as shocked as anyone when a cuss word escaped her mouth. "Even after I told Hud she was after him?"

"You had to be there," Colt said. "She's playing Rick's death to the hilt. She said she needs someone to talk to and has questions that only Hud can answer.... You get the idea."

Unfortunately she did. "We have to get her fingerprints soon."

"I promise you we will. Just be patient. I'll be back tonight. I was wondering if we could have dinner?"

Was he asking her on a date? Or was he just worried about her? "I'd like that."

He sounded relieved. "Good. I could pick you up by seven. I thought we'd go up to Mountain Village, get away for a while."

She felt a shiver of excitement race through her. "I look forward to it." She hung up feeling like a schoolgirl. It was all she could do not to dance around the shop.

Hilde might have let herself go and danced, but the bell over the door jangled and she turned to see Dana's cousin step inside. As Dee entered, she flipped the sign from Open to Closed and locked the door before turning to face Hilde.

"DON'T MAKE A fool of yourself," Dee snapped, as she saw Hilde fumble for her cell phone. Hilde looked so much like a deer in the headlights that Dee had to laugh. "What are you going to tell the marshal? That I came into your shop to try to kill you again? Really, Hilde. You must realize how tiresome you've become."

"Don't come any closer," Hilde said, holding up the phone.

"You're wasting your time. Hud is in Bozeman, Colt is on his way to West Yellowstone—and what's that other deputy's name?"

"Liza."

"Right. She just got a call and is headed up the mountain. By the time any of them get here, I will have unlocked the door and left you safe and as sound as you can be under the circumstances and you'll only look all the more foolish."

"What do you want?" Hilde demanded. But she lowered the cell phone as she stepped behind the counter.

Dee couldn't help being amused as Hilde snatched up a pair of deadly-looking scissors from behind the counter. "You aren't going to use those. Even if you had it in you, everyone would just assume you went off the deep end. You've been teetering on the brink for several days now."

"What. Do. You. Want?" Hilde repeated.

Dee had to hand it to the woman. She was tougher than she looked. "I want you to leave me alone."

"Don't you mean you want me to leave Dana alone?"

"Just let me enjoy this vacation with my family."

"Are they really your family? Rick didn't seem to think so."

Finally. She'd known Rick had shot off his mouth on the phone with Hilde. She'd just needed to know what he'd told her, and apparently Hilde was more than ready to tell anyone who'd listen.

"Rick was on drugs."

"How convenient," Hilde snapped. "He was going to tell me all about you and I have a feeling he knew plenty."

"But ten thousand dollars' worth?" Dee shook her head as she moved closer to the counter and Hilde.

"Dana told you about that?" Hilde didn't sound so sure of herself suddenly.

"She told me everything—how you were convinced that I'd killed Rick—and right before you were finally going to learn all my deep, dark secrets. How frustrating that must have been for you."

Hilde brandished the scissors. "You really don't want to come any closer."

Dee smiled, but stopped moving. "So if I'm not Dee Anna Justice, then who did Rick say I was?" She saw the answer at once on Hilde's face. The woman wasn't good at hiding her emotions. She would never survive in Dee's world. "So he didn't say. You just got the *feeling* I wasn't Dee?" She shook her head. "Yep, you're teetering on the brink. One little push and I'm afraid you're going over the edge. It's going to break Dana's heart. She really does care for you, her *best* friend."

"But you'll be there to pick up the pieces, right?"

"That's what I came here today to tell you," Dee said. "I'm not going anywhere. Accept it. If you don't, I'm afraid of what it will do to you mentally. You seem so fragile as it is."

"You're wrong," Hilde said. "I'm a lot stronger than I look."

Dee didn't expect Hilde to lunge at her with the scissors. It wasn't much of a lunge. Her reaction was to grab Hilde's arm and twist it. The scissors clattered to the floor to the sound of Hilde crying out in pain.

As the shop owner stumbled back, rubbing her wrist and looking scared, Dee bent down and picked up the scissors from the floor by the blades.

"If you're going to try to kill someone, it works better if they don't see you coming at them," Dee said in disgust. As she placed the scissors on the counter, she studied Hilde, realizing she was much closer to the edge of insanity than she'd thought. It would take hardly anything to push her over.

"I need to get to Bozeman," Dee said. "I have a lunch date with Hud. I suggest you close up shop and get some rest. You might want to see someone about that wrist. I hope it's not sprained. How will you ever explain what happened?" She laughed as she turned toward the door. She almost wished that Hilde would grab up the scissors and come for her again.

At the door, she flipped the sign to Open, unlocked the door and let herself out. When she looked back, Hilde was still standing with her back against the wall, rubbing her wrist. The look in her eyes, though, wasn't one of fear. It was…triumph.

Dee stopped to look again, surprised and worried by what she'd glimpsed in Hilde's eyes just then. Was it just a trick of the light through the window? She couldn't shake the feeling that there was something she was missing. Hilde kept throwing her off balance. The woman was impossible. Anyone else would have taken the hint long before now.

But when she glanced into the shop again, she saw Hilde rush to the door to lock it and put up the Closed sign. Apparently the woman *had* taken her advice and was going to get some rest.

HILDE WAITED UNTIL she saw Dee drive away before she carefully slid the scissors into a clean plastic bag. She was positive she'd gotten the woman's fingerprints because Dee had picked up the scissors by the blades, holding them out as if she wanted to seem nonthreatening.

What a joke. Everything about Dee was threatening.

Once she had the scissors put away, it was all she could do not to call Colt and tell him, but he was working. She would have to wait until dinner tonight since in order for him to run Dee's prints, he would have to do it under Hud's radar. Hilde realized what a chance he would be taking.

Just the thought of Colt made her heart beat a little harder.

He would have a fit when she told him how she'd managed to get Dee's prints. She'd been pretty sure that Dee would take the scissors away from her. She had hoped that Dee wouldn't use them on her, had bet that Dee wasn't ready to kill again. Not yet, anyway. Even if Dee would have claimed self-defense, few people would have believed it.

Well, they wouldn't have believed it before the past few days. Now Hilde wasn't sure what her friends thought of her. That she was mentally unbalanced? That like Dee said, she was teetering on the edge?

Wait until Dee's prints came back. She'd see what they thought then.

What if she is *Dee Anna Justice?* Hilde tried to remember what Dana had told her about Dee Anna and her family. Maybe Dana's grandparents had had a good reason for disinheriting Walter Justice and demanding that his name never be spoken again.

The thought gave her a chill. If there had been something wrong with Walter, wasn't it possible Dee Anna had inherited it?

"No, she's not Dee Ana Justice," she said to herself now. "And I'm going to prove it." If she had a good set of Dee's prints on the scissors. Now she was worried that she might not have.

Hilde started to open her shop when a thought struck her. Dee had gone into Bozeman to have lunch with Hud. That meant Dana would be at the house alone with the kids.

"You promised Colt you wouldn't go near the ranch," she reminded herself, as she went into the back to stuff several plastic bags into her purse. "Colt meant don't go near Dee, not the ranch, and I might not have this opportunity again."

As she started for the door, she realized she was talking to herself. Dee was right. She was teetering on the edge. She was starting to scare herself.

Locking up behind herself and leaving the Closed sign in the window of the sewing shop—something she never did—Hilde headed for Cardwell Ranch.

CHAPTER NINE

"Dee," Hud said the moment there was a lull in the conversation.

She'd chosen a private booth at the back of the local bistro and had been doing her best to entertain him with fabricated stories about her life.

He'd laughed at the appropriate times and even blushed a little when she'd told him how she'd lost her virginity. Well, how she *could* have lost it if it wasn't for her real life. Her fabricated story was cute and sad and wistful, just enough to pluck at his heartstrings, she hoped. She had Dana where she wanted her. Hud was another story.

She'd noticed that he'd seemed a little distracted when he'd sat down, but she'd thought she'd charmed away whatever was bothering him.

"Dee," he repeated when she'd finished one of her stories. "I have to ask you. How much do you know about Rick?"

The bastard was dead, but not forgotten. She'd been relieved earlier when she'd stopped by Needles and Pins to learn that Rick hadn't had a chance to tell Hilde anything of importance. Had he lived much longer, though, he would have spoiled everything.

"What do you mean?" she asked, letting him know

he'd ruined her good mood—and her lunch—by bringing up Rick.

"I found three different forms of identification on him in three different names."

The fool. Why had he taken a chance like that? Because it was the way they'd always done it. So she knew he was planning to start over somewhere else—once he got money from her. If she could have sent him straight to hell at that moment, she'd have bought him a first-class ticket.

"I don't understand." It was the best she could do. Now the marshal would look into Rick's past. It was bound to come out who he really was. Damn him for doing this to her. He really was going to ruin everything.

"Did you suspect he might not be who he said he was?"

She let out a nervous laugh. "He's Rick Cameron. I met his friends. He even had me talk to his mother one time on the phone. She sounded nice."

"I think he lied to you," Hud said gently.

She let him take her hand. His hands were large and strong. She imagined what they might feel like on the rest of her bare skin, and she did her best to look brokenhearted. She even worked up a few tears and was pleased when Hud pulled out a handkerchief and handed it to her.

"Thank you. I don't know what I would have done if this had happened in New York. I have friends there, but at a time like this it is so good to be around *family*." She gave him a hug, but not too long since she felt him tense.

Hilde. The blasted woman had warned him. Of course she had.

"You are so lucky to have such a wonderful family," she said. "Dana is amazing and the kids…what can I say?"

He nodded and relaxed again. "I *am* lucky. And Dana is so happy to have found a cousin she didn't know she had."

"I feel as if I'm wearing out my welcome, though." He started to say something. Not to really disagree, but to try to be polite. "I'll be taking off Saturday. Dana's invited me back for a week next year. I hope she and Hilde regain their friendship. I know it's not my fault, but still…"

Hud smiled. "They'll work it out. I'm just glad you came out to the ranch. You'll have to keep in touch."

"I'll try," she said, furious that between Rick and Hilde, they'd managed to ruin her lunch with Hud and force her to move up her plan—because she wasn't leaving Cardwell Ranch.

WHEN DANA OPENED the door, Hilde saw her expression and felt her heart drop. She thought of all the times she'd stopped by and her best friend had been delighted to see her. Today wasn't one of those days.

"Hilde?" She looked leery, almost afraid. How ironic.

Hilde wanted to scream, *I'm not the one you should fear!* Instead she said, "I bought those ice cream sandwiches the kids like."

Dana glanced at the bag in her hand, but didn't move.

"I won't stay long. I just haven't seen the kids for a few days now. I've missed them."

"Auntie Hilde?" Mary cried and came running to the door. She squeezed past her mother and into Hilde's arms.

She held the adorable little girl close. Mary looked just like the pictures Hilde had seen of Dana at that same age. Was that another reason Dee had been able to fool Dana? Because there was a resemblance between Dana and Dee, one no doubt Dee had played on?

"We're making pies!" Mary announced, as Hilde let her go. "Come on, I'll show you."

Hilde took the child's hand and followed her through the house. Dana had been forced to move out of the doorway, but she looked worried as Hilde entered. What did she think Hilde was going to do? Flip out in front of the kids?

"These are beautiful," Hilde said when she saw the pies. The kitchen looked like a flour bomb had gone off in it. Dana was so good at letting the kids make as big a mess as they had to. She was a great mother, Hilde thought as she looked up at her friend and smiled.

Dana seemed to soften. "Would you like a pie?"

Hilde shook her head. Only a few days ago, Dana would have asked her to stay for dinner and have pie then. Now she seemed anxious that Hilde not stay too long. Dee would be returning.

"We'd better put these in the freezer," Hilde said, handing Dana the bag with the ice cream sandwiches.

"What do you say to Auntie Hilde?"

"Thank you, Auntie Hilde," Mary and Hank chimed in. Dana stepped out on the old back porch to put the ice cream in the freezer.

"I'm taking off now," Hilde called. She said goodbye to the kids, then hurried back into the living room and up the stairs. She assumed Dana had put Dee in the guest bedroom. Hilde had stayed over enough; she almost thought of it as her own.

The door was closed. She opened it quickly and stepped inside. The curtain was drawn so it took her a moment before her eyes adjusted. She knew she had to move quickly.

Dee's cosmetic bag was on the antique vanity. She hurried to it, trying not to step on the floorboards that creaked. Taking the plastic bags out of her purse, she used them like gloves. They were awkward, but she managed to pick up a bottle of makeup, then spied Dee's toothbrush. DNA. She grabbed it, stuffed both into her purse again and hurriedly moved to the door.

Opening it, she stepped out and was partway down the hall headed for the stairs when Dana came up them.

"Hilde?"

"I'm sorry, I just needed to use your bathroom. I hope you don't mind. I drank too much coffee this morning."

Dana relaxed a little. She, of all people, knew about Hilde's coffee habit.

"Thank you for letting me see the kids."

Tears filled her friend's eyes. "I hate this," Dana whispered.

"Me, too. But we'll figure it out. We have to."

Dana nodded, looking skeptical. Who could blame her?

Hilde smiled and touched her shoulder as they passed. She practically ran down the stairs. Dee would realize her makeup and toothbrush were missing. And knowing Dee, she would figure it out.

As Hilde climbed into her SUV, she saw Dana watching her leave. Colt would be furious. He'd realize what was just sinking in for her. Dee had warned her numerous times. The next time they crossed paths, Dee would make sure Hilde Jacobson was no longer a problem.

Hilde just hoped before that time came that she would have the proof she needed to stop Dee Anna Justice—or whoever the woman was.

DEE CALLED STACY after her unsuccessful lunch with Hud. Dana had told her that Stacy had a part-time job as a nanny. Dee was hoping that meant Stacy could get away long enough to talk.

"I was just in town and thought maybe we could have a cup of coffee somewhere," she said when Stacy answered. Dee had gotten her number from the little book Dana kept by the downstairs phone. She'd gotten Hilde's cell phone number out of the book as well.

"Coffee, huh?" Stacy asked.

"Okay, you found me out. I do have some questions about the family."

Stacy laughed. "So you called me. Sure, I know where all the bodies are buried. Do you know where the Greasy Spoon is, off Main Street?"

"No, but I can find it. Ten minutes?"

"I'll have to bring the kids, but they have a play area at the café."

Dee was waiting when Stacy came in with two toddlers: Ella, who she said was now over a year old, and Ralph, the two-year-old she babysat. Stacy deposited the two kids in the play area and came back to sit down with Dee. She could watch the children from where they sat.

"Who names their kid *Ralph?*" Dee asked.

Stacy shrugged and helped herself to the coffee and mini-turnovers Dee had ordered for them. "Named after his wealthy grandfather."

"Then I can see why they love the name," she said and laughed. "I hope I'm not putting you on the spot."

Stacy's laugh was more cutting. "You want to know about me and Dana and Hud, right?"

Dee lifted a brow before she could stop herself. "You and Hud?"

"Dana didn't tell you?"

She lied. "She hinted at something, but I never thought—"

"To make a long story short, Hud and Dana were engaged. I was strapped for money, and truthfully, I was always jealous of Dana. Someone offered me money to drug Hud and get him into my bed so Dana would find him there. It was during a really stupid part of my life. Thankfully my sister forgave me, but it split Hud and Dana up for five years—until the truth came out."

"Wow." Dee hadn't expected this. "Dana mentioned a rift with you and her brothers after your mother died?"

Stacy's laugh held no humor. "We were all desperate for money. Or at least we thought we were. So we wanted to sell off the ranch and split the money. Since our mother's old will divided the ranch between us..."

"But then the new will turned up."

Stacy nodded. "We treated Dana really badly. Family had always meant so much to her... It broke her heart when we turned against her. I will never forgive myself."

"Families are like that sometimes," she said, thinking of her own. "I'm just so glad that Dana found me and I get to be part of yours. I can't tell you how much it means to me."

"Okay, now tell me the big secret with your side of the family." Stacy helped herself to another mini-turnover. "Dana said the family disinherited your father, Walter, because they didn't like who he married? There has to be more to it."

Dee had known Stacy might be more outspoken than her sister. She was a little taken aback by how much. Also, the real Dee Anna Justice had never told her about her father, so Dee was in the dark here.

"I had no idea I had other family," she said. "My father led me to believe my grandparents were dead. Clearly he'd never been close to them."

"And your mother?"

"She's a socialite and philanthropist."

"What?" Stacy cried. "She's not a tramp?"

"Far from it. The woman was born with a silver spoon in her mouth, can trace her ancestry to the *Mayflower* and has more money than she knows what to do with." Dee was offended the family had thought Dee Anna's mother was a skank, even though it wasn't her mother and she didn't like Marietta Justice. The woman was an uptight snob, colder than the marble entry at her mansion. But thanks to her, Dee would be getting her daughter's trust fund check soon.

"So why did the Montana Justice family disinherit his son for marrying wealth?" Stacy asked. "That makes no sense."

No, it didn't. As Stacy said, there had to be more to the story. Dee could only guess. "It's a mystery, isn't it?"

COLT COULDN'T WAIT to get back to Big Sky. He'd been anxious all day and having trouble concentrating on his investigation. It wasn't like him. He took his job seriously. Just like Hilde.

When he'd finally gotten a chance, he'd called Needles and Pins. The phone rang four times and went to voice mail. He doubted she was so busy waiting on a customer that she couldn't answer the phone.

So he waited ten minutes and tried again. Still no answer. He'd never known Hilde not to open the shop. His concern grew even more when he tried later in the afternoon.

He'd finally called Dana and asked for Hilde's cell phone number. "I tried the shop and couldn't reach her."

"That *is* odd," Dana agreed after she'd given him the number. "She stopped out earlier and brought the kids ice cream sandwiches."

Colt swore silently. "How did that go?"

"Okay. But she was acting…strange. Is she all right?"

"She's been through a lot the past few days," he said. "So she didn't stay long?"

"No."

"I'll give her a call and make sure she's all right," he said.

"You'll let me know if…if there is anything I can do?"

"Sure." He quickly dialed Hilde's cell and felt a wave of relief when she answered on the third ring. "You went out to the ranch." He hadn't meant for those to be the first words out of his mouth.

"Don't be mad. I got her fingerprints."

He bit back a curse. "Hilde."

"I know. But she stopped by the shop right after I opened this morning."

If he'd been scared before, he was petrified now. "What did she want?"

"To threaten me. Again. She made it clear that if I didn't back off—"

"So you went out to the ranch and got her finger-prints. I hate to even ask."

"I feel like we are racing against the clock," she said. "I had to do something. She's more dangerous than even I thought."

He agreed. "Okay, just do me a favor. Where are you now?"

"I'm at home. I was too antsy to work today."

"You have the items with her fingerprints on them at the house, right?"

"Yes."

"Okay, just stay there, lock the doors, don't open them for anyone but me. I'm on my way from West. I should be there in an hour. You don't happen to own a gun, do you? Sorry, of course you don't."

"You think you know me that well?" she demanded.

"Yep. Are you going to tell me you do own a gun and know how to shoot it?"

"No."

He laughed. "Go lock your doors. I'm on my way."

DEE WAS DISAPPOINTED when she reached the ranch and found out that Hud was working late at the office. He was the only bright spot in a dreary day.

"I see your ankle is better. That's good," Dana said when Dee came in with the small presents she'd brought the kids. She hadn't wanted to spend much, so she'd found some cheap toys. Mary and Hank thanked her, but she could tell she'd bought the wrong things.

Dinner was just the four of them. Dana had fed the twins and put them to bed. The house was deathly quiet since Mary and Hank were practically falling asleep in their dinner plates.

Dee walked around the ranch while Dana bathed the kids and got them to bed. The night was cool and dark. As she walked, something kept nagging at her about earlier at the sewing shop.

She hadn't been surprised when Hilde had picked up the scissors and lunged at her. Just as she wasn't surprised the woman was slow and uncoordinated, so much so that it had been child's play to take the scissors away from her. Often anger made a person less precise, even clumsy, right?

Coming at her with scissors had seemed a fool thing to do, but Dee hadn't questioned it. Until now.

She recalled how easily it had been to get Hilde to drop the scissors and how surprised she'd been when Hilde had stood there rubbing her wrist as if Dee had broken it.

Hilde hadn't been trying to stab her. Far from it. Then why—

The truth hit her like a ton of bricks.

The scissors.

She swore, stopping in her tracks, to let out her anger in a roar aimed at the night sky. All the pieces fell into place in an instant. The triumphant look in Hilde's eyes.

The woman had gotten her fingerprints!

All the implications of that also fell into place. Once she had her boyfriend Colt run the prints…

Dee slapped herself hard. The force of it stung her cheek. She slapped herself again and again until both cheeks burned as she chanted, "You fool. You fool. You fool." Just as her mother had done.

By the time she stopped, her face was on fire, but she knew what she had to do.

HILDE COULDN'T REMEMBER the last time she was this excited about a date. Well, not exactly a date, she supposed. Dinner. Still she wore an emerald-green dress she'd bought and saved for a special occasion.

Colt's eyes lit when he saw her. "You look beautiful."

She *felt* beautiful.

"I don't think you have any idea what you do to me," he said, his voice sounding rough with emotion. "You make me tongue-tied."

"I really doubt that," she said with a small nervous laugh. The desire in his gaze set her blood aflame.

He took a step to her, ran his fingers along one bare arm. She felt her heart jump. Goose bumps skittered across her skin. His gaze moved over her face like a caress before it settled on her mouth. If he kissed her now—

"We had better go to dinner," he said, letting out a breath as he stepped back from her. "Otherwise…" He met her gaze. "I want to do this right, you know."

She smiled. "I do, too."

"Then we'd better go. I made reservations up on the mountain. It's such a nice night.…"

She grabbed her wrap. Montana in the mountains was often cold, even in the summer after the sun went down. She doubted she would need it, though. Being this close to Colt had her blood simmering quite nicely.

They didn't talk about Dee Anna Justice or the scissors and other evidence locked up back at the house. Colt asked her about growing up in Chicago. She told him about her idyllic childhood and her loving parents.

"I had a very normal childhood," she concluded. "Most people would say it was boring. How about you?"

"Mine was much the same. It sounds like we were both lucky."

"So your parents are professors at the University of Montana."

"My mother teaches business," he said. "My father teaches math. They'd hoped I would follow in their footsteps, but as much as I enjoyed college, I had no interest in teaching at it. I always wanted to go into law enforcement, especially in a small town. I couldn't have been happier when I got the job here at Big Sky."

He had driven up the winding road that climbed to Mountain Village. There weren't a lot of businesses open this time of year, but more stayed open all year than in the old days, when there really were only two seasons at Big Sky.

The air was cold up here but crystal clear. Colt was the perfect gentleman, opening her door after he parked. Hilde stood for a moment and admired the stars. With so few other lights, the sky was a dark canopy glittering with white stars. A sliver of moon hung just over the mountains.

"Could this night be more perfect?" she whispered.

When she looked at Colt, he grinned and said, "Let's see." His kiss was soft and gentle, a brush across the lips as light as the breeze that stirred the loose tendrils of her hair. And then he drew her to him and deepened the kiss, breaking it off as the door of the restaurant opened and a group of four came out laughing and talking.

"We just keep getting interrupted," Colt said with a laugh. He put his arm around her waist and they entered the restaurant.

Hilde had never felt so alive. The night seemed to hold its breath in expectation. She could smell adventure on the air, feel it in her every nerve ending. She had a feeling that tonight would be one she would never forget.

OVER DINNER, they talked about movies and books, laughed about the crazy things they did when they were kids, and Colt found himself completely enthralled by his date.

Hilde was, as his grandfather used to say, the whole ball of wax. She was smart and ambitious, a hard worker, and yet she volunteered for several organizations in her spare time. She loved nature, cared about the environment and made him laugh.

On top of that, she was beautiful, sexy and a good dancer. After dinner, they'd danced out in the starlight until he thought he would go crazy if he didn't get her alone and naked.

"Is it just me, or do you want to get out of here?" Colt said after they took a break from the dance floor.

"I thought you'd never ask."

He laughed and they left. It was all he could do not to race down the mountain, but the switchback curves kept him in check.

Once out of the vehicle, though, all bets were off. They were in each other's arms, kissing as they stumbled toward her front door. Once inside, they practically tore each other's clothes off, dropping articles of clothing in a crooked path before making it only to the rug in front of the fireplace.

"Hilde," Colt said, cupping her face in his hands as he leaned over her. He couldn't find words to tell her how beautiful she was or how much he wanted her. Or that he had fallen in love with her. He couldn't even tell her the exact moment. He just knew that he had.

Fortunately, he didn't have to put any of that into words. Not tonight. He saw that she understood. It was in her amazing brown eyes and in the one word she uttered as he entered her. "Colt."

LATER, COLT CARRIED her to her bed and made love to her slowly. The urgency of their first lovemaking had cooled. He took his time letting his gaze and his fingers and his tongue graze her body as he took full possession of her.

Hilde cried out with a passion she'd never known existed as he cupped her breasts and laved her nipples with his tongue until she felt her whole body quake. She surrendered to him in a way she'd never given herself to another man. His demanding kisses took her to new heights.

And when he finished, his gaze locked with hers, she felt a release that left her sated and happier than she'd ever known.

As he lay curled against her, one arm thrown protectively over her, she closed her eyes and drifted off to sleep feeling…loved.

CHAPTER TEN

DEE WOKE FROM the nightmare in a cold sweat. For a few moments, she couldn't catch her breath. She swung her legs out of bed and stumbled to the window, gulping for air. Her heart felt as if it would pound its way out of her chest.

It was the same nightmare she'd had since she was a girl. She was in a coffin. It was pitch-black. There was no air. She was trapped, and even though she'd screamed herself hoarse, no one had come to save her.

She shoved open the screenless window all the way and leaned out to breathe in the night air. A sliver of moon hung over the top of the mountain. A million stars twinkled against the midnight-blue sky. She shivered as the cold mountain air quickly dried her perspiration and sent goose bumps skittering over her skin.

The nightmare was coming more frequently—just as the doctor had told her it would.

"Do night terrors run in your family?" he'd asked, studying her over the top of his glasses.

"I don't know. I never asked."

"How old did you say you were?"

She'd been in her early twenties at the time.

He'd frowned. "What about sleepwalking?"

"Sometimes I wake up in a strange place and I don't know how I've gotten there."

He nodded, his frown deepening as he tossed her file on his desk. "I'm going to give you a referral to a neurologist."

"You're saying there's something wrong with me?"

"Just a precaution. Sleepwalking and night terrors at your age are fairly uncommon and could be the result of a neurological disorder."

She'd laughed after she left his office. "He thinks I'm crazy." She'd been amused at the time.

But back then she was sleepwalking and having the nightmare only every so often.

Now...

She looked out at the peaceful night. "This is all I need. This place and Hud and I will be fine," she whispered. "Once I get rid of the stumbling blocks, I'll be fine for the first time in my life."

But that was the problem, wasn't it? There were more stumbling blocks than she'd ever run into before. More chances to get caught.

"It would be worth it, though," she said as she heard a horse whinny out in the corrals. All this could be hers. *Would* be hers. She deserved Dana's happiness. She deserved Dana's life—minus the kids.

After getting dressed, she sneaked out and made the walk into town. It was only a couple of miles and she'd walked it before and gotten away with it. If anyone discovered her missing, she'd say she'd gone out to the corral to check the horses. She wasn't worried. So far, they'd believed everything she told them.

THE NEXT MORNING, Colt tried to talk Hilde out of opening the shop. "Can't you have someone else man Needles and Pins for a few weeks?"

Hilde touched his handsome face, cupping his strong jaw, and smiled into those blue eyes of his. He'd been so gentle, so loving, last night when they'd made love. At least the second time. Before that, he'd let his passion run as wild as horses in a windstorm.

Her skin still tingled from the memory. She'd never known that kind of wild abandon. Just the thought thrilled her. She'd awakened feeling as if she could conquer the world. Hadn't she always known that she could be anything she wanted with the right man—in or out of bed?

"I am not going to let Dee or whoever she is keep me from doing what I love," she said, as she felt the rough stubble along his strong jawline. "Especially this morning when I'm feeling so…"

He laughed. "So…?"

"Invincible."

Colt pulled her to him and kissed her. As he drew back, he said, "I love seeing you like this, but Dee will figure out that you have her fingerprints and DNA. She isn't going to take this lying down. You have to know that."

She nodded. "Remember? I know what she's capable of. And I know she isn't finished. How long before we know who she is?" Colt had left for a while before daylight to go to the office to run Dee's fingerprints. He had a friend at the crime lab he'd called.

"You're counting on her fingerprints being on file. She might not have a record. Also, she might actually be Dee Anna Justice."

Hilde knew Dee was slippery. She might have avoided getting arrested. Might never have had a job that required she be fingerprinted. She might even be who she said she was. But all Hilde could do was hope that not only was she right about Dee being an impostor—but also that the woman had had at least one run-in with the law so her prints would come up. The sooner Dee was exposed, the sooner she would be gone from the ranch.

"I just don't want you getting your hopes up. The toothbrush was a good idea. We might be able to compare Dee's DNA to Dana's."

"I should have thought to get Dana's DNA while I was at it."

"Don't even think about," he said, holding her away from him so she couldn't avoid his gaze. "I'm serious. You have to stay away from Cardwell Ranch."

Hilde nodded. By now Dee would have realized that her makeup and toothbrush were missing. Hopefully she was running scared.

COLT HATED THAT he had to go back down to West Yellowstone on the burglary case today. He didn't like leaving Hilde alone.

"Can I see you for a minute?" the marshal asked, as he was getting ready to leave the office later that morning.

Colt stepped into Hud's office.

"Close the door, please."

He turned to close the door, worry making him anxious. Hud had always run the station in a rather informal way. Not that they all weren't serious about their jobs. But Hud had never seen the need to throw around his weight.

"Have a sit," he said now.

"Is something wrong?" Colt asked, afraid Hud had

somehow found out that he'd sent Dee's prints to his friend who worked at the crime lab.

"I wanted to talk to you about Hilde." Hud shook his head. "I know, it's not my place as your boss. Or even as your friend. But I feel I have to. Did you see her last night?"

Colt almost laughed. He figured Hud already knew that his patrol pickup had been parked in front of her house all night. News traveled fast in such a small, isolated community. Gossip was about the only excitement this time of year. It was too early for most tourists or seasonal homeowners, so things were more than a little quiet.

"Yes, I saw her," he said, keeping his face straight.

"I've known Hilde for a long time. I'm concerned about her."

"She's been a little distraught," Colt said. "She truly believes that Dee might be dangerous and is concerned about you and your family."

"I gathered that," Hud said with a curse, then studied him for a long moment. "I get the feeling you agree with her."

"I think there is cause for concern." He hurried on, before Hud could argue differently, knowing he was in dangerous territory. "You never laid eyes on this woman before she showed up at your door. You can't even be sure she is who she says she is."

"Dana sent her a certified letter that she had to sign for at her current address. And I've seen her identification."

That surprised Colt. "Then you *were* suspicious."

Hud sighed. "I had to be after the allegations Hilde was making. But she checks out, and Dana is enjoying her visit. She thinks Hilde is jealous. I can see that you don't agree."

"I'm just saying, you might want to keep an eye on her, that's all."

His boss looked as if there was more he wanted to say. Or more he was hoping his deputy would. But Colt held his tongue. His friend at the crime lab had promised to run the prints as quickly as he could.

Whatever the outcome, he hadn't figured out what to do after that. Until then, there was little he *could* do.

"We finally got a positive identification on Rick Cameron," Hud said, and tossed the man's file across his desk to Colt.

He opened it, glanced at the latest entry and jerked his head up in surprise. "Richard Northland?" So he hadn't been using his real name at all?

Hud nodded. "And before you ask, Dee had no idea he was lying about his name."

Colt let out a laugh as he tossed the file back. "As your friend? Get Dee out of your house. As your deputy? I really should get to work."

HILDE WAS LOST in the memory of last night with Colt as she unlocked Needles and Pins. Dinner had been magical. The lovemaking had been beyond anything she'd ever experienced. She'd been lost in a dream state all morning.

That's why it took her a moment to realize what she was seeing.

The shop had been vandalized.

Bolts of fabric were now scattered over the floor. Displays had been toppled, and spools of thread littered the areas of the floor that weren't covered by fabric bolts.

She fumbled her phone from her purse, her heart pounding as she realized whoever had done this could still be in the shop. That was when she noticed the back door standing open. The vandal had left a large roll of yellow rickrack trailing out the back door like the equivalent of a bread trail through the shop.

"911. What is your emergency?" she heard an operator say.

"My shop has been vandalized," Hilde said.

"You're calling from Big Sky?"

"Yes. Needles and Pins."

"Is the vandal still there?"

"No. I don't believe so."

"Please wait outside until the marshal or one of his deputies arrive. Do you need to stay on the phone with me?"

"No. I just can't imagine who would—" That's when Hilde saw the scissors. Six of them. All stabbed into the top of her counter just inches from where she'd pretended to attack Dee to get the woman's fingerprints.

"You look tired," Dana said when Dee came downstairs. "Did you sleep all right?"

"Like a baby." Once she got into bed again. Last night's exploits had left her exhausted. Clearly just what she'd needed since once she'd hit the sheets, she hadn't had the nightmare again.

Dana was busy with the kids as usual. "It might be just as well that I don't have anything planned for you today. Maybe a day just resting would do us all good."

Dee didn't know how the woman managed with four kids. She'd apparently just finished feeding the two oldest because she was only now clearing away their plates. She sent them off to the bathroom to wash up.

The two youngest were in some kind of contraptions that allowed them to roll around the kitchen. They'd gotten caught in a corner and one of them was hollering his head off.

Dana saved him, kneeling down to cajole him before she asked, "I made Mary and Hank pancakes, Dee. Would you like some?"

The kitchen smelled of pancakes and maple syrup. Dee heard her stomach growl. She was starved, also probably because of all the exercise she'd gotten last night. She'd been careful to stay away from any streetlights, and she was sure no one had seen her leaving and returning to the ranch.

"I'd love pancakes, but let me make them," Dee offered, knowing Dana wouldn't take her up on it.

"It's no trouble. Anyway, you're my guest."

Dee could hear something in Dana's voice, though. Her hostess was tiring of her guest. Probably all the drama. Dana would be glad when Dee left.

Well, there was nothing she could do about that, because the drama was far from over. Forced to move up her plan, she said, "I'm thinking I've stayed too long."

Dana turned from the stove. "No. I don't want you to feel that way at all. I'm just sorry. I really wanted you to have a good time."

"I *am* having a good time." Dee went over and gave Dana a hug. "But I need to get back home and look for a job. I can't be off work for too long." Sometimes she couldn't believe how easy lying came to her. She was more amazed by people who couldn't tell a lie. Maybe it was a talent you were born with.

Or maybe you had to learn it at your daddy's knee, she thought bitterly.

"I checked this morning about a flight," she said with equal effortlessness. "I'm booked for Saturday on a nonstop flight to LaGuardia." She knew Dana and Hud wouldn't check to see if it was true or not. But Colt might.

Dana didn't try to get her to change her mind. *Yep, it's time.* She just said, "Well, I hate to see you cut your trip short, but you know best."

"This isn't my only trip to Cardwell Ranch," Dee said.

"Well, I insist on paying for your flight." Dana held up her hand even though Dee hadn't protested. "No arguments. I want this trip to be my treat."

"That is so sweet of you. I'm going to pay you back, though, and then some." By booking the nonstop flight that was available only on Saturday, she had bought herself a little more time. It wasn't perfect timing, but she'd have to make it work, especially after finding her toothbrush and makeup missing. She'd already put the wheels in motion. *Hang on,* she thought, because she knew what was about to hit the fan.

Dana looked visibly relaxed now that she knew her guest was leaving. Dee hated Hilde at that moment. The woman had been a thorn in her side from the beginning. If she had just backed off… But it was too late for regrets, she thought, and checked her watch.

Any minute poor Hilde would be crying on the marshal's shoulder and no doubt blaming her.

Marshal Hud Savage stopped in the doorway of Needles and Pins and demanded, "What are you doing?"

"I'm cleaning up my shop," Hilde said, as she placed another bolt of fabric back where it went. She was thankful that most of the fabrics hadn't gotten soiled or ruined. Dee could have torn up the place much worse. Hilde knew she should be thankful for that.

She'd started cleaning up the moment she'd realized who'd done this. At that same moment, she'd known there was no reason to wait for the marshal. Hud wasn't going to believe Dee had done this. And the only way to try to change his mind would be to show him the scissors and explain why they were a message from Dee.

Hilde couldn't do that without telling what she'd done to get Dee's fingerprints and Colt's involvement. She wasn't about to drag him into this any more than he already was.

"You shouldn't have touched anything until I got here," Hud said behind her. "Hilde—"

She stopped working to look at him. Fueled by anger, she'd accomplished a lot in a short time. "The person broke in through the back. I haven't touched anything back there."

He looked toward the back of the shop, where she had a small kitchen she and her staff used as a break and storage room. She'd found a chair moved over against the wall under the open window. There appeared to be marks on the window frame where someone had pried it open.

When she'd stepped outside in the alley, she'd discovered the large trash container pulled over under the window.

Hud went back in the break room, then outside. "Is anything missing?" he asked when he came back in.

"I don't believe so. I don't leave money down here. I think it was just a malicious act of vandalism."

"Looks like it might have been kids, then," Hud said.

Hilde had stopped to look at him, after restoring almost all of the bolts of fabric to their correct places. She saw him staring at the countertop where the half-dozen new scissors had been stuck in the wood.

"Kids resort to this sort of thing just for something to do, I guess," he said.

"It wasn't kids." She crossed her arms because she was trembling and she didn't want him to see it. She thought that if she kept calm and didn't get upset or cry, he might believe her.

"Don't tell me Dee did this." He looked as resolute as she felt.

"Okay, I won't. You don't want to hear the truth, fine. Kids did it."

"Hilde," Hud said in that tone she was getting used to. "Dee went to bed last night before we did. If she had driven into town, I would have known it."

"Maybe she walked."

"It's a couple of miles. She can barely walk around the yard without twisting an ankle. You think she climbed up into that window back there?" He was shaking his head. "I'm sorry this happened. I'll file a report and you can turn it over to your insurance. I'm glad nothing was destroyed."

She laughed at that. Dee had destroyed so much—the shop was the least of it.

"Are you going to be okay?"

The concern and kindness she heard in his tone was

her undoing. The tears broke loose as if they had been walled up, waiting for the least bit of provocation to burst out.

He patted her shoulder. "Take the rest of the day off. Go home. Get some rest."

As if rest would make her world right again.

FORTUNATELY, THE REST of the day was busy at the shop. All the women who'd come in to sign up for quilting classes buoyed Hilde's spirits.

Dana called midmorning. "Just wanted to say hi."

Hilde figured she'd heard about the vandalism from Hud. He must not have told her about the allegations against her cousin.

"Fourteen women have signed up for the quilting classes so far," she told her silent partner in the shop.

"Oh, that's great. You must be excited to get them started."

"I am. It's going to be a good summer." Hilde said the last like a mantra, praying it was true.

"Dee's leaving Saturday," Dana said.

The words should have made her heart soar, but she heard sadness in her friend's voice. "I'm sorry her visit didn't go like you had hoped."

The bell over the door jangled as another customer came in.

Dana must have heard it. "You're busy. I'll let you go. I just wanted you to know I was thinking about you."

"Thank you for calling." It was the best she could do before Dana hung up.

The rest of the day slipped by. Hilde had moments when she would forget about the break-in. She knew she would have to replace the top of the counter. The scissor holes were a gut-wrenching reminder each time she saw them that it wasn't over with Dee.

Colt must have called when she was helping a customer by carrying her fabric purchases out to her car. He'd left a message that he hoped he could see her tonight.

She texted back that she was looking forward to it.

And suddenly it was time to close up shop. She gathered her things, trying hard not to look at the top of the counter. Thinking about Dee only made her blood boil.

A gust of wind caught the door as she started to lock up. She hadn't realized the wind had come up or that a storm was blowing in.

As she turned, she saw that her SUV parked across the street was sitting at a funny angle. Then she noticed the right back tire. Flat.

All she'd been thinking about the past few minutes was going home, taking a nice hot bath and getting ready for when Colt got back from West Yellowstone.

After finding her store vandalized first thing in the morning, she wasn't going to let a flat tire ruin her mood now, she thought. For a moment, she considered changing the tire herself, but she wasn't dressed for it, and her house was only a short walk from the shop.

As she started down the street, she saw that the storm was closer than she'd thought. Dark clouds rolled in, dimming the remainder of the day's light. She'd be lucky to get home before it started to rain, and in April the rain could easily turn to snow.

Hilde laughed, surprised that even the storm didn't bother her. She was seeing Colt again tonight and she couldn't wait. The only real dark cloud right now was

Dee Anna Justice, and apparently there wasn't a darned thing she could do about her.

When she looked up and saw Dee coming down the dark street toward her, she feared she'd conjured her. Because of the upcoming storm and the time of the year, the streets were deserted—something she hadn't noticed until that moment.

Stopping, she considered what to do. Dee had realized that she had her fingerprints and DNA. That was probably why she'd torn up the shop. Did that mean she'd realized whatever she'd been up to was about to come to a screeching halt? Or would the prints only prove that the woman really was Dee Anna Justice, a psychopath who would be able to keep fooling Dana unless Hilde and Colt could prove otherwise?

More to the immediate point, what was she doing here now? Hilde considered whether she should make a run for it. She didn't have that many options. Calling the marshal's office for help would be a waste of time.

"You don't have to look so scared," Dee called to her. "I came to give you some news that I think will make you happy."

Hilde let the woman get within a few feet of her. "That's close enough. What is it?"

"You win."

"You're the one who made it into a competition."

Dee chuckled as she took another step closer. "I've known women like you my whole life. Everything comes so easy to you. You've never had to fight for anything. You wouldn't have lasted two seconds in my world."

"I'm sorry you had a rough life, Dee, if that is really

your name. But that doesn't give you the right to take someone else's—literally."

"You're right," Dee said, not even bothering to deny anything. "I'm leaving. I just wanted you to know. That, and I'm sorry. I don't expect you to understand. I don't even understand why I'm like I am sometimes." She put her head down, actually sounding as if she meant it.

Hilde wondered what kind of life this woman really *had* lived through. Dee was right that her own had been cushy. As much as she hated it, she felt some sympathy for the woman. "You should try to get some help."

Dee slowly raised her head. It took Hilde an instant to realize Dee had stepped closer during all this. When she met her gaze, Hilde saw that something had changed in her eyes. It was an instant too long.

Before Hilde could react, Dee grabbed her right hand and raked Hilde's nails down her own left cheek.

Hilde let out a cry of shock and jerked her hand back.

Dee was smiling as she touched the four angry scratches down her face. Laughing at Hilde's reaction, she reached down and picked up a chunk of broken sidewalk at the edge of the street.

Hilde took a step back as Dee said, "You think I need help? Maybe I *should* see someone." She hit herself in the face with the piece of concrete and for a moment, Hilde thought Dee would buckle under the savage blow. But she straightened, dropped the chunk of sidewalk and, in the next instant, began to tear at her clothes.

"What are you doing?" Hilde cried. "Have you lost your mind?"

"Isn't this what you wish you were able to do to me?" Dee asked, smiling again. Her left eye was already swelling shut from where she'd hit herself. There was blood at the corner of her mouth and her lip was split and bleeding. The scratches down the left side of her face were bleeding now as well.

"No, I would never—" The rest of Hilde's words died on her lips as she realized exactly what Dee *was* doing. "No one will believe I did that to you!"

"Won't they?" Dee asked with a smirk. "Wanna bet?" With that she turned and ran screaming down the street.

CHAPTER ELEVEN

HILDE RUSHED BACK to Needles and Pins, fumbled the key in the lock and, once inside, relocked the door behind her. She was in shock, never having witnessed anything like that in her life.

Her hands shook as she took out her cell phone. She tried to call Colt but only got his voice mail. She left a message that it was urgent she talk to him. Only after she hung up did she remember he had to go back to West Yellowstone today.

She'd barely hung up when she saw Marshal Hud Savage pull up in his patrol pickup in front of the shop. Past him, across the street, she spotted her SUV with the flat tire. She hadn't had a flat in years. Why hadn't she realized it was a trap?

Because that wasn't how her mind worked. She'd never had to read evil into everything—until Dee arrived in town.

Hilde felt like a fool. She'd played right into the woman's hands, not once, but time and again. The more she protested, the worse it got. She knew that even if she hadn't started to walk home, Dee would have found an opportunity to make this happen.

Lightning cut a zigzagged line across the sky behind Hud as he headed for her front door. Thunder followed on its heels. Large drops of rain pelted the sidewalk as she put her cell phone back in her purse and hurried to unlock the shop door. "Hud, I—"

"I need you to come with me down to the station," he said, his voice hard as the sidewalk Dee had hit herself with.

"I didn't do any of that to her," Hilde cried. "Hud, you have to believe me."

He grabbed her right hand, holding it up. "Hilde, her skin is still under your fingernails."

"Hud, I know this sounds crazy, but that's the problem. Dee, or whatever her name is, *is* crazy. She's insane. She did all of that to herself."

He shook his head looking as sad as she had ever seen him. "Are you telling me you didn't attack her previously with a pair of scissors right here in your shop?"

Of course Dee would have told him about that, too. "No. I mean, yes, but—"

He began to read her rights to her. "Let's go," he said when he finished.

"You're really arresting me?" She couldn't believe any of this was happening. "You know me, Hud—"

"I thought I did. Dee Anna is pressing assault charges against you. Hilde, what is going on with you?"

She swallowed and shook her head. Even if she told him about the scissors incident, it wouldn't help her. Nor help Colt. She just had to put her faith in Colt to find out the truth about the woman—and soon.

COLT TRIED TO reach Hilde the moment he got her message. Her phone went straight to voice mail. He called the shop, just in case she was working late. She did that a lot, especially since she'd recently taken over the space next to Needles and Pins and expanded the business.

She was buying a line of sewing machines and would be starting quilting lessons, now that she had the room. He loved her work ethic. Loved a lot of things about her, he thought, reminded of last night.

With growing concern when she didn't answer at the shop, he realized he didn't know whom else to call. Not that long ago, he could have called Dana. She would have known where Hilde was. Dana and Hilde had been that close.

But not now. Thanks to Dee.

He was holding his phone, trying to decide what to do, when it rang. It was one of the dispatchers, Annie Wagner, a cute twentysomething redhead who was dating a Bozeman police officer he knew.

"I thought you'd want to know," Annie said in a hushed voice. "Hilde has been arrested."

"What?" His mind whirled. Hilde?

"Dee Anna Justice came screaming into the office thirty minutes ago saying Hilde had attacked her."

Colt groaned. He'd understood Hilde's thinking with the scissors, but—

"Dee was a mess. She looked like she'd gotten into a cat fight. Black eye, scratched up, bleeding."

He couldn't imagine Hilde doing that to anyone even if she was provoked. But if she was defending herself—

"Where is Hilde now?"

"Hud has her in his office. I just put through a call from Dee Anna Justice. Do you want me to call you if anything changes?"

"Thanks, Annie. I appreciate it. I'm on my way back from West Yellowstone. I should be there within the hour."

What had happened? He couldn't even imagine.

He'd told himself that Hud would see through Dee soon. Or Dee would give up once she realized Hud loved Dana and would never fall for her. He'd told himself that as long as Hilde stayed away from the ranch and Dee, this wouldn't escalate.

He'd been wrong. He also realized that until that moment, he hadn't really thought Dee had tried to kill Hilde. The scare at the falls had been just that. The incident under the raft? He thought Dee had probably pulled the same thing. Held Hilde under the raft then tried to save her, only this time Hilde had fought her off.

Now he was angry with himself for not truly believing what Hilde had known in her heart. Dee was capable of horrendous things. Even murder. Maybe she'd drugged Rick. What had she done to get Hilde arrested? Tried to kill her only to have Hilde fight back?

His heart was pounding as he switched on his lights and siren and raced toward Big Sky.

HILDE KNEW SHE was lucky that Hud hadn't brought her into jail in handcuffs. She figured that might be Dana's doing. Dana would go to bat for her even if she believed that her once best friend had attacked her cousin.

It still amazed her that anyone would believe Dee. But look at the extremes the woman would go to. She *was* insane. How else could Hilde explain it? Insane and desperate. This was a ploy to keep Hilde from getting her fingerprints run. Which had to mean that Dee really wasn't Dee Anna Justice—just as the now deceased Rick had insinuated.

But none of that helped Hilde right now, she thought, as she looked across the marshal's big desk. He was on the phone and had been for several minutes. From his tone of voice, she suspected it had been Dana who'd called, but Hilde now thought that Dana had put Dee on the line.

"I do understand," Hud was saying. "But I'd prefer that you came down here and we discussed this before you made any—" He listened for a moment, his gaze going to Hilde, before he said, "If you're sure. I would strongly advise you against this." More listening, then he said, "Fine," and hung up.

Hilde hadn't realized that she'd been holding her breath toward the end of his conversation until she let it out as he hung up.

Hud sat for a moment before he turned to her. "Dee is dropping the charges. I can still hold you, if I want to, and I'm certainly considering it."

She could tell that Dana had fought for her. Why else would Dee have dropped the charges? She felt tears sting her eyes. She knew better than to argue that she hadn't done anything to Dee. She'd already tried the truth and that had gotten her arrested, so she waited.

"Dee is filing a temporary restraining order that is good for twenty days. I assume you know what that is," he said.

A restraining order? It was all she could do not to scream. "It means I can't go near her." Which meant she couldn't go near the ranch or Dana. Her tears now were of frustration. Dee kept maneuvering her into impossible situations where Hilde always came out looking like the villain.

"That's going to be hard to do in Big Sky, Hilde," he said with a sigh. "Think about taking a vacation. Go see your mother in Chicago. Or go lay on a beach for a couple of weeks. Get out of here."

"For twenty days?" Wouldn't Dee love that. "Or maybe she'll make it a permanent restraining order, since she doesn't seem to be leaving, does she?"

"Hilde, I'm trying to help. I'd think you'd want to get out of here for a while."

"You don't know how tempting that is, Hud." She felt as beat-up as Dee was. She'd lost control of her life. She'd certainly lost her friends, her shop had been vandalized and she was losing faith that she would ever be able to fix any of this before things got worse.

"Dana is worried about you," he said, and she heard some of that old caring in his voice.

"And I'm worried about her. I wish I *could* leave, but I can't, Hud. I can't leave Dana knowing what's living in your house right now. I'm sorry," she said when she saw his expression harden. "So can I go now?"

He nodded. "Hilde? Stay away from Dee."

"Believe me, I'm doing my best. For the record, do you want to actually hear the truth?" She didn't wait for him to answer. "I came out of the shop after locking up to find I had a flat tire. I should have suspected something then, but I've never been a suspicious person. I started to walk home, no big deal, that's when I saw Dee. She called to me, said she had some news. When she got close, she told me she was leaving. She said she was sorry for what she'd done to me."

Hilde stopped for a moment, smiled and said, "You know I actually believed her. She is that good. And then she grabbed my hand, raked my fingernails down her face. I was so shocked I couldn't move. I jerked my hand back. That's when she picked up a chunk of broken sidewalk from the side of the street and hit herself in the face. I know," she said, seeing his disbelieving expression. "I had the same reaction. Right after that was when she began to rip her clothing. She said no one would believe me. So far, she's been dead-on, hasn't she?"

With that she turned and walked out, leaving Hud frowning after her.

ONLY A FEW miles out of Big Sky, Colt got the call that Dee was refusing to press charges, deciding to take out a temporary restraining order instead. He swore, anxious to get to Hilde and find out what had happened.

He found her at her house. She hadn't been home long when she opened the door. He saw that she had a stunned look on her face. Stunned and devastated. It was heartbreaking.

Without a word, he took her in his arms. She was trembling. He took her over to the couch, then went to her liquor cabinet and found some bourbon. He poured her a couple fingers' worth.

"Drink this," he said.

"Aren't you afraid what I might do liquored up?" she asked sarcastically.

"Terrified," he said and stood over her until she'd downed every drop. "You want to talk about it?" he asked, taking the empty glass from her and joining her on the couch.

She let out a laugh. "*I* hardly believe what happened. Why would I expect anyone else to?"

"I believe you. I believe everything you've told me."

Tears welled in her brown eyes. He drew her to him and kissed her, holding her tightly. "I'm sorry you had to go through this alone."

She nodded and wiped hastily at the tears as she drew back to look at him. "You're my only hope right now. We have to find out whatever we can about this woman." And then she told him everything, from finding the shop vandalized to what led up to her being nearly arrested.

When she finished, he said, "We shouldn't be surprised."

"Surprised? I'm still in shock. To do something like that to yourself…"

"You knew Dee was sick."

Hilde nodded. "What will she do next? That's what worries me."

Colt didn't want to say it, but that worried him, too. "Maybe Hud has the right idea. Isn't there somewhere—"

"I'm not leaving. Dee told me that I've never had to fight for anything. Well, I'm fighting now. I'm bringing her down. One way or another."

"Hilde—"

"She has to be stopped."

"I agree. But we have to be careful. She's dangerous." He felt his phone vibrate, checked it and saw that his boss had sent him a text. "Hud wants to see me ASAP." Not good. "I don't want to leave you here alone."

"I'll be fine. Dee won this round. She won't do anything for a while, and I'm not going to give her another chance to use me like she did today."

He heard the courage as well as the determination in her voice. Hilde was strong and, no matter what Dee had told her, she *was* a fighter.

"Would you mind if I came by later?"

Her kiss answered that question quite nicely.

HUD WAS WAITING when Colt arrived. He motioned him into his office. "What the hell do you think you're doing?" he said the moment Colt closed the door and sat down.

"I beg your pardon?" He had a pretty good idea what the problem was, but he wasn't about to hand him the rope to hang him.

"Tell me about the unauthorized request to run fingerprints you sent to the crime lab," the marshal said.

That's what Colt figured. Someone had caught his friend. He hated that he'd gotten the man into trouble. Sticking out his own neck was one thing. Sticking out someone else's was a whole other story.

"They're the woman's now staying at your house, the one you call Dee Anna Justice," he said.

Hud swore and slammed a hand down on his desk as he sat forward. "What the hell were you thinking sending an unauthorized request to the crime lab?"

"I was trying to protect you and your family."

"That isn't going to wash and you know it. Well, let me give you the news. There are no prints on file." Hud let that sink in. "That's right. Dee has no record. Satisfied?"

So she'd never been arrested. That didn't surprise him given what he'd seen of her maneuvers so far.

"This is about Hilde, isn't it?" Hud demanded. "You did this for her. This is so you can get closer to her."

Colt got to his feet. "If that's what you think—"

"You're suspended."

This, too, didn't come as a surprise. He met Hud's gaze. "If you really think I would use law enforcement resources to try get a woman in bed, then I think you should fire me."

"Damn it, Colt, you're a fine deputy marshal and I don't want to lose you. Two weeks without pay. Get out of here."

He left Hud's office, knowing there was nothing he could say. He'd taken a risk. It had cost him. Worse, it had only made Dee look more innocent.

"Colt," Annie whispered, as he started for the door out of the station. He could tell that she'd probably heard everything. The department was small, the walls thin. She motioned him over and secretly slipped him a folded sheet of paper. "I think you'll want to see this."

They both heard Hud come out of his office. Colt mouthed *Thank you* and quickly left. It wasn't until he reached home that he finally unfolded the sheet and saw what was written on it.

He went straight to his computer. It didn't take long before he found what he was looking for—and then some.

CHAPTER TWELVE

HILDE KNEW THINGS hadn't gone well at the marshal's office the moment she opened the door and saw Colt's face.

"What happened?" she asked, as she let him in.

"Nothing to worry about."

"He found out that you sent Dee's fingerprints to the crime lab."

"I knew there was a chance that might happen."

"Tell me he didn't fire you," she cried.

"He didn't. Suspended for two weeks. As it turns out, the suspension couldn't come at a better time. I've got some news."

They moved into the kitchen, where Hilde got him a beer and poured a glass of wine for herself. She had a feeling she was going to need it. "I hate getting you into trouble."

"You didn't. I'm in this just as deep as you are," he said, and kissed her as he took the cold bottle of beer she offered him. He took a sip. She watched him, desire making her legs weak as water.

She dropped into a chair in front of the fireplace, curling her legs under her and taking a drink of her wine. She'd built a small fire since he'd said he would be back. She'd tried not to count the minutes.

Colt didn't sit but stood in front of the fire. She could tell he was worked up, too antsy to sit.

"You have news?" she asked, afraid what he was about to tell her.

"Rick Cameron's real name was Richard Northland. Cameron was apparently one of a number of aliases he has used. He was a small-time con artist, been arrested a couple of times, but nothing that got him more than a little jail time. The person he cheated tended to drop the charges."

Hilde felt her eyes widen. "So he and Dee had a lot in common."

"I'm sure Dee was shocked by the news when Hud told her."

Hilde let out a humorless laugh. "I'm sure she was."

"There's more. Her fingerprints weren't on file. But when I did some digging online, I found a story about Richard and his sister, Camilla Northland."

"His *sister?*"

Colt nodded. "The two of them were the only survivors of a fire at their home in Tuttle, Oklahoma. Both parents were killed. Apparently there was some suspicion that one or both might have purposely started the fire. Richard was fourteen at the time, Camilla sixteen."

"Are you saying what I think you are?" Hilde asked.

"I'm trying hard not to jump to any conclusions. All we know for sure is that the man lying in the morgue is Richard Northland from Tuttle, Oklahoma. I'll know more once I get there."

"Get there?"

"I'm flying to Oklahoma tomorrow on the first flight out."

Hilde got up from her chair and moved to the fire as

a sudden chill skittered across her skin like spider legs. "You think there's a possibility that Dee is his sister?"

"A possibility based on nothing more than a feeling that the two of them knew each other longer than Dee said."

She recalled how Rick had turned around when the naked Dee had gotten out of the lake. "Dana thought Rick was Dee's boyfriend."

"Probably because that's what she told her. I haven't been able to find out much of anything about Camilla because she dropped off radar right after the fire. According to a newspaper account, the two were going to live with an aunt since their parents were the only family they had."

"She dropped off the radar because she's not using her real name?"

"That would be my guess. While I'm gone I want you to stay clear of Dee."

"If she finds out where you've gone…"

"She won't. I'll tell someone at the station that I'm going to Denver to see my brother. I'm sure by now they all know I've been suspended."

"Colt," she said, touching his strong shoulder. "I don't want to see you lose your job."

"I won't. I think whatever I find out in Oklahoma will change things drastically."

Hilde couldn't help being nervous. "Be careful. I'm just afraid what Dee might do if she thinks you're onto her. So far it's just me she's after."

"Yeah, that's what worries me. Look what happened to Rick," Colt said.

Hilde shivered and he took her in his arms. "I just don't want her moving up her plan, whatever it is."

"I'm more worried about you. I wish you were going with me."

"If we both went, it would look even more suspicious. Anyway, she's accomplished what she set out to do. Dana and I are hardly speaking."

"I hate seeing you like this," he said, and kissed her. "It's going to be all right. I know you're worried about Dana. But we're going to get this resolved."

She nodded. "Hopefully before something horrible happens."

"Hilde, I don't think Dee is through with you, so be careful."

"I will."

"Promise?"

She smiled and leaned up to kiss him. "I'll be careful."

"I'll call you from Oklahoma as soon as I know something. I won't be gone any longer than I have to. I'm going home to pack, but first…" He swung her up in his arms. "I don't want you to forget about me while I'm gone."

"Like that could happen," she said with a laugh, as he carried her into the bedroom.

COLT TRIED TO get on standby, but the earliest flight he could get on was that afternoon. He hated leaving Hilde. Last night he'd managed to talk her into letting Ronnie open the shop and man it until he got back. It had taken some talking, though. Hilde was one determined woman.

He tried not to speculate on what Dee might do. When he'd called Annie at the office, he'd told her he was flying to Denver to visit his brother. Of course, she knew he'd been suspended.

"Mrs. Savage was in earlier," Annie told him in a hushed whisper. "She and the boss had a row over your suspension. Seems her cousin has booked a flight to New York City for Saturday."

That had been news. Saturday was only two days away. If Dee was telling the truth. "I suppose there is no way to find out if she really did book that flight," he said to Annie.

She chuckled. "I'll see what I can do."

After he hung up, he wondered if this meant Dee was giving up. Maybe she'd realized that Hilde had her fingerprints and DNA, so it wouldn't be long before they knew who she really was. *Best to leave town before that happened, huh, Dee?*

His plane landed in Salt Lake City with a short layover before he flew into Oklahoma City, where he rented a car. It was too late to drive to Tuttle, so he got a motel. When he called Hilde, she sounded fine, anxious, but staying in the house. He breathed a sigh of relief.

"Try to get some sleep," he told her. "I won't know anything until tomorrow at the soonest." He didn't sleep well at all and early the next morning set off for Tuttle.

The town had once been a tiny suburb. Now the buildings along the former main street were boarded up. It was one of many small, dying towns across the country.

Colt stopped at the combination grocery and gas station and wandered inside. A fan whirred in the window near the counter behind an elderly woman who sat thumbing through a movie magazine.

"Can you believe all the divorces they have out in

Hollywood?" She looked up at him over her glasses as if actually expecting an answer.

"No, I can't."

She closed the magazine, studying him. "You aren't from around here."

He shook his head. "But I'm looking for someone *from* around here."

Her eyes widened a little. "I figured you were just lost. Who are you looking for? I know most everyone since I was born and raised right here."

That had been his hope. "Maybe you know them, then. Richard and Camilla Northland?"

The woman's expression soured in a heartbeat. She leaned back as if trying to distance herself from his words. "Well, you won't find them around here."

"Actually, I'm looking for their aunt, the one who raised them after their parents died."

"Didn't die. Were murdered." She shook her head. "What do you want with Thelma?"

"I have some news about her nephew."

"There isn't any news she'd want to hear except that he's six feet under," the woman snapped.

"Then I guess I have some good news for her."

HILDE TRIED NOT to go down to the shop the next day, but Ronnie called to say there was a problem with the new sewing machine invoice and the deliveryman wasn't sure what she wanted him to do.

"I'll be right there." She was thankful for the call. Sitting around waiting to hear from Colt was making her all the more anxious. She was also thankful that the sewing machines hadn't arrived before Dee vandalized the shop.

Once at the shop after taking care of the problem, Hilde showed Ronnie some of the ideas she had for quilting classes, and they began to work on a wall hanging for the sewing room.

Hilde loved the way the shop was coming together. She'd long dreamed of a place where anyone who wanted to learn to quilt could come and sew with others of like mind. Quilting was a restful and yet creative hobby at any age. She had great plans for the future and was so excited about them that she'd almost picked up the phone and called Dana to tell her.

Dana still had money invested in Needles and Pins. Hilde realized that might change now. She should consider buying her out if their friendship went any further south. The thought made her sad. If only they could prove that Dee wasn't her cousin.

She was mentally kicking herself for not thinking to take Dana's toothbrush as well as Dee's, when the bell over the door jangled and she turned to see Dana walk into the shop.

Hilde felt her face light up—until she saw Dana's expression. Her stomach fell with the memory of what had happened yesterday. Dana must be horrified. But how could her once best friend not realize that Hilde could never beat up anyone?

She felt a spark of anger, which she quickly tamped down as Dana stepped into the shop. Letting her temper flare was a surefire way to make herself look more guilty.

"Could we talk alone?" Dana asked quietly.

"Ronnie, would you mind watching the counter for a few minutes?" Hilde called. Ronnie said she'd be happy to. Hilde led Dana into the break room and closed the door. She didn't want Ronnie hearing this. But the news was probably all over town anyway. The shop had been unusually slow today.

"I don't know what to say to you," Dana said.

Hilde stepped to the coffeepot, fingers trembling as she took two clean glass cups and filled each with coffee. She handed one to Dana, then sat down, ready for a lecture.

Dana seemed to hesitate before she sat down. Hilde didn't help her by denying anything. Instead she waited, relieved when Dana finally took a drink of the coffee and seemed to calm down some.

"How long have we known each other?" Hilde asked.

Dana looked up from her cup in surprise. "Since you came to town about…six years ago. But you know that."

"So for six years we've been close friends. Some might even have said best friends."

Dana's eyes suddenly shone with tears.

"Would you have said you knew me well?" She didn't wait for an answer. "Remember that spider in my kitchen that time? I couldn't squish it. You had to do it."

"You can't compare killing a spider to—"

"Dana, what if Dee wasn't your cousin?"

"That's ridiculous because she *is* my cousin."

Hilde wasn't going to argue that. Not right now anyway. "What if she was just some stranger who ended up on your doorstep and things began happening and the next thing you knew you and I were…" She couldn't bring herself to say where they were. "Would you take a stranger's word over mine?"

Dana put down her cup. "She said you would say you didn't attack her."

Hilde sighed and put down her own cup. "That you

came here today makes me believe that there is some doubt in your mind. I hope that's true, because it might save your life."

"It's talk like that, Hilde, that makes me think you've lost your mind," Dana said, getting to her feet. "Why would Dee want to hurt me?"

"So she could have Hud."

Dana shook her head. "Hud loves *me*."

"But if you were gone…"

Dana reached into her jeans pocket and took out a piece of paper. Hilde recognized it as a sheet from the notepad Dana kept by the phone. "I called around. This is the name of a doctor everyone said was very good." When Hilde didn't reach for the note, Dana laid it on the table. "I think you need help, Hilde." Her voice broke with emotion.

"She doesn't just want you out of the way, Dana. Your children will have to go, too."

Dana's gaze came up to meet hers.

Hilde saw fear. "Trust me. Trust the friendship we had. You're in trouble. So are your babies."

A tear trailed down Dana's cheek. She brushed at it. "I have to go." She hurried out, leaving Hilde alone in the break room.

The moment she heard the bell jangle, Hilde got up, took a plastic bag from the drawer and carefully bagged Dana's coffee cup.

"What are you doing?"

She turned in surprise to find Dana standing in the doorway. She must have started to leave, but then changed her mind.

"I asked you what you were doing."

Hilde knew there was no reason to lie even if she

could have thought of one Dana might believe. "I need your DNA to check it against Dee's."

The shocked look on Dana's face said it all. That and what she said before turning and really leaving this time: "Oh, Hilde."

COLT DROVE OUT of Tuttle, took the third right and pulled down a narrow two-track toward a stand of live oak. He hadn't been in the South in years. Oklahoma wasn't considered the South to people from Georgia or Alabama, but anywhere that cotton grew along the road was the South to him.

He followed the directions the woman at the grocery and gas station had given him until the road played out, ending in front of a weathered, stooped old house that was much like the elderly woman who came out on the porch.

He parked and climbed out. Thelma Peters was Richard and Camilla Northland's aunt on their mother's side of the family, PJ Harris had told him.

"Everyone's called me PJ since I was a girl," the elderly woman at the store had told him. "Not because it has anything to do with my name, which by the way is Charlotte Elizabeth. No, I got PJ because that's what I was usually wearing when I would come down here, to this very store, in the morning so my father could make me breakfast. My mother had died when I was a baby, you see. He'd pour me a bowl of cereal, ask me if I wanted berries. I always said no, then he'd pour on some thick cream." Her eyes had lit at the memory. "I can still taste that cream. Can't buy anything like it anymore."

He'd finally managed to turn her back to Richard and Camilla's aunt.

"Thelma Peters. She's an old maid. I can see where having those two in her house turned her against ever having any of her own children." PJ had studied him again then. "Don't be surprised if she comes out on her porch with a shotgun. Don't take it personally. Just make sure she knows you aren't that no-'count nephew of hers. I'd hate to see you get shot."

"I'll keep that in mind," he'd promised.

"I'm here with some good news," Colt called out now to the elderly old maid holding the shotgun.

"If you're preaching the Gospel, I've already found the Lord. You wasted your gas coming out here," she called back.

"I'm a deputy marshal from Montana," he called to her. A slight exaggeration at the moment. He saw the change in her as if she was bracing herself for whatever bad news he was bringing. "Your nephew Richard has been killed."

Thelma Peters nodded, then took a step back and sat down hard in an old wooden chair on her porch. The barrel end of the shotgun banged against the worn wood flooring at her feet, but she held on to the gun as she motioned him to come closer.

Colt walked up to the house, shielding his eyes against the sun. The yard was a dust bowl. The weeds that had survived were baked dead. "I'm sorry to bring you the news."

She looked up then and, from rheumy but intelligent blue eyes, considered him for a long moment. "You certainly came a long way to give it to me."

"I need to ask you about Camilla."

Thelma let out a cough of a laugh. "You cross her path, too? Best say your prayers."

"I don't know if I've crossed her path or not. Do you happen to have a picture of her?"

The woman looked at him as if he was crazy. "Not one I keep out, I can tell you that."

"I sure would appreciate it if you could find one for me. I'm worried about a family in Montana that this woman has moved in with."

She grunted and pushed herself to her feet, using the shotgun like a crutch. "Better step inside. This could take a while."

WHEN DANA CAME back from town, she was clearly upset.

"You didn't go see Hilde," Dee said, wanting to wring her neck. She'd begged her to stay away from her former friend. "Dana, what were you thinking?"

Hud, who'd come home to watch the kids while she ran to the store, seconded Dee's concern.

"I had to see her," Dana cried, then shook her head.

Dee had been so excited when Dana had told her that Hud was coming home to help her watch the children. She knew that neither of them wanted to leave the little darlings with her. She'd made it clear she knew nothing about kids, especially babies.

But all the time Hud had been home, he'd been so involved with the children that he wasn't even aware Dee was in the room.

"I hope you didn't listen to Hilde's crazy talk," Dee said, worried that that was exactly what Dana had done. She'd felt Dana pulling away from her. Worse, Hud was doing the same thing, she feared.

If only Hilde had just drowned that day under the raft.

Dee touched her sore black eye. "You're just lucky you didn't end up like me."

Dana glanced at her, wincing at the sight. Dee had to admit she looked like she'd been run over by a truck. But she'd wanted to make a statement and she had. Dana had been so thankful when she'd dropped the charges against Hilde. Even Hud had seemed relieved when he'd come home that night.

"It's worse than I thought," Dana said and looked at Hud. "I sat down and had a cup of coffee with her at the shop…"

Dee gritted her teeth in anger. How could Dana do that after seeing what Hilde had done to her cousin?

"She seemed calm, even rational…" Dana glanced at Dee then back at Hud.

Dee felt her heart begin to race. Hilde had gotten to Dana. She'd started believing her.

"Then I got ready to leave, made it as far as the door, thought of something and went back." She stopped and took a breath. "Hud, she was bagging my coffee cup."

Dee let out a silent curse that was like a roar in her ears.

"I demanded to know what she was doing," Dana continued now in tears. "She told me she was going to check my DNA against Dee's. I'm sorry, Dee," Dana said, turning to her again. "I'm so sorry."

"Don't be. Clearly Hilde has had some sort of psychotic episode. How can she think I'm not your cousin? We look so much alike."

Dana nodded, still obviously upset.

"I'd ask who she thought she was going to get to run the tests, but I'm sure Colt is helping her," Hud said. "I can't imagine what he's thinking."

"I thought you said he went to Denver to see his brother?" Dee asked.

"That's what I heard, but I have my doubts. I can't see him leaving Hilde alone now. He must be as worried about her as we are."

THELMA PETERS'S HOUSE was small and cramped. She left him in a threadbare chair in the living room and disappeared into a room at the back. Periodically he would hear a bump or bang.

He looked around, noticing a picture of Jesus on one wall and a cross on another. A Bible lay open on the table next to his chair. He picked it up, curious what part she'd been reading. She had a passage underlined—Acts 3:19. *Repent therefore, and turn again, that your sins may be blotted out.*

"Here is the only one I could find." Thelma came back into the room with a snapshot clutched in her fingers. "I haven't seen Camilla in years, so I don't know what she looks like now. But this is what she looked like at sixteen."

CHAPTER THIRTEEN

COLT LOOKED DOWN at the photo. His heart sank. The photo was of two people, a young man and a girl with long dark hair. The young man was the same man still at the morgue in Montana—Rick Cameron, aka Richard Northland.

The girl—was definitely not Dee.

He told himself it had been a long shot, but now realized how much he'd been counting on Dee being Camilla Northland. Maybe Rick really was her boyfriend. Maybe she didn't even kill him.

"This isn't the woman in Montana," he told Thelma.

"Like I said, she was only sixteen. I have no idea what she looks like now." She took the photograph back. "You look disappointed. You should be thankful the woman in Montana isn't Camilla. You should be very thankful."

"Were she and her brother really that bad?" he had to ask.

The old woman scoffed. "They killed their parents. Burned them to a crisp. That bad enough for you? They tried to poison me. Camilla pushed me down the stairs once no doubt hoping I would break my neck. I hate to think what they would have done if I'd broken a leg and needed the two of them to take care of me. I finally ran them off." Still clutching the photo, she sat down in a chair across from him and patted her shotgun. "I've always felt guilty about that." Her gaze came up to meet his. "But I couldn't have killed them even knowing what I was releasing on the world."

He felt a chill at her words as she looked from him to the photograph and seemed startled by what she saw.

"I grabbed the wrong photograph. This isn't Camilla. This is that awful girlfriend of Richard's." She pushed to her feet, padded out of the room and returned a moment later.

This time she handed him a photo of Richard and a girl standing on the porch outside. The girl's face was in shadow, but there was no doubt it was the woman who called herself Dee Anna Justice.

At sixteen, she already had those dark, soulless eyes.

Dee had been waiting, so she wasn't surprised when Dana finally asked.

"I know nothing about your father," Dana said, as she was making dinner. "Do you have any idea why our families separated all those years ago?"

Mary and Hank were making a huge mess building a fort in the living room. The twins were in dual high chairs spreading some awful-looking food all over themselves and anything else within reach.

Dee moved so she wasn't in their line of fire. Dana had put her to work chopping vegetables for the salad. Now she stopped to look at the small paring knife in her hand. She tried to remember exactly what she'd told Stacy.

"I really have no idea," she said, thinking that if she had to cut up one more cucumber she might start screaming. Hud hadn't been around all day. Spending "free" time with Dana and the kids was mind-numbing.

"Can you tell me what your father was like?" Dana asked as she fried chicken in a huge cast-iron skillet on the stove. The hot kitchen smelled of grease. It turned Dee's stomach.

"He was secretive," Dee said, thinking of his daughter. The real Dee Anna had never talked about her family, her father in particular, which had been fine with her because she wasn't really interested. She liked her roommates to keep to themselves, just share an apartment, not their life stories.

"Secretive?" Dana said with interest. "And your mother?"

Dee gave her the same story she'd given Stacy. She had actually met Marietta Justice, so that made it easy.

"That surprises me. I can't imagine why my family wouldn't have been delighted to have Walter marry so well," Dana said.

"Maybe they didn't want him leaving here and they knew that was exactly what was going to happen," Dee said, as she chopped the last cucumber and dumped it into the salad. The entire topic of Dee Anna's family bored her. If Dana wanted to hear about an interesting family, Dee could tell her about hers.

"Tell me more about your side of the family," Dee said, knowing Dana would jump at the chance. She tuned her out as she ripped up the lettuce the way Dana had showed her and thought about her plan. She felt rushed, but she had no choice. In order to make this happen, she had to move fast.

Hilde had done a lot of damage, but Dee was sure

that after Dana and the kids were gone, Hud would lean on her. Eventually.

She thought of the man she'd met on the airplane. He was still over on the Yellowstone River for a few more days. All she had to do was pick up the phone and call him. She could walk away from here and never look back. All her instincts told her that was the thing to do.

Dee heard the kids start screaming in the other room, then the front door slam. A moment later Hud Savage came into the kitchen with Mary and Hank hanging off him like monkeys. All three were laughing.

"What smells so good?" he asked. Even the two babies got excited to see him and joined in the melee.

Dee watched him give Dana a kiss. She felt her heart swell. She'd never wanted anything more in her life than what Dana had. No matter how long it took, she would have this with Hud Savage. Only he would love her more than he'd ever loved Dana.

"So Camilla is the woman you mentioned back in Montana," Thelma Peters said, and added under her breath, "God help you all."

Colt's heart was pounding. "If you know for certain that she and her brother killed their parents, why weren't they arrested?"

"No proof. Those two were cagey, way beyond their years. She was far worse than her brother. Smarter and colder. She made it look like an accident. Anyone who knew Camilla knew what had really happened out at that house the night of the fire. She fooled everyone else, making them feel sorry for her."

He thought about the way she'd worked Hud and Dana. Even himself that day on the river. Camilla

Northland was a great actor. "And yet, you let them move in here."

"They were so young. I thought I could turn them around. I dragged the two of them to church." She shook her head. "It was a waste of time. The evil was too deep in her, and Richard was too dependent on her."

"Would you mind if I took this photograph?" he asked.

"Please do. For years, I've prayed never to see that face again. I've always worried that when I got old, she would come back here."

Thelma didn't have to say any more. He had a pretty good idea now of what Camilla might do to the aunt who had taken her in all those years ago.

"Do you believe in evil, Marshal?"

He didn't correct her. "I do now."

She nodded. "I assume she's already hurt people or you wouldn't be here."

He nodded, reminded that she'd gotten away with it, too. And might continue to get away with it because there was never any proof and she was very good at her lies.

"I pray you can stop her," Thelma said. "I couldn't. But maybe you can."

HILDE WAS AT the shop when Colt called. After Dana had left, she'd been so upset she'd thought about going home. But she couldn't stand the thought of her empty house. So she'd stayed and helped set up the new sewing machines with Ronnie.

When her cell phone rang, she jumped as if she'd been electrocuted. Ronnie shot her a worried look. Hilde saw that it was Colt calling and, heart racing, hurried into the break room and closed the door.

"Where are you?" she asked.

"On my way to the airport. I was able to get a flight out this afternoon. If I can make the tight connections, I'll be home tonight."

Home tonight. She thrilled at his words. "It is *so* good to hear your voice."

"Rough day?" he asked. "Hilde—"

"Don't worry, I haven't seen Dee. Dana stopped by. I'll tell you about it when you get back." She braced herself. "What did you find out?"

"First, I need you to remain calm. I almost didn't call you because I was afraid you'd go charging out to the ranch."

"She's this Camilla person who they think killed her own parents," Hilde said.

"Yes."

She closed her eyes, gripping the phone, emotions bombarding her from every direction. Relief that she'd been right about the woman. Terror since a killer was still out at the ranch with her best friend and her kids.

"Listen to me, Hilde. If you go charging out there or even call, they aren't going to believe you—and you could force Dee to do something drastic and jeopardize everyone, okay?"

She nodded to herself, knowing what he was saying was true. Dana wouldn't believe Colt any more than she had Hilde. "You've told Hud, though, right? So he's going to take care of everything."

"I've been trying to reach him. I've left him a message. He'll know how to handle this. I need your word that you'll sit tight. I'll be there by tonight and this will all be over."

She wished it were that simple. She prayed he was right. "Okay. I know what you're saying. I won't do anything."

"Where are you?"

"At the shop. I couldn't stay at the house."

"I wish you would go home and wait for me. Lock the doors. Don't leave for any reason."

She smiled, touched by his concern.

"Hilde, I...I love you."

His words brought tears of joy to her eyes. For years she'd waited for the right man to come along. Dana had been her biggest supporter.

"I want you to find someone like Hud so badly," Dana would say.

Hilde had wanted that, too, but she'd thought it could never happen.

"Are you crying?" he asked.

She gulped back a sob. This was the happiest moment of her life and she couldn't share it with her best friend. "I love you, too, Colt."

"Okay, baby," he said. "I have to go. I'll call you the moment I land. Be safe."

She hung up and let the tears fall that she'd been fighting to hold back all day.

A moment later, Ronnie opened the door a crack. "Are you all right?"

Hilde almost laughed. Dana and Hud weren't the only people looking at her strangely lately. "Colt Dawson just told me that he loves me."

Ronnie started to laugh, clearly relieved. "That's

wonderful. I guess you must be one of those people who cries when they're happy?"

Hilde nodded, although some of the tears were out of a deep sadness. In a matter of days, her life had changed so drastically it made her head spin.

"Do you want me to stay with you?" Ronnie asked. "If you don't feel like locking up tonight by yourself—"

Hilde hadn't realized it was so late. "No, I'm fine."

Ronnie hesitated. Of course she'd heard about Dee's alleged attack and probably even the restraining order.

"I don't think there will be any trouble tonight," Hilde said, thinking she should have gotten a restraining order against Dee. As if a restraining order would stop someone like her.

As Ronnie left, Hilde locked up behind her. She wasn't quite ready to go home yet. A part of her was still chilled by the news that the woman posing as Dee Anna Justice was actually Camilla Northland, sister of Richard Northland, both of them believed to be cold-blooded killers.

It was easy for Hilde to believe that of Dee. She knew firsthand what the woman was capable of. The fact that Dee was probably out on the ranch right now having dinner with Dana and Hud and the kids...

Colt was right, of course. Calling out there to warn Dana was a waste of breath. It could even make matters worse.

Hilde turned out the lights in the front of the store and walked to the break room. Closing the door, she pulled out her cell phone. At the touch of one button she could get Dana on the line.

She thought about what she could say. She hit the

button. The phone rang three times. They were eating dinner. Dana wasn't going to answer the call.

Hilde had just started to hang up when it stopped ringing. "Dana?" She could hear breathing. "Dana, I just called to tell you that Colt just told me he loved me."

"I'm sorry, but you have the wrong number." The line went dead.

For just an instant, Hilde thought she had gotten the wrong number because that hadn't been Dana's voice.

Then her mind kicked into gear.

It had been Dee's voice. She'd answered Dana's cell phone.

COLT COULDN'T BELIEVE he'd blurted it out like that. *I love you.* He'd said it without thinking. He let out a chuckle. He'd just said what was in his heart.

He considered calling her back to warn her again about doing anything crazy. He had debated telling her about Dee to start with, afraid of what Hilde would do. For a woman who he suspected had never been impulsive in her life, she had been doing a lot of things on the spur of the moment lately.

Like telling him she loved him, too.

He felt his heart soar at the memory of her words. He couldn't wait to get home for so many reasons.

The moment he walked into the airport terminal, though, he felt his heart drop. Something was wrong. He could feel it in the air as he hurried to the airline counter and saw that his flight had been canceled.

"What's going on?" he asked of a man waiting in line. He could hear a woman arguing that she had to get to Salt Lake.

"All flights into Salt Lake City have been canceled

for today because of a bad spring snowstorm," the man said. "Snow's falling at a rate of six inches an hour. I just saw it on the weather channel. Doesn't look good even for in the morning."

Colt felt like the woman arguing with the airline clerk. He desperately needed to get home. But unlike that woman, he realized he wasn't going to be flying.

He'd just reached the car rental agency when Annie called from the marshal's office in Big Sky. "Ready to be surprised? Dee Anna Justice *did* book a flight to New York City for tomorrow."

He *was* surprised. "You're sure?"

"I had the airline executive double-check. Because I called concerned about Dee Anna Justice, I figure they'll take her into one of those little rooms and do an entire cavity search," she said with a satisfied chuckle.

Colt was trying to make sense of this. Dee was really leaving tomorrow? Maybe she was just covering her bets.

"Not only that, Hud announced that he plans to take Dana on a trip to Jackson Hole beginning Sunday. Jordan and Liza are going to stay at the house for a couple of days and watch the kids."

"You're sure Dee isn't going with them?" he asked.

"Definitely not. He said he hoped things calmed down once Dana put Dee on the plane."

Colt bet he did. "Thanks for doing this, Annie. One more thing. I left a message for Hud—"

"There's been a break in the burglary case in West Yellowstone. He was up there today and he's coming back tomorrow. That's probably why he hasn't returned your call."

Either that or he'd seen who'd called and didn't want to deal with his suspended deputy right now. While

Hud had to be having his own misgivings about Dee, Colt knew that the marshal would be skeptical even if Colt gave him the information he'd gathered in Tuttle— until he saw the photograph of Camilla Northland and her brother.

"YOU'RE IN LUCK," the woman behind the counter told him. "I have one vehicle left. I'm afraid it's our most expensive SUV."

"I'll take it," he said, and pulled out his credit card. Getting the paperwork done seemed to take forever. He glanced at his watch. Not quite noon. While he was waiting for the woman to finish the paperwork, he'd checked.

It was twenty-two hours to Big Sky. That didn't take into account the bad weather ahead of him. He knew he wouldn't be able to make good time once he reached the snow. He would have to make up for it when he had dry roads.

But he could reach Big Sky by late morning. He just prayed that wouldn't be too late.

Finally, she handed him the keys. A few minutes later, he was in the leather, heated-seat lap of luxury and headed north.

Hilde had sounded disappointed when he'd called to tell her the news. "But I'm glad you're on your way. Just be careful. I checked the weather before you called. It looks like that storm is going to stay to the south of us."

Neither of them had mentioned what they had said to each other earlier.

"I can't wait to see you," he said.

"Me, too."

"I'd better get off and pay attention to my driving."

He'd hung up feeling all the more frustrated that he couldn't get to her more quickly. Hud still hadn't returned his call.

He pushed down on the gas pedal, hoping he didn't get pulled over.

DEE SAW HOW disappointed Dana was at dinner when Hud told her he had to go up to West Yellowstone the next day. Any other time, Dee would have felt the same way.

She touched the small vial in her pocket. Hud didn't realize how lucky he was. Now she could implement her plan without involving him. This was so much better.

"I should be back by late afternoon," Hud was saying. "What do you and Dee have planned?"

"She flies out tomorrow afternoon, so it's up to her," Dana said. She and Hud looked at Dee.

"I just want to spend the morning here on the ranch with Dana and the kids," Dee said. "I don't know when I'll get to see them again, so I want to make it last. If it's nice, I'd love to take the kids on a walk. I saw those tandem strollers you have out there. I thought we could hike up the road, pick wildflowers…"

"That's a wonderful idea," Dana said. "I could pack a lunch."

"You're not going," Dee said. "You are going to stay here and put your feet up and relax. You have been waiting on me for days. It's my turn to give you a break. The kids and I can pack the lunch, can't we?"

Mary and Hank quickly agreed. "I want peanut butter and jelly," Mary said.

"Mommy's strawberry jelly," Hank added, and Mary clapped excitedly.

"Good, it's decided," Dee said. "You aren't allowed to do any work while we're gone. When was the last time you had a chance to just relax and, say, read a book or take a nap?"

Dana smiled down the table at her, then reached to take her hand to squeeze it. "Thank you. I really am glad you came all this way to visit us. I'm just sorry—" Her eyes darkened with sadness.

"None of that," Dee said, giving her hand a squeeze back. "I can't tell you how thankful I am that you invited me."

As she sat picking at her food, the rest of the family noisily enjoying the meal, Dee counted down the hours. She could feel time slipping through her fingers, but she was relatively calm. Once she'd decided what she was going to have to do, she'd just accepted it.

She'd learned as a child to just accept things the way they were—until she could change them. There was nothing worse than feeling trapped in a situation where you felt there was nothing you could do.

That had been her childhood—feeling defenseless. She'd sworn that the day would come when she would never feel like that again. It took a steely, blind determination that some might have thought cold.

But the moment she'd lit that match so many years ago, she'd sworn she was never going to be a victim again.

CHAPTER FOURTEEN

Hud had been in such a good mood after dinner that he'd suggested one last horseback ride.

Dee couldn't contain her excitement once she'd heard that it would be just the two of them. Dana had considered calling Liza to see if she would babysit, but one of the twins was teething and cranky, so she'd told Hud and Dee to go and have a good time.

"Oh, here," Hud had said. "I picked up the mail on my way in. You had something, Dee." Mail was delivered to a large box with Cardwell Ranch stenciled on the side. The box sat at the edge of Highway 191, a good quarter mile from the ranch house.

She took the envelope with the name Dee Anna Justice typed on it. The trust fund check. She hoped she would never have to use it. But it was always good to have money tucked away—just in case she had reason to leave town in a hurry.

Hud watched her open it, peek inside, then stuff the folded envelope into the hip pocket of her jeans. Having mail come to her in Dee Anna Justice's name seemed to seal the deal as far as who she was. At least for Hud.

While he went out to saddle two horses, Dee insisted on staying in the house and helping Dana with the dishes. She could tell Hud had liked that.

Hud smiled at her now as she walked out to the corral where he was waiting. She smiled back, warmed to her toes. He seemed comfortable and at ease with her. She wouldn't let herself think that his good mood had to do with her plans to fly out the next day.

It was the perfect evening, the weather cool but not cold. The sky was still bright over the canyon, the sun not yet set.

Dee let him help her into the saddle, loving being this close to him. She felt comfortable in the saddle. Hud could never love a woman who didn't ride.

"I think I could get into horseback riding," she said, as the two of them left the ranch behind and headed up into the mountains.

"You should check into riding lessons when you get home," he suggested. "I'm sure they're offered in New York."

"Yes," she agreed, reminded again that there was nothing waiting for her back in the city. She'd given up the apartment. Given up that life.

She considered what the real Dee Anna Justice would do once she realized Dee had borrowed her name. The best thing to do was send the check back. Put "Wrong Address" on the envelope. Dee Anna would never have to know.

That decided, Dee began to relax and enjoy the ride and the man riding along next to her. At that moment she was so content, so sure that everything was going to work out the way she'd planned it, that she couldn't have foreseen the mistake she would make just minutes later on top of the mountain.

COLT MADE GOOD time, and by seven that night he wasn't far outside Denver. He stopped for gas and coffee, figuring he had at least another fourteen hours minimum to go.

Hilde answered on the second ring as if she'd been waiting by the phone. "Where are you?"

He told her. "The roads haven't been bad. I expect they will be worse the closer I get. I should be there by nine or ten in the morning. Get some sleep."

"What about you?" she asked.

"I'm okay. When I first got into law enforcement I had to work some double shifts. I learned how to stay awake. Anyway, I'll be thinking of you the whole time."

He could hear the smile in her voice when she said, "Same here."

He stretched his legs and got back into the SUV. He tried Hud again. His call went straight to voice mail. Cussing under his breath, he headed for the interstate.

His thoughts were with Hilde. What Camilla's aunt had told him had him scared.

"Even when she was a little girl, if another child had a toy she wanted, she'd take it from her," Thelma Peters had said. "If that child got hurt in the process, Camilla was all the more happy for it. I remember one time scolding her for that behavior. She must have been four or five at the time. She and her family had come for a visit. Her father was often out of work. I'll never forget the way she turned to look at me. I remember my heart lurching in my chest. I was actually frightened."

Thelma had taken a moment, as if the memory had been too strong, before she continued. "That child looked at me and said, 'She should have given the toy to me when I told her to. If she got hurt, it's her own fault. Next time, she'll give it to me when I ask for it.'"

"What about her mother and father? They must have

seen this kind of behavior and tried to do something about it."

Thelma had shook her head sadly. "I mentioned what I'd seen to my sister. Cynthia wasn't a strong woman. She said to me, 'Leave her be. Camilla's just a child.' Herbert? He smacked her around, then would hold her on his lap and pet her like she was a dog." The aunt had wrinkled her mouth in disgust. "That child worked him. Cynthia was too weak to stand up to her husband or her daughter."

"And Richard?"

"He idolized his sister, did whatever she wanted. The two were inseparable. I'm not surprised they were together in Montana when he died."

"There's a chance she killed him," he'd told her.

Thelma's hand had gone to her heart. "It is as if something is missing in her DNA. A caring gene. Camilla has no compassion for anyone but herself. I always wondered what she would do with Richard when she got tired of him."

"If she was responsible, why did she want her parents dead?"

Thelma had looked away. "I have my suspicions, ones I've never voiced to anyone."

"You think Herbert was abusing her?"

Her face had filled with shame. "I tried to talk to my sister. I even called Social Services. Herbert swore it wasn't true. So did Camilla."

"You think your sister knew and just turned a blind eye."

"That's why Camilla killed them both," Thelma had said. "I saw that girl right after the police called and told me about the fire and that my sister and brother-in-law were dead. Richard? He's crying his eyes out. Camilla? Cool as a cucumber. She waltzes into the house and asks me what I have to eat, that she's starving. She sat there eating, smiling to herself. I tried to tell myself that we all grieve in our own way. But it was enough to turn my blood to ice."

AS THE SUN sank lower behind the adjacent mountains, Dee and Hud reached a spot where aspens grew thick and green.

They reined in and climbed off their horses to walk to the edge of the mountain. This view was even more spectacular than the one she'd seen on the four-wheeler ride into the mountains.

"It's so peaceful here," Dee said, as she breathed in the evening. The air was scented with pine and the smell of spring. She hugged herself against the cool breeze that whispered through the trees. Shadows had puddled under them.

Unconsciously, she stepped closer to Hud as she thought of the bears and mountain lions that lived in these mountains. Hud seemed so unafraid of anything. She loved his quiet strength and wondered what her life would have been like if she'd had a father like him. Or even a brother like him.

As she glanced at him, she told herself that life had given her another chance to have such a man to protect her.

"Hud." Just saying his name sent a shiver through her.

He looked over at her expectantly as if he thought she was about to say something.

She didn't think. At that moment, she felt as if she

would die if she didn't kiss him. No matter what happened, it was all she told herself she would ever want.

The kiss took him by such surprise that he didn't react at first. She felt his warm lips on hers as she pressed her chest into his hard, strong one.

One of his arms came around her as if he thought she'd stumbled into him and was about to fall off the edge of the mountain.

Several seconds passed, no more, before he pushed her away, holding her at arm's length. "What the—" His eyes darkened with anger. "What was that, Dee?" he demanded.

"I…I just—" She saw the change in his expression and knew that Hilde had warned him that she was after him. He hadn't believed her—until this moment.

Hud shoved her away from him.

She felt tears burn her eyes and anger begin to boil deep in her belly. She wanted to scream at him, *Why not me? What is so wrong with me?*

Instead, she said, "I'm so sorry," and pretended to be horrified by what she'd done when, in truth, she was furious with him.

"It was all of this," she said, motioning to the view. "I just got swept up in it and, standing next to you…" She looked away, hating him for making her feel like this.

"We should get back," he said, and turned to walk toward the horses where he'd left them ground tied by the aspens.

She tried to breathe out her fury, to act chastised, to pretend to be remorseful. It was the hardest role she'd ever played.

They rode in silence down the mountain through the now dark pines.

Dee thought about the kiss. She'd been anticipating it for days and now felt deeply disappointed. Hud had cut her to the quick. She could never forgive him.

Worse, he would now suspect that everything Hilde had said was true. Good thing she'd made that plane reservation for tomorrow. She couldn't wait to get away from here.

HILDE GOT THE text from Dana the next morning as she was starting to open the shop.

u r rght abt D Im so—

She hurriedly tried to call her friend. The phone went straight to voice mail. "Dana, call me the moment you get this."

Hilde stood inside the shop for a moment. The apparently interrupted text scared her more than she wanted to admit.

She called the sheriff's office. If Hud was home… But she was told that Hud had been called away on a case in West Yellowstone.

So Dana was alone out at the ranch with the kids… and Dee.

Colt was on his way, but she couldn't wait for him. She had to make sure Dana was all right.

Locking the shop, she headed for her vehicle, thankful Colt had changed her flat and retrieved it for her. Her mind was racing. The text had her terrified that something had happened. She drove as fast as she could to the ranch, jumping out of the SUV and running inside the house without knocking.

"Dana!" she screamed, realizing belatedly that she should have at least thought to bring a weapon. But she didn't have a gun, let alone anything close to a weapon at the house or shop other than a pair of scissors. She shuddered at the thought.

Dana appeared in the kitchen doorway looking startled. She was wearing an apron and had flour all over her hands. "What in the—"

"Are you all right?" Hilde said, rushing to her.

"I'm fine. What's wrong?"

"I got your text."

"My *text?* I didn't send you a text. In fact, I haven't been able to find my cell phone all morning."

Belatedly, Hilde remembered who'd answered Dana's cell just the afternoon before. She looked around the kitchen as that slowly sank in. Dee must still have the cell phone. Dana hadn't sent the text. But why would Dee send her a text that said she was right unless… *"Where are the kids?"*

"Hilde, you're scaring me. The kids just left with Dee for a walk up the road."

Hilde glanced around, didn't see Angus and Brick. "The twins, too?"

"She took them in the stroller to give me some time to myself this morning."

"No one is with her?" She saw the answer in her friend's face. "We have to find them. *Now.*"

"Hilde, Dee might have her problems but—"

"Colt called me from Oklahoma."

"Oklahoma? I thought he went to Denver?"

"He went down there to find out what he could about Rick. The woman you thought was Dee is his *sister,* Dana. When they were teenagers, the two of them were suspected of torching their house and killing their parents, but it could never be proven."

Dana paled. "Dee is Rick's *sister?*"

"Her name isn't Dee Anna Justice. It's Camilla Northland. Or at least it was."

"Then where is Dee Anna Justice?"

"I have no idea, but right now we have to get the kids." For all Hilde knew, the woman calling herself Dee had killed Dana's cousin and taken over her life.

"You can't really believe she'd hurt my—"

"*She wants Hud, Dana.* She's been after your life since the moment she saw Hud. Do you really think she wants the kids as well?"

Dana seemed to come out of the trance Dee'd had her in since arriving in Montana. Surely she'd seen the way Dee fawned over her husband.

"Hud told me she has a crush on him, but… You *have* to be wrong about her," Dana cried. But she grabbed the shotgun she kept high on the wall by the back door.

As they ran outside, Hilde prayed the babies were all right. She told herself that if Dee stood any chance of getting away with this, then she couldn't have hurt them. But the woman had apparently already gotten away with murdering her own parents—and her brother. Possibly Dana's cousin as well. Who knew what she'd do to get what she wanted.

Dee and the kids were nowhere in sight.

"She must have gone up the road," Dana said.

"There!" Hilde cried as she spotted the stroller lying on its side in front of the barn. Dana rushed into the barn first, Hilde right behind her. They both stopped, both breathing hard.

"Mary! Hank!" Dana called, her voice breaking. Silence. She called again, her voice more frantic.

A faint cry came from one of the stalls.

Rushing toward it, they found Mary and Hank holding the twins in the back of the stall. Hilde heard the relief rush from Dana as she dropped to the straw.

"What are you two doing?" Hilde asked, fear making her voice tight.

"We're playing a game," Hank said.

"Auntie Dee told us to stay here and not make a sound," Mary said in a conspiratorial whisper.

"But Mary made a sound when she heard you calling for her," Hank said. "Now Auntie Dee is going to be mad, and when she's mad she's kind of scary."

"Where is Auntie Dee?" Hilde asked.

Hank shook his head and seemed to see the shotgun his mother had rushed in with. "Are you and Auntie Hilde going hunting?"

"We are," Hilde said. "That's why we need you and your sister to stay here and keep playing the game for just a little longer. Can you do that?"

Dana shot her friend a look, then picked up the shotgun. "Be very quiet. We'll be back in just a minute, okay?" Both children nodded and touched fingers to their lips.

Hilde stepped out of the stall and looked down the line of stalls. The light was dim and cool in the huge barn. Dee could be anywhere.

As they moved away from the stall with the children inside, Dana whispered, "Maybe it *is* just a game."

Hilde bit back a curse. Dana was determined to see the best in everyone—especially this cousin who'd ingratiated herself into their lives. But Hilde had to admit whatever game Camilla Northland was playing, it didn't make any sense.

They both jumped when they heard the barn door they'd come through slam shut. An instant later, they heard the board that locked it closed come down with a heart-stopping thud.

"She just locked us in," Hilde said, her voice breaking.

Dana had already turned and was racing toward the back door of the barn. Hilde knew before she saw Dana reach it that she would find it locked.

Only moments later did she smell the smoke.

CHAPTER FIFTEEN

"I'M ABOUT TEN minutes outside of Big Sky," Colt said when he'd called Hilde's phone and gotten voice mail. "I don't know where you are or why you aren't picking up." He didn't know what else to say so he disconnected and tried to call her at the shop.

His anxiety grew when the recording came on giving the shop's hours. He glanced at his watch. Hilde was a stickler for punctuality. If she'd gone to the shop, there was no way she would be thirty minutes late for work unless something was wrong.

When his phone rang, he thought it was Hilde. Prayed it was. He didn't even look to see who was calling and was surprised when he heard Hud's voice.

"I can't get into all of it right now," he told Hud, "but I have proof the woman at the ranch isn't Dee Anna Justice, and I can't reach Hilde at the shop or on her cell. I can't reach the ranch, either."

"I'm on my way home from West Yellowstone," Hud said. "I haven't been able to reach Dana, either. I was hoping you had heard something."

"I'm five minutes out," Colt said. "I'm going straight to the ranch."

"I'm twenty minutes out. Call me as soon as you know something."

He hung up and called the office, asked if there was

any backup, but Deputy Liza Turner Cardwell was in Bozeman testifying in a court case and Deputy Jake Thorton was up in the mountains fishing on his day off.

"Liza should be back soon," Annie had told him.

Not soon enough, he feared. He tried Dana's brother Jordan. No answer. No surprise. Jordan was busy building his house and probably out peeling logs.

He disconnected as he came up behind a semi, laid on his horn and swore. The driver slowed, but couldn't find a place to pull over and the road had too many blind curves to pass.

Colt felt a growing sense of urgency. He needed to get to Cardwell Ranch. *Now.* All his instincts told him that Hilde was there and in trouble. Which meant so were Dana and the kids.

Mentally, he kicked himself as the vehicles in both lanes finally pulled over enough to let him through. He shouldn't have told Hilde what he found out in Oklahoma. She must have gone out to the ranch to warn Dana. He wouldn't let himself imagine what the woman calling herself Dee Anna Justice would do if cornered.

ALONG WITH THE smell of smoke, Hilde caught the sharp scent of fuel oil. She could hear the crackling of flames. The barn was old, the wood dry. Past the sound of fire they heard an engine start up.

For just an instant Hilde thought Dee might be planning to save them—the way she had her at the falls and possibly the way she had tried on the river.

But they heard the pickup leave, the sound dying off as the flames grew louder.

They rushed back to the children. Hilde dug in her pocket for her cell phone, belatedly realizing she'd left it in the SUV when she'd jumped out. She looked up at Dana. "You said you haven't been able to find your cell phone?"

Dana shook her head. The smoke was getting thicker inside the barn. Hilde could see flames blackening the kindling dry wood on all sides. It wouldn't be long before the whole barn was ablaze.

"Let's try to break through the side of the barn," Hilde said, grabbing up a shovel. She began to pound at the old wood. It splintered but the boards held.

Dana joined her with another shovel.

Hilde couldn't believe Dee thought she could get away with this. But at the back of her mind, she feared Dee would. Somehow, she would slip out of this, the same way she had as a kid. The same way she had killed her brother and gone free. And it would be too late for Hilde and Dana and the kids.

"I can't believe she would hurt innocent children," Dana said, tears in her eyes.

"What's wrong, Mommy?" Mary asked.

"Is the barn on fire?" Hank asked.

Hilde and Dana kept pounding at the wood at the back of the stall. If she could just make a hole large enough for the kids to climb out.

The wood finally gave way. She and Dana grabbed hold of the board and were able to break it off to form a small hole. Not large enough for them, but definitely large enough to get the children out.

What would happen to them if Dee saw them, though? They'd heard the sound of the pickup engine, but what if she hadn't really left? The question passed silently between the two friends.

"We're going to play another game," Dana said,

crouching down next to Mary and Hank. "You and your sister are going to crawl out. I am going to hand you Angus and Brick. Then you're going to go hide in that outbuilding where we keep the old tractor. You can't let Dee see you, okay?"

Hank nodded. "We'll sneak along the haystack. No one will see us."

"Good boy," Dana said, her voice breaking with emotion. "Take care of the babies until either me or Daddy calls you. Don't make a sound if Dee calls you, okay? Now hurry."

Hilde looked out through the hole. No sign of Dee. She helped Hank out and Dana handed him Angus. Mary crawled out next and took Brick. They quickly disappeared from sight.

The smoke was thick now, the flames licking closer and closer as the whole barn went up in flames.

"Oh, Hilde, I'm so sorry for not trusting you," Dana cried, and hugged her.

"Right now, we have to find a way out of here."

The two of them tried to find another spot along the wall where they could get out. The barn was old but sturdily built, and the smoke was so thick now that staying low wasn't helping. They could hear the flames growing closer and closer.

With a *whoosh* the back of the barn began to cave in.

The rest of the structure groaned and creaked. But over the roar of the flames and the falling boards, Hilde heard another sound. A vehicle headed in their direction.

DEE HAD LEFT Dana a note. "I couldn't find you and the kids when I got ready to leave for the airport, so I borrowed your pickup. Thank you for everything. I'll leave the truck in long-term parking. Dee."

Then she'd taken the keys from where she'd seen Dana hang them on a hook by the door and left.

After they'd finished their horseback ride yesterday, Hud had unsaddled the horses and put everything away. Then she'd heard him go upstairs, his boots heavy on the steps, as if he dreaded telling his wife about her cousin.

She'd listened hard but hadn't heard a sound once he entered his and Dana's bedroom, confirming what she'd suspected. That he hadn't awakened Dana last night to tell her.

Earlier this morning when Dee had come downstairs, she'd seen Hud and Dana with their heads together. He had definitely told her something. She'd seen how reluctant he was to leave his wife. They'd done their best to act normal. But she could tell they were counting down the hours until she left.

She'd helped herself to a cup of coffee. Dana had made French toast and sausage for breakfast and offered her a plate. Dee ate heartily as Dana took care of the kids and nibbled at the food on her plate. "You should eat more breakfast," Dee told her.

"I'm fine. Anyway, I still need to lose a few pounds after the twins."

But this is your last breakfast, Dee had wanted to say. She hoped on her last day on earth she ate a good breakfast, since she would never be eating again.

As she drove away from the ranch, she glanced at the barn. Flames were licking up the sides. She looked away, thinking how sad it was that things hadn't worked out differently.

She looked back only once more as she drove past Big Sky. Smoke billowed up into the air across the river, an orange glow behind the pines. She gave the pickup more gas. She had a plane to catch, and there was no going back and changing things now.

She turned on the radio and began to sing along. She had no idea where she was going or what she would do when she got there, but she had Dee Anna Justice's trust fund check and options. She would find another identity and disappear.

What amazed her as she left the canyon was that she'd ever thought she could be happy living on Cardwell Ranch with Hud.

COLT SAW THE smoke and flames in the distance the moment he came out of the narrow part of the canyon. He felt his heart drop. He raced up the highway, calling the fire department as he went, and turned onto the ranch road.

At first he thought it was the house on fire, but as he came up over a rise, he saw that it was the barn. For a moment he felt a wave of relief. Then he saw Hilde's SUV parked in front of the house. Dana's ranch pickup was gone. Maybe they'd all left to take Dee to the airport. Maybe they were all fine.

But his gut told him differently.

When he saw the stroller lying on its side in front of the barn and the door barred, he knew. Holding his hand down on the horn, he hit the gas and raced toward the burning front door of the barn.

The bumper smashed through the burning wood as the expensive rental SUV burst into the barn. Pieces of burning wood hit the windshield, sparks flew all around him and then there was nothing but dark thick smoke.

The moment the SUV broke through the door, he hit his brakes. *It's too late,* he thought when he saw the entire shell of the barn in flames, the smoke so thick he couldn't see his hand in front of his face. He leaped from the rig, screaming Hilde's name. The heat was so intense he felt as if his face were burning. He feared the vehicle's gas tank would explode any moment.

Then he heard her answer.

She and Dana came out of the smoky darkness silhouetted against the walls of flames.

"Where are the babies?" he yelled over the roar of the flames.

"They got out!" Hilde yelled back.

He shoved them both into the SUV and threw it in Reverse. The heat was unbearable. He knew if he didn't get the rig out now…

The hood of the SUV, the paint peeling and blackened, had just cleared the edge of the barn when he heard the loud crash, and the barn began to collapse.

If he'd been just a few minutes later…

He wouldn't let himself even imagine that as he slammed on the brakes back from the inferno. Hilde and Dana were coughing and choking, but he could hear fire trucks and the ambulance on its way.

"My babies," Dana choked out.

"They're in that outbuilding," Hilde said, pointing a good ways from the burning remains of the barn.

"Where's Dee?" he asked them.

"She left after she started the fire," Hilde said.

"I heard her take my truck," Dana added. She was already getting out of the SUV to go after her children,

Hilde at her heels. Colt ran ahead and found the children all safe, huddled together in a back corner of the outbuilding.

Later, as the fire department and EMTs took care of Hilde and Dana and the kids, he told Hilde, "I have to go after Dee. I can't let her get on that plane."

"I'm fine," she told him. "Go!"

CHAPTER SIXTEEN

THE RIDE TO the airport outside of Bozeman was the longest one of Colt's life. He called ahead and asked that Dee Anna Justice be detained, but he was told that she'd already gone through security. Two airport officials were looking for her, but so far they hadn't found anyone matching the description he'd given them.

Camilla's plane was scheduled to board within twenty minutes.

"Don't let her get on that plane," Colt ordered. "Hold her there until I get there. Consider her armed and dangerous."

"Armed? She just went through security. I'm sure if she was—"

"You don't know this woman. She's dangerous. Have your officers approach her with extreme caution."

He was just outside of Belgrade when Hud called.

"I'm on my way to the airport," Hud said. "Make sure that woman doesn't get away, Deputy."

"I'm doing my best," Colt said. "But I'm on suspension."

"Your suspension was lifted hours ago," Hud said. "About the time you saved my wife's life. We'll talk about that later. Where are you?"

Colt told him he was turning onto the airport road. He was only minutes away from confronting Camilla Northland.

DEE LOOKED INTO the women's restroom mirror, appraising herself. She'd brushed out her hair. Since it was naturally curly, it flowed around her head like a dark halo.

She'd applied makeup, especially eye shadow, mascara and blush, sculpting her face. It amazed her how different she looked from the woman who'd been staying at Cardwell Ranch.

As she studied herself in the mirror, she liked what she saw. She'd been able to cover most of the damage she'd done to herself. But maybe when she got wherever she was going, she'd change her hair. Something short and blond. Yes, she liked that idea. A whole new her.

That thought made her laugh. When she'd first left Oklahoma, she'd believed in her heart that she could put the past behind her, become whoever and whatever she wanted.

She hadn't realized then how deep the past had embedded itself in her. It ate at her like a parasite, a constant reminder that she was broken and while she might be able to put back the pieces, she would never be whole.

One of the female security guards stuck her head in the restroom door. Camilla saw her out of the corner of her eye but continued to carefully apply another coat of bright red lipstick.

"Excuse me," the woman said. "We're checking boarding passes. May I see yours?"

"Of course," Camilla said. She took her time putting the lipstick back into her purse. "Here it is."

The woman started to take it, her attention on the slip of paper. More important the *name* on the paper. No Dee Anna Justice but Amy Matthews.

Dee Anna's boarding pass was buried at the botton of the trash container.

The security officer looked from the boarding pass to Camilla, then handed the paper back. "Have a nice flight, Ms. Matthews. I believe your flight is boarding now," the woman said.

"Thank you." Camilla walked out and got into line for the flight to Seattle. In a few minutes she would be onboard.

She had hoped to catch an earlier flight, but it hadn't worked out. Fortunately, she'd planned for this, making several flights in three different names. One in the name of Dee Anna Justice to New York. Another as Amy Matthews to Seattle. And a third flight earlier that day to Las Vegas under the name Patricia Barnes.

Like Rick, she had three different identities ready. She'd just been smart enough not to get caught with them on her, though.

She'd missed the flight to Vegas by only minutes. Finishing up her business at the ranch had taken longer than she'd hoped.

Not that it mattered now. Within minutes she would be on her way to Seattle. No one was looking for Amy Matthews.

She figured Hud must have come home sooner than expected. Or that deputy, Colt Dawson, had showed up. Either way, it would be too late.

It wasn't as if she'd thought for a moment they wouldn't suspect her given everything that had happened. But they had no proof.

Anyway, she would be long gone before they could get to the airport. Even if they should somehow track her down, they still couldn't do anything except get her for using an alias. Or yes, and pretending to be Dee Anna Justice.

She'd cried her way out of more of those situations than she could remember. If tears didn't work, then her life story definitely did. Of course she was messed up. Imagine living your life with such suspicions hanging over you.

It had worked every other time. It would now, too, because without proof, they couldn't touch her. With Dana, Hilde and the kids gone…

She left the restroom and walked to her gate. The woman taking her boarding pass told her to hurry, her flight was about to leave.

She hurried down the ramp and into the plane just moments before the flight attendant was about to shut the door. She'd timed it close, but she hadn't wanted to risk sitting at the gate in case anyone she knew was looking for her.

As she slipped into her first-class seat next to a businessman in a nice suit, she told herself her luck might be changing.

"Hello," she said and extended her hand. "I'm Amy Matthews."

"Clark Evans."

The flight attendant asked her what she would like to drink.

"I'd love a vodka Collins," she said. "I'm celebrating. Today's my birthday. Join me?" she asked the business executive, taking in his gold cuff links, the cut of his suit and the expensive wristwatch.

"How can I say no?" he said, already flirting with her.

"Yes, how can you?" she asked, flirting back. "I have a feeling that this could be a very interesting flight."

COLT RAN INTO the airport. The head of security met him the moment he came through the door.

"Dee Anna Justice hasn't checked in for her flight. It was supposed to leave ten minutes ago," the man told him. "We've held it as long as we can. So far, she's a no-show."

"Dee Anna Justice definitely isn't on the flight? You checked all the passengers?"

"No one matching her description is on the flight, and everyone is accounted for," he assured Colt.

Colt had been so sure she would make her flight. As gutsy as the woman was and as bulletproof as she'd been, she would think she had nothing to fear.

She'd already gone through security, so she'd been here. But that didn't mean she didn't change her mind and leave.

Maybe she was running scared, though he highly doubted it. Camilla had an arrogance born of getting away with murder.

"What other flights have left in the last hour?" he asked.

"Only one, but it's to Seattle. The plane is taxiing down the runway right now."

"Stop that plane."

"I'm not sure—"

"This woman just tried to kill six people, four of them children, by burning them alive. Stop the plane. *Now.*"

CAMILLA WAS SIPPING her drink, smiling at her companion, when the pilot announced they would be returning to the terminal because of an instrument malfunction.

She looked past the man next to her out his window. Sunlight ricocheted off the windows of the terminal, reminding her of the day she'd flown in here. If she'd gone fishing on the Yellowstone River with Lance...

Still, even though she knew there was nothing wrong with the instruments, she wasn't worried. The barn had been burning so quickly, the boards locking the doors would be ashes—all evidence gone.

Even the spilled fuel oil she'd used to get the barn burning fast would look like nothing more than an accident—at first. She'd started the fire with several candles she'd found in the back of Hilde's sewing shop, complete with the cute little quilted mats that went with them.

Everyone knew that Hilde had been losing her mind lately. But to do something this horrible because Dana turned against her? It was almost unthinkable—unless her behavior had been so out of character lately that everyone feared she was having a nervous breakdown. But taking her own life and her friend's along with Dana's four children? This story would make headlines across the country.

The plane taxied back to the small terminal. It wasn't but a few minutes after she'd heard the door being opened that Deputy Colt Dawson appeared.

She turned to the man next to her and asked him a question. Out of the corner of her eye, she saw Colt start to move through the plane. He was almost past her when he stopped and took a step back until he was right at her elbow. "Camilla," he said.

She looked up at him, frowned and said, "I'm sorry. You're mistaken. My name is Amy Matthews."

"Miss...Matthews. I'd like you to come with me. *Now,*" he said when she hesitated. "You won't be taking this flight today."

She sighed and, picking up her bag, got to her feet. "We'll have to celebrate another time," she told the businessman. Colt took her bag from her and quickly frisked her, which made her smile as if she was amused.

"I never noticed how cute you are," she said, as he escorted her off the plane to four waiting security guards. He insisted on cuffing her once she was out of sight of the passengers.

"Is that really necessary?" she asked. "What is this about, anyway? So I didn't use my real name. I have an old boyfriend who I don't want to find me. So sue me."

"This is about the attempted murder of six individuals, four of them children." Colt appeared to be fighting to keep his emotions in check.

Camilla was silent for a moment, then she frowned and said, "Attempted?"

"That's right. They're all alive. Hilde and Dana will be testifying against you in court."

Camilla let out a little laugh. "I suppose you're the one I should thank for this?"

"Be my guest," Colt said, as he led her up the ramp. They were almost to the boarding area when Marshal Hud Savage appeared.

Colt felt Camilla tense. They all did at the look in the marshal's eyes. Colt knew exactly how he felt. In the old West she would have been strung up from the nearest tree.

But this wasn't the old West, and he and Hud didn't mete out justice. All they could do was hope and pray that this woman never saw the outside of a cell for the rest of her life.

ONCE AT THE law enforcement center, Camilla Northland's story was that she'd left the ranch right after Hilde arrived. Dana was with the kids on the front porch as she drove away and had asked Hilde if she wanted to go on a walk with them. That was the last she said that she saw of them.

She'd seemed surprised that Dana and Hilde had told another story. "I don't know why they would lie, except that Hilde has been telling lies about me ever since I came to Montana, and Dana must be confused."

"It's over, Camilla," Colt said, as they all sat in the interrogation room. He tossed the photo of her as a teenager on the table. "Your aunt told me everything. She said she would fly up here if need be."

She stared at the photo of herself and her brother. When she looked up, she suddenly looked tired—and almost relieved.

"It would appear I'm going to need a lawyer," she said.

"Just tell me this. How was it that you ended up here pretending to be Dee Anna Justice?"

For a moment, she didn't look as if she would answer. "Dee Anna was my roommate in New York City for a while," she said with a shrug. "The letter came after she'd moved out."

"And you decided to take her identity?"

"I'd never been to Montana," she said. "I liked the idea of having a cousin I'd never met." She looked unapologetic as her gaze locked with Hud's. "And I'd never met a real cowboy."

"Where is Dee Anna Justice?" Hud demanded, clearly not amused by her flirting with him.

She looked away for a moment, and Colt felt his heart drop. He now knew what extremes this woman would go to and feared for the real Dee Anna Justice.

"She's in Spain visiting some friend of hers. Her mother, Marietta, probably knows how to contact her."

"Marietta's family is from Spain?"

"Italy." Camilla smiled. "No one told you that Dee Anna is half-Italian?" She laughed. "Dana asked me why her grandparents disinherited their son. He married a *foreigner.* Apparently a woman who spoke Italian and wanted to live in the big city wasn't what they wanted for their son. But you'd have to ask Dee Anna if that is really why they disinherited him." She shrugged. "Dee Anna and I were never close. She was a lot like Hilde. For some reason, she didn't like me." Camilla laughed at that. "I'll take that lawyer now."

EPILOGUE

HILDE HELD IT all together until a few weeks after Camilla's arrest. Suddenly she was bombarded with so many emotions that she finally let herself cry as the ramifications of what had happened—and what had almost happened—finally hit her.

Over it all was a prevailing sadness. She and Dana were trying to repair their relationship, but Hilde knew it would take time—and never be the same. She felt as if someone had died and that made her all the sadder.

"Hilde, can you ever forgive me?" Dana had cried that day, as they'd watched the rest of the barn burn from the back of the ambulance. "I should have listened to you. I'm so sorry. I'm just so sorry."

"There is nothing to forgive," she'd told Dana, as they'd hugged. But in her heart, she knew that something was broken. Only time would tell if it could be fixed.

Hud was going through something even worse, Colt had told her. He blamed himself for not seeing what was right in front of his eyes.

"I was just so happy that Dana was enjoying her cousin, I made excuses for Dee's behavior just like Dana did. I didn't want to see it," he kept saying. "I almost lost my family because of it. And what I did to Hilde—"

She'd told him and Dana both that she understood.

Camilla had been too good at hiding her true self. Hilde didn't blame them. But a part of her was disappointed in them that they hadn't believed her—the friend they'd both known for years. That was going to be the hard part to repair in the friendship.

Colt was wonderful throughout it all. He'd saved her life and Dana's. Neither of them would ever forget that.

Hilde, who'd always thought of herself as strong, had leaned on him, needing his quiet strength to see her through. Both she and Dana had recovered from the smoke inhalation. It was the trauma of being trapped in a burning barn with a psychopath trying to kill them that had residual effects.

Jordan and Liza had a housewarming a few months after everything settled down. Their new home was beautiful, and Hilde could see the pride they shared with all the work they'd done themselves. Hilde gave them a quilt as a housewarming present.

"I'd like to take your beginner quilting class," Liza said, making both Hilde and Dana look at her in surprise. She was a tomboy like Dana and had never sewn a thing in her life.

Liza grinned and looked over at Jordan, who nodded. "We're going to have a baby! I want to make her a baby quilt."

Cheers went up all around, and Hilde said she would be delighted to teach her to quilt, and she also had some adorable baby quilt patterns for girls.

"Stop by the shop and I'll show you," she said.

AT THE PARTY, Dana told Hilde that she'd called Marietta Justice, only to receive a return call from the woman's assistant confirming that the real Dee Anna Justice was alive and well in Spain traveling with friends.

Hilde could tell that Dana had been disappointed the woman hadn't even bothered to talk to her herself. But fortunately, Dana hadn't taken it any further. Whatever was going on in that part of the Justice family, it would remain a mystery.

At least for now, since Hilde knew her friend too well. Dana had a cousin she'd never met. Maybe more than one. She wouldn't forget about the very real and mysterious Dee Anna Justice and family. One of these days, Dana wouldn't be able to help herself and she would contact her cousin.

Hilde hated to think what might happen—but then again, she wasn't as trusting as Dana, was she?

The party was fun, even though things were still awkward between all of them.

"THEY'LL GET BETTER," Colt promised her. "You and the Savages were too good of friends before this happened. Right now everyone is a little bruised and battered, especially you. I can see how badly they both feel when they're around you."

That was what was making things so awkward. They wore their regrets on their sleeves.

"Are you still worried about Hud?" she asked him on their way back to her house.

"He's really beating himself up. I think he's questioning whether he should remain marshal. He's afraid he can't trust his judgment."

"That's crazy. He's a great marshal."

"He let a psychopath not only live with them, but also take his children for a walk the morning of the fire."

"He didn't know she was a psychopath."

"Yeah. I think that's the point. He overlooked so much because he wanted Dana to have a good time with her cousin. You told me how excited she was about finding a cousin she'd never met."

Hilde nodded. "They both tried to make the woman he thought was Dee Anna Justice fit into their family. Dana was at odds with her siblings for years, so I understand her need for family."

Colt looked over at her. "What about you?"

"Me?"

"How do you feel about a large family?"

She laughed. "As an only child, I've always yearned for one."

"Good," he said with a smile. "Because I have a large family up north, and they're all anxious to meet you."

She looked at him. "You want me to meet your family?"

He slowed the truck, stopping on a small rise. In the distance, Lone Mountain was silhouetted against Montana's Big Sky. Stars glittered over it. A cool breeze came in through his open window, smelling of the river and the dense pines. The summer night was perfect.

Colt cut the engine and turned toward her. "I can't wait for my family to meet you. I'm just hoping I can introduce you as my fiancée."

Hilde caught her breath as he reached into his pocket and pulled out a small black jewelry box.

"Hilde Jacobson? Will you marry me?" He opened the box, and the perfect emerald-cut diamond caught in the starlight.

For a moment she couldn't speak. So much had happened, and yet they'd all come out of the ashes alive with their futures ahead of them.

"I know this is sudden, but we can have a long engagement if that's what you want," Colt added when she didn't answer him.

She shook her head. She'd always been a woman who never acted impulsively. Until recently. She believed in taking her time on any decision she made. Especially the huge ones.

But if she'd learned anything from all this, it was that she had to follow her instincts—and her heart. "I would love to marry you, Colt Dawson. I can't wait to be your bride."

He let out a relieved laugh and slipped the ring on her finger. It fit perfectly. As he pulled her into his arms and kissed her, Lone Mountain glowed in the starlight.

"I was so hoping you would say that," he whispered.

Wrapped in his arms, she knew whatever the future held, they would face it together. Time and love were powerful healers. With Colt by her side, she could do anything, she thought, as her heart filled to overflowing.

* * * * *

BIG SKY
STANDOFF

This one is for Harry Burton Johnson Jr.
Who knows how different our lives
would have been had you lived.

CHAPTER ONE

DILLON SAVAGE SHOVED back his black Stetson and looked up at all that blue sky as he breathed in the morning. Behind him the razor wire of the prison gleamed in the blinding sunlight.

He didn't look back as he started up the dirt road. It felt damn good to be out. Like most ex-cons, he told himself he was never going back.

He had put the past behind him. No more axes to grind. No debts to settle. He felt only a glimmer of that old gnawing ache for vengeance that had eaten away at him for years. An ache that told him he could never forget the past.

From down the road past the guardhouse, he saw the green Montana state pickup kicking up dust as it high-tailed toward him.

He shoved away any concerns and grinned to himself. He'd been anticipating this for weeks and still couldn't believe he'd gotten an early release. He watched the pickup slow so the driver could talk to the guard.

Wouldn't be long now. He turned his face up to the sun, soaking in its warmth as he enjoyed his first few minutes of freedom in years. Freedom. Damn, but he'd missed it.

It was all he could do not to drop to his knees and kiss the ground. But the last thing he wanted was to have anyone know how hard it had been doing his time. Or just how grateful he was to be out.

The pickup engine revved. Dillon leaned back, watching the truck rumble down the road and come to a stop just feet from him. The sun glinted off the windshield in a blinding array of fractured light, making it impossible to see the driver, but he could feel the calculating, cold gaze on him.

He waited, not wanting to appear overly anxious. Not wanting to get out of the sun just yet. Or to let go of his last few seconds of being alone and free.

The driver's side door of the pickup swung open. Dillon glanced at the ground next to the truck, staring at the sturdy boots that stepped out, and working his way up the long legs wrapped in denim, to the firearm strapped at the hip, the belt cinched around the slim waist. Then, slowing his eyes, he took in the tucked-in tan shirt and full rounded breasts bowing the fabric, before eyeing the pale throat. Her long dark hair was pulled into a braid. Finally he looked into that way-too-familiar face under the straw hat—a face he'd dreamed about for four long years.

Damn, this woman seemed to only get sexier. But it was her eyes that held his attention, just as they had years before. Shimmering gray pools that reminded him of a high mountain lake early in the year, the surface frosted over with ice. Deeper, the water was colder than a scorned woman's heart.

Yep, one glance from those eyes could freeze a man in his tracks. Kind of like the look she was giving him right now.

"Hi, Jack," he said with a grin as he tipped his battered black Stetson to her. "Nice of you to pick me up."

STOCK DETECTIVE Jacklyn Wilde knew the minute she saw him waiting for her beside the road that this had been a mistake.

Clearly, he'd charmed the guards into letting him out so he could walk up the road to meet her, rather than wait for her to pick him up at the release office. He was already showing her that he wasn't going to let her call the shots.

She shook her head. She'd known getting him out was a gamble. She'd foolishly convinced herself that she could handle him.

How could she have forgotten how dangerous Dillon Savage really was? Hadn't her superiors tried to warn her? She reminded herself that this wasn't just a career breaker for her. This could get her killed.

"Get in, Mr. Savage."

He grinned. Prison clearly hadn't made him any less cocky. If she didn't know better, she'd think this had been his idea instead of hers. She felt that fissure of worry work its way under her skin, and was unable to shake the feeling that Dillon Savage had her right where he wanted her.

More than any other woman he'd crossed paths with, she knew what the man was capable of. His charm was deadly and he used it to his advantage at every opportunity. But knowing it was one thing. Keeping Dillon Savage from beguiling her into believing he wasn't dangerous was another.

The thought did little to relieve her worry.

As she slid behind the wheel, he sauntered around to the passenger side, opened the door and tossed his duffel bag behind the seat.

"Is that all your belongings?" she asked.

"I prefer to travel light." He slid his long, lanky frame into the cab, slammed the door and stretched out, practically purring as he made himself comfortable.

She was aware of how he seemed to fill the entire cab of the truck, taking all the oxygen, pervading the space with his male scent.

As she started the truck, she saw him glance out the windshield as if taking one last look. The prison was small by most standards—a few large, plain buildings with snow-capped mountains behind them. Wouldn't even have looked like a prison if it wasn't for the guard towers and razor-wire fences.

"Going to miss it?" she asked sarcastically as she turned the truck around and headed back toward the gate.

"Prison?" He sounded amused.

"I would imagine you made some good friends there." She doubted prison had taught him anything but more ways to break the law. As if he needed that.

He chuckled. "I make good friends wherever I go. It's my good-natured personality." He reached back to rub his neck.

"Was it painful having the monitoring device implanted?" A part of her hoped it had given him as much pain as he'd caused her.

He shook his head and ran his finger along the tiny white scar behind his left ear. "Better anyday than an ankle bracelet. Anyway, you wanted me to be able to ride a horse. Can't wear a boot with one of those damn ankle monitors. Can't ride where we're going in tennis shoes."

She was willing to bet Dillon Savage could ride bareass naked.

His words registered slowly, and she gave a start. *"Where we're going?"* she asked, repeating his words and trying to keep her voice even.

He grinned. "We're chasing cattle rustlers, right? Not the kind who drive up with semitrucks and load in a couple hundred head."

"How do you know *that?*"

He cocked his head at her, amusement in his deep blue eyes. "Because you would have caught them by now if that was the case. No, I'd wager these rustlers are too smart for that. That means they're stealing the cattle that are the least accessible, the farthest from the ranch house."

"It sounds as if you know these guys," she commented as the guard waved them past the gate.

Dillon was looking toward the mountains. He chuckled softly. "I'm familiar with the type."

As she drove down the hill to the town of Deer Lodge, Montana, she had the bad feeling that her boss had been right.

"What makes you think a man like Dillon Savage is going to help you?" Chief Brand Inspector Allan Stratton had demanded when she told him her idea. "He's a *criminal.*"

"He's been in prison for four years. A man like him, locked up…" She'd looked away. Prison would be hell for a man like him. Dillon was like a wild horse. He needed to run free. If she understood anything about him, it was that.

"He's dangerous," Stratton had said. "I shouldn't have to tell you that. And if you really believe that he's been masterminding this band of rustlers from his prison cell… Then getting him out would accomplish what, exactly?"

"He'll slip up. He'll have to help me catch them or he goes back to prison." She was counting on this taste of freedom working in her favor.

"You really think he'll give up his own men?" Stratton scoffed.

"I think the rustling ring has double-crossed him." It was just a feeling she had, and she could also be dead wrong. But she didn't tell her boss that.

"Wouldn't he be afraid of them implicating him?"

"Who would believe them? After all, Dillon Savage has been behind bars for the past four years. How could he mastermind a rustling ring from Montana State Prison? Certainly he would be too smart to let any evidence of such a crime exist."

"I hope you know what you're doing," Stratton said. "For the record, I'm against it." No big surprise there. He wasn't going down if this was the mistake he thought it was. "And the ranchers sure as hell aren't going to like it. You have no idea what you're getting yourself into."

Stratton had been wrong about that, she thought, as she glanced at Dillon Savage. She'd made a deal with the devil and now he was sitting next to her, looking as if he already had her soul locked up.

She watched him rub the tiny scar behind his left ear again. It still surprised her that he'd agreed to the implanted monitoring device. Via satellite, she would know where he was at any second of the day. That alone would go against the grain of a man like Dillon Savage. Maybe she was right about how badly he'd wanted out of prison.

But then again, she knew he could very well have a more personal motive for going along with the deal.

"So the device isn't giving you any discomfort?" she asked.

He grinned. "For a man who can't remember the last time he was in a vehicle without shackles, it's all good."

As she drove through the small prison town of Deer Lodge, past the original jail, which was now an Old West museum, she wondered what his life had been like behind bars.

Dillon Savage had spent his early life on his family's cattle ranch, leaving to attend university out East. Later, when his father sold the ranch, Dillon had returned, only to start stealing other people's cattle. Living in the wilds, with no home, no roots, he'd kept on the move, always one step ahead of her. Being locked up really must have been his own private hell.

Unless he had something to occupy his mind. Like rustling cattle vicariously from his prison cell.

"I'm surprised you didn't work the prison ranch," she said as she drove onto Interstate 90 and headed east.

"They worried that their cattle would start disappearing."

She smiled not only at his attempt at humor, but also at the truth of the matter. It had taken her over two years to catch Dillon Savage. And even now she wasn't sure how that had happened. The one thing she could be certain of was that catching him had little to do with her—and a whole lot to do with Dillon. He'd messed up and it had gotten him sent to prison. She'd just given him a ride.

REDA HARPER STOOD at the window of her ranch house, tapping the toe of her boot impatiently as she cursed the mailman. She was a tall, wiry woman with short-cropped gray hair and what some called an unpleasant disposition.

The truth? Reda Harper was a bitch, and not only did she take pride in it, she also felt justified.

She shoved aside the curtain, squinting against the glare to study her mailbox up on the county road. The red flag was still up. The mailman hadn't come yet. In fact, Gus was late. As usual. And she knew why.

Angeline Franklin.

The last few weeks Angeline had been going up the road to meet mailman Gus Turner, presumably to get her mail. By the time Angeline and Gus got through gabbin' and flirtin' with each other, Reda Harper's mail was late, and she was getting damn tired of it.

She had a notion to send Angeline one of her letters. The thought buoyed her spirits. It was disgraceful the way Angeline hung on that mailbox, looking all doe-eyed, while Gus stuttered and stammered and didn't have the sense to just drive off.

The phone rang, making Reda jump. With a curse, she stepped away from the window to answer it.

"Listen, you old hateful crone. If you don't stop—"

She slammed down the receiver as hard as she could, her thin lips turning up in a whisper of a smile as she went back to the window.

The red flag was down on her mailbox, the dust on the road settling around the fence posts.

Reda took a deep breath. Her letters were on their way. She smiled, finally free to get to work.

Taking her shotgun down from the rack by the door, she reached into the drawer and shook out a half-dozen shells, stuffing them into her jacket pocket as she headed to the barn to saddle her horse.

A woman rancher living alone had to take care of herself. Reda Harper had had sixty-one years of practice.

"I WANT TO MAKE SURE we understand each other," Jacklyn Wilde said, concentrating on her driving as an eighteen-wheeler blew past.

"Oh, I think we understand each other perfectly," Dillon commented. He was looking out at the landscape as if he couldn't get enough of it.

A late storm had lightly dusted the tops of the Boulder Mountains along the Continental Divide to the east. Running across the valley, as far as the eye could see, spring grasses, brilliantly green, rippled in the breeze, broken only by an occasional creek of crystal clear water.

"I got you an early release contingent on your help. Any misstep on your part and you go back immediately, your stay extended." When he said nothing she looked over at him.

He grinned again, turning those blue eyes on her. "We went over this when you came to the prison the first time. I got it. But like I told you then, I have no idea who these rustlers are. How could I, given that I've been locked up for four years? But as promised, I'll teach you everything I know about rustling."

Which they both knew was no small thing. Jacklyn returned her gaze to her driving, hating how smug and self-satisfied he looked slouched in her pickup seat. "If at any time I suspect that you're deterring my investigation—"

"It's back to the slammer," he said. "See, we understand each other perfectly." He tipped his Stetson down, his head cradled by the seat, and closed his eyes. A few moments later he appeared to be sound asleep.

She swore softly. While she hadn't created the monster, she'd definitely let him out of his cage.

DILLON WOKE WITH A START, bolting upright, confused for an instant as to where he was.

Jacklyn Wilde had stopped the truck in a lot next to a café. As she cut the engine, her gaze was almost pitying.

"Prison makes you a light sleeper." He shrugged, damn sorry she'd seen that moment of panic. Prison had definitely changed his sleep patterns. Changed a lot of things, he thought. He knew the only way he could keep from going back to jail was to keep the upper hand with Ms. Wilde. And that was going to be a full-time job as it was, without her seeing any weakness in him.

"Hungry?" she asked.

He glanced toward the café. "Always." It felt strange opening the pickup door, climbing out sans shackles and walking across the open parking lot without a guard or two at his side. Strange how odd freedom felt. Even freedom with strings attached.

He quickened his step so he could open the restaurant door for her.

Jacklyn shot him a look that said it wasn't going to be *that* kind of relationship. He knew she wanted him to see her as anything but a woman. Good luck with that.

He grinned as she graciously entered, and he followed her to a booth by the window as he tried to remember the last meal he'd had on the outside. Antelope steak over a campfire deep in the mountains, and a can of cold beans. He closed his eyes for a moment and could almost smell the aroma rising from the flames.

"Coffee?"

He opened his eyes to find a young, cute waitress standing next to their table. She'd put down menus and two glasses of water. He nodded to the coffee and made a point of not letting Jacklyn see him noticing how tight the waitress's uniform skirt was as he took a long drink of his water and opened his menu.

"I'll have the chef salad," Jacklyn said when the waitress returned with their coffees.

Dillon was still looking at his menu. It had been four years on the inside. Four years with no options. And now he felt overwhelmed by all the items listed.

"Sir?"

He looked up at the waitress and said the first thing that came to mind. "I'll have a burger. A cheeseburger with bacon."

"Fries?"

"Sure." It had been even longer since he'd sat in a booth across from a woman. He watched Jack take off her hat and put it on the seat next to her. Her hair was just as she'd worn it when she was chasing him years ago—a single, coal-black braid that fell most of the way down her slim back.

He smiled, feeling as if he needed to pinch himself. Never in his wildest dreams did he ever think he'd be having lunch with Jacklyn Wilde in Butte, Montana. It felt surreal. Just like it felt being out of prison.

"Something amusing?" she asked.

"Just thinking about what the guys back at the prison would say if they could see me now, having lunch with Jack Wilde. Hell, you're infamous back there."

She narrowed her gaze at him, her eyes like slits of ice beneath the dark lashes.

"Seriously," he said. "Mention the name Jacklyn Wilde and you can set off a whole cell block. It's said that you always get your man, just like the Mounties. Hell, you got me." He'd always wondered how she'd managed it. "How exactly *did* you do that?"

He instantly regretted asking, knowing it was better if he never found out, because he'd had four long years to think about it. And he knew in his heart that someone had set him up. He just didn't know who.

"I'll never forget that day, the first time I came face-to-face with you," he said, smiling to hide his true feelings. "One look into those gray eyes of yours and I knew I was a goner. You do have incredible eyes."

"One more rule, Mr. Savage. You and I will be working together, so save your charm for a woman who might appreciate it. If there is such a woman."

He laughed. "That's cold, Jack, but like I said, I understand our relationship perfectly. You have nothing to worry about when it comes to me." He winked at her.

Jack's look practically gave him frostbite.

Fortunately, the waitress brought their lunches just then, and the burger and fries warmed him up, filling his belly, settling him down a little. He liked listening to the normal sounds of the café, watching people come and go. It had been so long. He also liked watching Jacklyn Wilde.

She ate with the same efficiency with which she drove and did her job. No wasted energy. A single-minded focus. He hadn't entirely been kidding about her being a legend in the prison. It was one reason Dillon was so damn glad to be sitting across the table from her.

He'd been amazed when she'd come to him with her proposition. She'd get him out of prison, but for his part, he had to teach her the tricks of his trade so she could catch a band of rustlers who'd been making some pretty big scores across Montana. At least that was her story.

He'd seen in the papers that the cattlemen's association was up in arms, demanding something be done. It had been all the talk in the prison, the rustlers becoming heroes among the cellies.

What got to him was that Jack had no idea what she was offering him. He hadn't agreed at first, because he hadn't wanted to seem too eager. And didn't want to make her suspicious.

But what prisoner wouldn't jump at the chance to get out and spend time in the most isolated parts of Montana with the woman who'd put him behind bars?

"Where, exactly, are we headed?" he asked after he'd finished his burger. He dragged his last fry through a lake of ketchup, his gaze on her. It still felt so weird being out, eating like a normal person in a restaurant, sitting here with a woman he'd thought about every day for four years.

Her gray eyes bored into him. "I'd prefer not to discuss business in a public place."

He smiled. "Well, maybe there's something else you'd like to discuss."

"Other than business, you and I have nothing to say to each other," she said, her tone as steely as her spine.

"All right, Jack. I just thought we could get to know each other a little better, since we're going to be working together."

"I know you well enough, thank you."

He chuckled and leaned back in the booth, making himself comfortable as he watched her finish her salad. He could tell she hated having his gaze on her. It made her uneasy, but she did a damn good job of pretending it didn't.

He'd let her talk him into the prerelease deal, amused by how badly she'd wanted him out of prison. She needed to stop the rustlers, to calm the cattlemen, to prove she could do her job in a macho man's West.

Did she suspect Dillon's motives for going along with the deal? He could only speculate on what went through that mind of hers.

She looked up from her plate, those gray eyes cold and calculating. As he met her gaze, he realized that if she could read his mind, it would be a short ride back to prison.

She said nothing, just resumed eating. She was wary, though. But then, she had every reason to be mistrustful of him, didn't she.

CHAPTER TWO

RANCHER SHADE WATERS looked across the table at his son, his temper ready to boil over—lunch guest or not.

In fact, he suspected Nate had invited her thinking it would keep Shade from saying anything. He hadn't seen his son in several days, and then Nate had shown up with this *woman*.

"I suppose you heard," Shade said, unable to sit here holding his tongue any longer. "Another ranch was hit last night by that band of rustlers. If they don't catch those sons of—"

"Do we always have to talk ranch business at meals?" Nate snapped. "You're ruining everyone's appetite."

Nate's appetite seemed to be fine, and Shade couldn't have cared less about Morgan Landers's. From what he could tell, she ate like a bird. Their guest was like most of the women his son dated: skinny, snobby and greedy. He'd seen the way she'd looked around the ranch house. As if taking inventory of the antiques, estimating their worth at an auction.

Shade had no doubt what Morgan Landers would do with the ranch and the house if she got the chance.

But then, he wasn't about to let her get her hands on either one.

"Please don't mind me," Morgan said. "This rustling thing is definitely upsetting."

"No one can stop them. They've fooled everyone and proved they're smarter than the ranchers and especially that hotshot stock inspector, Wilde," Nate said, clearly amused by all of it.

"I beg your pardon?" Shade snapped, no longer even trying to keep his temper under control. How could his son be so stupid? "You sound like you admire these thieves."

"Well, they haven't hit our ranch, so what do you care?"

Shade was speechless. He'd never understood his son, but it had never crossed his mind that Nate was just plain stupid.

He heard his voice rising as he said, "As long as those men are out there stealing cattle, this ranch is at risk. I won't rest until they are all behind bars. And as for the man who's leading this ring, I'd like to see him hanged from that big tree down by the creek, like he would have been if your grandfather was still alive."

Nate chuckled and looked at Morgan, the two sharing a private joke. "As if he can be caught."

"Do you know something I don't?" the rancher asked between gritted teeth.

"The leader of the rustlers is already behind bars," Morgan said. "Everyone knows it's Dillon Savage. Who else could it be?"

"Really?" Shade looked at his son.

"Who else *could* it be?" Nate said. He had the irritating habit of parroting everything Morgan said.

"Well, for your edification, Dillon Savage is not behind bars anymore. Jacklyn Wilde got him out of prison."

Nate had the sense to look surprised—and worried. "Why would she do that?"

"Supposedly to help her catch the rustlers. Isn't that rich?" Waters said, and swore under his breath.

Nate looked upset, but Shade doubted his concern was for their cattle. No, he thought, looking over at the woman beside his son, Nate had other worries when it came to Dillon Savage.

"The whole damn thing was kept quiet," Shade said, fighting his anger. "For obvious reasons." He would have fought it tooth and nail had he known.

"Like I said, do we have to talk about this now?" Nate asked pointedly.

"Your *guest* might have more of an interest in the topic than you think," he replied. "After all, she was Dillon Savage's…" he looked at Morgan as if he wasn't sure what to call their relationship "…girlfriend."

Nate shot him a warning look as the cook came in with another basket of warm rolls. Morgan was picking at her salad. It galled Waters that while he and Nate were having beefsteaks, Morgan had opted for rabbit food. The woman was dating a cattle rancher, for hell's sake.

The rancher cursed under his breath, angry at his son on so many levels he didn't even know where to begin. Nate not only looked like his mother—blond with hazel eyes, and an aristocratic air about him—he'd also gotten her softness, something Shade had tried to "cowboy" out of him, although, regretfully, he hadn't succeeded.

He wished he hadn't let Nate's mother spoil the boy so. Now in his early thirties, Nate stood to inherit everything Shade had spent his life building. Nate had no idea the sacrifices his father had made, the obstacles he'd had to overcome, the things he'd had to do. Still had to do. Nate, like his mother, would have been shocked and repulsed if he'd known.

Fortunately, Elizabeth had always turned a blind eye to anything her husband did, although Shade wondered if it wasn't what had put her in an early grave. That and the loss of her firstborn son, Halsey.

While Halsey had loved everything about ranching, Nate never took to it. And just the thought of ever turning the W Bar over to him was killing Shade.

Nate leaned toward Morgan now, whispering something in her ear that made her chuckle coyly—and turned Shade's stomach.

"I'm sorry, Morgan, is talk of Dillon Savage making you uncomfortable?" he asked innocently.

Nate shot him a warning look.

"It's all right, Nate," she said, smiling at the older Waters. "Yes, I knew Dillon…well." Her smile broadened. "Do I care that he's out of prison? Not in the least. Dillon and I were over a long time ago."

Shade looked at his son to see if he believed any of that bull. Nate had never had any sense when it came to women. Apparently, he was buying everything Morgan told him, probably because he had a good view of the woman's breasts in that low-cut top.

"Then you didn't write him while he was in prison or go see him?" Shade asked, ignoring the look his son gave him.

"No," Morgan said, her smile slipping a little. "We'd gone our separate ways long before Dillon went to prison."

She was lying through her teeth. He suspected that

she'd been keeping Dillon up on everything going on in the county, especially at the W Bar.

"Well," Shade said, with exaggerated relief, "I guess the only thing Nate and I have to worry about with Savage out is losing our cattle." He dug into his steak as he noted with some satisfaction that his son had lost *his* appetite.

As JACKLYN WILDE DROVE east past one small Montana town after another, Dillon realized he didn't have any idea where they were headed or what she had planned for him.

But that was the idea, wasn't it? She wanted to keep him off balance. She didn't want him to know too much—that had been clear from that first day she'd come to see him in prison.

He glanced over at her now. Back when she'd been trying to catch him rustling, he'd known only what he'd heard about her. It wasn't until he'd come face-to-face with her and the gun she had leveled at him that he'd looked into her steel-gray eyes and realized everything he'd heard about her just might be true.

She was relentless, clever and cunning, cold and calculating. Ice water ran through her veins. In prison, anyone who'd crossed her path swore she was tougher than any man, but with a woman's sense of justice, and therefore more dangerous.

He couldn't argue the point, given that she was the one who'd put him behind bars.

"So when are you going to tell me the real reason you got me out?" he asked now.

Outside the pickup, the landscape had changed from mountains and towering, dark green pines to rolling hills studded with sagebrush. Tall golden grasses undulated like waves in the breeze and the sky opened up, wide and blue from horizon to horizon. It truly was Big Sky Country.

"I thought I made myself clear on that point," she said, keeping her eyes on the road. "You're going to help me catch rustlers."

He chuckled and she finally looked over at him. "Something funny about that?"

"You didn't get me out of prison to catch rustlers. You are perfectly capable of catching any rustler out there and we both know it." He met her gray eyes. In this light, they were a light silver, and fathomless. The kind of eyes that you could get lost in. But then the light changed. Her gaze was again just a sheet of ice, flat and freezing.

"I need your expertise," she said simply.

Right. "Well, I'll be of little help to you if you keep me in the dark," he said, smiling wryly as he changed tactics. "Unless you have something besides rustling on your mind. I mean, after what happened the first time we met…"

Her eyes narrowed in warning. "The only reason you aren't still behind bars is because you were good at rustling. That's the only talent of yours I'm interested in."

He lifted a brow, still smiling. "That's too bad. Some of my other talents are even more impressive. Like my dancing," he added quickly. He could see she hadn't expected that was where he was headed.

"I'm surprised you had the time, given how busy you were stealing other people's cattle."

He shrugged. "All work and no play… What about you, Jack? What do you do for fun?"

"Mr. Savage, I told you, our discussions will be restricted to business only."

"If that makes you more comfortable... How about you tell me where we're headed then, Jack."

"You'll be updated on a need to know basis, Mr. Savage, and at this point, the only thing you need to know is that I'm Investigator Wilde or Ms. Wilde. Not Jack."

"Still Ms., huh? I guess it's hard to find a cowboy who's man enough to handle a woman like you."

Her jaw tightened, but she didn't take the bait.

He gazed out the windshield, enjoying himself. There were all kinds of ways to get even, he realized. Some of them wouldn't even get him sent back to prison.

Too bad he'd so often in the past four years revisited the day she'd caught him. It was like worrying a sore tooth with his tongue. He'd lost more than his freedom that day.

There'd been only one bright spot in his capture. After she'd cuffed him, he'd stumbled forward to steal one last thing: a kiss.

He'd taken her by surprise, just as she had him with the capture. He'd thought about that kiss a lot over the years. Now, as he glanced over at her, he wondered if he'd be disappointed if he kissed her again. *When* he kissed her again, he thought with a grin. And he *would* kiss her again. If only goodbye.

"Is there a problem, Mr. Savage?" she asked.

"Naw, just remembering the day you caught me," he said, and chuckled.

"Lewistown," she said irritably, making him laugh. "We're headed for Lewistown."

"Now that wasn't so hard, was it?" The center of the state. A hub of cattle ranches. How appropriate, given that rustlers had run rampant there back in the 1800s. It had gotten so bad that some ranchers took matters into their own hands. On July 4, 1884, a couple of suspected rustling ringleaders, "Longhair" Owen and "Rattlesnake Jake" Fallon, were busy shooting up the town when a band of vigilantes gunned them down in the street. Longhair Owen took nine bullets and Rattlesnake Jake eleven.

Dillon wondered how long it would be before a band of vigilantes started shooting first and asking questions later, given how upset the ranchers were now over this latest ring of rustlers. Was that why Jack had gotten him out? Was she hoping some ranchers would string him up?

Staring out at the landscape, he knew that the only reason she'd told him where they were headed was because he wouldn't be getting an opportunity between here and there to call anyone and reveal their destination.

"Your lack of trust cuts me to the core," he said as he ran his finger along the tiny scar behind his left ear, where the chip was embedded under his skin.

Much like Jacklyn Wilde had gotten under his skin and been grating on him ever since. He told himself he'd be free of both before long. In the meantime, he tried not to think about the fact that Jack as well as her superiors would know where he was at any given moment.

"You sure that monitoring chip isn't bothering you?" she asked, frowning at him.

He hadn't realized she'd been watching him. Apparently she planned to keep a close eye on him—as well as monitor his every move.

"Naw," he said, running his finger over the scar. "I'm good."

Her look said he was anything but, and they both knew it.

SHADE WATERS always made a point of walking up the road to the mailbox after lunch, even in the dead of winter.

While it was a good half mile to the county road and he liked the exercise, his real motive was to get to the mail before anyone else did.

The letters had been coming for years now. He just never knew which day of the week, so he always felt a little sick as he made the hike up the road.

Even after all this time, his fingers shook a little as he pulled down the lid and peered inside. The envelope and single sheet of stationery within were always a paler lavender, as if the paper kept fading with the years.

Today he was halfway up the ranch lane when he saw Gus come flying down the county road, skidding to a stop and almost taking out the mailbox.

"What the hell?" Waters said under his breath as he watched the carrier hurriedly sort through the mail, open the box and stuff it inside. He had been running later and later recently.

Gus saw him, gave a quick wave and sped off almost guiltily.

Waters shook his head, already irritated knowing that his son and Morgan Landers were back at the house together. He had to put an end to that little romance. Maybe Dillon Savage being out of prison would do the trick.

At least something good would come of Savage being on the loose again.

When Shade finally reached the mailbox, he stopped to catch his breath, half dreading what he might find inside. Fingers trembling, he pulled down the lid, his gaze searching for the pale lavender envelope as he reached for the mail.

Even before he'd gone through the stack, he knew the letter hadn't come. A mixture of disappointment and worry washed over him as he slammed the box shut. He hadn't realized how much he anticipated the letters. What if they stopped coming?

He shook his head at his own foolishness, wondering if he wasn't losing his mind. What man looked forward to a blackmail letter? he asked himself as he tucked the post under his arm and headed back up the lane.

JACKLYN HAD JUST LEFT the town of Judith Gap when her cell phone rang and she saw with annoyance that it was her boss. She glanced over at Dillon, wishing she didn't have to take the call in front of him, because more than likely it would be bad news.

"Wilde."

"So how did it go?" Stratton asked, an edge to his voice. He was just waiting for things to go badly so he could say I told you so.

"Fine," she said, and glanced again at Dillon. He was chewing on a toothpick, stretched out in the seat as if he was ready for another nap.

"I hope you aren't making the biggest mistake of your career. Not to mention your life," Stratton said.

So did Jacklyn. But they'd been over this already. She waited, fearing he was calling to tell her the rustlers had hit again. She knew he hadn't phoned just to see how she was doing. Stratton, too, had a receiver terminal that told him exactly where Dillon Savage was at all times. Which in turn would tell her boss exactly where she was, as well.

"Shade Waters wants to see you," Stratton said finally.

She should have known. Waters owned the W Bar, the largest ranch in the area, and had a habit of throwing his weight around. "I've already told him I'm doing everything possible to—"

"He's starting what he calls a neighborhood watch group to catch the rustlers," Stratton said.

"Vigilante group, you mean." She swore under her breath and felt Dillon Savage's gaze on her.

"Waters has all the ranchers fired up about Savage being released. He's got Sheriff McCray heading up a meeting tomorrow night at the community center. I want you there. You need to put a lid on this pronto. We can't have those ranchers taking things into their own hands. Hell, they'll end up shooting each other."

She groaned inwardly. There would be no stopping Waters. She'd already had several run-ins with him, and now that he knew about her getting Dillon Savage out of prison, he would be out for blood. Hers.

"I'll do what I can at the meeting." What choice did she have? "Will you be there as well?"

"I'm not sure I can make it." The chicken. "You do realize by now that you've opened up a hornets' nest with this Savage thing, don't you?" He hung up, but not before she'd heard the self-satisfied "I told you so" in his voice.

DILLON WATCHED JACK from under the brim of his Stetson, curious as to what was going on. Unless he missed his guess, she was getting her butt chewed by one of her bosses. He could just imagine the bureaucratic bull she had to put up with from men who sat in their cozy offices while she was out risking her life to protect a bunch of cows.

And from the sounds of it, the ranchers were doing exactly what he'd expected they would—forming a vigilante group and taking the law into their own hands. This situation was a geyser ready to go off. And Dillon had put himself right in the middle of it.

He watched her snap shut the phone. She squared her shoulders, took a deep breath and stared straight ahead, hands gripping the wheel as she drove. He knew she was desperate. Hell, she wouldn't have gotten him out of prison if she hadn't been. She'd stuck her neck out and she would have to be a fool not to realize she was going to get it chopped off.

For a split second, he felt sorry for her. Then he reminded himself that Jacklyn Wilde was the enemy. And no matter how intriguing he found her, he would do well to remember that.

"Everything all right?" he asked innocently.

She shot him a look that said if he wanted to keep his head he wouldn't get smart with her right now.

Unfortunately, he'd never done the smart thing. "Why do you do it?"

"What?" she snapped.

"This job."

She seemed surprised by the question. "I *like* my job."

He scoffed at that. "Putting up with rich ranchers,

not to mention your arrogant bosses and all that bureaucrat crap?"

"I'm good at what I do," she said defensively.

"You'd be good at anything you set your mind to," he said, meaning it. She was smart, savvy, dedicated. Plus her looks wouldn't hurt. "You could have any job you wanted."

"I like putting felons behind bars."

"You put *cattle rustlers* behind bars," he corrected. "Come on, Jack, most people see rustling as an Old West institution, not a felony. Hell, it was how a lot of ranchers in the old days built their huge spreads, with a running branding iron, and a little larceny in their blood. Rustling wasn't even a crime until those same ranchers started losing cattle themselves."

"Apparently that's an attitude that hasn't changed for two hundred years," she snapped. "Rustling, with all its legends and lore." She shook her head angrily, her face flushed. "It's why rustlers are seldom treated as seriously as burglars or car thieves."

He shrugged. "It comes down to simple math. If you can make ten grand in a matter of minutes easier and with less risk and more reward than holding up a convenience store, you're gonna do it." He could see that he had her dander up, and he smiled to himself, egging her on. "I see it as a form of living off the land."

"It's a *crime*."

He laughed. "Come on, everyone steals."

"They most certainly do not." Her hands gripped the wheel tightly, and she pressed her foot on the gas pedal as her irritation rose. He saw that she was going over the speed limit, and grinned to himself.

"So you're telling me that you've never listened to

bootleg music?" he asked. "Tried a grape at the supermarket before buying the bunch? Taken a marginal deduction on your taxes?"

"No," she said emphatically.

"You're *that* squeaky clean?" He shook his head, studying her. "So you've never done *anything* wrong? Nothing you've regretted? Nothing you're ashamed of?" He saw the flicker in her expression. Her eyes darted away as heat rose up the soft flesh of her throat.

He'd hit a nerve. Jack had something to hide. Dillon itched to know what. What in her past had her racing down the highway, way over the speed limit?

"You might want to slow down," he said quietly. "I'd hate to see you get a ticket for breaking the law."

Her gaze flew to the speedometer. A curse escaped her lips as she instantly let up on the gas and glared at him. "You did that on purpose."

He grinned to himself yet again as he leaned back in the seat and watched her from under the brim of his hat, speculating on what secret she might be hiding. Had to have something to do with a man, he thought. Didn't it always?

Everyone at prison swore she was an ice princess, cold-blooded as a snake. A woman above reproach. But what if under that rigid, authoritarian-cop persona was a hot-blooded, passionate woman who was fallible like the rest of them?

That might explain why she was so driven. Maybe, like him, she was running from something. Just the thought hooked him. Because before he and Jacklyn Wilde parted ways, he was determined to find her weakness.

And use it to his advantage.

RANCHER TOM ROBINSON had been riding his fence line, the sun low and hot on the horizon, when he saw the cut barbed wire and the fresh horse tracks in the dirt.

Tom was in his fifties, tall, slim and weathered. He'd taken over the ranch from his father, who'd worked it with *his* father.

A confirmed bachelor not so much by choice as circumstances, Tom liked being alone with his thoughts, liked being able to hear the crickets chirping in the sagebrush, the meadowlarks singing as he passed.

Not that he hadn't dated some in his younger days. He liked women well enough. But he'd quickly found he didn't like the sound of a woman's voice, especially when it required him to answer with more than one word.

He'd been riding since early morning and had seen no sign of trouble. He knew he'd been pushing his luck, since he hadn't yet lost any stock. A lot of ranchers in this county and the next had already been hit by the band of rustlers. Some of the ranchers, the smaller ones, had been forced to sell out.

Shade Waters had been buying up ranch land for years now and had the biggest spread in two counties. He had tried to buy Robinson's ranch, but Tom had held pat. He planned to die on this ranch, even if it meant dying destitute. He was down to one full-time hired man and some seasonal, which meant the place was getting run-down. Too much work. Not enough time.

On top of that, now he had rustlers to worry about. And as he rode the miles of his fence, through prairie and badlands, he couldn't shake the feeling that his luck was about to run out. This latest gang of rustlers were a brazen bunch. Why, just last month two cowboys had driven up to the Crowley Ranch to the north and loaded up forty head in broad daylight.

Margaret Crowley had been in the house cooking lunch at the time. She'd looked out, seen the truck and had just assumed her husband had hired someone to move some cattle for him.

She hadn't gotten a good look at the men or the truck. But then, most cowboys looked alike, as did muddy stock trucks.

Tom could imagine what old man Crowley had said when he found out his wife had just let the rustlers steal their cattle.

Tom was shaking his head in amusement when he spotted the cut barbed wire. Seeing the set of horseshoe prints in the dirt, he brought his horse up short. He was thinking of the tracks when he heard the whinny of a horse and looked up in time to see a horse and rider disappear into a stand of pines a couple hundred yards to the east.

Tom was pretty sure the rider had seen him and had headed for the trees just past the creek. From the creek bottom, the land rose abruptly in rocky outcroppings and thick stands of Ponderosa pines, providing cover.

"What the hell?" Tom said to himself. He looked around for other riders, but saw only the one set of tracks in the soft earth. He felt his pulse begin to pound as he stared at his cut barbed wire fence lying on the ground at his horse's feet.

Tom swore, something he seldom did. He squinted toward the spot where he'd last seen the rider. This part of his ranch was the most isolated—and rugged. It bordered the Bureau of Land Management on one corner and Shade Waters's land on the other.

The man had to be one of the rustlers. Who else would cut the fence and take to the trees when seen?

Still keeping an eye on the spot where the horse and rider had disappeared, Tom urged his mount forward, riding slowly, his hand on the butt of his sidearm.

CHAPTER THREE

JACKLYN SILENTLY CURSED Dillon Savage as she drove, glad she hadn't gotten a speeding ticket. Wouldn't he have loved that? It was bad enough she'd proved his point that everyone broke the law.

She couldn't believe she'd let him get to her. Like right now. She knew damned well he wasn't really sleeping. She'd bet every penny she had in the bank that he was over there smugly grinning to himself, pleased that he'd stirred her up. The man was impossible.

She tried to relax, but she couldn't have been more tense if she'd had a convicted murderer sitting next to her instead of a cattle rustler. But then, she'd always figured Dillon Savage was only a trigger pull away from being a killer, anyway.

She could hear him breathing softly, and every once in a while caught a whiff of his all-male scent. With his eyes closed, she could almost convince herself this had been a good idea.

Desperate times required desperate measures. She had her bosses and a whole lot of angry cattlemen demanding that the rustlers be stopped. Because of her high success rate in the past—and the fact that she'd brought in the now legendary Dillon Savage—everyone expected her to catch this latest rustling ring.

She'd done everything she could think to do, from

encouraging local law enforcement to check anyone moving herds late at night, to having workers at feed-lots and sale barns watch for anyone suspicious sell-ing cattle.

Not surprisingly, she'd met resistance when she'd tried to get the ranchers themselves to take measures to ward off the rustlers, such as locking gates, check-ing the backgrounds of seasonal employees and keep-ing a better eye on their stock.

But many of the ranches were huge, the cattle miles from the house. A lot of ranches were now run by absen-tee owners. Animals often weren't checked for weeks, even months on end. By the time a rancher realized some of his herd was missing, the rustlers were long gone.

Everyone was angry and demanding something be done. But at this point, she wasn't sure anyone could stop this band of rustlers. These guys were too good. Almost as good as Dillon Savage had been in his hey-day.

And that was why she'd gotten him out of prison, she reminded herself as she turned on the radio, keep-ing the volume down just in case he really was sleep-ing. She liked him better asleep.

Lost in her own private thoughts, she drove toward Lewistown, Montana, to the sounds of country music on the radio and the hum of tires on the pavement. Ahead was nothing but trouble.

But the real trouble, she knew, was sitting right be-side her.

DILLON STIRRED as she pulled up in front of the Yogo Inn in downtown Lewistown and parked the pickup.

He blinked at the motel sign, forgetting for a moment where he was. His body ached from the hours in the pickup, but he'd never felt better in his life.

Opening his door, he breathed in the evening air. A slight breeze rustled the leaves on the trees nearby. He stretched, watching Jack as she reached behind the seat for her small suitcase.

"I can get that," he said.

"Just take care of your own," she replied, without looking at him.

Inside the motel, Dillon felt like a kept man. He stood back as Jack registered and paid for their two adjoining reserved rooms, then asked about places in town that delivered food.

"What sounds good to you?" she asked him after she'd been given the keys, both of which she kept, and was rolling her small suitcase down the hallway.

She traveled light, too, it appeared. But then, he expected nothing less than efficiency from Jack.

"What sounds good to me?" He cocked a brow at her, thinking how long it had been.

"For *dinner*," she snapped.

"Chinese."

She seemed surprised. "I thought you'd want steak."

"We had steak in prison. What we didn't have was Chinese food. Unless you'd prefer something else."

"No, Chinese will be fine," she said as she opened the door to his room.

He looked in and couldn't help but feel a small thrill. It had been years since he'd slept in a real bed. Past it, the bathroom door was open and he could see a bathtub. Amazing how he used to take something like a bathtub for granted.

"Is everything all right?" Jack asked.

He nodded, smiling. "Everything's great." He took a deep breath, surprised how little it took to make him feel overjoyed. "Would you mind if I have a bath before dinner? In fact, just order for me. Anything spicy."

Her look said she should have known he'd want something spicy. "I'll be right next door," she said, as if she had to warn him.

The last thing on his mind was taking off. All he could think about was that bathtub—and the queen-size bed. Well, almost. He looked at Jack. Past her, down the hall, he spotted a vending machine.

"Is there something else?" she asked.

He grinned. "Do you have some change? I'd really like to get something out of the vending machine."

She glanced behind her, then reached into her shoulder bag and handed him a couple of dollars.

"Thanks." He looked down at the money in his hand. He hadn't seen money for a while, either. He tossed his duffel bag into the room and strode down the hallway, knowing she was watching him. From the machine, he bought a soda and, just for the hell of it, a container of sea scent bubble bath.

She was still standing in the hallway, not even pretending she wasn't keeping an eye on him.

"You'll ruin my reputation if you tell anyone about this," he said, only half joking as he lifted the package of bubble bath. "But when I saw that bathtub… We only had showers in prison," he added when he saw her confusion.

"I hadn't realized…"

"It's scary enough in the showers," he said with a

shake of his head. "Can't imagine being caught in a bathtub there."

She ducked her head and put her key into the lock on her room door, as if not wanting to think about what went on in prison. "I'll let you know when our dinner arrives." She opened her door, but didn't look at him. "Enjoy your bath."

He chuckled. "Oh, I intend to."

JACKLYN SWORE as she closed her room door. The last thing she wanted to do was imagine Dillon Savage lounging in a tubful of bubbles.

Bubble bath? Clearly, he didn't worry about his masculinity. Not when he had it in spades. But she knew that hadn't been his reason for buying the bubble bath. He'd wanted her imagining him in that tub.

She opened her suitcase and took out the small receiver terminal with the built-in global positioning system, turning it on just in case the bath had been a ruse. The steady beep confirmed that he was just next door. In fact, she could hear the water running on the other side of the adjoining door.

In the desk drawer, she found a menu for the local Chinese restaurant, and ordered a variety of items to be delivered, all but one spicy. It seemed easier than going out, since after they ate, she wanted to get right down to business.

With luck, she'd be ready when the rustlers struck again.

Her cell phone rang. She checked the number, not surprised that it was her boss again. "Wilde."

"Is he there?"

"No. He's in the adjoining room."

"He's probably using the motel room phone to call his friends and let them know where he is and what your plans are," Stratton said, sounding irritated.

"The phone in his room is tapped," she said. "If he makes a call, he'll be back in prison tomorrow. But he isn't going to call anyone and warn them. I haven't told him anything."

"Good. I didn't want him to hear this," Stratton said. "The rustlers hit another ranch. Bud Drummond's."

The Drummond ranch was to the north, almost to the Missouri River. Jacklyn swore under her breath. "When?"

"He's not sure. He'd been out of town for a few days. When he got back, he rode fence and found where the rustlers had cut the barbed wire and gotten what he estimates was about twenty head."

Less than usual. "Why didn't they get more? Is it possible someone saw them?"

"Doubtful. It's at the north end of his ranch, a stretch along the river," Stratton said. "I told him you were going to be up that way tomorrow, anyway, so you'd stop by."

It had rained the day before. Any tracks would be gone. She doubted there would be anything to find—just like usual.

"Savage giving you any trouble?" Stratton asked.

"No." No trouble, unless you counted the psychological games he played. She had a mental flash of him in the tub, sea scent bubbles up to his neck. Exactly the image she knew Dillon had hoped she'd have when he'd bought the bubble bath.

"I shouldn't have to remind you how clever he is or

how long it took you to catch him the last time. Don't underestimate him."

She heard the water finally shut off next door. She checked the monitor. Dillon was exactly where he'd said he would be.

"Trust me," she said, "I know only too well what Dillon Savage is capable of."

TOM ROBINSON DISMOUNTED in the dry creek bottom and pulled out his handgun. He hadn't realized how late it was. He was losing light. A horse whinnied somewhere above him on the hillside. He moved behind one of the large pines and listened, trying to determine if the horseback rider was moving.

He knew the man was still up there. This was the only cover for miles. At the very least he was trespassing. But Tom knew that, more than likely, the rider was one of the rustlers. Since the man was alone, maybe he was just checking out the ranch layout, finding the best access to the cattle in this section of pasture.

Tom had gotten only a glimpse of him, but that glimpse was more than anyone else had gotten of the rustlers. His heart began to pound at the thought of catching the man, being the one who brought down the rustling gang.

He had two options. He could wait for the intruder to break cover and try to make a run for it.

Or he could flush him out.

Leaving his horse, Tom worked his way up the steep incline, taking a more direct route on foot than the horseback rider had. Pebble-size stones rolled under his boots and cascaded down with every step he took.

Halfway up, he stopped, leaning against one of the

large rocks to thumb off the safety on his weapon. His hands were shaking. It had crossed his mind belatedly that there might be more than one rider now on his spread. Maybe they'd planned to meet here in the trees. There could be others waiting in ambush at the top of the hill.

He considered turning back, but this was his land and he was determined to defend it and his livestock. He knew he had at least one man cornered. Once he broke from the shelter of trees, Tom would see him. With luck, he would be able to get off a shot. Unless the intruder was waiting for the cover of darkness.

This, Tom knew, was the point where the cops on television called for backup. But even if he'd had a cell phone, he wouldn't have been able to get service out here. Nor could he wait for someone to arrive and help him even if he could call for assistance.

No, he was going to have to do this alone.

Would the man be armed? Tom could only assume so.

He was breathing hard, but his hands had steadied. He had no choice. He had to do this.

Climbing quickly upward, staying behind the cover of rocks and trees as best he could, Tom topped the hill, keeping low, the gun gripped in both hands.

He knew he couldn't hesitate. Not even an instant. The moment he saw the rustler he would have to shoot. Shoot to kill if the individual was armed. He'd never killed a man. Today could change that.

As Tom Robinson moved through the trees at the edge of a small clearing, he heard a horse whinny off to his left, and spun in that direction, his finger on the trigger.

The moment he saw the animal, and the empty saddle, he realized the mistake he'd made. He spun back around and came face-to-face with the trespasser. Shocked both by who it was and by the tree limb in the man's hands, Tom hesitated an instant too long before pulling the trigger.

The shot boomed among the trees, echoing over the rocks, the misguided bullet burying itself in the bark of a pine off to the trespasser's left.

It happened so fast, Tom didn't even realize he'd fired. He barely felt the blow to his head as the man swung the thick limb like a baseball bat. Instead, Tom just heard a sickening thud as the limb struck his temple, felt his knees give out under him and watched in an odd fascination as the dried needles on the ground came up to meet his face, just before everything went black.

JACKLYN WILDE STARTED at the sound of a knock on the hall door to her motel room. "Delivery."

She sat up in confusion, horrified to realize that she'd dozed off. After the phone call from Stratton, she'd lain down for only a minute, but must have fallen asleep.

She rushed to the receiver terminal, half expecting to see that Dillon was no longer in his room.

But the steady beep assured her he was right next door. Or at least his tracking device was.

She thought about knocking on his door to check, using the food as an excuse. But instead she went to tip the deliveryman, closing her door behind him.

As she placed the Chinese food sacks on the table in the corner of her room, she heard a soft tap on the door between their rooms.

"Dinner's here," she called in response. Unconsciously, she braced herself as he stepped into her room.

His hair was wet and curled at his neck, his face flushed from his bath, and he smelled better than sweet and sour shrimp any day of the week. On top of that, he looked so happy and excited that anyone with a heart would have felt something as he made a beeline for the food.

She knew she was considered cold and heartless with no feelings, especially the female kind. It made it easier in her line of work to let everyone think that.

But how could she not be moved to see Dillon like a kid in a candy store as he opened each of the little white boxes, making delighted sounds and breathing in the scent of each, all the time flashing that grin of his?

"I can't believe this. I think you got all my favorites," he said, turning that grin on her. "You must have read my mind." The look in his eyes softened, taking all the air from the room.

She turned away and pretended to look in her suitcase for something.

"Come on," he said. "Let's eat while it's hot. Work can wait. Can't it?"

She pulled out the map she'd planned to show him later, and glanced toward the small table in the corner and Dillon. "Go ahead and start."

He shook his head. "My mother taught better than that."

Reluctantly, she joined him as he began to dish up the rice. "I just want a little sweet and sour shrimp."

He looked up. "You can't be serious. Who's going to eat all this?"

She couldn't help her smile. "I figured you would. You did say you've been starved for Chinese food."

His grateful expression was almost her undoing—and his subsequent vulnerability as well. He ducked his head as if overcome with emotions he didn't want her to see, and spooned sweet and sour shrimp onto a plate for her.

She made a job of putting the map on the chair beside her, giving him a moment. Maybe she'd underestimated what four years in prison had done to him. Or what it must be like for him to be out.

When she looked up, however, there was no sign of anything on his face except a brilliant smile as he dished up his own plate. She warned herself not to be taken in by any of his antics as she took a bite of her meal and watched him do the same.

He closed his eyes and moaned softly. She tried to ignore him as she pretended to study the map on the chair next to her while she nibbled her food.

"You have to try this."

Before she could react, he reached across the table and shoved a forkful of something at her. Instinctively, she opened her mouth.

"Isn't that amazing?" he asked as he intently watched her chew.

It *was* amazing. Spicy, but not too hot. "Which one is that?" she asked, just to break the tense quiet in the room as he stared at her.

"Orange-peel beef." He was already putting some on her plate. "And wait until you try this." He started toward her with another forkful.

She held up her hand, more than aware of how intimate it was to be fed by a man. She was sure Dillon

Savage was aware of it, too. "Really, I—" But the fork had touched her lips and her mouth opened again.

As he dragged the fork away slowly, she felt a rush of heat that had nothing to do with the spicy food.

She met his gaze and felt a chill run the length of her spine. The smile on his lips, the teasing tilt of his head, couldn't hide what was deep in those pale blue eyes.

She had forgotten that she'd been the one to put him behind bars, but clearly, Dillon Savage had not.

CHAPTER FOUR

DILLON STARED INTO Jack's gray eyes. For a moment there he'd been enjoying himself, so much that he'd forgotten who she was: the woman who'd sent him to prison. His mood turned sour in an instant.

He dragged his gaze away, but not before she'd seen the change in him. Seen his true feelings.

She shoved her plate aside, her appetite apparently gone, and spread the map out on the table like a barrier between them. "We need to get to work, so as soon as you've finished eating…"

He ate quickly, but his enjoyment of foods he'd missed so much was gone. He told himself it was better this way. Jack had to be aware of how he felt about her. She would have been a fool not to, and this woman was no fool.

But he doubted she knew the extent of his feelings. Or how he'd amused himself those many hours alone in his bunk. He'd plotted his revenge. Not that he planned to act on it, he'd told himself. It had just been something to do. Because he would need to do *something* about the person who'd betrayed him. And while he was at it, why not do something about Jack?

Only he would have to be careful around her. More careful than he'd been so far.

Food forgotten, he shoved the containers aside and

stood to lean over the map. But his attention was on Jack. He could tell she was still a little shaken, and wanted to reassure her that he was no longer a man driven by vengeance. No easy task, given that he didn't believe it himself.

But that wasn't what bothered him as he pretended to study the map. As a student of human nature, he couldn't help but wonder why, when he'd been so careful to mask his feelings for years, he had let that mask slip—even for an instant—around the one woman who controlled his freedom.

Jacklyn watched his eyes. They were a pale blue, with tiny specks of gold. Eyes that gave away too much, including the fact that behind all that blue was a brain as sharp as any she'd run across. And that made him dangerous, even beyond whatever grudges he still carried.

On the map, she'd marked with a small red *x* each ranch that had lost cattle. Next to it, she'd put down the number of livestock stolen and the estimated value.

Some of the cattle had been taken in broad daylight, others under the cover of night. The randomness of the hits had made it impossible to catch the rustlers—that and the fact that they worked a two-hundred-mile area, moved fast and left no evidence behind.

Dillon had been leaning over the table, but now sat back and raked a hand through his still-wet hair.

"Something wrong?" she asked. Clearly, there was. She could see that he was upset. If he was the leader of the rustlers, as she suspected, none of this would come as a surprise to him. Unless, of course, his partners in crime had hit more ranches than he was aware of. Had they been cheating him? What if they'd been double-crossing him? She could only hope.

She reminded herself that there was the remote chance Dillon Savage wasn't involved, which meant whoever was leading this band of rustlers was as clever as he had been. Another reason Dillon might have looked upset?

"Just an interesting pattern," he said.

She nodded. She'd been afraid he was going to start lying to her right off the bat. "Interesting how?"

He gave her a look that said she knew as well as he did. "By omission."

"Yes," she agreed, relieved he hadn't tried to con her. "It appears they are saving the biggest ranch for last."

He smiled at that. "You really think they're ever going to stop, when things are going so well for them?"

No. That was her fear. Some of the smaller ranchers were close to going broke. The rustlers had taken a lot of unbranded calves this spring. Based on market value, the animals had been worth about a thousand dollars a head, a loss that was crippling the smaller ranches, some of which had been hit more than once.

Worse, the rustlers were showing no sign of letting up. She'd hoped they would get cocky, mess up, but they were apparently too good for that.

"What do you think?" she asked, motioning to the map.

He leaned back in his chair. "I'm more interested in what you think."

She scowled at him.

"I'm not trying to be difficult," he contended. "I'm just curious as to your take on this. After all, if we're going to be working together…"

She fought the urge to dig in her heels. But he was right. She'd gotten him out of prison to help her catch the rustlers. It was going to require some give and take. But at the same time, if he was the leader…

"I think they're going to make a big hit on Shade Waters's W Bar Ranch. It's the largest spread in the area and the rustlers have already hit ranches around him for miles, but not touched his."

Dillon lifted a brow.

"What?"

"I suspect that's exactly what they want you to think," he said.

She had to bite her tongue. Damn him and his arrogance. "You have a better suggestion as to where they'll go next?"

He leaned forward to study the map again. After a long moment, he said, "Not a clue."

She swore under her breath and glared at him.

"If you're asking me what the rustlers will do next, I have no idea," he said, raising both hands in surrender.

"What would *you* do?" she snapped.

Dillon shrugged, pretty sure now he knew why Jack had gotten him out of prison. "Like I told you back at the prison weeks ago, I'm not sure how I can help you find these guys."

He saw that she didn't believe that. "Look, it's clear that they are very organized. No fly-by-night bunch. They move fast and efficiently. They know what they're doing, where they're going to go next."

"So?" she asked.

"If you think I can predict their movements, then you wasted your time and your money getting me an early release. You might as well drive me back to prison right now."

"Don't tempt me. You said you think they want me

to assume they're going to hit Waters's ranch. What does that mean?"

"They wouldn't be that obvious. Sorry, but isn't the reason this bunch has been so hard to catch the fact that they don't do what you expect them to? That gives them the upper hand."

"Tell me something I don't know, Mr. Savage."

He sighed and looked at the map again. "Are these the number of cattle stolen per ranch?" he asked, pointing to the notations she'd made beside the red *x*'s.

She gave him an exasperated look, her jaw still tight.

He could see why she thought the ring would be looking for a big score. The rustlers were being cautious, taking only about fifty head at a time, mostly not-yet-branded calves that would be hard to trace. Smart, but not where the big money was.

Jacklyn got up from the table as if too nervous to sit still, and started clearing up their dinner.

"It's not about the money," he said to her back.

She turned as she tossed an empty Chinese food box into the trash. "Stop trying to con me."

"I'm not. You're looking at this rationally. Rustling isn't always rational—at least the motive behind it isn't. Hell, there are a lot of better ways to make a living."

"I thought you said it was simple math, quick bucks, little risk," she said, an edge to her voice.

So she had been listening. "Yeah, but it's too hit-or-miss. With a real job you get to wear a better wardrobe, have nicer living conditions. Not to mention a 401 K salary, vacation and sick pay, plus hardly anyone ever shoots at you."

"Your point?" she said, obviously not appreciating his sense of humor.

She started to scoop up the map, but he grabbed her hand, more to get her attention than to stop her. He could feel her pulse hammering against the pad of his thumb, which he moved slowly in a circle across the warm flesh. His heart kicked up a beat as her eyes met his.

What the hell was he doing? He let go and she pulled back, her gaze locked with his, a clear warning in all that gunmetal-gray.

"All I'm saying is that you have to think like they think," he said.

She shook her head. "That's *your* job."

"The only way I can do that is if I know what they really want," he said.

"They want *cattle*."

He laughed. "No. Trust me, it's not about cattle. It's always about the end result. The cattle are just a means to an end. What we need to know is what they're getting out of this. It isn't the money. They aren't making enough for it to be about money. So what do they really want?"

"The money will come from a big score. Waters's W Bar Ranch."

"After they've telegraphed what they are going to do so clearly that it's what you're expecting?" He snorted. "No, they have something else in mind."

She shook her head as if he was talking in riddles. "I won't know what they want until I catch them."

He grinned. "Catching them is one thing. Finding out who they are is another."

She was glaring at him again.

"You've been trying to catch an unnamed ring of cattle rustlers," he said patiently. "What do these men do when they aren't rustling cattle? You can bet they work on these ranches," he said, pointing at the map.

She sat back down very slowly. He could tell she was trying to control her temper. She thought he was messing with her.

"Look," he said softly. "You already know a lot about these guys." He ticked items off on his fingers. "One, someone smart is running this operation. That's why these characters seem to know what they're doing and why they haven't made any mistakes. Two, they know the country." He nodded. "We're talking some inside jobs here. They know not only where to find the cattle, but which ones to take and when. They either work on the ranches or have a connection of some kind."

She crossed her arms, scowling but listening.

"Three, they're cowboys. They're too good at working with cattle not to be, and they've used horses for most of their raids. I'll bet you these guys can ride better at midnight on a moonless night in rough terrain than most men can ride in a corral in broad daylight."

She actually smiled at that.

He smiled back, then asked, "What's so humorous?"

"You. You just described yourself," she said, her gaze locking with his. "We're looking for someone just like you. How about that."

WHEN THE CALL CAME hours later, Jacklyn was in the middle of a nightmare. She jerked awake, dragging the bad dream into the room with her as she fumbled for her cell phone beside the bed.

"Tom Robinson's in the hospital," Stratton said without preamble. "He's unconscious. The doctors aren't sure he's going to make it."

Jacklyn fought to wake up, to make sense of what he was saying and what this had to do with her. Although she couldn't remember any specifics of the nightmare, she knew it had been about the leader of the rustling ring. He'd been trying to kill her, stalking her among some trees. She could still feel him out there, feel the danger, the fear, sense him so close that if she looked over her shoulder… It had been Dillon, hadn't it?

"It seems like he might have stumbled across the rustlers," Stratton said. "His hired hand found him near a spot where someone had cut the fence."

She glanced at the clock next to the bed. It was just after midnight.

"Are you there?" Stratton asked irritably. Like her, he'd obviously been awakened by the call about Tom. "When Tom didn't return home for dinner, his hired hand tracked him down, and got him to the hospital. You know what this means, don't you?"

Jacklyn threw off the covers and sat up, trying to throw off the remnants of the dream and the chilling terror that still had her in its grip, too. Snapping on the light beside the bed, she asked, "Did they get any cattle?"

"No. He must have scared the rustlers away."

More awake, she said, "You told everyone to stay out of the area, right? To wait until I got there before they fix the fence?"

"Sheriff McCray already went out to the scene tonight."

She swore under her breath.

"I told Robinson's hired man that you'd be there first thing in the morning. The rustlers have moved up a level on the criminal ladder. If Tom dies, they've gone from rustling to murder." With that he hung up.

She closed her cell phone and, bleary-eyed, glanced again at the clock, then at the monitor. She'd turned it down so there was no steady beep indicating where Dillon Savage was at the moment.

But she could see that he was in the room next door. Probably sleeping like a baby, without a care in the world.

With both a real nightmare and a bad dream hanging over her, she fought the urge to wake him up and ruin his sleep, just as hers had been. She wondered what Dillon Savage's reaction would be to the news.

She turned out the light and crawled back under the covers, even though she doubted she'd get back to sleep. Silently, she prayed that Tom Robinson would regain consciousness and be able to identify his assailants.

The rustlers had messed up this time. They'd been seen. It was their first mistake.

CHAPTER FIVE

THE DRIVE NORTH the next morning was like going home again for Dillon Savage. Except for the fact that he had no home. Which made seeing the land he knew so well all that much harder to take.

Not to mention that Jack wasn't talking to him. She'd broken the news at breakfast.

"You all right?" he'd finally asked, over pancakes and bacon. She'd seemed angry with him all morning. He couldn't think of anything he'd done recently that would have set her off, but then, given their past...

She'd looked up from her veggie omelet and leveled those icy gray eyes on him. "Tom Robinson was found near death yesterday evening on his ranch. Apparently, he stumbled across the rustlers. He's in the hospital. His ranch hands found him—along with a spot in the fence where the barbed wire had been cut." She'd stared at Dillon, waiting.

"I'm sorry to hear about Tom. I always liked him," he had said, meaning it. But his words only seemed to make Jack's mood more sour, if that was possible.

Tom Robinson was one of the few neighbors who still had his place. Dillon had often wondered how he'd managed to keep his spread when almost all the other ranchers around the W Bar had sold out to Shade Waters.

"If Tom was attacked by the rustlers, then they just

went from felony theft to attempted murder," Jack had pointed out. "But the good news is that when Tom regains consciousness, he'll be able to identify them."

"Good," Dillon had said, seeing that she was bluffing. She had no way of knowing if Tom Robinson had gotten a good look at whoever had attacked him, let alone if it was the rustlers. "Sounds like you got a break." She was staring at him, so he frowned at her. *"What?"*

"Come on, Dillon," she'd said, dropping her voice. It was the first time she'd called him by his first name. "You and I both know you're the leader of this rustling ring. Once Tom identifies who attacked him, your little house of cards is going to come tumbling down. Tell me the truth now and I will try to get you the best deal I can."

He had laughed, shaking his head. "Jack, you're barking up the wrong tree. I'm not your man." He'd grinned and added, "At least not for that role, anyway. I told you. I've gone straight. No more iron bars for me."

She hadn't believed him.

He should have saved his breath, but he'd tried to assure her she was wrong. "There's a lot of injustice in the world. I'm sorry Tom got hurt. But Jack, if you think I have anything to do with this—"

"Don't even bother," she'd snapped, throwing down her napkin. Breakfast was over.

Since then, she hadn't said two words to him.

He stared out his window. The golden prairie was dotted with antelope, geese and cranes, and of course, cows. This was cattle country and had been for two hundred years. Ranch houses were miles apart and towns few and far between.

It amazed Dillon how little things had changed over the years. He kept up on the news and knew that places like Bozeman had been growing like crazy.

But this part of Montana had looked like this for decades, the landscape changing little as the population diminished. Kids left the farms and ranches for greener pastures in real towns or out of state.

But as isolated and unpopulated as this country was, there was a feeling of community. While there had been little traffic this morning, everyone they passed had waved, usually lifting just a couple of fingers from the steering wheel or giving a nod.

There was so much that he'd missed. Some people didn't appreciate this land. It was fairly flat, with only the smudged, purple outline of mountains far in the distance. There was little but prairie, and a pencil-straight, two-lane road running for miles.

But to him it was beautiful. The grasses, a deep green, undulated like waves in the wind. The sky was bluer than any he'd ever seen. Willows had turned a bright gold, dogwood a brilliant red. Everywhere he looked there were birds.

God, how he'd missed this.

He'd known it would be hell coming back here. Especially after his four-year stint in prison. He'd never dreamed he'd return so soon—or with Jack—let alone have a microchip embedded behind his left ear. Life was just full of surprises.

The farther north Jacklyn drove, the more restless

Dillon became. He'd hoped the years in prison had changed him, had at least taught him something about himself. But this place brought it all back. The betrayal. The anger. The aching need for vengeance.

"I'm sorry, where did you say we were going?" he asked. Jack, of course, hadn't said.

"Your old stompin' grounds," she said.

That's what he was afraid of. They'd gone from the motel to pick up a horse trailer, two horses and tack. He couldn't wait to get back in the saddle. He was just worried where that horse was going to take him. Maybe more to the point, what he would do once he and Jack were deep in this isolated country, just the two of them.

JACKLYN HAD HER OWN reasons for not wanting to go north that morning. The big one was that Sheriff Claude McCray had sent word he had to see her.

Claude was the last man she wanted to see. And with good reason. The last time she'd been with him they'd gotten into an argument after making love. She'd broken off their affair, knowing she'd been an idiot to get involved with him in the first place. She was embarrassed and ashamed.

When Dillon had asked her if she didn't regret something she'd done, she'd thought of Sheriff McCray. Since the breakup, she'd made a point of staying out of his part of Montana.

But today she had no choice. And maybe, just maybe, the reason McCray wanted to see her had something to do with Tom Robinson and the men who had attacked him, given the fact that the sheriff had gone to her crime scene last night.

The day was beautiful as she drove out of Lewistown pulling the horse trailer. Behind her, in her rearview mirror, she could see the Big Snowy Mountains and the Little Belts. Once she made it over the Moccasins and the Judiths, the land stretched to the horizon, rolling fields broken only occasionally by rock outcroppings or a lone tree or two.

Jack stared at the straight stick of a road that ran north, away from the mountains, away from any town of any size, and dreaded seeing Sheriff Claude McCray again—especially with Dillon Savage along.

She'd never forgive herself for foolishly becoming involved with someone she occasionally worked with. Not a good idea. On top of that, she'd gotten involved with Claude for all the wrong reasons.

Jacklyn turned off the two-lane highway onto a narrow, rutted dirt road. As far as the eye could see there wasn't a house or barn. Usually this open land comforted her, but not this morning, with everything she had on her mind. She felt antsy, as if she were waiting for the other shoe to drop.

She'd called the hospital before she'd left the motel. Tom Robinson was in critical condition. It was doubtful he would regain consciousness. She was angry and sickened. She liked Tom.

Selfishly, she'd wanted him to come to in the hopes that he could ID at least one of the rustlers. With just one name, she knew she could put pressure on that individual to identify the person running the ring. Dillon Savage.

She glanced over at him. She'd give him credit; he'd seemed genuinely upset over hearing about Tom. But was that because he'd known and liked the man, as he'd said? Or because his little gang of rustlers had gone too far this time and now might be found out?

He didn't look too worried that he was going to be caught, she thought. He was slouched in the seat, gazing out the window, watching the world go by as if he didn't have a care. Could she be wrong about him? Maybe. But there *was* something going on with him. She could feel it.

"So we're heading to the Robinson place," Dillon said, guessing that would be at least one of their stops today.

"After that we're going to the W Bar."

He could feel her probing gaze on him again, as if she was waiting for a reaction.

But he wasn't about to give her one. He just nodded, determined not to let her see how he felt about even the thought of crossing Shade Waters's path. He hadn't seen Waters since the day Jack had arrested him.

The truth was she'd probably saved his life, given that Shade had had a shotgun—and every intention of killing Dillon on the spot that day.

"Waters know you got me out of prison?" he asked.

"Probably the reason he wants to see me."

Dillon chuckled. "This should be interesting then."

"You'll be staying in the pickup—and out of trouble.

Your work with me has nothing to do with Shade Waters," she said in that crisp, no-nonsense tone.

He smiled. "Just so I'm there to witness his reaction when you tell him that. Unless you want to leave me at the bar in Hilger and pick me up on your way back."

She shot him a look. "Until this rustling ring is caught, you and I are attached at the hip."

"I do like that image," he said, and grinned over at her.

She scowled and went back to her driving. "Any animosity you have for Waters or any other ranchers, you're to keep to yourself."

"What animosity?" he asked with a straight face. "I'm a changed man. Any hard feelings I had about Shade Waters I left behind that razor wire fence you broke me out of."

She gave him a look that said she'd believe that when hell froze over. "Just remember what I said. I don't need any trouble out of you. I have enough with Waters."

"Don't worry, Jack, I'll be good," Dillon said, and pulled down the brim on his hat as he slid down in the seat again. He tried not to think about Tom Robinson or Shade Waters or even Jack.

Instead, he thought about lying in the bathtub last night at the motel, bubbles up to his neck. And later, sprawled on the big bed, staring up at the ceiling, trying to convince himself he wasn't going to blow his freedom. Not for anything. Even justice.

The bath had been pure heaven. The bed was huge and softer than anything he'd slept on in years. In prison, he'd had a pad spread on a concrete slab. A real bed had felt strange, and had made him wonder how long it would take to get used to being out.

How long did it take not to be angry that normal no longer felt normal? Maybe as long as getting over the fact that someone owed him for the past four years of his life.

SHERIFF CLAUDE MCCRAY wasn't in, but the dispatcher said she was expecting him, and to wait in his office.

Ten minutes later, Claude walked in. He was a big man, powerfully built, with a chiseled face and deep-set brown eyes. He gave Jacklyn a look that could have wilted lettuce. His gaze turned even more hostile when he glanced at Dillon.

McCray chuckled to himself as he moved behind his desk, shaking his head as he glared at Jacklyn again. "Dillon Savage. You got the bastard out. What a surprise."

She met his eyes for only an instant before she looked away, not wanting to get into this with him. Especially in front of Dillon, given what Claude had accused her of nearly four years ago.

"You're obsessed with Dillon Savage," McCray had said.

"Excuse me? It's my job to find him and stop him," she'd snapped back.

"Oh, Jacklyn, it's way beyond that. You admire him, admit it."

"Wh-what?" she'd stammered, sliding out of bed, wanting to distance herself from this ridiculous talk.

"He's the only one who's ever eluded you this long,"

Claude had called after her. "You're making a damn hero out of him."

She had been barely able to speak, she was so shocked. "That's so ridiculous, I don't even— You're jealous of a cattle rustler?"

He'd narrowed his eyes at her angrily. "I'm jealous of a man you can't go five minutes without talking about."

"I'm sorry I bothered you with talk about my job," she'd snapped as she jerked on her jeans and boots and looked around for her bra and sweater.

Claude was sitting up in the bed, watching her, frowning. "I'd bet you spend more time thinking about Dillon Savage than you do me."

She'd heard the jealousy and bitterness in his voice and had been sickened by it. He'd called her after that, telling her he'd had too much to drink and didn't know what he was saying.

For all his apologies, that had been the end of their affair. She'd caught Dillon a few days later and had made a point of staying as far from Sheriff Claude Mc-Cray as possible, even though he'd tried to contact her repeatedly over the past four years.

Now, as Claude settled into his chair behind the large metal desk, she noticed that he looked shorter than she remembered, his shoulders less broad. Or maybe she couldn't help comparing him to Dillon Savage. They were both close to the same age, but that was where the similarities ended.

"What's the world coming to when we have to get

criminals out of prison to help solve crimes?" McCray said as if to himself, looking from Dillon to Jack.

"Is there anything new on the Robinson case?" she asked, determined to keep the conversation on track.

"Why don't you ask your boyfriend here," McCray quipped.

Dillon was watching this interplay with interest. She swore under her breath, wishing that she'd come alone. But she didn't like letting Dillon out of her sight. Especially now that the stakes were higher, with Tom Robinson critical.

"Sheriff, I just need to know if you have any leads. I understand you went out to the crime scene last night." She had to bite her tongue to keep from saying how stupid it was to go out there in the dark and possibly destroy evidence. "I'm headed out there now."

"Don't waste your time. There's nothing to find."

She would be the judge of that. "What about the Drummond place?"

Claude was shaking his head. "Wasn't worth riding back in there for so few head of cattle."

Bud Drummond might argue that, she thought.

She rose from her chair, anxious to get out of Claude's office. She'd thought about not even bothering to come here, but he'd sent word that he wanted to see her. She should have known it wasn't about the Robinson case.

Her real reason for coming, she knew, was so he wouldn't think she was afraid to face him. Perish the thought.

"If Tom Robinson dies, it will be murder," McCray said, glaring at Dillon. "This time you'll stay in prison."

Dillon, to his credit, didn't react. But she could see that this situation could escalate easily if they didn't leave. Claude seemed to be working himself up for a fight.

"We're going," Jacklyn said, moving toward the door.

The sheriff rose, coming around the desk to grab her arm. "I need to speak with you alone."

Jacklyn looked down at his fingers digging into her flesh. He let go of her, but she saw Dillon leap to his feet, about to come to her defense.

That was the last thing she needed. "Mr. Savage, if you wouldn't mind waiting by the pickup..." She had no desire to be alone with Claude McCray, but if she was anything, she was no coward. And he just might have something to tell her about the investigation that Dillon shouldn't hear.

Dillon frowned, as if he didn't like leaving her alone with McCray. Obviously, she wasn't the only one who thought the man could be dangerous.

She indicated the door and gave Dillon an imploring look.

"I'll be right outside if you need me," he said as he opened the door and stepped out, closing it quietly behind him.

"That son of a bitch." The sheriff swore and swung on her. "He acts like he owns you. Are you already sleeping with him?"

"Don't be ridiculous. What was it you had to say to me?"

He glared at her, anger blazing in his eyes. "If you're not, it's just a matter of time before you are. You've had something for him for years."

"If that's all you wanted to say…" She started for the door.

He reached to grab her again, but this time she avoided his grasp. "Don't," she said, her voice low and full of warning. "Don't touch me."

He drew back in surprise. "Jackie—"

"And don't call me that."

He stiffened and busied himself straightening his hat, as if trying to get his temper under control.

What had she ever seen in him? She didn't want to think about why she'd ended up with McCray. And it wasn't because she hadn't known what kind of man he was. She'd been looking for an outlaw during the day and had wanted one at night, as well.

Too late she'd realized Claude McCray was a mean bastard with even less ethics than Dillon Savage.

"Was there something about the case?" she asked as she reached for the doorknob.

He glared at her for a long moment, then grudgingly said, "My men found something up by where the rustlers cut the barbed wire of Robinson's fence last night," he said finally. "I'm sure it's probably been in the dirt for years and has nothing do with the rustlers, but I was told to give it to you." He reached toward his desk, then turned and dropped a gold good-luck piece into her palm.

"You have any idea who this might belong to?" she asked.

"Someone whose luck is about to turn for the worst," McCray said cryptically. "At least if I have anything to do with it."

CHAPTER SIX

"You ALL RIGHT?" Dillon asked as Jack came out of the sheriff's office.

"Fine," she said, whipping past him and heading for the truck.

He followed, thinking about what he'd seen in there. Definitely tension between the lawman and Jack. Dillon had never liked that redneck son of a bitch, McCray. He'd seen plenty of guys like him at prison. What he'd witnessed in the office hadn't made Dillon dislike him any less.

In fact, it had been all he could do not to punch the man. But if Dillon had learned anything it was that you didn't punch out a sheriff. Especially when you had just gotten a prerelease from prison and were treading on thin ice as it was.

Jack started the pickup as Dillon slid in and slammed the door. She seemed anxious to get out of town. He knew that feeling.

"So what did the bastard do to you?"

She jerked her head around to look at him and almost ran into the car in front of them.

He saw the answer in her expression and swore. "McCray. Oh man." Dillon had hoped the animosity between them just had to do with work, but he'd known better. He just hadn't wanted to believe she'd get involved with Claude McCray, and said as much.

"Don't," she warned as she gripped the wheel. The light changed and she got the pickup going again. "You and I aren't getting into this discussion."

He shook his head. "I've made some big mistakes in my life, but Claude McCray?"

She slammed on the brakes so hard the seat belt cut into him. "I will not have this discussion with you," she said, biting off each word. The driver behind them laid on his horn. Jack didn't seem to notice. She was clasping the wheel so tightly her knuckles were white, her eyes straight ahead, as if she couldn't look at him.

"Okay, okay," Dillon said, realizing this had to be that big regret he'd sensed in her. Jack's big mistake.

It was so unlike her. She had more sense than to get involved with McCray. Something must have caused it. "When was it?"

"I just said—"

He swore as he remembered something he'd overheard while in the county jail. "You were seeing him when you were chasing me."

She groaned and got the pickup going again. "Could we please drop this? Can't you just sit over there and laugh smugly under your breath so I don't have to hear it?"

She still hadn't looked at him.

He reached over and touched her arm. Her gaze shifted to him slowly, reluctantly. He looked into her eyes and saw a pain he couldn't comprehend. No way had McCray broken it off between them. No, from the way the sheriff had been acting, Jack had dumped *him*.

So what was with this heartache Dillon saw in her eyes?

TOM ROBINSON'S RANCH house was at the end of a narrow, deeply rutted road. The ranch was small, a wedge of land caught between Waters's huge spread and Reda Harper's much less extensive one.

The ride north had been pure hell. Though Dillon finally shut up about her and Sheriff McCray, Jack knew he was sitting over there making sport of her entire affair. She hated to think what was going through his mind.

After a few miles, she stole a glance at him. He had his hat down over his eyes, his long legs sprawled out, his hands resting in his lap. To all appearances, he seemed to be sleeping.

Right. He was over there chortling to himself, pleased that he'd stirred her up again. Worse, that he now had something on her. The man was impossible.

She would never figure him out. Earlier, when he'd forced her to look at him, she'd thought she'd seen compassion in his eyes, maybe even understanding.

But how could he understand? She didn't herself.

Dillon Savage was like no man she'd ever known. When she'd been chasing him before, she'd been shocked to learn that he didn't fit any profile, let alone that of a cattle rustler. For starters, he was university educated, with degrees in engineering, business and psychology, and he'd graduated at the top of his class.

If that wasn't enough, he'd inherited a bundle right before he started rustling cattle. He had no reason to commit the crime. Except, she suspected, to flout the law.

Dillon stirred as she pulled into Tom Robinson's yard. She felt the gold good-luck coin in her pocket. She'd almost forgotten that she'd stuck it there, she'd been so upset about McCray—and Dillon.

She knew it might not be a clue. Anyone could have dropped it there at any time. While the coin did look old, that didn't mean it was. Nor would she put it past Claude McCray to lie about where he'd found it, just to throw her off track. Worse, she suspected it might be fairly common, even something given out by casinos, since Montana had legalized gambling.

If it had belonged to one of the rustlers, any fingerprints on it had been destroyed with McCray handling it.

She sighed and reached into her pocket for the coin, thinking about what McCray had said about luck changing for the person who'd been carrying it.

"I need to ask you something," she said, turning to Dillon. "I need you to tell me the truth."

He nodded and grinned. "Did I tell you I never lie?"

"Right."

Dillon looked at the hand she held toward him, her fingers clasped around something he couldn't see, her eyes intent on his face.

He felt his stomach clench as she slowly uncurled her fingers. He had no idea what she was going to show him. And even though he suspected it wasn't going to be good, he wasn't prepared for what he saw nestled in her palm.

"You recognize it!" she accused, wrapping her fingers back around it as if she wanted to hit him with her fist. "So help me, if you deny it—"

"Yeah, I've seen it before. Or at least one like it."

She was staring at him as if she was surprised he'd actually admitted it. "Who does it belong to?"

"I said I'd seen one like it, I didn't say—"

"Don't," she snapped, scowling at him.

"Easy," he said, holding up his hands. "A friend of mine used to have one like it, okay? He carried it around for luck. But he's dead."

"And you don't know what happened to his?"

Dillon couldn't very well miss her sarcasm. "May I look at it?"

She reluctantly opened her hand, as if she thought he might grab it and run.

He plucked the good-luck coin from her warm palm, accidentally brushing his fingertips across her skin, and saw her shudder. But his attention was on the coin as he turned it in his fingers. The small marks were right where he knew they would be, leaving no doubt. His heart began to pound.

"Where did you say you got this?" he asked as he handed it back.

Her gaze burned into him. "I didn't."

Dillon could only assume that, since she'd gone to the sheriff about Tom Robinson, McCray had given it to her. Which had to mean that she suspected one of the rustlers who'd attacked Tom had dropped it.

"So who was the deceased friend of yours who had one like it?" she asked, clearly not believing him.

"Halsey Waters. And as for what happened to his coin," Dillon said, "I personally put it in his suit pocket at his funeral."

"Halsey *Waters?* Shade's oldest son?"

"That's the one." Out of the corner of his eye, Dillon

saw the ranch house door open and a stocky cowboy step out. Arlen Dubois.

It was turning out to be like old home week, Dillon thought. All the old gang was back in central Montana. Just as they had been for Halsey Waters's funeral.

ARLEN DUBOIS WAS all cowboy, long and lanky, legs bowed, boots run-down, jeans worn and dirty. He invited them into the house, explaining that he was looking after everything with Tom in the hospital.

Jacklyn watched Arlen take off his hat and nervously rake a hand through short blond curls. His skin was white and lightly freckled where the hat had protected it from the sun. The rest of his face was sunburned red.

He looked from Jacklyn to Dillon and quickly back again. "I'd offer you something to drink…"

"We're fine," Jacklyn said, noticing how uncomfortable the cowboy was in the presence of his old friend. Arlen had a slight lisp, buckteeth and a broad open face. "I just want to ask you a few questions."

He shifted on his feet. "Okay."

"Do you mind if we sit down?" she asked.

Arlen got all flustered, but waved them toward chairs in the small living room. Jacklyn noticed that the fabric was threadbare, and doubted the furnishings had been replaced in Tom's lifetime.

Arlen turned his hat in his hands as he sat on the edge of one of the chairs.

"You work for Tom Robinson?" she asked.

"Yep, but you already know that. If you think I had anything to do with what happened to Tom—"

"How long have you worked for Mr. Robinson?"

Arlen gave that some thought, scraping at a dirty

spot on his hat as he did. "About four years," he said, without looking up. The same amount of time Dillon Savage had been behind bars.

"You and Mr. Savage here have been friends for a long time, right?"

Arlen started. "What does that have to do with this? If you think I ever stole cattle with him—"

"I was just asking if you were friends."

Arlen shrugged, avoiding Dillon's gaze. "We knew each other."

Yeah, she would just bet. She'd long suspected Dillon hadn't done the rustling alone. He would have needed help. But would he have involved a man like Arlen Dubois? Word at the bar was that Dubois tended to brag when he had a few drinks in him, although few people believed even half of what he said.

"Have you seen anyone suspicious around the ranch? Before Tom was attacked?" she asked, knowing that most of her questions were a waste of time. She had just wanted to see Arlen and Dillon together.

Dillon seemed cool as a cucumber, like a man who had nothing to hide.

"Nothin' suspicious," Arlen said, with a shake of his head.

"You know of anyone who had a grudge against Tom?"

The cowboy shook his head again. "Tom was likable enough."

Dillon was studying Arlen, and making him even more nervous. Maybe she should have left him in the truck.

"If you think of anything…"

Arlen looked relieved. "Sure," he said, and rose from his chair. "You ready to ride out to where I found Tom?"

Jacklyn nodded. "One more thing," she said as she stood and reached into her pocket. "Ever seen this before?"

Arlen reacted as if she'd held out a rattlesnake. His gaze shot to Dillon's, then back to the coin. "I might have seen one like it once."

"Where was that?" she asked.

"I can't really recall."

Both of Arlen's responses were lies.

"Mr. Savage, would you mind waiting for me in the pickup?" she asked.

"Not at all, Ms. Wilde."

She ground her teeth as she waited for him to close the front door behind him. "Anything you want to tell me, Arlen?"

"About what?" he asked, looking scared.

"Did you happen to be at Halsey Waters's funeral?"

All the color left his face. "What does that have to do with—"

"Yes or no? Or can't you remember that, either?"

He had the good grace to flush. "I was there, just like all his other friends."

She detected something odd in his tone. Today was the first time she'd heard anything about Halsey Waters. But then, she wasn't from this part of Montana. "How did Halsey die?"

Arlen looked down at his boots. "He was bucked off a wild horse. Broke his neck."

ALL THE OLD DEMONS that had haunted him came back with a vengeance as Dillon rode out with Arlen and

Jacklyn, across rolling hills dotted with cattle and sagebrush. He breathed in the familiar scents as if to punish himself. Or remind himself that even four years in prison couldn't change a man enough to forget his first love. Or his worst enemy.

The air smelled so good it made him ache. This had once been his country. He knew it even better than the man who owned it.

They followed the fence line as it twisted alongside the creek, the bottomlands thick with chokecherry, willow and dogwood. Jacklyn slowed her horse, waiting for him.

The memories were so sharp and painful he had to look away for fear she would see that this was killing him.

Or worse, that she might glimpse the desire for vengeance burning in his eyes.

"I've always wanted to ask you," she said conversationally. Arlen was riding ahead of them, out of earshot. "Why three university degrees?"

Dillon pretended to give her question some thought, although he doubted that's what she'd been thinking about. She'd made it clear back at the ranch house that she thought he and Arlen used to rustle cattle together. It hadn't helped that Arlen had lied through his teeth about the good-luck coin.

Shoving back his hat, Dillon shrugged and said, "I was a rancher's son. You know how, at that age, you're so full of yourself. I thought the last thing I wanted to do was ranch. I wanted a job where I got to wear something other than jeans and boots, have an office with a window, make lots of money."

She glanced over at him, as if wondering if he was

serious. "You know, I suspect you often tell people what you think they want to hear."

He laughed and shook his head. "Nope, that's the real reason I got three degrees. I was covering my bets."

She cut her eyes to him as she rode alongside him, their legs almost touching. "Okay, I get the engineering and business degrees. But psychology?"

He wondered what she was really asking. "I'm fascinated by people and what makes them tick. Like you," he said, smiling at her. "You're a mystery to me."

"Let's not go there."

"What if I can't help myself?"

"Mr. Savage—"

He laughed. "Maybe before this is over I'll get a glimpse of the real Jack Wilde," he said, her gaze heating him more than the sun beating down from overhead.

He could see that she wished she hadn't started this conversation when she urged her horse forward, trotting off after Arlen Dubois.

As Dillon stared after her retreating backside, he suspected he and the real Jacklyn Wilde were more alike than she ever wanted to admit—and he said as much when he caught up to her.

JACKLYN PRETENDED NOT TO hear him. His voice had dropped to a low murmur that felt like a whisper across her skin. It vibrated in her chest, making her nipples tighten and warmth rush through her, straight to her center.

Dillon chuckled, as if suspecting only too well what his words did to her.

She cursed her foolishness. She should have known

better than to try to egg Dillon Savage on. He was much better at playing head games than she was.

In front of her, Arlen brought his horse up short. She did the same when she noticed the cut barbed wire fence. Dismounting, she handed the cowboy her reins and walked across the soft earth toward the gap.

There was one set of horseshoe tracks in the dirt on the other side of the cut fence, a half-dozen on this side, obliterating Tom's horse's prints. Sheriff McCray and his men. She could see where they had ridden all over, trampling any evidence.

But she no longer thought McCray had planted the lucky gold coin. Not after both Dillon's and Arlen's re-actions. She just didn't know what a coin belonging to the deceased Halsey Waters had to do with this ring of rustlers. But she suspected Dillon and Arlen did.

Bending down, she noted that there was nothing unique about the trespasser's horse's prints. She could see where Tom had followed the man toward the creek bottom.

Arlen Dubois had tracked Tom and found him. At least that was the cowboy's story. Unfortunately, Mc-Cray and his men had destroyed any evidence to prove it.

She swung back into her saddle. "Show me where you found Tom," she said to Arlen. Turning, she looked back at Dillon. He seemed lost in thought, frowning down at the cut barbed wire.

"Something troubling you?" she asked him.

He seemed to come out of his daze, putting a smile on his face to cover whatever had been bothering him. If he was the leader of the rustlers, then wouldn't he feel something for a man who might die because of him and his partners in crime?

She followed the trampled tracks in the dust, feeling the hot sun overhead. It wasn't until she reached the trees and started up the hillside that she turned, and wasn't surprised to see Arlen and Dillon sitting astride their horses, engaged in what appeared to be a very serious conversation below her.

At the top of the ridge, she found bloodstained earth and scuffed tracks—dozens of boot prints. There was no way to distinguish the trespasser's. Had that been Sheriff McCray's intent? To destroy the evidence? Her one chance to maybe find out who the rustlers were? McCray would do it out of spite.

But there was another explanation, she realized. McCray might be covering for someone. Or even involved…

She couldn't imagine any reason Claude McCray would get involved in rustling. But then, she wasn't the best judge of character when it came to men, she admitted as she looked down the slope to where Dillon and Arlen were waiting.

By circling the area, she found the trespasser's tracks, and followed them to where he'd made a second cut in the barbed wire to let himself and his horse onto state grazing land.

Then she headed back to where she'd left the two men. As she approached, she noticed that Dillon had ridden over to a lone tree and was lounging under it, chewing on a piece of dried grass, his long legs stretched out and crossed at the ankles, his hat tilted down, but his eyes on her. He couldn't have looked more relaxed.

Or more sexy. She couldn't help but wonder what he'd been talking about with Arlen.

Back at the ranch, she let Dillon unsaddle their horses while she went out to the barn, where Arlen was putting his own horse and tack away. He seemed surprised to see her, obviously hoping that she'd already left.

"Thanks for your help today," she said, wondering what he would do for a job if Tom Robinson didn't make it. "Looks like you could use a new pair of boots."

Arlen looked down in surprise. "These are my lucky boots," he said bashfully. He lifted one leg to touch the worn leather, and Jack saw how the sole was worn evenly across the bottom.

Lucky boots. Good-luck coin. Cowboys were a superstitious bunch. "You'll be walking on your socks pretty soon," she said. "I saw you talking to Dillon. Mind telling me what you two were chatting about?"

Arlen gave a lazy shrug. "Nothin' in particular. Just talking about prison and Tom and—" he dropped his gaze "—you. Don't mean to tell you your business, but if I were you, I'd be real careful around him. When he's smiling is when he's the most dangerous."

DILLON WATCHED JACK COME out of the barn, and knew Arlen had said something to upset her.

Dillon had loaded the horses into the trailer and was leaning against the side, waiting for her in the shade. He hadn't been able to get Halsey's good-luck coin off his mind.

"Get what you needed?" he asked as Jack walked past him to climb behind the wheel.

He opened his door and slid in.

"I saw you and Arlen talking. Looked pretty serious," she said, without reaching to start the truck.

"Think we were plotting something?" He laughed.

"You said yourself that the rustlers might work for the ranchers they were stealing cattle from."

Dillon let out a snort. "Arlen? That cowboy can't keep his mouth shut. If he was riding with the gang, you'd have already caught them. The guy is a dim bulb."

Maybe. Or maybe that's what Dillon wanted her to believe. She looked back at Arlen. He was standing in the shade of the barn, watching them.

Dillon sighed. "I was asking him what he was going to do now. He said even if Tom regains consciousness, his injuries are such that he won't be running the ranch anymore. Waters has offered Arlen a job."

"What's wrong with that?" Jacklyn asked, as she heard Dillon curse under his breath.

"Arlen? He's worthless. Tom just kept him on because no one else would hire him. The only reason Waters would make the offer is so Arlen keeps him informed on everything that's going on with Tom and the ranch." At her confused look, Dillon added, "Waters has been trying to buy the Robinson ranch for years."

"Tom is in no condition to sell his ranch—"

"Tom has a niece back East, his only living relative. In his will, apparently he set it up so if anything happened to him and he couldn't run the place or he died…."

"You think she'll sell to Shade Waters."

"Waters will make sure she does."

Jacklyn could understand how Shade might want Tom Robinson's ranch. With it, he would own all the

way to the Missouri on this side of the Judith River.
The Robinson spread had been the only thing standing in his way.

CHAPTER SEVEN

JACKLYN FOLLOWED THE county road as it wound around one section of land after another, until she saw the sign that marked the various directions to ranches in the area.

At one time there'd been a dozen signs tacked on the wooden post. But over the years, most ranches had been bought out, all of them by Shade Waters.

Now there were only three signs on the post, pointing to Shade Waters's W Bar Ranch, Tom Robinson's ranch and Reda Harper's RH Circle Cross.

Jacklyn saw Dillon glance at the signs, his gaze hardening before it veered away. Not far up the road, she turned to drive under an arched entry with W Bar Ranch carved into the graying wood.

"I'll stay in the pickup," he said as she pulled up in the ranch yard.

She looked at him, then at the sprawling ranch house. Shade Walters had come out onto the porch. Always a big man, he wasn't quite as handsome as he'd been in his younger days, but he was still striking. He stood in the shadow of the porch roof, an imposing figure that demanded attention.

The front door opened again and his son Nate came out, letting the door slam behind him. She saw Shade's irritated expression and the way he scowled in Nate's direction.

Nate was in his early thirties, big boned and blond. Unlike his father, his western clothing was new and obviously expensive. Shade Waters looked like every working rancher she'd known, from his worn western shirt to his faded jeans and weathered boots.

She couldn't help but think that whoever had attacked Tom Robinson had come by way of the W Bar, Shade Waters's land.

Nate was staring toward her passenger, and it dawned on her that Dillon and he were close in age and must have gone to school together. The old Savage place had been up the road. Had they once been friends, as had Dillon and Nate's brother, Halsey?

Nate's frown and the intense silence coming from the man next to her made it clear that the two were no longer friends, whatever their relationship had been in the past.

"You won't get out of the pickup no matter what happens?" she asked quietly, without looking at Dillon.

"Nope."

As Jacklyn started to open her door, a pretty, dark-haired woman joined the two men on the porch. Jacklyn felt Dillon tense beside her. The woman looped her arm through Nate's and gazed out at the pickup, as if daring anyone to try to stop her—including Shade Waters. Judging from his expression, he wasn't happy to see the woman join him, any more than he had been his son.

But it was Dillon's reaction that made Jacklyn hesitate before she climbed out of the truck.

Dillon knew the woman. Not just knew her. His left hand was clenched in a fist and his jaw was tight with anger.

She knew he blamed Shade Waters for what had happened not just to his family ranch but to his father. But was there more to the story? Was there a woman involved?

This dark-haired beauty?

"Holler if you need me," Dillon said as she started to climb out of the truck.

She shot him a look as he drew the brim of his hat down over his eyes and leaned back as if planning to sleep until she returned.

Right. As if he wouldn't be watching and listening to everything that was said. She noticed that he'd managed to power down his window before she turned off the pickup engine.

"Enjoy your nap," she said, knowing he wouldn't.

His lips tipped up in a smile. He wasn't fooling her and he knew it.

As Jacklyn closed the truck door, she noticed that the woman had her own gaze fixed on the passenger side of the pickup. On Dillon.

Jacklyn knew there'd been women in Dillon's life. Probably a lot of them. Had he turned to crime because of one of them? Maybe this one?

Jacklyn approached the porch slowly, afraid all hell was about to break loose. She just hoped Dillon Savage wasn't going to be in the middle of it.

MORGAN LANDERS. Dillon couldn't believe his eyes. He'd heard she'd gone to California. Or Florida. That she'd snagged some old guy with lots of bucks.

But as he watched her lean intimately into Nate Waters, Dillon knew he shouldn't have been surprised that Morgan had come back—or why.

What did surprise him was his reaction to seeing her. He hadn't expected ever to lay eyes on her again. Especially not here. It felt like another betrayal, but then he suspected it wasn't her first. Or her last.

What bothered him was that he knew Jack had seen his reaction. She missed little. Now she would think he still felt something for Morgan.

From under his hat, he watched Jack walk to the bottom step of the porch. Clearly, Shade Waters wasn't going to invite her inside the house. Manners had never been the man's strong suit. No, Waters wanted to intimidate her. How better than to stand on the porch, literally looking down on her?

Dillon smiled to himself. He'd put his money on Jack anyday, though. Not even Shade Waters could intimidate a woman like Jacklyn Wilde.

The rancher glanced at the pickup, no doubt seeing that Dillon had has side window down. Another reason Waters wouldn't invite Jack inside. He'd want Dillon to hear whatever he had to say. And Dillon was sure Waters had a lot to say, given that he'd demanded Jack stop by to see him.

Also, Dillon thought with a grin, Waters wouldn't want to go in the house knowing that a Savage was on his property, alone. Waters would be afraid of what Dillon might do.

As Dillon shifted his gaze from Morgan Landers to the elderly man he'd spent years hating, he thought Waters was wise to worry.

JACKLYN LOOKED UP at the three standing on the porch. They made no move to step aside so she could enter the house—or even join them in the shade.

"I can handle this," Shade said, scowling over at his son. But Nate didn't move. Nor did the woman beside him.

Jacklyn couldn't help being curious about the woman, given that Dillon obviously had some connection to her. "I don't believe we've met," she said. "I'm Jacklyn Wilde."

The brunette had the kind of face and body that could stop traffic, but that had nothing to do with the dislike Jacklyn had felt for her instantly.

"Morgan Landers." She flicked her gaze over Jacklyn dismissively, her brown eyes lighting again on the pickup and no doubt the passenger sitting in it.

"If we're through with introductions…" Shade Waters snapped.

Jacklyn waited. She could see how agitated the rancher was, but wasn't entirely certain it had anything to do with her.

"Do you people have any idea what you're doing?" he finally demanded, tilting his head toward the pickup and Dillon.

"You want the rustlers caught?" she asked, resenting him trying to tell her how to do her job.

Waters smirked. "The rustler was *already* behind bars. That is, until you got him out. What the hell were you thinking?"

"Dillon Savage is my problem."

"You're right about that," the big man said angrily. "You going to try to tell me he doesn't know anything about what's been going on?"

She wasn't. Nor was she about to admit that she suspected the same thing he did when it came to Dillon Savage.

"It's his boys who are stealing all the cattle," Waters said with a curse. "That bunch he used to run around with. He's been orchestrating the whole thing from prison, and now you go and get him out so he can lead you in circles. You don't really think he's going to help you catch them, do you?"

"What bunch are we talking about?" she asked, ignoring the rest of what he'd said.

"Buford Cole, Pete Barclay, Arlen Dubois—that bunch," Waters snapped.

"What makes you think it's them? Or are you just making unfounded accusations? Because if you have some evidence—"

Waters let out another curse. "Hell, if I had evidence I'd take it to Sheriff McCray and the rustlers would be behind bars. Everyone in the county knows that Buford Cole and Arlen Dubois were riding with Savage before he went to prison."

"There was never any evidence—"

"Don't give me that evidence bull," Waters snapped. "Just because you couldn't prove it."

"I'm confused. Arlen Dubois just told me you offered him a job. If you really believe he's one of the rustlers…"

Waters's smile never reached his eyes. "Sometimes it's better to have the fox living in the henhouse so you can keep an eye on him. That's one reason I hired Pete Barclay. He also used to run with Savage."

That was also never proved, but she decided not to argue the point. "What about Buford Cole?"

"He's working at the stockyard," Waters stated, and raised a brow as if that said everything.

She looked at Nate. "Didn't you used to run with those same cowboys?"

Nate appeared surprised that she'd said anything to him. "What?"

"I heard you were all friends, including Dillon and your brother, Halsey."

The older Waters's face blanched and he looked as if he might suddenly grab his chest and keel over.

"Now just a minute," Nate said.

"What the hell are you trying to do?" Waters interrupted, taking a step toward her. "Don't you ever bring up Halsey's name in the same breath as those others!"

She noticed he was fine with Nate's name being mentioned with the others. Nate had noticed it, too, and was scowling in his father's direction.

"I'm just saying that because this group used to be friends, there is no evidence they are now involved in rustling cattle together." Her gaze went to Morgan Landers. She was smiling as if enjoying this.

"The damn rustlers are closing in on my ranch. Even you should be able to see that." Waters's face was now flushed, his voice breaking with emotion. "I can't protect my land or my livestock, not even if I hire a hundred men. Not when half of the range is badlands and only accessible by horseback."

She wanted to point out that the rustlers would have the same problem. But Waters was right. Huge sections of his land were inaccessible except by horseback, and given the size of the place, it would take several days to ride across the length of the W Bar. No amount of men could protect it completely.

"Your ranch hasn't been hit by the rustlers," she

pointed out. "Do you have some reason to believe it will be?"

Waters looked flustered, something she didn't think happened often. "They must know I'll shoot to kill if they try to take my cattle."

"I wouldn't advise that," Jacklyn said.

"Then what are you going to do to stop them?" he demanded.

"I'm going to catch them, but I'll need your help. Tell me where your cattle are, what precautions you've taken and what men you have available to guard the key borders."

Waters looked at her, then glanced toward the pickup and laughed. "You don't really think I'm going to give you that information, do you? Why don't I just run it in the newspaper so the rustlers know exactly when and where to steal my cattle?"

"If this is about Mr. Savage—"

"You can try to explain until you're blue in the face why you got Dillon Savage out of prison, young woman, but I'm not giving you a damn thing. I'll take care of my stock as best I can. Just know I'll do whatever I have to, and that includes killing the sons of bitches." He was looking toward the truck again. "I have the right to protect my property."

"Mr. Waters—"

"I don't have time for this," he said, and thumped down the steps and past her, headed toward the barn.

"Like we're going to hold our breaths and wait for you to catch the rustlers," his son muttered.

"Shut up, Nate," Waters snapped over his shoulder.

"Mr. Waters," Jacklyn said, trailing after him. "I

want your permission to put some video devices on your ranch. If you're right, the rustlers have probably been watching your operation already."

"No," he said, without stopping or looking back. "I told you I was going to take care of things my own way."

"If your own way is illegal—"

He swung around so fast she almost ran into him. "Listen, maybe you will catch the rustlers. But it won't be on my ranch. I won't be spied on."

"Spied on?"

"Videos and all that paraphernalia. No. Maybe that's the way it's done nowadays, but I don't want a bunch of your people on my land, and I know for a fact you can't force them on me."

Jacklyn glanced back at the truck. She couldn't see Dillon's face through the sunlight glinting off the windshield, but she knew he hadn't missed a thing.

Then she followed Shade Waters into the barn, determined to do her job despite him.

DILLON WATCHED MORGAN give him a backward glance before she followed Nate Waters into the house. She'd stared in his direction, as if she'd been expecting to see him.

Unlike him, who hadn't been prepared to see her again ever. As the front door closed, he sat without moving, bombarded by memories of the two of them.

Morgan. There'd been a time when she'd made him think about buying another ranch and settling down. But even Morgan couldn't still the quiet rage inside him. Not that Morgan had wanted him to be anything but a rustler. She liked the drama. She'd never wanted him to quit rustling.

She was hooked on the danger, never knowing when he would sneak into town and into her bed, never knowing if her house would be raided by the sheriff's men.

And since Morgan had no way of knowing about Dillon's inheritance, she'd just assumed he would never have enough money to keep her in the way she wanted to live, so she'd never even mentioned marriage. And he'd never told her different.

He wondered idly if she was serious about Nate Waters. Or if she was only serious about his money. Morgan would like the power that came with the Waters name, as well.

As Jacklyn disappeared into the barn with the rancher, Dillon fought the turmoil he felt inside. Seeing Morgan had brought back the past in a blinding flash. All his good intentions not to let what had happened drag him back into trouble again seemed to fly out the window. He felt the full power of the old bitterness, the resentment, the injustice that burned like hot oil inside him.

Worse, while he'd always suspected that he'd been set up four years ago, that someone close to him had betrayed him, he hadn't wanted to believe it.

In prison, he'd told himself it didn't matter. That all of that was behind him.

But as he thought about the look Morgan had given him before going back into the house, the image now branded on his mind, he knew it *did* matter—would always matter. He'd been kidding himself if he thought he could forgive and forget—at least not until he found out who had betrayed him.

And Morgan was as good as any place to start.

JACKLYN SHOULD HAVE SAVED her breath. Shade Waters was impossible. She'd tried to talk to him, but he seemed distracted as he looked in on one of the horses. She saw him frown and touch the horse's side, apparently surprised to find that it was damp, as if recently ridden.

"Is something wrong?" she asked, noting that he seemed upset.

He shook his head irritably. "I told you. I don't have time for this. Shouldn't you be out looking for the rustlers instead of driving me crazy?" he snapped, then sighed, looking his age for a moment. "I just got a call a few minutes before you got here. Tom Robinson's condition is worse."

Her heart dropped, and instantly she felt guilty, because she'd been praying he would regain consciousness. She'd been counting on Tom being able to identify at least one of the rustlers.

"I'm sorry to hear that," she said, a little surprised how hard Waters was taking the news, given that he would now probably get the Robinson ranch, just as Dillon had said. Was Tom's worsened condition really what had Waters upset?

The rancher didn't seem to hear her as he began to wipe down the horse. Jacklyn wondered where Pete Barclay was.

She let herself out of the barn, knowing she wasn't going to get anywhere with him. But she couldn't shake the feeling that Dillon Savage might be right. Maybe there was more going on than she'd thought.

As she started toward her pickup, what she saw stopped her dead. The truck was empty. Dillon Savage was gone.

CHAPTER EIGHT

JACKLYN COULDN'T BELIEVE her eyes. No. For just an instant there, she'd believed Dillon, believed she'd been wrong about him, believed he really was trying to help her catch the rustlers.

What a fool she was!

"Excuse me," she said as she spotted a man trimming a hedge that ran along one side of the ranch house. "Did you happen to notice the man who was waiting in the pickup?" She pointed to her truck.

He nodded, shoving back his hat to wipe the sweat from his forehead. "He said to tell you he'd meet you in town if he missed you."

She raised a brow. Town was twenty miles away. Trying not to show her panic or her fury, she asked, "And how, exactly, was he planning to get back to town? Did he say?"

The man shrugged. "He said he needed to take a walk."

Take a walk? Oh, he'd taken a walk all right. She would kill him when she found him. And she *would* find him.

She thanked the gardener and, hoping Shade Waters wasn't watching, tried not to storm to the pickup. There were going to be enough people saying I told you so, starting with Waters.

As she climbed in and started the engine, she looked down the long dirt road. Empty. Just like the truck.

Still fighting panic and fury, she drove until she topped a hill and couldn't see the ranch house anymore. Pulling over, she opened the tracking receiver terminal and started to push the on button, afraid of what she would find.

She knew Dillon Savage. Better than she wanted to. He was too smart. Too charming. Too arrogant for words. But there was something about him, something wounded that had softened her heart to him four years ago, when she'd captured him.

How could he do this? Didn't he realize it was going to get him sent back to prison? Unless he thought he could evade her as he had for so long before.

But the only way he could do that was to disable the monitoring device or cut the thing out. If he had, she'd be lucky if she ever saw him again.

She wasn't even thinking about her career or her anger as she turned on the receiver terminal, her heart in her throat. In those few seconds, she felt such a sense of dread and disappointment that she only got more angry—angry at feeling anything at all for this man.

Until that moment, she hadn't realized how badly she wanted to believe in his innocence.

The steady beep from the terminal startled her. "I'll be…" According to this, he was still on the ranch—and moving in her direction.

Or at least his monitoring device was.

If she drove on up the road, she should connect with him about a half mile from here.

Why would he head for the road, when he could have gotten lost in the mountains and led her on a wild-goose chase? One that she wouldn't have been able to hide from her boss?

As she topped the next rise, she spotted a figure walking nonchalantly across open pasture, headed for the road. He had to have heard the pickup approaching, and yet he didn't look up. Nor did he make any attempt to run away.

He vaulted over the barbed wire fence as she brought the truck to a dust-boiling stop next to him.

She was out of the vehicle, her hand on the butt of her pistol, before he reached the road.

"Don't you ever do that again," she shouted at him.

He held up both hands in surrender.

Had he grinned, she feared she would have pulled the pistol and shot him.

"I'm sorry. I couldn't very well tell you where I was going under the circumstances," he said contritely.

"Circumstances?"

"You were with Shade Waters, and I didn't want him to know I was following one of his stock trucks."

She stared at Dillon. "Why would you follow one of the Waters's stock trucks?" she demanded suspiciously.

"To see what was going on." He glanced up as if he heard someone coming. "Could we talk about this somewhere besides the middle of a county road?"

She sighed, torn between anger and overwhelming relief. She removed her hand from her gun butt and turned back toward the pickup. She'd left the driver's door open. As she slid behind the wheel, he climbed in the passenger side and saw the monitoring device on the seat between them.

"Thought I'd skipped out on you, did you?" He chuckled. "So much for trust. You want me to help you catch these guys? Then you have to give me a little leeway. Keep me on too short a leash and I'm useless to you."

She wasn't so sure he wasn't useless to her, anyway. "So why did you follow the stock truck?"

"I went for a little walk. Took your binoculars," he said, handing them back to her. "Hope you don't mind. I just happened to see a couple of ranch hands loading something into the back of a stock truck. They acted suspicious, you know? Looking around a lot. I made sure they didn't see me, and when the truck stopped so one could open the gate, I hopped in the back."

As she got the pickup moving, she looked over at Dillon, convinced he was either lying or crazy or both. Then she caught a whiff of his clothing and wrinkled her nose. "Let me guess what was in the back. Something dead."

"Half-a-dozen dead calves."

She shot him a look, the truck swerving on the gravel road. "They were probably just taking them to the dump."

He shook his head. "They were headed north. Waters's dump is to the south."

"He probably has a new dump since you've been here," she said irritably. "Why would you get in the truck with the dead calves?"

He lifted a brow. "*Six* dead calves. Doesn't that make even *you* suspicious?"

Everything made her suspicious. Especially him. "Every rancher loses a few calves—"

"Six all dead at the same time? Not unless they're sick with something."

She glanced over at him. "What do you think killed them?"

"Lead poisoning." He grinned at her obvious surprise. "That's right, Jack, they each had a bullet hole right between their eyes. But that's not the best part. They were missing a patch of hide—right where their brands should have been—and notches had been cut in their ears. You guessed it, no ear tags."

She slammed on the brakes, bringing the truck to another jarring stop. "What are you talking about?"

He nodded, still grinning. "I knew Shade Waters was still up to no good."

Jacklyn was shaking her head. "You went looking for trouble, didn't you? This walk you took, you just happened along on a stock truck with six possibly rustled dead calves? Where was this?"

"A mile or so from the ranch house."

Her brows shot up.

"I walk fast. I figured I'd be back before you finished with Waters. I told the gardener so you wouldn't worry. I'm telling you the truth, Jack. I swear."

She glared at him and turned back to her driving, not believing anything he said. "So who were these ranch hands?"

"I didn't get a good look at them. When the truck started moving, I took off running, so I could jump in the back."

"Right. But you're sure they work for Waters?" she asked, trying to rein in her temper.

"They were on his land, driving one of his stock trucks," Dillon said.

She could hear the steel in his voice. She shot him a suspicious look. He had to realize that all she had was his word for this, and right now her trust in him was more than a little shaky.

"And you have no idea where they were taking the calves," she said.

"No," he replied through gritted teeth. "North. I would assume to bury them. Look, under other circumstances, I would have stayed with that truck till the end. But I knew you'd flip if you came out and found me gone." His gaze narrowed. "And you did."

"I could have tracked you and the truck," she pointed out.

"I thought of that. But I also really didn't want every lawman in the county coming after me, ready to shoot to kill, before I got to explain that I hadn't just taken off. Even you believed that's what I'd done, didn't you?"

He was right. Even if she'd had faith that he wouldn't run off, Stratton would have had a warrant out on Dillon Savage before the ink dried.

"Plus I had no weapon and was a little concerned about when the truck got to its destination," Dillon said. "I didn't want to end up buried with those calves. For all I knew they might have been meeting more ranch hands up the road."

If he was telling the truth, he'd done the only thing he could do. And if so, he'd certainly made more progress than she had in the case.

"I'm sorry," she said. "You did the right thing." She could feel his gaze on her.

"You believe me then?"

She glanced back at him. "Let's say I'm considering the possibility that you're telling the truth."

To her surprise, he laughed. "Jack, you're killing me. But at least that's progress." He turned toward her.

"Don't you see, this proves what I've been saying. Waters is your man. He's behind this rustling ring."

She met his gaze, knowing he was capable of making up this whole thing to even the score with his archenemy. "You can't be objective when it comes to Waters."

"There's a reason his ranch hasn't been hit by the rustlers and you know it," Dillon said.

She shook her head. All she knew was that if Dillon was behind the rustling, then by not stealing from Waters, he would make him look guilty. Just as coming up with a story about a stock truck filled with bullet-ridden calves missing their brands would do.

"You're trying to tell me that Waters is rustling cattle from his neighbors, then killing them, cutting off the brands and ear tags and burying them? Why? He's not even making any money, that I can see, on the deal."

Dillon rolled his eyes. "Waters doesn't need the money. I told you there was another motive. He's getting something out of this, trust me."

She shook her head. "I know you believe he was the cause of your father losing his ranch, but you have to realize there were other factors." She saw his jaw tighten.

"I do. Dad made some business mistakes after my mother died. But ultimately, Waters wanted our ranch and he got it."

"Exactly. He's bought up almost all of the ranches around him, so what—"

"There are still two he wants. And with Tom Robinson gone, he's got that one. That leaves the Harper place."

"Reda will never sell," Jacklyn said, remembering her visit to the Harper ranch when she was talking to local folks about the rustlers. "She hates Waters. Maybe worse than you do."

Dillon lifted a brow. "We'll see. Tom said he'd never sell, either. Jack, we have to get on Waters's ranch and find out where they're taking those calves. You want evidence? It's on the W Bar."

"And what do you suggest I do? Trespass? Waters has already said he won't have us on his ranch."

Dillon grinned. "We need to make Waters think we aren't anywhere near his ranch."

"If you're suggesting—"

"You have to make sure everyone believes you've gotten a new lead and will be to the south, nowhere near the W Bar."

She shook her head. "Stratton would never let me do that."

"That's why you have to tell him you got a tip that the Murray ranch is going to be hit."

"Lie?" Jacklyn fought the sick feeling in the pit of her stomach. "Are you trying to set me up?" she asked, her voice little more than a whisper.

Dillon didn't answer. She looked over at him and saw anger as hard as granite in his blue eyes. "Waters is your man. You want to catch the rustlers?"

She couldn't even acknowledge that with a response.

"When are you going to trust me? I'll tell you what. Let's put something on it. A small wager."

"I don't want your money."

"Don't worry, you won't get it. No, I was thinking of something more fun."

She shot him a warning look.

"A dance. If I'm right, you'll owe me a dance."

"And if you're wrong and it turns out you're involved with this rustling ring?" she asked, studying him as she headed for Lewistown.

He grinned. "Then I'll be back in prison. What do you have to lose? One dance. Deal?"

Was he that sure she'd never prove he was involved? Or was he really innocent—this time? "Deal," she said, ninety-nine percent certain she would never be dancing with Dillon Savage, and a little sad about it.

"So are you going to take my advice?" he said as they shook on their bet.

Not a chance. Waters didn't want her on his ranch. She'd have to get a warrant to go there and she had no evidence to get Stratton to go along with it, not to mention a judge.

"There's a meeting of the ranchers this evening in town," she said noncommittally. "Let's see how that goes."

REDA HARPER CHECKED the time on the dash of her pickup as she cut across her pasture, opened a gate posted with No Trespassing signs and, thumbing her nose at Waters and his W Bar Ranch, drove along what once had been a section road between his spread and the Savage Ranch.

The road had long since grown over with weeds, but Reda was in one of her moods, and when she got like this, she just flat-out refused to drive past the W Bar ranch house. She not only didn't want to see Shade Waters, she also didn't want him seeing her.

As she drove, darkness settled in, forcing her to turn on her headlights. The last thing she wanted was to be caught trespassing on Shade's land. Her own fault. As it would be if she was late for the meeting Shade Waters had called about the rustling problem.

"If you're late, it's your own blamed fault for being so stubborn," she told herself as her pickup jostled along. "You should have taken the main road. Shade is probably already in town, anyway. Damn foolish woman."

On the other hand, it aggravated her that she had to take the back roads to town to avoid seeing Shade Waters. Just the thought of him angered her. She would blame him if she got caught trespassing on his land. But then, she blamed him for most everything that had happened to her in the last forty years.

She blamed herself for being a fool in the first place. What had she ever seen in Shade? Sure, he'd been handsome back then. Hell, downright charming when he'd wanted to be.

She swore at even the thought of him. It still made her sick to think about it. She hated to admit she could have been so stupid. Shade Waters had played her. Tempting her with sweet words and deeds, then reeling her in. His professed love for her nothing more than an attempt to take her ranch.

But in the end, she'd outfoxed him, she reminded herself.

As she came over a rise in the road, she saw a light flicker ahead, off to her left. She frowned as the light flashed off, pitching the terrain back into darkness— but not before her headlights had caught a stock truck pulling behind a rock bluff a good twenty yards inside the fence line.

There was nothing on this road for miles. Nothing

but sagebrush and rock. Shade didn't run cattle up here. Never had. Too close to the badlands. Too hard to round 'em all up. Not to mention he had so much land he didn't need to pasture his cattle in the vicinity.

So what would a stock truck be doing up here? As far as she knew, no one used this road. Hadn't since Waters bought the Savage Ranch.

She slowed. In her headlights, she could see where the truck had trampled the grass as it drove back between the bluffs. How odd.

Reda powered down her window, pulling the pickup to a stop to stare out. The night was black. No moon. The stars muted by wisps of clouds. She couldn't see a damn thing. If she hadn't seen the light, she would never have known there was a truck out there among the rocks.

What had her curiosity going was the way the truck had disappeared, as if the driver didn't want to be seen.

The air that wafted in the window was warm and scented with dust and sage. She listened. Not a sound. And yet she'd seen the light. Knew there was a truck in there somewhere.

She felt a cold chill and shuddered as a thought struck her. Whoever was there hadn't expected anyone on this road tonight. The driver had turned out the lights when he'd seen her come flying over the rise. For some reason he hadn't heard her approaching.

Whatever he was doing, he didn't want a witness.

Reda knew, probably better than anyone in four counties, what Waters was capable of. But she had a feeling this wasn't his doing.

On a sudden impulse, she reached for the gearshift

and the button to power up her window, telling herself she wanted no part of whatever was going on.

But as the window started to glide upward, she heard a sound behind her pickup, like the scuff of a boot sole on a rock.

Her foot tromped down on the gas pedal. The tires spat dirt and chunks of grass as she took off, her blood pounding in her ears, her hands shaking.

When she glanced into her rearview mirror, she saw the black outline of a man standing in the middle of the road.

He'd been right behind her truck.

She was shaking so hard she had trouble digging her cell phone from her purse while keeping the pickup on the road between the fence posts.

Was it possible he was one of the rustlers?

Her cell phone display read No Service. She swore and tossed the phone back into her purse. Worthless thing. She only used the damn gadget to call from town to the ranch. Only place she could get any reception.

She glanced behind her again, afraid she'd see lights. Or worse, the dark silhouette of a stock truck chasing her without its headlights on.

But the road behind her was empty.

She drove as fast as she dared, telling herself she had to notify someone. Not Shade Waters, even though it was his property. It would be a cold day in hell if she ever spoke to him again.

No, she'd drive straight to the meeting. Sheriff Mc-Cray would be there. She'd tell him what she'd seen.

Her pulse began to slow as she checked her mirror again and saw no one following her. Even in the dark, she would have been able to see the huge shape of a stock truck on the road. She was pretty darn sure she could outrun a cattle truck.

As she swung into the packed lot at the community center, she felt a little calmer. More rational.

Maybe it had been rustlers. Maybe not. Shade Waters was the only rancher who hadn't lost cattle to that band of thieves she'd been hearing about. It made sense that the rustlers had finally gotten around to stealing some of his livestock.

Except that Waters wasn't running any cattle in that area.

Reda parked and headed for the meeting. As she pushed open the door to the community center, the first man she saw was Sheriff Claude McCray. She started to rush to him, her mouth already open as she prepared to tell him about what she'd seen on the road.

But then she saw the man he was deep in conversation with: Shade Waters. Their heads were together as if they were cooking up something.

Her mouth snapped shut, the words gone like dead leaves blowing away in the wind. She walked past both men, her head held high. The sheriff didn't seem to notice her, but Shade Waters did.

She could feel his gaze on her, as intense and burning as a laser beam. She waltzed right on past without even a twinge of guilt. She hoped the rustlers cleaned Shade Waters out. Hell, she wished she had stopped and helped them.

ON THE DRIVE BACK to Lewistown, Jack had seemed lost in thought, which was just fine with Dillon. He tried not to think about Waters or the fact that Jack didn't believe him. Those problems aside, he couldn't get Morgan Landers off his mind—or the fact that she was apparently now with Nate Waters.

Jack stopped by the hospital to see how Tom Robinson was doing, and Dillon went in with her even though he hated to. The last time he'd been in a hospital was after his father's heart attack.

The moment he walked in, he was hit by the smell. It took him back instantly, filling him with grief and guilt. His father would have been only fifty-eight now, young by today's standards, if he had lived. If Shade Waters hadn't killed him as surely as if he'd held a gun to his head.

Tom was still unconscious. His recovery didn't look good, which meant that the chances of him identifying the rustlers wasn't good, either.

Dillon could see the effect that had on Jack. She'd been counting on a break in the rustling case. As they left the hospital, he could feel her anger and frustration.

"Would you please stop looking at me as if I was the one who put Tom in that hospital bed?" Dillon said as she drove back toward the motel.

"Aren't you?"

He groaned. "Jack, I'm telling you I have nothing to do with this bunch of rustlers. You've got to believe that." But of course, she didn't have to.

She shot him a quizzical look. Clearly, she didn't believe anything he said.

"How can I convince you?" he asked. "We already know who the rustler is, but you don't believe that, either. I told you what we have to do to catch him, except you aren't willing to do that. So what else can I say?" He shook his head.

"Don't you find it interesting that some of your old friends are working ranches around here?" she asked.

So she'd been thinking about some of the cowboys he'd run around with: Pete Barclay, Buford Cole, Arlen Dubois.

"*Former* friends," he said. "We haven't been close for years. A lifetime ago."

"I know for a fact that Buford Cole came to visit you in prison."

It shouldn't have taken him by surprise, but it did. Of course she would have checked to see who his visitors had been during his four years at Montana State Prison.

"Buford and I used to be close," he admitted. "He only came that one time. I haven't heard from him since."

"What about Pete Barclay?"

Dillon chuckled. "Yeah, he came to visit me in prison several times."

"He works for Waters."

"I'm aware of that. You want to know why he came to see me?" Dillon asked. "To deliver threats from his boss about when I got out."

She swung her gaze to him. "Is that true?"

"I told you I don't lie."

"Right. How could I forget?" She pulled into the motel parking lot and glanced at her watch. "We have to get to the ranchers' meeting. I just need to change." She settled her gaze on him. "Maybe you shouldn't go. You could stay in the motel room. You'd be monitored the whole time, of course."

"Of course," he said disagreeably. He hated to be reminded of how little freedom he had. Or how little trust she had in him. Not that he could blame her. He hated being constantly watched. But that was the deal, wasn't it?

"I'm going with you," he said, meeting her gaze head-on.

"I'm not sure that's a good idea."

"I'm not afraid of any of them, and I have nothing to hide."

She gave him one of her rock-hard looks, as if nothing could move her.

"Jack, come on. You think I have that much control over everything that is happening now?" He couldn't help but smile and shake his head. "You give me too much credit."

"On the contrary. I think you are capable of just about anything you set your mind to."

He made a face, recognizing his own words to her earlier. "That almost sounded like a compliment," he joked. "So you got me out of prison thinking you'd give me enough rope that I'd hang myself? That's it, isn't it?" He saw that he'd hit too close to home, and chuckled at her expression.

"If not you, then who?" she demanded. "And don't tell me Shade Waters." She cocked an eyebrow at him, her eyes the color of gunmetal. There was a pleading in her expression. "Whoever is leading this band of rustlers is too good at this. Is it possible there is someone who's even better than the great Dillon Savage?"

He shrugged, but admitted to himself that she had a point. Waters was a lot of things, but what did he know about rustling? Whoever was leading the ring knew what he was doing. But if it wasn't Shade Waters, was it someone who worked for him?

CHAPTER NINE

THE LOT WAS full of pickups as Jacklyn tried to find a place to park at the community center. Clearly, many ranchers had arrived early, not about to miss this.

She couldn't help but think it was the last place Dillon wanted to be. She looked around for a large tree, figuring one of the ranchers might have a rope and this could end in a hangin' before the night was over. And it would be Dillon Savage's neck in the noose.

"I'd prefer if you don't say anything during the meeting," she said as she cut the engine and looked over at him.

"No problem." He glanced toward the building. All the lights were on and a muted roar came from inside. A few ranchers were out on the steps, smoking and talking in the darkness. They'd all glanced toward the state pickup as she'd parked.

"You sure about this?" she asked.

"If I don't go in," Dillon said, "they'll assume you're trying to protect me."

That was exactly what she hoped to do. "Maybe I'm trying to protect us both."

He smiled at that. "We're both more than capable of taking care of ourselves."

She wasn't so sure. The ranchers were furious. Shade Waters had them all stirred up about Dillon being out of prison. And unfortunately, Dillon had enemies in there waiting for him—and so did she.

Jacklyn stepped from the pickup, her hand going to the gun at her hip as she started toward the community center and the angry-looking men now blocking the doorway. Dillon walked next to her. She dreaded the moment he would come face-to-face with Shade Waters, not sure what either of them would do.

The men on the steps finally parted so she and Dillon could enter. The room was already buzzing as she pushed open the door. She wasn't surprised to find the center packed, a sea of Stetsons.

As she started down the aisle between the chairs, she could feel Dillon right behind her. A wave of stunned silence seemed to fill the place, followed at once by a louder buzzing of voices as heads turned. They hadn't expected her to bring Dillon. He'd been right about coming.

She didn't look at any of them as she made her way toward the front of the room. But Shade Waters stopped her before she could reach it. "No one invited you. Or your *friend*."

Dillon Savage was far from her friend, but she wasn't here to debate that with Waters.

"I'm here to clear up a few things," she said over the drone of voices.

"Things are damn clear," Waters said angrily. "The state isn't doing a thing to protect us ranchers."

"What's this *us?*" called a female voice from near the front. "Your cattle haven't been stolen. So what are you all worked up about?"

Jacklyn recognized the strident voice as Reda Harper's.

"You think my ranch isn't next?" Waters demanded

to the crowd, apparently ignoring Reda. "Only it won't be fifty head of cattle. The bastards will hit me harder than any of you, and we all know it."

"That's why I'm here," Jacklyn said. "So that doesn't happen. But just this afternoon you denied me access to your land."

There were murmurs from the crowd.

"And you know damn well why," Waters snapped, glaring at Dillon.

Was Dillon the reason? Or was he telling the truth and there was a lot more going on here than missing cattle.

"You didn't protect *my* ranch," said an angry male voice.

"You're finally going to do something because it's the W Bar?" called another. "What about the rest of us?"

"Let her talk," cried one of the ranchers.

"Yeah, I'd like to hear what she has to say," Reda declared.

Waters scowled at Jacklyn, visibly upset that she'd come, and maybe even more upset that Reda Harper had been heckling him. He turned his scowl on Dillon and cursed. "I'd like to hear what Dillon Savage has to say for himself," Waters bellowed.

A few in the crowd were agreeing with him as Jacklyn stepped up on the stage. She glanced around the room, recognizing most of the faces. Waters's son, Nate, was slumped in the first row, looking bored.

As she stepped behind the podium, Dillon joined her, standing back but facing the angry crowd.

"Yeah, what the hell is the story?" called out one of the ranchers. "You get a rustler out to catch rustlers? What kind of sense is that?"

She raised a hand. When the room finally quieted, she waited for Shade Waters to sit down, glancing at him pointedly until he took his seat.

"Most of you know me. I'm Stock Detective Jacklyn Wilde," she began. "And I know most of you. Because of that you know I'm doing everything I can to catch the rustlers." She hurried on as the room threatened to erupt again.

"Dillon Savage is helping with the investigation of the rustling ring operating in this area." As expected, a wave of protests rang out. Again she raised a hand and waited patiently for the room to go quiet.

"I will not debate my decision to have Mr. Savage released early to help in that investigation. You want the rustlers caught?" she demanded, above the shouts and angry accusations. "Then listen to me."

"We've listened to you long enough," Shade Waters said, getting to his feet again. "It's time we took matters into our own hands."

"That's right!" A dozen ranchers were on their feet.

She saw her boss and several others come in through the back door. Chief Brand Inspector Allan Stratton walked up the aisle to the stage and stepped to the podium, practically shoving her aside.

Jacklyn edged back, hating the son of a bitch for upstaging her in front of the ranchers.

"Finally we're going to get some answers," Waters called. "You sent us a damn woman, when we need a man for *this* job."

Others began to applaud Stratton, echoing Waters's sentiments.

Jacklyn felt her face flame. It was all she could do not to walk off the stage. She felt Dillon move to her side, as if in a show of support for her. The move would only antagonize the ranchers, and worse, Sheriff Mc-Cray, whom she spotted standing on the sidelines, glaring at her.

Stratton raised his arms and waited for the room to quiet down before he spoke. "I don't have to tell any of you how hard it is to stop rustlers. Livestock are a very lucrative source of income."

There were nods across the room, some murmurs.

"A thief who breaks into a house and steals a television or CD player can try to sell the equipment either at a pawnshop or on the black market, but will likely only get about ten percent of the actual value of the property," Stratton continued. "Someone who steals a cow, on the other hand, can sell the animal at a packing plant or an auction market and receive one hundred percent of the value."

There were more murmurs of agreement, but some restless movement as the smarter ranchers began to realize Stratton wasn't telling them anything they didn't already know.

"Improvements in transportation, the interstate, bigger cattle trailers, all make it easier for criminals to load up cattle and haul them across state lines before you even realize the animals are missing," he continued. "I don't have to tell you that thieves can steal more and move farther and faster than in the old days. A rustler can steal cattle here today, and this afternoon or early tomorrow morning be in Tennessee or California."

"Don't you think we know all that?" one of the ranchers demanded.

"What I can tell you is that we need to work together to stop these rustlers," Stratton said.

"You know a lot of us can't afford to hire more hands or buy special equipment," a man said from the front row.

"The state can't afford to hire staff to watch your cattle, either," Stratton said, as if it hurt him personally to say that. "That's why we need each of you to help us. Experienced cattle thieves will watch a ranch for a while, get to know the schedule of the owner and hired hands, and the times of day when no one will be around. You can keep an eye out for strangers hanging around or hired help that's too curious."

Jacklyn couldn't believe Stratton thought the rustling gang was that stupid. They weren't like some bumbling amateurs who left a gas receipt or wallet at the scene of the crime. These guys always got away clean. Except possibly for a good-luck coin. And even that could have been dropped by anyone at any time.

But for sure, the rustlers wouldn't be asking stupid questions of ranchers.

"You can also run checks on the men you hire," Stratton was saying, over an uproar from the floor. "I know society is so mobile that you're lucky to get a ranch hand to stay a season, let alone longer, and most ranches don't keep good records when it comes to seasonal help."

The crowd was getting restless.

Stratton had to raise his voice as he explained how every rancher should brand even dairy cows. "One white or black cow looks exactly like another. We have no way of telling them apart."

"I thought some states were using DNA?" a rancher asked over the growing murmuring.

"It's expensive, and we have to have some idea where the cow was stolen so we can try to match the DNA," he replied. "The best place to stop rustlers is at livestock sales. We need those people to be attentive. There are also radio-frequency chips that we're looking into. It's an expense for all of you, I know, but—"

"It sounds like you're expecting everyone else to do your job," a rancher called.

"Yeah," Waters agreed. "What's the bottom line here? You're telling us you aren't going to do a damn thing?"

"The only way we can beat the rustlers is to work together." Stratton was forced to yell to be heard over the uproar. "You have to trust—"

Jacklyn walked over to the podium and kicked it over. Stratton jumped back as if he'd been shot. The boom as the podium hit the floor sent a shock wave through the room, instantly quieting everyone. All attention was fixed on her.

She barely had to raise her voice. "You want to know how easy is it to steal your cattle? Simple as hell. If there is nobody watching them tonight, the rustlers are out there taking a dozen, two dozen, three dozen right now. You probably won't even know for weeks, maybe months, that they're gone. As for the rustlers, they made a quick getaway. Your cattle *could* be in another state. Or already butchered. Doesn't matter, because they aren't going to turn up. You just lost ten, twenty thousand dollars."

She looked out at the stunned audience of ranchers. "*That's* the reality. I plan to catch these rustlers. But even if I do, there will be others. Unless you help, we'll never be able to protect your property. That, Mr. Waters, is the bottom line."

With that she turned and walked off the stage as the

room went from stunned silence to a clamor of voices. She saw a group of ranchers corner Stratton, blocking his exit, as she and Dillon slipped out the side into the cool darkness.

DILLON LET OUT a low whistle as he joined her outside. "You all right?"

She'd stopped at the street, as if she'd forgotten where she'd parked the truck. When he touched her shoulder, he could feel her shaking.

"I'm fine." She took a step forward to break the contact, but made no move toward the pickup.

"That was great back there. You got the respect of every man in that room."

A small sound like a chuckle came out of her. "*That* just cost me my job."

"No way. The bastard tried to make you look bad, and only succeeded in ticking off everyone in the center. He won't come at you like that again. And once you catch the rustlers…"

She spun on him, her face contorting in anger. "You know damn well I'm not going to catch the rustlers. It's the only reason you agreed to pretend to help me."

"You're wrong."

"Damn it, Dillon, I know you're the one who's leading them. It's how they keep one step ahead of me. Just like you used to."

He shook his head. "You're wrong about that, too."

The anger was gone as quickly as it had appeared. "It doesn't matter now, anyway."

"The hell you say. Come on, Jack. We can do this. I'll help you. Really help you. After all, it's the only way I can prove to you how wrong you are about me."

She seemed to study him in the lamplight. Behind him, the community center was in an uproar. "How can I trust you?"

He smiled. "You can buy me a steak. Come on," he said again, as some of the ranchers began to leave the meeting. "There's a steak house just a short walk from here. I don't know about you, but I could use some fresh air." He took her arm before she could object, and they started down the street. It was a good walk, but he figured they both could use it.

Also, he didn't want a run-in with the ranchers. Not for himself, but for Jacklyn. She'd been through enough tonight. He saw her look over at him as if trying to make up her mind about him.

Funny, but at that moment he wanted to be the man his father always told him he could be. The last thing Dillon wanted to do was disappoint Jacklyn Wilde.

Unfortunately, there was little chance of him doing anything *but* disappointing her.

JACKLYN COULDN'T BELIEVE she'd let Dillon talk her into this.

"After everything you've been through tonight, I say we celebrate," he'd said as they walked into the steak house.

"Celebrate?" Had he lost his mind?

"You still have a job. I'm not on my way to prison. Yet," he added with a grin. "Tell me that isn't cause for celebration."

She might have argued that keeping her job was nothing to celebrate. Maybe Dillon was right. Maybe she was a fool for thinking that her job mattered. Right now not even the ranchers thought so.

The steak house was crowded, especially at the bar. They were shown to a booth in the rear. She noticed that Dillon made a point of sitting with his back to the wall rather than the room. Something he'd picked up in prison?

To her surprise, the waitress put a bottle of her favorite wine on the table and a cold beer in front of Dillon, no glass.

She looked up at him in surprise.

He grinned. "I grabbed a waitress on the way in and told her it was urgent."

"How did you—"

"Know your favorite wine?" His grin broadened. "It's not my psychic ability. I asked. It's what you ordered the last time you were in here. Apparently, you made an impression."

She groaned inwardly. The last time was right before she'd gotten Dillon out of prison. She'd been feeling anything but confident about her decision, and had definitely imbibed more than she should have. No wonder the waitress remembered what wine she'd ordered.

Dillon poured her a glass of wine, then lifted his bottle of beer in a toast, his gaze locked with hers. "To a successful collaboration."

She slowly picked up the glass, clinked it softly against his beer bottle and took a sip, not any more sure of the appropriateness of the toast than she was about drinking even one glass of wine with Dillon Savage.

He took a long swallow of his beer, then stared at the bottle, his thumb making patterns on the sweating glass. "I can't remember the last beer I had." He looked up, scanning the noisy steak house and bar. "It still all feels surreal."

Just then a man who'd had too much to drink stumbled into their table, startling them both and jostling her glass and spilling some of the wine. But it was Dillon's instant reaction that startled her the most.

In a flash, he'd grabbed the beer bottle by its neck, brandishing it like a weapon as he shot to his feet, ready to defend himself and her.

The drunken man raised both hands. "Sorry. My apologies," he said, backing away. "Just clumsy. No harm done, right?"

Dillon sat back down, turning the bottle as he did and gently setting it on the table as beer spilled down the sides. He'd gone pale, his eyes wide. She thought she saw his hand shaking as he rubbed it over his face. "Old habits die hard," he said quietly. "Sorry."

She stared at him, shocked by how quickly he'd changed when he'd felt threatened. "Was it that dangerous in there?" she asked, before she could stop herself.

He looked up at her, his grimace slow and almost painful. "Prison? Dangerous? With people who are crazy, mean, strung out?" He shook his head. "What makes it dangerous is a lack of hope. A lot of those people will never see the outside again and they know it. Because of that, they have nothing to lose."

He smiled as if to lighten his words. "If you're smart, you do your time, stay out of trouble, make the right friends." He grinned. "Like I said, I make friends easily, and you know what they say. What doesn't kill you makes you stronger."

She heard something in his tone that tore at her heart.

The waitress hurried over to mop up the mess, then returned with another beer for Dillon. "That gentleman over there sends his apologies," she said.

Dillon looked in the drunken man's direction and gave a nod.

Jacklyn took a drink of her wine to try to wash down the lump in her throat, and busied herself with her menu. What was wrong with her, having sympathy for a criminal? A criminal *she'd* put behind bars? Dillon had the same options as everyone else. He didn't have to rustle cattle. He'd chosen the route that had led him straight to prison. He had only himself to blame.

So how could she feel sorry for him?

Because, she thought, lowering her menu to peer across the table at him, Dillon Savage wasn't the criminal stereotype. Instead he was educated, smart, from a good family. And, she suspected, a man with his own code of ethics. So what had made him turn to crime?

She tried to concentrate on her menu, but when she looked up again, she saw that Dillon was no longer gazing at his. Instead, he was staring toward the bar, a strange expression on his face.

She turned to follow his gaze. A few cowboys were standing together, the back door closing as someone left. All she caught sight of was one denim-clad shoulder and a glimpse of a western hat.

She searched the group at the bar and recognized only Arlen Dubois, from earlier today on Tom Robinson's ranch.

Was that who Dillon had noticed? Or had it been whoever had just left? In any case, Dillon looked upset.

"Who was that?" she asked, turning back to him.

His expression instantly changed, to an innocent look. "I beg your pardon?"

"You saw someone, someone you recognized?" He'd spotted someone he hadn't wanted to see. She was sure of it. She tried to read his expression, but his eyes showed only the vast blue of an endless sky. She would have thought she was wrong about him seeing someone he knew if it hadn't been for the twitch of a muscle along his jaw.

He was looking at her now, studying her the way she'd been studying him. He always seemed slightly amused—and wary.

THE WOMAN WAS PERCEPTIVE. Much more than Dillon had realized. He smiled at her, meeting her gaze, cranking up the charm as he tried to mask whatever had alerted her.

"What makes you think I wasn't just staring off into space, thinking about the meeting tonight and Shade Waters?"

She cocked her head, her look one of disappointment. "How about the truth? Try it, you might like it."

He rubbed the back of his neck and smiled faintly at her.

"The person who just left. You knew him."

He frowned. "What would make you think that?"

"Don't play games with me," she snapped. "And stop answering my questions with one of your own."

"Okay," he said. "What say we flip for it?" He pulled a quarter from his pocket and spun it between his fingers. "A little wager of sorts. Truth for truth."

"You like to gamble, don't you?"

He grinned. "I like to take my chances sometimes, yes. And I never lie, remember?"

She drew a breath, her gaze on the silver flicker of the quarter in the dim light of the restaurant. "Is it that hard for you to tell the truth that you have to flip for it?"

He did his best to look offended. "Don't assume just because I have a proclivity for cattle rustling that I'm a liar—and a gambler."

"Of course not."

He turned serious for a moment. "Have I ever lied to you?"

She met his gaze. "How would I know?"

"You could look into my eyes." His gaze locked with hers. "So what do you say? A flip of the coin. Heads, I tell you whatever you want to know. Tails, you tell me something I'd like to know."

She watched the quarter for a moment, then held out her hand. "I'll flip the coin if you don't mind."

He pretended to be hurt by her lack of trust.

"You'll answer truthfully?"

He nodded. "And you?"

"I'm always honest."

He smiled at that. "I guess we'll see about that."

Jacklyn didn't like the gleam in his eyes, but anything was better than talking about his prison stay. She'd seen a side of him with the drunken man that had scared her, and at the same time made her want to comfort him.

Fear of Dillon Savage was good—and appropriate. Sympathy on any level was dangerous.

Probably as dangerous as this game he had her playing. But against her better judgment, she believed him when he said he'd tell her the truth if she won the coin toss. And since she was no doubt going to get fired before the night was over, and Dillon would be going back to prison, what did it hurt?

He was watching her, humor dancing in his eyes, as she inspected the coin. "You're the least trusting woman I've ever known."

"Then the women you've known didn't know you very well."

He laughed. It was a nice sound. He took a long drink of his beer and seemed to relax. She hadn't noticed, but apparently he'd refilled her wineglass.

It crossed her mind that he might be trying to get her drunk. She met his gaze, then tossed the coin up, catching it and bringing it down flat on the tabletop.

He took on an excited, eager look as he stared down at her hand and waited for her to lift it from the coin.

Drawing a breath, she did so, instantly relieved to see it was heads.

She smiled at him and took a drink of her wine.

He leaned back, raising his hands in defeat and grinning. "You win, and I'm a man of honor whether you believe it or not. So what do you want to know? The truth, I swear."

"Who did you see earlier going out the back door?"

He glanced toward the bar, clearly hesitating, then slowly said, "Truthfully? I'm not even sure. I just caught a glimpse of the man. Actually, it was the way he moved. It reminded me of someone I used to know. But it couldn't have been him, because he's dead."

She eyed Dillon suspiciously. "What was his name?"

"Halsey Waters." Dillon met her gaze, and she saw pain and anger. "I guess it's because I've been thinking about him."

"He was a good friend?"

Dillon nodded. "We were best friends. He was like a brother to me. I've never been that close to anyone since." He smiled ruefully. "Just one of those regrets in life, you know what I mean?"

"Yes," she said, and looked toward the bar, wondering who Dillon had seen that might remind him of Halsey Waters. Or if he'd made up the whole thing.

"Trust," he said, with his usual amusement.

Then Morgan Landers walked in the door with Nate Waters.

CHAPTER TEN

JACKLYN COULDN'T VERY well miss the instant that Dillon saw Morgan. His entire demeanor changed. Like him, she watched the two come in on a cool gust of night air, Morgan laughing, Nate totally absorbed in her.

When Jacklyn turned back to Dillon, he was on his feet, excusing himself to go to the restroom. He walked away, not looking back. Jacklyn turned, pretty sure she'd find Morgan watching Dillon go, but her view was blocked by a man standing next to her table.

"Jacklyn Wilde?" he asked, but before she could answer he slid into the seat Dillon had just vacated. "I'm Buford Cole. A friend of Dillon's."

She studied the man across from her. He looked like most of the other cowboys, wearing jeans, boots, a western shirt and hat. His face was weathered from a life outdoors, and crow's-feet bracketed his brown eyes.

"How much do you know about Dillon Savage?" Buford asked before she could comment.

His question took her by surprise. "Not much," she said, telling herself how true that was.

"He ever tell you how he got into rustling cattle?" Buford didn't wait for an answer. "Dillon believes that his family's ranch was stolen."

"Stolen?" she asked, even though she knew that's how Dillon felt.

Buford nodded. "Cattle disappeared, others got accidentally closed off from water and died. There were a lot of strange accidents around the ranch, including his father's near-death accident that left him dependent on a cane. After that his dad just gave up. His spread was bought by Shade Waters. Dillon's always believed his father died of a broken heart. That ranch was his life."

She'd suspected as much.

"But even if Dillon believed that Shade Waters stole his family ranch, why not alert the authorities or just steal cattle from the W Bar if he wanted revenge?" she asked. "Why steal from all his neighbors?"

"Dillon's father tried to get the neighboring ranchers to join forces and fight Waters. They all turned a blind eye to what was happening on the Savage Ranch. By the time it started happening to them, Dillon's old man was dead, the ranch lost. Then Waters bought up one ranch after another, usually after each had had its share of bad luck."

"Are you trying to tell me that Waters—"

"I'm trying to tell you what Dillon believes," Buford interrupted, glancing toward the hallway to the restrooms where Dillon had disappeared. "In the end, all but two of the ranchers sold out to Waters."

"Why, if what Dillon believes is true, weren't those two forced to sell as well then?"

"You ever meet Reda Harper? As for Tom Robinson, he was barely hanging on by a thread. Now after what happened…" The cowboy shook his head. "Word is that Waters has already bought it from Tom Robinson's niece. As for Reda… She's old. Waters can wait her out."

"You sound as if you don't like Shade Waters any more than Dillon does."

"I don't like fighting battles I know I can't win. Dillon's an idealist. He still believes in justice. And vengeance."

"You think Dillon is out for revenge?" she asked, thinking about the ranchers that Dillon had rustled cattle from. They'd all later sold out to Waters. When she'd finally caught him, he'd been on the W Bar, Shade's own ranch. She'd thought Dillon had gotten greedy and that had been his downfall. Now she wondered.

She'd seen how much Waters and Dillon hated each other, but the big rancher's hatred of Dillon seemed out of proportion to the amount of cattle he'd lost over the years.

"Why does Shade hate Dillon so much?" she asked, feeling the effects of the wine.

"Did you ask Dillon?"

She shook her head.

"Shade Waters blames him for his son's death."

"Halsey," she murmured, frowning to herself. "But he was Dillon's best friend."

Buford smiled at that. "We were all friends. Did you ever wonder what happened to the cattle Dillon rustled?" he asked. "Dillon put them in with Waters's herd."

She stared at him. Wouldn't she have heard this from Waters if that were true?

The cowboy chuckled. "The cattle just seemed to disappear. Who knows what Waters did with them."

Jacklyn thought about the dead calves in the stock truck that Dillon swore had been shot. Is that what

Shade Waters had done with the rustled cattle he'd found among his herd?

And then what? Just taken them out and buried them?

What a waste. And for what?

She couldn't believe the lengths Dillon had gone to. But was any of this true? Or was it just the way he rationalized his thieving ways to his friends?

"You seem to know a lot about Dillon's rustling activities," she said.

Buford smiled. "You aren't going to ask me if I was in on it with him, are you?"

"You were one of his closest friends, right? This gang of rustlers—you think he has anything to do with them?"

Buford looked wary. "I wouldn't know."

"But you think it's possible."

He sighed, still not looking at her. "I just know Dillon isn't finished with Waters." He shook his head as he rose from the booth. "He won't be, either, until Waters is either behind bars or dead. Unfortunately, Dillon Savage is the kind of man who takes a grudge to the grave. I would just hate to see him in an early grave."

Why was Buford telling her all this? Buford appeared to be genuinely worried about his old friend. But didn't he realize this only made Dillon look guilty of being the leader of this latest band of cattle rustlers?

As Buford walked away, Jacklyn saw that Nate Waters was sitting alone. Where was Morgan? And why hadn't Dillon returned?

MORGAN GASPED as Dillon stepped directly into her path. Her hand went to her throat, her eyes looking around wildly as if searching for a way to escape the dim restaurant hallway.

"Dillon."

He smiled as he moved so close he could see the fear in her eyes. "Morgan."

She licked her lips and smiled back nervously. "What are you doing here?" Without Nate Waters beside her, she'd lost a lot of her haughtiness.

"I wanted to see you, Morgan. Don't tell me you didn't expect to meet up with me again."

"I didn't think you could...that is, I thought you weren't allowed to go anywhere alone."

He smiled at that. "Is that what you thought?"

She swallowed, looking again for a way to escape, but he was blocking the hallway. She'd have to go over him to get back to Nate.

"We should get together sometime," she said, shifting nervously. "To talk. A lot has happened since you've been gone."

"So I gather. You and Waters." Dillon shook his head. She would turn Nate any way but loose before she was through.

"Nate and I are getting married."

"You're perfect for each other."

She frowned, thinking he was being facetious.

"Seriously, I wish you all the best."

"You're not upset?" She was eyeing him now, obviously not wanting to believe that he'd gotten over her.

"I had a lot of time to think in prison," he said, his gaze locking with hers. "It cleared up a lot for me. Like, for instance, how I just happened to get caught."

She shifted again, pulling her shoulder bag around to the front, her hand going to it.

He put his hand over hers and smiled. "Carrying a gun now? You have something to fear, Morgan?"

Her gaze hardened as she jerked her hand away from his.

"You set me up that day, didn't you?"

She was shaking her head. "You're wrong. I swear to you."

"Come on, Morgan, you were the only person who knew where I would be."

"No, the others knew. It had to be one of them. Or maybe your luck just ran out."

"Yeah, maybe that was it." He reached into her purse and pulled out the gun, swinging the barrel around until the end was pointed at her forehead. Her eyes widened as she heard him snap off the safety.

"Here's the one-time deal," he told her. "The truth for your life. Because, Morgan, I'm going to find out who set me up. Tell me the truth now and I walk away. No foul, no harm. For old time's sake, I'll give you this chance. But," he added quickly, "if I find out you lied, I'll come back and all bets are off. So what's it going to be?"

"I'm telling you the truth. I didn't say a word to anyone. I swear. It wasn't me, Dillon. I couldn't do that to you."

He would have argued the latter, but his time was up. Jacklyn would have realized by now that he was missing. He couldn't chance her finding him holding a gun on Morgan.

He emptied the gun, snapped the safety back on and dropped the weapon into her purse, pocketing the bullets. "Wouldn't want you to accidentally shoot anyone," he said with a grin.

It would have been like Morgan to shoot him in the back and say it was self-defense. And with the Waters family behind her, she would have probably gotten away with it.

"I'm sure we'll be seeing each other again," he said.

"Not if I see you first," Morgan snapped back.

He chuckled to himself as he turned and walked away. Behind him, Morgan let out a string of curse words. That's what he'd loved about her: she was no lady.

Back at the table, Jack seemed relieved to see him. As Morgan returned to her own table, Jack shot Dillon a suspicious look.

He picked up his menu and studied it. But he could feel both Jack and Morgan looking in his direction. He'd known what kind of woman Morgan was. The kind who would lie through her teeth. The fact that she was carrying a gun didn't bode well in the truth department. She was afraid of someone. Him, no doubt. Which led him to believe she had something to hide.

She'd said the others knew where he'd be that day.

Yes, the others. His friends, his partners, the men he'd trusted with his life. He'd have to have a little talk with each of them. If he helped Jack bust up this rustling ring, he'd get the opportunity, he was sure.

"Have you made up your mind?" Jack asked.

He couldn't help but wonder if Morgan might not be involved. She was carrying a gun and had hooked up with the son of one of the richest and most influential ranchers in the state of Montana.

He looked up from his menu. "Definitely," he said, smiling at her.

"About what you're going to order," she said, but not with her usual irritation at his foolishness.

The wine had mellowed her some. Her cheeks were a little flushed. She looked damn good in candlelight. Dillon had the wildest urge to reach across the table and free her hair from that braid.

The waitress appeared at that moment, saving him. After they'd ordered, he stole a glance in the direction of Morgan's table.

Morgan and Nate were gone.

JACKLYN COULDN'T HELP thinking about everything Buford Cole had told her as she ate her dinner. The wine had left her feeling too warm, too relaxed, too intent on the man across the table from her.

Dillon was his usual charming self. And she found herself enjoying not only the meal, but also the company.

But what difference did it make? She was sure she'd lost her job tonight. In fact, she was surprised that Stratton hadn't already called to fire her.

After dinner they walked back toward the community center, both falling into silence as if a spell had been broken. The night was dark and cold. Lewistown was close to the mountains, so that often made nights here chilly, especially in spring.

Without a word, Dillon took off his jacket and put it around her shoulders. She thought about protesting, but was still in that what-the-heck mood.

Tonight he'd sweet-talked her, stood up for her, wined and dined her, and she'd liked it. In the morning, she'd be her old self again. Not that it mattered. She was sure Stratton would be picking up Dillon to take him back to prison, and would fire her.

What would *she* do? She didn't have a clue. But for some reason not even that bothered her right now.

"Pretty night," Dillon said, as he stopped to look up at the stars.

She stopped, too, taking a deep breath of the clean air, feeling strangely happy and content. A dangerous way to be feeling this close to Dillon Savage.

His hand brushed her sleeve, and she turned toward him like a flower to the sun. They were so close she couldn't be sure who made the first move. All she knew was that when his lips brushed hers, she felt sparks.

She leaned into him, wanting more even as the sensible Jacklyn Wilde tried to warn her that she'd regret it in the morning. Heck, she'd probably regret it before the night was over.

Dillon pulled back. "Jack, you sure you know what you're doing?"

"This isn't the first time I've kissed someone," she said.

He laughed. "No, I didn't think it was. It's just that—" He looked past her and let out a curse.

She turned and saw her pickup sitting alone in the community center parking lot. Sitting at an odd angle.

"Someone slashed your tires," Dillon said, sounding miserable.

To her surprise, she found she was fighting tears. The slashed tires were the last straw. She marched toward her pickup, angry at the world.

"I'm sure you had nothing to do with this, either," she snapped over her shoulder.

He caught up to her as she reached the truck. She

started to open the driver's door to get out her insurance card and call for towing, but he slammed it shut, flattening her back to the side of the vehicle.

"How can you say that?" he demanded, his voice hoarse with emotion. "I was with you all night."

"Right, you have the perfect alibi. You were getting me drunk."

He raised a brow. "Is that what that kiss was about? You just had too much to drink?"

She didn't answer, couldn't. She wanted to push him away, to distance herself from him. Every instinct told her that Dillon Savage was nothing but trouble. And these feelings she had for him, had had for him years ago when she'd spent days learning everything she could about him, chasing him across Montana and finally coming face-to-face with him, well, they were feelings she was damn determined not to have. Especially now.

"Jack?"

She pushed on his chest with both hands, but he was bigger and stronger than she was, and he had her pinned against the truck with his body.

"Trust me, Jack," he said, his eyes dark with emotion. "I know you want to. Let me prove to you that I'm through with that life."

Her eyes filled with tears. She wanted to believe him. But she'd seen the other look in his eyes, the hatred, the need for vengeance. He would never forget that she'd put him in prison. No matter if she believed anything Buford had told her, she believed Dillon Savage was a man who held a grudge.

"Damn it, Jack," he said with a groan. He dragged

her to him, his mouth on hers, his arms surrounding her and pulling her in.

He caught her off guard. Just like the first time he'd kissed her, the day she'd captured him. Her lips parted now of their own accord. Just as they had the first time. And just like the first time, she felt the stars and planets fall into line.

Noise erupted from a bar down the street. Dillon stepped back as abruptly as he'd kissed her. She followed his gaze, surprised and disappointed that he'd ended the kiss.

That is, until she saw the lone man standing outside the bar, watching them. As he scratched a match across his boot and lifted the flame to the cigarette dangling from his mouth, his face was caught in the light.

Sheriff Claude McCray.

DILLON FELT SHAKEN. He'd seen the look on the sheriff's face. All Dillon had done was bring Jack more trouble—as if she needed it.

Worse, she'd given him nothing but silence and distance ever since. But at that moment he would have done anything to convince Jack she was wrong about him. As if a kiss would do that! And yet, it had been one hell of a kiss. He'd felt a connection between them. Just as he had the first time. It had haunted him for the past four years, locked up in prison.

Just as this kiss would haunt him.

He mentally kicked himself on the way back to the motel. She was skittish again when it came to him. Distrustful.

He almost laughed at the thought. Hell, as it was,

she didn't trust him as far as she could throw him. How could it be any worse?

But he knew the answer to that.

She could send him back to prison.

He was probably headed back there for another year, anyway. If she lost her job, which appeared likely, then this deal was over. He knew Stratton hadn't wanted him out to begin with, and with pressure from Shade Waters…

But that wasn't what worried him. It was Sheriff Claude McCray. McCray had seen the two of them together by the truck. He would make trouble for Jack. Dillon didn't doubt that for a second.

The tow truck driver finally arrived. Jack had been leaning against the side of the disabled pickup, arms crossed, a scowl on her face.

Dillon had had the good sense to leave her alone. Now he listened to Jack give the tow truck operator instructions to take the pickup to a tire shop, have the slashed tires replaced, the state billed, and the truck delivered to the motel in the morning.

The driver, a big burly guy with grease-stained fingers, grunted in answer before driving off with the pickup in tow.

"Pleasant fellow," Dillon commented as he and Jack were left alone in the dark parking lot.

She grunted in answer and started walking toward the motel. He guessed she needed the fresh air so he accompanied her and kept his mouth shut.

They hadn't gone a block, though, when her cell phone rang. She shot him a look. He felt his gut clench. It was the call they'd both been expecting all night.

Once Stratton fired her, Dillon would be on his way back to Montana State Prison.

Well, at least he'd gotten a kiss, he told himself. And Chinese food. Sometimes that was as good as it got.

He could tell that Jack didn't want to talk to anyone, after everything that had happened tonight. As she checked her caller ID, he figured that, like him, she was worried it would be the sheriff.

"It's Stratton," she said, and gazed at Dillon. They'd both been expecting this. He sure was calling late, though.

Was there some reason it had taken him so long? Maybe like he was giving it some consideration—until he got a call from the sheriff?

She snapped open the phone. "Wilde."

Dillon watched her face. A breeze stirred the hair around her face, and her eyes went wild, like those of a deer caught in headlights.

"I see." She listened for a while, then stated, "Fine. No, I understand. If that's what you want." She snapped the phone shut.

Dillon stared at her, trying to gauge the impact of the call. She looked strange, as if all evening she'd been preparing herself for the worst. Earlier, he'd had the feeling that she'd already given up the job. There'd been a freedom in her that had drawn him like a moth to a flame. "Well?"

"The rustlers hit again. Leroy Edmonds's ranch, to the east. Stratton thinks it was the same bunch. One of the ranch hands just found where the barbed wire fence was cut. Not sure when or how many head were stolen."

"Did Stratton...?"

"Fire me? No." She shook her head, as if this had

been the last thing she'd expected. Maybe still couldn't believe it. "Waters apparently talked him out of it. Seems Waters has had a change of heart."

"Not likely," Dillon said with a curse, wondering what the bastard was up to.

Just as she had earlier, Jack looked to be close to tears. Tears of relief? Or just exhaustion? This day had to have played hell on her. He wished there was something he could do to make things easier for her. But he wasn't going to make the mistake of trying to kiss her again.

That woman at the steak house, the one who'd laughed and drank wine and seemed free, was gone. This one was all-business again.

"So you're telling me Waters has agreed to let us on his ranch?" Dillon asked, more than a little surprised.

"Sounds that way."

"Why the change of heart?" he had to ask.

"Shade says one of his ranch hands saw someone watching a grazing area with binoculars. He's agreed to let us talk to the hired hand and even have access to that section," she said. "That's a start."

She seemed relieved that she hadn't been fired. But there was also a sadness about her. Dillon felt a stab of guilt for denigrating her job earlier.

"The sneaky son of a bitch," he said with a laugh. "He's that sure we won't catch him at whatever he's up to. Tell me this doesn't feel like a setup."

"I have to treat it like a legitimate lead," she said, sounding as if she wasn't any more happy about this than he was.

"I know. It's your job. But just do me one favor. No

matter how sure you are that Waters is innocent, don't ever underestimate the bastard."

Jacklyn smiled. "Funny, that's what everyone keeps telling me about you."

CHAPTER ELEVEN

THE NEXT MORNING, with new tires on the truck, Jacklyn filled up the gas tank, then picked up the horse trailer and enough supplies to last a good three days.

"So we're headed for Leroy Edmonds's place?" Dillon asked, as Jack pointed the rig north again. "I thought you said his ranch was to the east?"

"First stop is Waters's spread. I need to talk to the hand who says he saw someone up in the hills scoping out the herd," she said.

He nodded, but sensed there was more going on with her this morning. Unless he was mistaken, there'd been a change in Jack. Not quite a twinkle in her eye, but close. He'd bet money she was up to something.

It was one of those blue-sky days that was so bright it was blinding. There wasn't a cloud in the sky and the weather was supposed to be good for nearly a week.

Dillon still couldn't believe he wasn't headed back to prison. It made him a little uneasy. "So who's the ranch hand?"

"Pete Barclay. He's worked for Waters ever since you went to prison," she said, glancing over at him.

She wasn't fooling him. All his old cowboy buddies were back in central Montana. Neither of them thought that was a coincidence.

He sighed deeply. "Pete Barclay."

"What? I thought Pete was your friend? Or are you going to tell me that he's now in cahoots with Waters?"

Dillon shook his head. There was no telling her anything. "Pete actually saw one of the rustlers?"

"The person was up in the hills. He saw a flash of light up in the rocks that he believes came from binocular lenses. When he went up to investigate, he found tracks. Look, I'm not sure what I believe at this point. That's why I want to talk to Pete."

"Right." There was more to it, sure as hell.

"If it makes you feel any better, I don't trust Waters," she admitted, as if the words were hard to say.

Dillon looked at her in surprise. That was the most honest she'd been with him. Not to mention that she'd just taken him into her confidence. Maybe he was finally making inroads with her. Or maybe she was just telling him what she thought he wanted to hear.

REDA HARPER HAD NEVER been good at letting sleeping dogs lie. She hadn't slept well last night, tossing and turning, her mind running over the meeting at the community center and, even more, what she'd seen on the W Bar.

She'd made a few calls first thing this morning to find out if the rustlers had struck again.

She'd been shocked to hear that, sure enough, they had hit another ranch. One to the east, though, not Waters's. How was that possible, when she'd have sworn she saw them on the W Bar last night? Unless she'd seen them *after* they'd hit Edmonds's ranch.

But what had she really seen?

"Isn't any of my business," she said to herself, even as she sat down at her desk and pulled out the pale lavender stationery. Caressingly, she ran her fingertips over the paper. Nicer than any paper she would have bought for herself. The stationery had been a gift from her lover.

"The no-good son of a bitch," she said under her breath. Her lips puckered, the taste in her mouth more sour than lemons as she picked up her pen and, with a careful hand, began to compose one of her infamous letters.

The mistake she'd made wasn't in mailing the letter, she realized later. It was in not leaving well enough alone and *only* sending the letter.

Even as she was pocketing shells and picking up her shotgun, she knew better. Not that she'd ever drawn the line at butting into other people's business. In fact, it was the only thing that gave her any satisfaction in her old age.

No, it was not leaving well enough alone when it came to Shade Waters. Her mother, bless her soul, had always said that Reda's anger would be the death of her.

Of course, her mother had never known about Reda's affair with Shade, so she'd never witnessed the true extent of her daughter's fury.

Had there been someone around to give Reda good advice, he or she would have told her not to get into her pickup armed with her shotgun. And maybe the best advice of all, not to go down that back road to where she'd seen that stock truck last night.

JACKLYN TURNED AT THE gate into the W Bar Ranch, taking a breath and letting it out slowly.

Last night she hadn't been able to sleep—not after the ranchers' meeting, everything she'd learned at the steak house with Dillon, and finally Stratton's call.

At least that's what she told herself. That it had been Dillon who gave her a sleepless night—and not just the kiss.

The night before had left her off balance. Even a little afraid. That wasn't like her, and she knew part of it was due to Dillon Savage. She'd known he was dangerous, but she'd underestimated his personality. Even his charm, she thought with a hidden smile.

But last night, unable to sleep, she'd realized what she had to do. As she drove into the W Bar, she knew the chance she was taking. She was no fool. She'd gotten Dillon out of prison for the reason he suspected: to give him enough rope that he would hang himself. She'd been that sure he was the leader of the rustling ring.

Now she suspected that Stratton was doing the same thing with her.

This morning before they left, she'd called Shade Waters. He'd been almost apologetic. She'd questioned him why this was the first time she'd heard about one of his men seeing someone on the ranch. Why hadn't he mentioned it yesterday at his place? Or last night at the meeting?

"I just heard about it. I guess he told Nate and—" Waters let out a low curse "—Nate had other things on his mind and forgot to mention it until late last night."

"I want to talk to the ranch hand."

"I'll make sure he's here in the morning."

She'd wondered even then if Waters was making

things too easy for her, setting her up, just as Dillon suspected. Or was she just letting Dillon sway her, the same way she'd let him kiss her last night?

As she parked in front of the ranch house, she was glad to see there wasn't a welcoming reception on the porch this time. "I need to talk to Pete alone."

"I'll be right here," Dillon said, lying back and pulling his hat down over his eyes. He gave her a lazy grin.

"Make sure you stay here," she said.

He cut his eyes to her. They seemed bluer today than she'd ever seen them. Just a trick of the light. "At some point, you might want to give me more to do than sleep."

Soon, she thought. Very soon.

DILLON'S INTENTION had been to stay in the pickup. The last thing he wanted to do was make Jack mad again, he thought, as he watched her walk toward the barn. She did fill out her jeans nicely, he decided. He groaned, remembering the hard time he'd had getting to sleep last night, just thinking about their kiss.

He'd figured this early release would be a cakewalk. Just hang back, let things happen, do as little as he could. Jack was good at her job. She didn't need him.

But that had been before last night. Now he felt frustrated, on too many levels. He couldn't sit back and let Jack make the biggest mistake of her life.

The thought made him laugh. The biggest mistake of her life would be falling for him.

Yeah, like that was ever going to happen.

No, Jack was going at this all wrong. She was never

going to catch the rustlers at this rate. She needed to investigate the W Bar and Waters.

Was she dragging her feet because of Dillon's own past with the rancher? He swore under his breath and sat up. The place was quiet. Maybe too quiet?

He told himself he had to think of what was best for him as well as Jack. She needed his help. He wondered how long it would be before he was headed back to prison, if she didn't get a break in this case.

Something shiny caught his eye. Grillwork on an old stock truck parked in tall weeds, behind what was left of a ramshackle older barn.

He thought of Jack for a moment. She'd disappeared into the new barn, closer to the house. He knew why she had balked at investigating Waters on the q.t. behind her supervisor's back. Because she didn't have a criminal mind.

But he did, he admitted with a grin, as he popped open his door and slipped out of the pickup. He wouldn't go far, but he definitely wanted to have a look at that truck. He was betting it was the same one he'd hitched a ride in just the day before.

Sneaking along the side of the building, Dillon kept an eye out for Jack. He hated to think what she would do if she caught him.

The W Bar definitely seemed too quiet as he neared the front of the truck. He hesitated at the edge of the building, flattening himself against the rough wood wall to listen. He could hear crickets chirping in the tall weeds nearby, smell dust on the breeze, mixed with the scents of hay and cattle, familiar smells that threatened to draw him back into that dark hole of his past.

After a moment, he inched around the corner of the barn and along the shady side of the stock truck. It was cool here, wedged between the truck and the barn. He stayed low, just in case he wasn't alone. Strange that no one was around, other than the hired hand Jack was meeting with in the other barn. Pete Barclay, she'd said. He and Pete had never been close. Pete was a hothead.

That fact made Dillon nervous about Jack being in the barn alone with him. He reminded himself that she was wearing a gun, this was what she did for a living, and he had to trust her judgment.

Still, he was worried as he moved past the driver's door and along the wooden bed of the truck. He grabbed hold of one of the boards and climbed up the side, hesitating before he stuck his head over the top. He still hadn't heard any vehicles. No tractors. No ranch equipment. Not even the sound of a voice or the thunder of horses' hooves. Where was everyone?

As he finally peered over the top of the stock rack, Dillon wasn't all that surprised by what he found. The back of the truck had been washed out. There was only a hint of odor from the dead calves that had been in it yesterday.

Climbing down, he noticed that the truck was older than he'd realized yesterday. Probably why it was parked back here. Because it was seldom used.

He started around the corner of the barn, sensing too late that he was no longer alone.

JACKLYN FOUND Pete Barclay where Waters had told her he would be. In the barn. On her walk there, she saw no one else. She hadn't seen Waters's car, nor Nate's, for that matter, and suspected they might have gone into town to avoid her.

Which was fine with her.

Pete Barclay was a long, tall drink of water. He had a narrow face that she'd once heard called horsey, and he wore a ten-gallon Stetson that he was never going to grow into. His long legs were bowed, his clothing soiled, she noted, when she found him shoveling horse manure from the stalls.

"Mornin'," he said when he saw her, and kept on working.

"Shade told you I was coming out?"

Pete nodded.

"I just wanted to ask you a few questions."

"Sure." He shoveled the manure into a wheelbarrow, not looking at her.

"Shade said you saw someone watching the ranch?"

Pete dumped another shovelful into the wheelbarrow, the odor filling the air. Had Waters purposely told him to do this job this morning, because she would be talking to him?

"Can't say I saw anyone, just kind of a reflection. You know—like you get from binoculars."

"So you investigated?"

He nodded as he scooped up more manure. "Just found some boot and horseshoe prints. The ground was kind of trampled. Looked like someone had been hanging around behind a rock up there."

"And where was this, exactly?"

He told her. He still hadn't looked at her.

"Shade said you told Nate?"

He gave another nod.

"How many cattle would you say Mr. Waters has in that area?" she asked. She couldn't see Pete's face, but his neck flushed bright red.

"Mr. Waters said I wasn't to be giving out any numbers. Truth is he's talking about moving the cattle closer to the ranch house until the rustlers are caught."

"That's a good idea," she agreed, wondering if Shade had any idea what a terrible liar Pete was.

"He said to tell you to take the Old Mill Road. The country back in there is pretty rough. It's a good day's ride on horseback."

"Then I'd better get started," Jacklyn said.

SHADE WATERS STEPPED OUT in front of Dillon, blocking his way, as he came around the corner of the barn.

Dillon had often thought about what he would do if he ever caught the rancher in a dark alley, just the two of them alone, face-to-face.

"You and I need to talk," Waters said.

Dillon cocked his head, studying the man. Did the rancher have any idea how much danger he was in right now? Up close, Waters looked much older than he remembered him. He had aged, his skin sallow and flecked with sun spots. But there was still power in his broad frame. Shade Waters was still a man to be reckoned with.

"What could you and I possibly have to talk about?"

"Your father."

Dillon couldn't hide his surprise. He glanced toward the pickup, but didn't see Jack. "I don't think you want to go down that road."

"You're wrong about what happened," Waters said, sounding anxious. "I liked your father—"

"Don't," Dillon said, and pushed past the older man, striding toward the pickup, telling himself not to look back. His hands were shaking. It was all he could do not to turn around and go back and—

"I have a proposition for you," Waters said from behind him.

Dillon stopped walking. He took a deep breath and slowly turned.

"You want your father's ranch back? It's yours."

Dillon could only stare.

"I'll throw in the old Hanson place, as well."

Dillon took a step toward him, his fists clenched at his sides, anger making his head throb. "You think this will make up for the past?"

"I don't give a rat's behind about the past," Waters snapped. "This isn't a guilty gesture, for hell's sake. This is a business deal."

Dillon stopped a few yards from Waters. "Business?"

He couldn't believe this old fool. Waters had no idea the chance he was taking. In just two steps Dillon could finally get vengeance, if not justice.

"I give you the ranch, you take Morgan Landers off my hands," Waters said.

Dillon couldn't have been more astonished. "I beg your pardon? Off *your* hands?"

"Don't play dumb with me, Savage. What I always admired about you was your intelligence. You know damn well what I'm asking. I want her away from my son. Name your price."

Dillon shook his head, disbelieving. "My price?" he asked, closing the distance between them. This was the man who had destroyed his family, stolen his ranch and now thought he could buy him as well.

Dillon reached out and grabbed the man's throat so quickly Waters didn't have a chance to react. He shoved the rancher against the side of the barn. "My price?"

"Dillon," Jacklyn said calmly, from behind him.

Waters's face had turned beet-red and he was making a choking sound.

"Dillon," Jacklyn repeated, still sounding calm and not overly concerned.

Dillon shot a look over his shoulder at her, saw her expression and let go of the rancher's throat.

Waters slumped against the side of the barn, gasping for air. "I'll have you back in prison for assault," he managed to wheeze as he clutched his throat.

"No, you won't," Dillon said to him quietly. "Or I'll tell your son what you just tried to do. Better yet, I'll tell Morgan."

Waters glared at him. "Get him the hell off my property," he growled to Jacklyn.

"We were just leaving," she said.

Next to her, Dillon walked toward the pickup, neither looking back.

"What was that about?" she asked under her breath, sounding furious.

"The bastard offered to give me back my ranch." She shot him a look.

"And the old Hanson place thrown in."

"He admitted he'd stolen your ranch?" she said, once they were at the pickup and out of earshot.

"Yeah, right." Dillon glanced back. Waters was still standing beside the barn, glaring in their direction. "It was a business deal. He wanted me to take Morgan Landers off his hands."

As Jack opened her door, she glanced toward him in surprise. "You aren't serious."

"Dead-on," Dillon said as he joined her in the cab. He was still shaking, his heart pounding, at how close he'd come to going back to prison for good.

"He wants her out of his son's life that badly?"

Dillon laughed and leaned back in his seat as she started the engine and got rolling. "Waters is one manipulative son of a bitch. But I'd say he's met his match with Morgan Landers."

JACKLYN WATCHED Dillon's face as he glanced out in the direction of what had once been his family's ranch. "Tempted?" she asked.

He smiled but didn't look at her. "That train has already left the station."

She thought about the lovely Morgan Landers, heard the bitterness in his voice. Jacklyn had little doubt that Dillon could get the woman back if he wanted. Nate was no match for Dillon Savage.

"The sooner we catch these guys, the sooner you can get your life back," she said.

"What life?" He looked over at her and sighed. "I guess I do need to start thinking about the future."

She nodded. "Have you thought about what you want to do?"

"Sure." He looked out at the rolling grasslands they were passing. "I thought about leaving Montana, starting over."

"Using one of your degrees?"

He nodded, his expression solemn.

"But you can't leave here, can you?"

He turned to her again, then smiled slowly. "I don't think so."

But he couldn't stay here unless he let go of the past, and they both knew it.

Ahead, Jacklyn spotted the turnoff to the Old Mill Road. She slowed the truck. "You wouldn't have killed him."

Dillon laughed. "Don't bet the farm on it."

She shook her head. "You're not a killer, Dillon Savage."

He looked over at her and felt a rush of warmth that surprised him. Whether true or not, he liked that she seemed to believe it. He reminded himself that while she might not consider him capable of murder, she *did* believe he was behind the rustling ring. Or did she really?

Jacklyn turned down the road, amazed by the lengths Shade Waters would go to get what he wanted. Was it possible Dillon had been right about him all along?

The road was rutted and rough, and obviously didn't get much use. But clearly, a vehicle had been down here recently. There were fresh tire tread patterns visible in the dust.

As she topped a small rise, the huge old windmill, with only a few of the blades still intact, stood stark against the horizon. Near it, she spotted two vehicles parked in the shade of a grove of trees.

She swore under her breath as she recognized both of the people standing beside the vehicles, having what appeared to be an intimate conversation.

"And what do we have here?" Dillon said, as Sheriff McCray turned at the sound of the truck coming over the hill.

Jacklyn saw the sheriff's angry expression. He left Morgan and walked over to stand in the middle of the road, blocking it.

"Tempted?" Dillon said with amusement when Jacklyn brought the pickup to a stop just inches from McCray's chest.

With a groan, she powered down her window as the sheriff walked around to her side of the vehicle. He didn't look happy to see her. Or was it that he wasn't happy to be caught out here with Morgan?

"What are you doing here?" McCray demanded, glancing from her to Dillon. "You spying on me?" Clearly, he was upset at being caught. But caught doing what?

She glanced toward Morgan, who had gotten into her SUV and was now leaving. "Shade said one of his men noticed someone watching this end of the ranch. I told him I'd check it out."

McCray frowned. "Why would he tell you that?

There's no cattle in here." His eyes narrowed. "You're going to have to come up with a better story than that."

No she wasn't. "My mistake." She shifted the pickup into Reverse and, backing up the horse trailer into a low spot, turned around.

But McCray wasn't done with her. He stepped up to her window. "Or maybe you had another reason for coming out here," he said, scowling at Dillon.

"I could ask what *you* are doing out here," Jacklyn snapped, before she could stop herself.

"I'm doing my job," he retorted defensively. "Shade asked me to keep an eye on his place."

"Really?" She glanced toward the retreating Morgan Landers. "Or did he make you an offer you couldn't refuse?" Claude ignored that.

"I see you got yourself some new tires," he said with snide satisfaction, no doubt to let her know he'd seen Dillon kissing her last night in the community center parking lot.

"Don't let me keep you from your...*work*," she said as she let the clutch out a little quicker than she'd planned. The pickup lurched forward, the tire almost running over the sheriff's foot.

He jumped back with a curse. As she turned the wheel and left, she saw him in her rearview mirror, mouthing something at her. She gave the pickup more gas and heard Dillon chuckle.

"I wonder what Waters offered *him?*" Dillon said. "That looked like a lovers' tryst to me. I just hope I'm around when Morgan finds out that Shade Waters is trying to sell her to anyone who'll take her."

As Jacklyn drove back the way they'd come, she only momentarily wondered just how far Shade would go to protect his son from Morgan Landers—and what Nate would do if he found out.

But her mind was on what McCray had said about Waters not running any cattle in that section of the ranch. She'd known Pete Barclay was lying, but now she knew that Waters was, as well.

CHAPTER TWELVE

As JACKLYN REACHED the county road, a truck whizzed past, headed in the direction of the W Bar Ranch.

"That's odd," she said, as she caught a glimpse of the man behind the wheel. Buford Cole had to have seen them, but appeared to turn away, as if not wanting to be recognized.

"Looks like he's headed for Waters's ranch," Dillon said, lifting a brow.

She was reminded of what Buford had told her at the steak house. "He's a friend of yours." She hadn't meant to make it sound so much like an accusation.

Dillon looked away. "I lost some friends when I went to prison. Buford was one of them."

That surprised her. "Why was that?"

He turned to smile at her. "You tell me. Was he the one who helped you capture me? I've always wondered who betrayed me."

She heard the pain in his voice. But it was the underlying anger that worried her. "No one helped me."

He gave her a look that said he didn't believe that for a minute.

"Buford used to rustle cattle with you, didn't he?"

Dillon didn't reply. But then, she thought she knew the answer. Buford had known too much about Dillon's motives not to have helped him.

And what about Dillon's other buddies, Pete Barclay and Arlen Dubois? Dillon hadn't seemed happy to see any of them. And now that she thought about it, they were giving him distance, as well. Because they didn't want her to know that they were still involved in rustling together?

"If I were you, I wouldn't trust anything Buford told you," Dillon said finally.

"Why?"

He looked at her as if she wasn't as smart as he'd thought. "Because he can't be trusted."

"Unlike you. Is Buford smart enough to be running this latest rustling gang?"

Dillon shook his head without hesitation. "He's smart enough, but he has no imagination."

"Rustling requires imagination?" she asked, half-mockingly.

He grinned. "As a matter of fact, it does. Whoever is running this gang has imagination. Look what they pulled off at the Crowleys'. Stealing the cattle in broad daylight right in front of the house. That took imagination. And bravado."

She heard admiration in his voice.

"Don't be giving me that look," he said. "If I was the one behind this gang, do you think I'd be bragging on myself?"

"As a matter of fact…."

DILLON GLANCED UP as she pulled off the road. Out the windshield, all he could see was pasture beyond the barbed wire fence gate. He shot Jack a questioning look. She appeared to be waiting for him to get out and open a gate that hadn't been opened for some time. The fence posts on both sides were clearly marked with orange paint.

In Montana any fool knew that a fence post painted orange meant no trespassing. It meant prosecution under the law if caught on that land. And up here, especially with a band of rustlers on the loose, the rancher would be prone to shoot first and ask questions later.

Especially this rancher, because the land on the other side of that gate was W Bar property, belonging to Shade Waters.

"What the hell?" Dillon asked quietly as he met her gaze.

"I called Stratton this morning and told him we would be going north up by the Milk River for a few days, to follow a lead," she said.

Dillon felt an odd ache in his chest. She'd lied to her boss, just as he'd suggested she should do. "Are you sure about this?"

"No," she said without hesitation. "If you want to know the truth, I suspect you're setting me up. But Waters lied about having cattle down by the old windmill and Pete lied about seeing someone in that area. I can only assume Shade was just trying to keep me busy. And that makes me wonder if he isn't trying to keep me away from another part of his ranch. You said that stock truck was headed north, right?"

Dillon nodded slowly.

"Toward your old ranch."

"Looked that way."

"Any thoughts on why he would get rid of the rustled calves on your family's old place?"

Dillon smiled at that. "For the same reason you're

thinking. To make it look like I had something to do with it."

She nodded.

"So when I told you about the calves in the back of the stock truck, you *believed* me?" he asked.

"I wouldn't go that far. I wanted to do a little investigating on my own first." She reached into the glove box, pulled out a map and spread it on the seat between them. "Okay, Waters's ranch house is here. Most of his cattle are in this area." She looked up at Dillon. "I had a friend who owns a plane fly over it early this morning."

He met her gaze. "You are just full of surprises."

"The problem is there's no way to get to your old ranch anymore without driving right past Waters's house." She pointed to the map. "Reda Harper's place is past his. According to the map, there used to be a section road that connected with another county road to the east, but that's now part of the W Bar."

"Waters closed the road after he bought our ranch," Dillon said, trying to keep the emotion out of his voice. Waters had had his family's ranch house razed.

"Can I ask you something?"

Her tone as much as her words surprised him. And he knew before she asked that her question wasn't about cattle rustling business.

"This bad blood between you and Shade Waters, am I wrong in suspecting it goes deeper than his ending up with your ranch?" she asked.

Dillon chuckled and looked toward the mountains in the distance. "I told you Nate had an older brother. He was killed trying to ride a wild horse." His voice sounded flat over the painful beating of his heart.

"Halsey was my best friend." He looked at her. "It happened on our ranch."

She let out a breath as if she'd been holding it, compassion and understanding in her eyes. "Shade blamed you."

He nodded. "And my family. Halsey was…" He chewed at his cheek for a moment. "Well, there just wasn't anyone like him. A day hasn't gone by that I haven't missed him."

"It must be worse for Shade," she said.

"Halsey was definitely his favorite of the two boys." Dillon looked down at the map. "So what we need is a way to get to my old ranch without Waters or his men seeing us, right?" he asked, hoping she'd let him change the subject.

"Right," she said, to his relief. "I thought you might have some ideas."

He managed a grin. "You know me. I'm just full of good ideas."

"Let's see if we can find those calves," Jack said. "Open the gate, Mr. Savage. You're about to get us both arrested for trespassing."

JACKLYN WOUND HER WAY among rocks and sage, across open grasslands. As soon as she reached a low spot where she was sure the truck and horse trailer couldn't be seen from the county road, she cut the engine.

The former Savage Ranch land was miles away, but the only way to get there without being seen was by horseback. Water and wind had eroded the earth to the north, carving canyons and deep ravines that eventually spilled into the Missouri River. It was badlands, inaccessible by anything but horseback, and isolated.

They would have a long ride. That's why she'd brought provisions in case they had to camp tonight.

Jacklyn didn't doubt for an instant that Waters would have them arrested for trespassing if he caught them before they could find the evidence they needed to open up an investigation.

"You suspected the calves are buried on my family's former ranch the minute I told you about the dead calves, didn't you?" Dillon said with a grin as they saddled up their horses and loaded supplies into the saddlebags.

She just smiled at him. The truth was she'd had a hard time believing his story. Why kill the calves? What was the point of rustling them in the first place?

But the more she'd pondered the topic, the more she couldn't help thinking about what Dillon had said regarding motive. Was there a chance it had nothing to do with money? That the rustlers didn't want the calves—they just wanted them stolen?

It made no sense to her, but it seemed to make sense to Dillon. If what Buford had told her was true, Dillon had rustled cattle as retribution against his neighboring ranchers and Waters. He hadn't wanted the cattle, either.

Which made her suspicious, given that the current rustlers appeared to have a similar, nonmonetary motive.

"Don't you wonder why the rustled calves are being dumped on my former land?" Dillon asked.

"Like you said, it makes you look guilty."

"But you know I'm too smart for that," he said, grinning at her.

Again Jack smiled back. "Right. You're so smart you would have the rustled cattle put on your land to frame Waters, by making it look like he was trying to frame you."

Dillon laughed, shaking his head.

But the truth was he looked worried. And maybe with good reason. If DNA tests were run on the dead calves he'd seen, she'd bet it would match cattle stolen from the same ranches that he had stolen from in the past.

"What if you never get justice?" she asked seriously.

Dillon seemed surprised by her question. "Isn't that the reason you do the job you do? To make sure justice is served?" He winked at her. "See, you and I aren't that different after all, Jack. We just have our own way of getting the job done."

She watched Dillon ride on ahead of her. He looked at home in the saddle. She'd come to realize there was little Dillon Savage wasn't capable of doing. Or willing to do for justice. Was that why he was helping her now?

As if he felt her eyes on him, he slowed his horse, turning to look back at her. Their gazes locked for a moment. He smiled as if he knew that she'd been studying him.

She looked away, hating that he made her heart beat a little faster. Worse, that he knew it. Dillon Savage was arrogant enough without seeing any kind of interest in her eyes.

"Everything all right?" he asked, reining in his horse to ride next to her again.

"Fine."

His grin broadened. "You don't have to always play the tough guy."

"Who's playing?"

He laughed. "You know, Jack, I like you. I don't care what other people say about you."

It was an old joke, but it still made her smile. Maybe because she knew at least the part about other people was true.

"Some men may hold a grudge toward you," he said as he rode alongside her. "But you and I understand each other."

She glanced at him, wondering if that was true.

SHADE WATERS STOOD at the front window, watching his son's SUV barrel up the road. Nate hadn't come home last night. Where had he been? Shade could only guess. He'd been with Morgan Landers.

Waters waited anxiously, having made a decision. He had to tell Nate exactly what would happen if he persisted in dating this woman.

As the car came to a stop, Shade saw that Nate wasn't alone, and swore. Morgan. Well, he'd have one of the ranch hands take her back to town, because he couldn't put off this talk with his son. He wouldn't.

Waters didn't turn at the sound of footfalls on the porch or the opening and closing of the door. He realized he was shaking, his entire body trembling.

"Nate." He cleared his voice, raising it. "Nate. I need to talk to you. Alone."

He finally turned as Nate entered the room. His son looked like hell. Obviously hungover, as if he'd pulled an all-nighter. Waters felt disgust as he stared at his youngest offspring. If only his elder son, Halsey, had lived.

"Dad…" Nate said, and Morgan appeared at his side,

looping her arm through his, a big, victorious smile on her face.

Shade felt his heart drop. "I want to speak to my son alone." He saw Morgan give a little tug on Nate's arm.

"Dad," Nate began again. "There's something I need to tell you." He didn't sound happy about it. Or was he just afraid of Shade's reaction? "Morgan and I got married last night."

Shade felt the floor beneath him threaten to crumble to dust. He watched his every dream fly out the window. He'd always hoped that Nate would change, that he'd grow up and want to take the ranch to the next level. He'd hoped Nate would make the Waters name known not only all across Montana, but also the Northwest. Maybe even farther. Anything would have been possible.

But as he looked at his son's hangdog face, Shade knew that Nate would only run the ranch into the ground. And Morgan... He looked at her self-satisfied expression and knew she would bleed the place dry, then dump Nate for someone with more to offer.

He saw every dream he'd ever had for the W Bar disappear before his eyes.

"Congratulations," he said, hoping the break in his voice didn't give him away. He stepped to his son and shook his hand, squeezing a little too hard.

Then he kissed Morgan on the cheek, embracing her, even smiling. Both newlyweds were surprised and taken aback. They'd run off to get married, afraid he'd try to stop them. Now they expected him to be upset, even to rant and rave and threaten them.

Clearly, neither knew him very well.

"I wish you both the best," he said, almost meaning

it. "This calls for champagne. You will join me for dinner tonight, won't you?"

They both readily agreed, and Waters smiled to himself.

He'd break the news at dinner.

JACKLYN RODE THE HORSE across sun-drenched, rolling hills miles from the nearest road, the grasses vibrant green, the air sharp with the scents of spring. Dillon rode next to her, his gaze more often than not on the horizon ahead—on land that had once been in his family for five generations.

For a long time, neither spoke. She could see how much Dillon was enjoying this. There was a freedom about him even though she had the tracking monitor in her saddlebag.

They stopped for lunch in a stand of trees, letting their horses graze while they ate their sandwiches. Out here, Jacklyn felt as if she was a million miles from civilization.

After lunch, they rode on again, across land starting to change from prairie to badlands.

"So tell me about your childhood," Dillon said out of the blue once they were back in the saddle. "Come on, Jack, we've got a long ride today. If you don't want me to sing—and believe me, you don't—then talk to me. You a Montana girl or a transplant?" When she didn't answer, he said, "Okay, if you want me to guess—"

"Montana. I grew up around West Yellowstone. I was an only child. My mother taught school. My father was a game warden."

Dillon let out a low whistle. "That explains a lot. Now I see where you get it."

"The game warden father," she said sarcastically.

"No, the schoolteacher mother," he joked, and she had to smile. "See? That wasn't so hard."

"So tell me about you," she said.

"Come on, Jack, you know my whole life story. What you didn't already know I'm sure Buford Cole filled you in on the other night at the steak house."

She couldn't hide her surprise.

He grinned. "Yeah, I saw him talking to you. I can just imagine what he had to say."

"Can you? He said you're a man who holds a grudge."

His grin broadened. "Buford should know. We're cut from the same cloth."

"He also said he wouldn't be surprised if you were leading this gang of rustlers."

Dillon laughed. "You don't believe that anymore," he said as he rode on ahead.

When she caught up to him, Dillon could tell she had something on her mind. "Come on, let's have it," he said.

"I was just thinking how different you are from your cousin Hud."

Oh boy, here it comes. As if he hadn't heard that his whole life. "How is Hud?" he asked, although he knew.

"He married his childhood sweetheart, Dana Cardwell. She owns a ranch in the Gallatin Canyon."

Dillon nodded. He liked her voice, her facial expressions when she spoke. "I heard something about a lost will," he said, encouraging her.

"Dana's mother had told her she made up a new will

leaving the ranch to her, with some of the income divided among the siblings, along with some other assets. For a while Dana couldn't find the document leaving her the ranch, and it looked like she would have to sell to settle with her sister and brothers."

"But the ranch was saved," Dillon said, hating the bitterness he heard in his voice.

Unfortunately, Jack heard it, too. "Weren't you away when your father sold the family ranch?"

He gave her a self-deprecating grin. "You know I was. But then, like I said, you know everything about me. You probably know when I had my first kiss, my first—"

"I know it is hard to lose something you love," she said quickly, to cut him off, no doubt afraid of where he was headed.

"Have you ever lost something you loved?" he asked, studying her.

"Dana's pregnant." Jack looked away as she changed the subject. "She and Hud are expecting their first child this fall."

That surprised Dillon. He hadn't seen his cousin in years. But Uncle Brick had stopped up to the prison a few times a year to give Dillon a lecture and tell him how glad he was that his brother and sister-in-law weren't still alive to see their son behind bars. Brick had also shared the going-ons with the family. The pregnancy must have been a recent development.

"I'm happy for Hud and Dana," Dillon said, meaning it. "A baby." Hud would make a great father. For the first time, Dillon felt a prickle of envy. Hud with a wife and a baby and living on Dana's family ranch.

Settling down had been the last thing Dillon had imagined doing. He'd always told himself he would be bored to death with that kind of life. He needed excitement, adventure, challenge.

Hell, apparently he needed to be running from the law.

"If you don't buy a ranch in the future, what will you do?" she asked.

He'd had plenty of time to think about what he would do once he was really free. "Can you see me behind a desk, wearing a three-piece suit?"

"Yes."

He laughed. "Liar." This felt good between them. Lighter. Freer. He liked it. He liked her, in spite of everything. That surprised him.

"So I guess you'll ranch, since apparently cattle are in your blood."

"Raising cattle so someone can steal them?" He chuckled to hide how close she'd come to the truth. "But then, you'd be around to catch the rustlers, right?"

She looked away.

"Hey, don't worry about me," he said, moving into her range of vision to smile at her.

"I'd hate to see you go back to rustling," she said quietly.

"I'm sure you're aware that my grandfather left me money," Dillon said. "It's not like I need to find a job."

"Everyone needs a job," she said adamantly. "You need something to occupy your mind. Especially *your* mind."

I have something to occupy my mind, he thought as he looked at her.

"How much farther?" she asked, as if feeling the heat of his gaze.

"I think I know where the calves are buried and how to get there." Dillon had been trying to think like Shade Waters. He regretted to realize that it wasn't that hard. He'd gotten to know the man too well. Maybe had even become too much like him over the years.

"On the other side of the canyon," he said. He'd been mulling over why Waters would be rustling cattle. It made no sense. Especially just to kill them. Was he trying to force out ranchers in the county so he could buy their land like he had Dillon's father?

The W Bar was so huge now that Waters had to be having trouble running it all. Dillon doubted Nate was of any help. Nate had never been much of a cowboy, let alone a rancher. Unlike his brother, Halsey, who had loved ranch life as much as Dillon had.

Also what didn't make sense—if he was right and Waters was dumping some of the stolen cattle on the old Savage Ranch—was why? Sure, he and the big rancher couldn't stand the sight of each other, but Dillon was small potatoes. Waters was too smart to risk everything to try to get even with Dillon after all this time. And hadn't he just offered to give back the ranch if Dillon got Morgan out of his life?

But what really worried him was why Buford Cole would be going to the W Bar. Buford had hated Waters as much as Dillon did. Or at least Dillon had thought so.

Ahead, the rolling prairie rose to rocky bluffs. "The canyon will be hot, but the route is shorter this way."

She glanced over at him. Was that suspicion he saw in her eyes?

"It isn't like we've been followed," he said, looking over his shoulder. He could see for miles. No one knew they were here. And yet he couldn't shake the feeling that Waters was one step ahead of them, laying a trap they were about to walk into.

As they rode between the rocks and into the narrow canyon, rocks and trees towering on each side, Dillon felt even more unease.

"Just a minute," he said, reaching out to touch Jack's hand on the reins.

She brought her horse up. "What's wrong?"

He wished he knew what to tell her. How could he explain this feeling? "Let me go first," he said, adding, "I know the way."

The look she gave him said she doubted there was a chance of getting lost in the narrow canyon, but she let him ride ahead of her.

He urged his horse among the rocks. There was no breeze in here, only heat. It felt stifling. That and quiet. He was regretting coming this way when a shadow fell over him.

He glanced up in time to see a hawk soar low over the rocks, its shadow flickering over the canyon for a few seconds before it was gone.

Dillon was literally jumping at shadows. What the hell was wrong with him?

As he turned to look back at Jack, he felt his horse stumble and heard a metal ping like the snapping of a guitar string.

"Get back!" he yelled, and jerked his mount's head around, digging his boot heels into its flanks.

He grabbed her reins as his horse rushed past hers, pulling her with him as the first rocks began to fall.

Their horses bounded along the canyon floor as the air filled with dust and the roar of a rockslide.

CHAPTER THIRTEEN

JACKLYN BENT OVER her horse as Dillon charged ahead
on his, drawing her after him through the tight canyon.

Behind her she could hear the crash of rocks. Dust
filled the air, obliterating everything. Then, suddenly,
they were riding out of the dust, out of the canyon. The
breeze chilled her skin as Dillon brought the horses to
a stop in the open.

"Are you all right?" he cried, swinging around to
look at her.

She nodded. "What was that back there?" she demanded, knowing it was no accident.

"A booby trap."

She stared at him, not comprehending. "You're telling me someone was waiting for us in the canyon? How
is that possible? No one knew we were headed this way."

"The booby trap was wired to set off the rockslide if
anyone tried to come up through the canyon."

"Who would do such a thing?"

Dillon gave her a knowing look. "Who do you
think?"

"You aren't going to try to tell me that Shade Waters
rigged that, are you?"

He gave her a cold stare. "No. I doubt he knows how."

She felt a chill. "But you do." She remembered six

years ago almost getting caught in a rockslide when she was chasing him.

"Oh, my God," she said, drawing back from him.

"The difference is that mine was just to slow you down," he said. "There was no chance of you being hurt."

She shook her head, wondering if she would ever really know this man. It was an odd thought, since more than likely he would be going back to prison. Where he belonged.

"I never did it again," he said, his gaze holding hers. "Too many things can go wrong. I didn't want your death on my conscience."

She realized she was still trembling inside at their near tragedy as she glanced back up the canyon. "You know who rigged that, don't you," she said quietly.

"No, but I used to know some men who were acquainted with the technique."

She turned in her saddle to look at him. "You're talking about the men who rode with you. I've never understood why you didn't give up their names. You could have gotten less time in prison if you had."

"Don't you know me better than that?" With a shake of his head, he added, "I made a lot of mistakes before I went to prison."

"You mean like getting caught."

He locked eyes with her, his expression intense even though he was smiling. "No, before that. I started off with what I felt was a damn good reason for what I did. But if prison taught me anything, it was that, while vindicated, I lost more than my freedom. I'm trying to get that back."

"What do we do now?" she asked, glancing at her

watch. They had been riding most of the day. They were losing light.

"We'll have to go around the bluffs. It will take longer, but it will be safer."

"You expect other booby traps?"

"No. But I'm not taking any chances. The good news is that the rockslide confirmed what we suspected. They had to have gotten rid of the stolen calves on the other side of the canyon. That's why they booby-trapped it from this side."

"Either that or they were expecting us because they know you," she said.

Dillon's eyes narrowed as he looked toward the canyon. "Yeah, that's another possibility, isn't it?"

THE SUN HAD MADE its trip from horizon to horizon by the time they reached the other side of the canyon. The shadows of the bluffs ran long and dark. The air had cooled. They still had a couple of hours of daylight. Jacklyn hoped they'd find the evidence, then ride out to the road, and avoid being forced to camp tonight.

She'd made sure they had the supplies they needed, just in case. There was no telling how long it would take to find where the calves had been buried. She refused to consider the possibility that Dillon was wrong, that Waters had too much land to hide in, that it might be impossible to find the dead calves—let alone that they didn't exist, that she'd been taken in by Dillon.

She concentrated her thoughts on Shade Waters. As arrogant as the man was, he would feel safe, if he was behind the rustling. This part of the ranch was isolated, far from a public road and all his land. He would feel confident doing whatever he wanted back here, she told herself. No matter what happened in this remote section, no one would be the wiser.

And there would be some poetic justice in dumping the cows on what had been the Savage Ranch.

At the top of a hill, Dillon reined in his horse. She joined him, glad to see that they'd finally made it to the old section road. Jacklyn could make out the hint of tracks, faint as a memory, through the grass.

"They left us a trail," Dillon said.

From this point, they could see for miles to the west. Almost as far as Waters's ranch house, but not quite. The good news was there were no vehicles in sight.

They rode down the hill and followed the faint tracks through the deep grass along what had once been a section road between the Savage and Waters ranches. Someone had definitely been using it lately.

There had been a barbed wire fence along both sides of the road, but Waters had it taken down after he'd bought out Dillon's father.

Jacklyn could feel the change that came over Dillon. The land off to their left had once been his. He would have probably been ranching it now if not for Waters.

She saw him looking ahead to the rocky bluffs, and wished she'd known him before he became a cattle thief.

"There's been more than one rig on this road," Dillon said.

"Can you still get out this way?" she asked, thinking that the road must dead-end a few miles from here.

"You can reach the county road, if you know where you're going," he said, pointing to the southeast.

The road wound through the badlands. To the right ahead was the opening to the canyon they'd tried to come up. To the left were more deep ravines and towering bluffs, then miles of ranch land.

As they rode closer to the canyon entrance, she saw the distinct track through the grass where someone had driven off the road back into the rocks. She could hear a meadowlark's sweet song, feel the day slipping away as the air cooled around her and the light dimmed.

She felt an urgency suddenly and rode out ahead, following the tracks. Along with the urgency was an overwhelming sense of dread. How many cattle had been buried back here? She hated to think.

She reined in in surprise where one set of vehicle tracks veered off to the left, while the other headed to the right, toward the canyon entrance.

As Dillon joined her, he reached over and touched her shoulder. "Look," he said, his voice a low, worried murmur.

She followed his gaze to a rock outcropping and saw the glint of light off a windshield. Her gaze met his as she unsnapped the holster on her weapon. Sliding off her horse to the ground, she whispered, "Wait here."

"Not a chance," he whispered back.

Ground-tying her horse, Jacklyn moved cautiously toward the vehicle hidden among the rocks. Dillon walked next to her, as quietly as a cat. The air that had felt cool and smelled sweet just moments before became stifling as she entered the shadow of the bluffs. Crickets chirped from the nearby grass, overhead a hawk cried out as it soared in a wide circle, and yet there was a deathly quiet that permeated the afternoon.

"It's Reda Harper's pickup," Jack said as they rounded the rocks and saw where someone had hidden the truck.

Dillon peered inside. Empty. "You don't think Reda is behind the rustling, do you?"

Jack shrugged. She wouldn't have put anything past the ranchwoman, even rustling cattle. "You have to admit she's smart enough to be the leader of the rustling ring. Otherwise, what is her truck doing here?" She glanced up as if the words had just hit her, and shook her head, dread in every line of her face.

"I'll go have a look, and if everything checks out—"

"Not a chance," she said, echoing his words. "I got you into this. I won't be responsible for you getting killed while I stand by."

He smiled at that. "Be careful," he said softly. "You're going to make me think you're starting to like me."

"Don't you wish," she joked as she strode toward her horse.

Yeah, he did wish, he thought as he watched her swing into the saddle. He reminded himself that this was the woman who'd captured him and helped send him to prison. But the memory didn't carry the usual sting. He smiled to himself as he caught his reins and swung up onto his horse. He was starting to like her. More than he should.

"I forgot that you see me only as a means to an end," he said as he looked at her. "I need to keep reminding myself of that."

She didn't glance at him, but he saw color heat her throat. Had he hit a little close to home or had their relationship changed since she'd gotten him out of prison?

He told himself, as he led the way, that he must be crazy if he thought he might be getting to Jack. True, she wasn't calling him Mr. Savage anymore. She was still ordering him around, but he wasn't paying any attention. And she hadn't sent him back to prison even though they hadn't caught the rustlers. Yet.

All in all, he hadn't made much progress with her. But then, he supposed that depended on what kind of progress he wanted to make. His plans had changed, he realized. He no longer felt any anger toward her. If only he felt the same way about Shade Waters…

The canyon was wider at this end. A few aspens grew in clumps along the sides of the bluffs, their leaves whispering in the breeze as he and Jack rode past.

They hadn't gone far, following the tire tracks in the soft earth, when he spotted the backhoe and the freshly turned earth a dozen yards down a small ravine at one side of the canyon. That the rustlers had used a backhoe to bury the calves didn't surprise him.

It was the pile of rocks that had cascaded down from the canyon wall along one side of the ravine that brought him up short. He let out a curse as Jack rode ahead of him, dismounting near the tumbled heap.

He went after her, already pretty sure he knew what she was about to find when he saw the shotgun lying to one side.

She let out a small cry and dropped to her knees beside the pile. The fallen rocks were shot with color.

"Jack, don't!" Dillon yelled as she frantically began throwing stones to one side. "It's too late."

JACKLYN DIDN'T REMEMBER dismounting and rushing to the rocks. Didn't remember falling to her knees beside the pile or reaching out to touch the bright fabric of a shirtsleeve.

All the time, she must have known what was trapped underneath, but it wasn't until she moved one of the rocks and saw first a hand, the nails short but bright red with polish, then a face contorted in pain and death, that she let out a cry and stumbled back.

Dillon grabbed her, pulling her to him. "There's nothing you can do. She's dead."

Jacklyn pressed her face against his chest, his shirt warm, his chest solid. She needed solidity right now. In her line of work, she took chances. She carried a gun. She knew how to shoot it, but she'd never had to use it. Nor was she in the habit of finding dead bodies. Cows, yes. People, no.

She just needed a moment to catch her breath, to get her emotions under control, to stop shaking. That's all it took. A moment listening to Dillon's steady heartbeat, feeling his arms wrapped protectively around her. She stepped back, nodding her thanks, under control again even if she was still shaking inside.

"We have to call someone," she said, as she dug out her cell phone.

Dillon watched, looking skeptical. "I doubt you'll be able to get service—"

She swore. "No service."

He nodded.

She glanced at the pile of rocks, then quickly turned her head away. "What was she doing here? She must have seen the backhoe in here and walked back to investigate."

Dillon shook his head. "What was she doing on Waters's ranch to begin with?"

That was the question, wasn't it. Everyone in the county knew there was no love lost between the two of them.

"I need to see if I can get the phone to work higher up

in the hills," Jacklyn said, reaching for her horse's reins so she could swing up into the saddle. "I'll ride up—" She heard Dillon call out a warning, but it was too late.

She was already spinning her horse around, only half in the saddle, headed for a high spot on the bluffs, when she heard a sound that chilled her to the bone.

SHADE WATERS LOOKED UP from his plate in the middle of dinner and realized he hadn't been listening. He'd insisted they eat early because he had some things to take care of.

"Shade," Morgan said in that soft, phony Southern drawl of hers. "I asked what you thought about my idea."

"What idea is that, Morgan?"

"Redecorating the house. It's so…male. And so…old-fashioned. Don't you think it's time for some changes around here?"

He could well imagine the changes she really meant. "Definitely," he said. "In fact, that's what I was doing, thinking it was high time for some changes around here."

Morgan looked a little surprised. He was taking this all too well. He knew she kept wondering why he wasn't putting up a fight.

"My first suggestion," he said, looking over at his son, "is that you both move into town."

Nate started in surprise. "What?"

"I'm changing my will in the morning," Shade announced. "I'm not going to leave you a dime. Oh, I know you'll spend years fighting it, but I can assure you, the way I plan to change my will, you'll lose. You'll never have the W Bar," he said, his gaze going to Morgan. "Or any of my money."

For once Morgan appeared speechless.

"Dad, you can't—"

"Oh, Nate, I can. And I will. You have no interest in the ranch. You never have. As for your...*wife*—"

"I think your father might be getting senile," Morgan said, glaring at Shade. "Clearly he is no longer capable of making such an important decision."

The rancher laughed. "I wondered how long it would take before you'd try to have me declared incompetent. Understand something, both of you. I will burn this place to the ground, lock, stock and barrel, before either of you will ever have it." He tossed down his napkin. "I have an appointment with my lawyer in the morning. I suggest you find a nice apartment in town to redecorate, Mrs. Waters. And Nate, you might want to find a job."

With that, he left the room, doing his best not to let them see that his legs barely held him up and he was shaking like the leaves on an aspen. The moment he was out of the house, he slumped against the barn wall and fought to control his trembling as he wiped sweat from his face with his sleeve.

He'd done it. There was no turning back now.

JACKLYN'S HORSE SHIED an instant after she heard the ominous rattle. Both caught her by surprise. She only had one foot in a stirrup as the animal reared. The next thing she knew she was falling backward, her boot caught there.

"Jack!" she heard Dillon yell as he lunged for her and her horse.

She hit the ground hard and felt pain shoot through

her ankle as it twisted. Her horse shied to the side, dragging her with it, the pain making everything go black, then gray.

When her vision cleared she saw Dillon leap from his horse and grab her mount's reins, dragging the mare to a stop before he gently freed Jacklyn's boot from the stirrup.

She would have cried out in pain, but the fall had knocked the air from her lungs. She lay in the dust, unable to breathe, the throbbing in her ankle so excruciating it took her a moment to realize the real trouble she was in.

Out of the corner of her eye, she saw the rattlesnake coiled not a foot from her. The snake's primeval head was raised, tongue protruding, beaded eyes focused on her as its tail rattled loudly, a blur of movement and noise as it lunged at her face.

The air filled with a loud boom that made her flinch.

The snake jerked. Blood splattered on the rocks behind it, then the serpent lay still.

In that split second before she saw the rattler lunge at her, and heard the deafening report of the gun, Jacklyn had seen her life pass before her eyes, leaving her with only one regret.

The boom of her gun startled her into taking a breath. She gasped, shaken, the pain in her ankle making the rest of her body feel numb and disconnected.

Dillon dropped to the ground next to her, her gun still in his hand. Later, she would recall the brush of his fingers at her hip in that instant before the snake struck.

She took deep ragged breaths, eyes burning with tears of pain and relief and leftover fear.

"How badly are you hurt?" Dillon asked as he looked

into her beautiful face. There was no doubt that she was hurting, even though she tried to hold back the tears. Her body was trembling, but he couldn't tell if it was from pain or fright.

"I'm fine," she managed to say, lying through her teeth. He could see that she was far from fine. But he let her try to get to her feet, ready to catch her when she gave a cry of pain and was forced to sit back down.

He handed her the gun. "Let's try my question again. How badly are you hurt?"

"It's my ankle," she said, replacing the pistol in her holster with trembling fingers.

"Let me take a look." He gently urged her to lie down, watching her face as he carefully eased her jeans up her leg. "I don't want to take off the boot yet." She wouldn't be able to ride without it. Also, it would keep the swelling down.

As he carefully worked his way down one side of her boot with his warm fingers, tears filled her eyes. She tried to blink them back and couldn't.

"I don't think it's broken. But if it's not, it's one nasty sprain." He looked past her and saw that both horses had taken off, skittish over the rattlesnake or the gun blast.

"I need to go round up the horses. Will you be all right for a few minutes?"

"Of course."

He nodded, glancing around to make sure there were no more rattlers nearby. "I'll be right back."

"Take your time. I'm fine."

He rose to his feet, then leaned back down. "Do not try to walk on that ankle. You'll only make matters worse if you do."

"I'm aware of that." She sounded as if she would have cried if he hadn't been there.

THE MOMENT DILLON WAS gone, Jacklyn eased herself as best she could away from the dead snake, putting her back to a warm rock. She prayed that her ankle wasn't broken, but the pain of just moving it almost made her black out again.

As Dillon disappeared from view, she felt a sob well up inside her, then surface. She swore, fighting back the urge to give in to the pain, to the despair. How was she going to be able to find the evidence now, let alone ride out of here?

Not only that, the receiver terminal for Dillon's tracking device was on her horse. This would be the perfect opportunity for him to take off. She couldn't very well chase after him. She couldn't even walk, and if he didn't return with her horse...

She looked up to see him leading both horses toward her, and relief made her weak. She was reminded of how gentle he'd been moments before as he'd checked her leg.

"You all right?" he asked, as he knelt down in front of her again.

She nodded, unable to speak around the lump in her throat. He had to have known she'd be worried he might not come back for her.

He reached out and brushed his fingers across her cheek. "Let me help you up on your horse."

She nodded and let him ease her up onto her good leg. His big hands were gentle as he put them around her waist and lifted her up into the saddle.

The cry escaped her lips even though she was fighting to keep it in as she tried to put her injured foot into the stirrup.

"Okay, you aren't going to be able to ride out of here," he said.

"No, I—"

"It's miles to the nearest ranch—and that ranch belongs to Shade Waters. You'd never make it. Anyway, it will be getting dark soon. We'll make camp for the night up there on that hill, and take the road out in the morning," he said, pointing to the southeast.

Clearly, he'd given this some thought already. She shook her head, close to tears. "I can ride. We have to tell someone about Reda."

Dillon pulled off his hat and raked a hand through his hair as he looked up at her. "Won't make any difference to Reda if we tell someone tonight or in the morning."

"You could ride out for help," she said through the pain.

"I'm not leaving you here alone. Tom Robinson is dead. So is Reda. The men behind this have nothing to lose now in killing anyone else who gets in their way."

She met his gaze.

He gave her a slow smile. "Finally starting to trust me? Scary, huh?"

Very. She looked toward the top of the bluff, where he planned to make camp. They would be able to see for miles up there. That's why he was insistent on camping on the spot, she realized. "You think they'll be back, don't you?"

"Let's just say I'm not taking any chances." He swung up into the saddle and looked over at her. "Come on. It's flat up there, with a few trees for shade and wood for a fire."

She wanted to argue, but as her horse began to move and she felt the pain in her ankle, she knew he was right. She wasn't going far. Nor could she leave here without evidence that would finally bring this rustling ring down.

As she let Dillon lead her up the steep bluff, she had one clear thought through the pain: her life was now literally in his hands.

CHAPTER FOURTEEN

THE SUN HAD dipped behind the mountains, leaving them a purple silhouette against the sunset. The air smelled of pine and aspens.

After Dillon had set up the tents and taken care of the horses, he made them dinner over a fire.

Jacklyn watched from where he'd settled her. He worked with efficiency, his movements sure, a man at home in this environment.

She felt herself relax as she watched him. The world seemed faraway, almost as if it no longer existed. Plus the pills he'd given her hadn't hurt.

"Looks like you're always prepared," Dillon had said when he'd found pain pills in the first aid kit she'd brought along with the other supplies.

"I try to be," she'd said, but in truth nothing could have prepared her for Dillon Savage.

A breeze stirred the leaves of the aspen grove where he'd chosen to camp. She stared at his broad back, surprised how protective he was.

"I feel so helpless," she said as he handed her a plate.

"It gives me a chance to wow you with my culinary talents, since dancing is out."

She tasted the simple food she'd brought and looked up at him in surprise. "It's wonderful."

He smiled, obviously pleased. "I had a lot of practice cooking over a fire." He sat down beside her with his own plate. She ate as if it had been days since she'd last tasted food.

He laughed. "I love a woman with a good appetite."

The fire crackled softly, filling the air with a warm glow as blackness settled around them. A huge sky overhead began to blink on as, one after another, stars popped out in the great expanse.

"I've lived in town for too long," she said, leaning back to gaze up at them. She found the Big Dipper, the constellation that had always been her guide since her father had first pointed it out to her as a child.

"This was the part I liked best," Dillon said from beside her.

She knew he was talking about his rustling days. He'd stayed in the wilds, seldom going into a town for anything except supplies. Or maybe to see some woman.

Mostly, she knew, he'd killed what he needed for food. Illegally, of course. She'd found enough of his camps, the coals still warm and the scent of wild meat in the air, but Dillon had always been miles away by that time.

"You know when I left here to go away to college, I never thought I'd come back," Dillon said. "Too many bad memories."

"Halsey's death," she said.

He nodded. "I thought I wouldn't miss Montana. But then, I always thought the ranch would be there if I ever changed my mind."

She glanced over at him, hearing his pain, remembering her own. After she'd left for college, her parents had divorced and gone their separate ways, the life she'd known, her childhood home and her family, dissolving.

She and Dillon fell into a comfortable silence, the fire popping softly, the breeze rustling the pine boughs and carrying the sweet scents of the land below them.

DILLON WAS SURPRISED when Jacklyn began to tell him about her parents, the divorce, the new families they'd made, how hard it was to accept the changes, to bond with the strangers that were suddenly her family.

He sat quietly as she opened up to him. Then he talked about Halsey, something he never did.

But it was a night for confidences, he decided. A night for clearing the air between them. Here, on this high bluff, they weren't an ex-con rustler and a stock detective. They had no shared past. They were just a man and a woman, both with histories they wanted to let go of.

Their talk turned to more pleasant things, like growing up in Montana. Both had spent most of their time as kids wading through creeks, climbing rocks and trees, daydreaming under a canopy of stars.

As the fire burned down, he saw there were tears in Jack's eyes. "How's the ankle?"

"Better."

He couldn't tell if she was lying or not. "Cold?"

She shook her head, her gaze holding his.

"I better check the horses," he said, dragging his eyes away as he got to his feet. She dropped her gaze as well, but he could still feel the warmth of it as he walked down the steep slope to the creek. The horses were fine, just as he knew they would be.

His real reason for coming down here was to make sure the area was secure. Earlier he'd rigged a few devices that would warn him if anyone tried to come up the bluff tonight. He didn't like surprises and he couldn't shake the bad feeling that had settled in his belly the minute he saw Reba Harper's shotgun lying beside the rock pile.

JACKLYN STARED INTO the fire. Sparks rose from the flames, sending fiery light into the air like fireflies. She could feel the effects of the pills Dillon had given her, but she knew they weren't responsible for the way she was feeling about him.

No, just before the rattlesnake had lunged, before Dillon had killed it, before she'd taken the pills, she'd acknowledged she would have only one regret if she were to die at that moment.

When Dillon touched her shoulder, she jumped. She hadn't heard him return.

"Sorry. I didn't mean to scare you." He threw some more wood on the fire.

She gazed into the flames again, too aware of him as he sat down beside her. Her heart was pounding, and all the oxygen seemed to be sucked up by the fire.

"You're trembling," he said softly, his breath stirring the hair at her temple. "Your ankle is worse than you said."

"No, it's not my ankle," she managed to say around the lump in her throat. She turned her face up to the stars, feeling free out here, as if there were no rules. Was that how Dillon had felt? With society so far away, was it as if that life didn't exist? "Dillon…"

"We should get some sleep," he said, rising to his feet.

She grabbed his shirtsleeve and pulled him back down to her, landing her mouth on his.

He let out a soft chuckle. "What do you think you're doing?"

"I'm seducing you," she said, and began to unbutton his shirt.

He placed a hand over hers, stopping her. "I don't think that's a good idea."

"I do." She unbuttoned her own shirt and let it slide off her shoulders.

SHADE WATERS HEARD the creak of the barn door. The ranch hands were all in town, a little treat he'd given them for the night. He listened to the soft, stealthy movements and waited.

He'd thought it would take longer. He smiled to himself and felt his eyes flood, the bittersweet rush of being right.

"Dad?" Nate's voice was tenuous. "Shade?" he called a little louder. "We need to talk."

Shade gave himself a little longer.

"Dad, I know you're in here," Nate said, irritation mixing with the anxiety.

Shade was just glad Elizabeth wasn't here to see the kind of man her son had turned into. Or what lengths Nate would go to. Or for that matter, Shade himself.

"I'm back here," he finally called, and waited. He'd purposely sat on the bench next to the tack room. The only light was the overhead one a few yards down the aisle. He liked being in the dark as Nate came toward him, his son's face illuminated in the harsh yellow light, his in shadow.

"We need to talk."

"There isn't anything to talk about. I've made up my mind."

Nate stopped a few yards from him and didn't seem to know what to do with his hands. He finally stuck them into the back pockets of his jeans and shifted nervously from boot to boot. He looked young and foolish. He looked afraid.

"I know you don't want to cut me out of your will."

"No, I don't," Shade admitted. "But I'm going to."

"This is about Morgan, isn't it?"

"No, Nate, it's more about you."

"What can I say to you to make you change your mind?"

Shade shook his head. "You wanted Morgan. You have her. Or did you get her only because she thought that the W Bar would be hers someday?"

Nate glared at him, fury in his eyes. "You think I can't get a woman without buying her with *your* money?"

Shade said nothing. The answer was too obvious.

"Can't we at least talk about this?" Nate's voice broke.

"There's nothing to talk about, Nate. You made your bed. Now lie in it."

"Like you made your bed when you cheated on my mother?" Nate snapped.

Waters saw an image of Reda Harper flash in his mind. She'd been so young, so beautiful and alive, so trusting. He would never forgive himself for what he'd done to her. He'd made her the angry, bitter woman she was today.

"I gave her up for you boys and your mother." He turned away, hoping that was the end of it.

"Do you think monsters are made or born?"

Waters turned back to stare at his son. "Are you crazy?"

Nate laughed. "Crazy? I'm just like you."

"You're nothing like me," Waters snapped.

"Oh, you might be surprised."

"I doubt that," he said. "Nothing you could do would surprise me."

"How could I not be like you? All these years of watching the way you just took whatever you wanted. You didn't think I knew." Tears welled in his eyes. "You made me who I am today."

Shade felt sick just looking at his son.

"I only wanted something of my own. Morgan—" His voice broke and he sounded close to tears.

"For hell's sake, if you wanted something of your own why would you marry a woman who's been with half the men in the county, including Dillon Savage?" Shade demanded.

Nate nodded, smiling through his tears. "I have to ask you since I won't get another chance. If Halsey had died before you hooked up with Reda Harper…"

"What are you trying to say?" Waters demanded, knowing exactly where Nate was going with this.

"You would have left me and Mom, wouldn't you?"

The big rancher rose to his feet. "I've heard enough of this. A man has to make sacrifices in this life. You need to learn that." He couldn't help the bitterness he heard in his voice. How could he explain true love to a man who'd just married a woman like Morgan Landers?

Nor could he tell Nate what giving up Reda had cost him. That he still regretted it every day of his life and would take that regret to his grave with him. And maybe worse, he'd had to let her go on hating him, let her go on believing that he'd only been after her ranch all those years ago, that he'd never loved her.

Nate would never understand that kind of loss. But he would someday, when Shade was dead and couldn't walk up the road to the mailbox to get the letters in the faded lavender envelopes, trying to keep his secrets.

"So what would you like me to sacrifice?" Nate asked. "Morgan? Maybe my life? Because you and I both know that I will never measure up to Halsey, will I, *Dad*? Isn't that what this is about? Halsey."

"I loved Halsey. He was my son." Just saying his son's name made him ache inside.

"Admit it," Nate said, stepping closer. "If you had the choice, if you could wave your hand through the air and change everything, you'd want it to be me who died instead of my brother."

There it was. "Yes," Shade said, and looked away in shame.

SHE WAS BEAUTIFUL, the black lacy bra cupping her perfect breasts, her skin creamy and smooth. Dillon felt an ache in his belly and felt himself go instantly hard.

Leaning down, he brushed his lips across hers. "Jack, do you have any idea what the sight of you half-naked is doing to me?"

She grinned in the firelight. "I noticed, actually."

"Does this mean you trust me?" he had to ask as he looked into her eyes.

"With my life," she said.

He laughed and shook his head. "I just wanted you to believe that I wasn't behind the rustling. I'm not sure you should trust me with your life, Jack," he added seriously.

"Too late. I already have," she said, and he saw naked desire in her gray eyes.

It was the last thing he expected. And, he realized, the only thing he wanted. "Jack—"

She pulled him to her and kissed him. He dropped to his knees in front of her, being careful not to brush against her hurt ankle as he took her in his arms and kissed her the way he'd been wanting to since the first time he'd laid eyes on her.

Damn, but this woman had gotten in his blood. For the past four years he'd told himself he wanted to get even with her. But as usual, he'd been lying to himself.

He just wanted Jacklyn Wilde. Wanted her in his arms. Wanted her in his bed. He drew back from the kiss to trail a finger over her lips as he searched her eyes, his heart beating too fast.

"There's no going back," he said as he unbuckled her gun belt. "Unlike you, I take no prisoners."

JACKLYN FELT HER BLOOD run hot as he drew his palm down her throat to her breasts. She leaned back, closing her eyes as she felt his fingers slip aside the lace of her bra, his touch warm and gentle.

Her eyes flew open, heat rushing to her center, when he traced around her rock-hard nipple, then bent to suck it through the thin lace, his mouth as hot as the fire he'd started inside her.

She arched against his mouth, wanting him as she had never wanted anything in her life.

He scooped her up in his arms and carried her to one of the small tents, setting her gently down inside it and crawling in after her.

She could see the firelight glowing through the thin

nylon, could still smell the smoke and the pines. It was cold in the tent, but in Dillon's arms she instantly warmed.

He unhooked her bra, baring her breasts to his touch. She hurriedly unbuttoned his shirt, desperate to feel his chest against hers, skin to skin. It was hard and hot, just as she knew it would be.

His hand slipped under her waistband and she gasped as he touched her, finding her wet and ready. Their eyes met. Slowly he unbuttoned her jeans.

"We have to leave your boot on," he said. "I've never made love to a woman wearing her boots. But you know me, I'm up for anything." His smile faded. "Are you sure this won't be too painful?"

She grabbed his shoulders and pulled him down in answer. He wrapped his arms around her and kissed her, teasing her tongue with his, his movements slow and purposeful, as if they had all night. They did.

IT WAS ALMOST DAYLIGHT when Dillon heard a sound and sat up with a start. They'd left the tent flap open. He could see the cold embers in the fire pit and smell the smoke as a light wind stirred the ashes and rustled the leaves on the nearby trees.

But he knew that wasn't what he'd heard. Someone was out there.

Feeling around in the darkness, he found Jack's weapon and slid it from the holster, careful not to wake her. He could hear her breathing softly and was reminded of their lovemaking. Desire for her hit him like a fist. He would never get enough of her even if he lived to be a hundred.

He edged away from her warm body with reluctance,

not wanting to leave her even for a moment. Stopping at the door, he leaned back to brush a kiss over her bare hip, and then rose and stepped from the tent.

Reaching back in, he withdrew his jeans and boots, then put them on, tucking the pistol into the waistband of his pants as he straightened and listened.

Just as he'd feared, he heard a limb snap below him on the hillside. He'd set up some small snare traps to warn him if anyone approached their camp, and knew that was what had awakened him. Now it sounded as if someone was trying to make his way up the slope.

It would be light soon, but Dillon knew he couldn't wait. The noise he'd heard could have been made by an animal. There were deer and antelope here, and smaller creatures that could have released one of the traps.

But his instincts told him this animal was larger and more cunning. This one would find a way up the steep bluff. Unless Dillon stopped him.

How had someone found them so quickly?

He could only assume that one of Waters's men had seen where they'd driven across the pasture. Once they found the hidden truck, they would tell Waters. And he would know exactly where they were headed.

Dillon heard one of the horses whinny. He thought about waking Jack. All he wanted to do was get back to bed with her as quickly as possible. And maybe he was wrong. Maybe there was nothing to worry about.

Moving through the trees, he headed toward the creek and the horses. If someone had found them, he'd be smart enough to take their mounts. It was much easier to run down a man on foot.

As he neared the creek, Dillon stopped to listen again. Not a sound. Was it possible it had just been the wind in the trees? Moving on down the bluff, he saw both horses were still tied to the rope he'd strung between two tree trunks beside the narrow stream. The animals would be reacting if there were any other horses around. But probably not to a man on foot.

Dillon tried to convince himself that everything was fine. And yet as he started to turn, he felt a rush of apprehension. He couldn't wait to get back to Jack.

"Dillon." The voice was soft. One of the horses whinnied again, moving to one side.

In the dim light of morning, Dillon watched Buford Cole step from the shadows. He'd wondered why Buford was going out to Waters's place when he'd seen him earlier. Now he had a pretty good idea.

"You work for Waters." Dillon's words carried all of his contempt.

Buford chuckled, still keeping one of the horses between him and Dillon. "Put down the gun and we can talk about it."

"Doesn't seem like there is much to say," Dillon commented, his heart in his throat. Had Buford come alone? Not likely. Dillon glanced back up the bluff toward the camp.

"She's fine. I thought you and I should talk."

"Too bad you didn't want to talk in town, where we could have sat down with a beer," Dillon said.

"I'm serious, Dillon. Put down the gun and make this easy on both of us."

The last thing he wanted to do was make things easy for Buford. He brought the gun up fast, knowing he would probably only get one shot. Unless he missed his guess, Buford would be armed.

Dillon fired just a split second before he was struck

from behind. He tumbled headlong toward the creek, out before he even hit the ground.

JACKLYN CAME AWAKE instantly, sitting up in the tent and reaching for Dillon as she tried to make sense of what she'd just heard. A gunshot?

The bedroll beside her was empty, but still warm. Dillon was gone, but he hadn't been for long.

Her pulse raced as she scrambled in the semidarkness of dawn to find her holster. Her heart fell even though she'd known what she was going to find. The holster was empty.

Where was Dillon? Her pulse took off at a gallop. The gunshot. Oh God. He would have returned to her if he could have. Her heart was pounding so hard in her ears she almost didn't hear it.

A limb cracked below her on the steep bluff. She froze. A squirrel chattered off in the distance. A bird belted out a short song in a tree directly overhead. One of the horses whinnied. Another answered.

Move! Move!

As she hurriedly pulled on her jeans, she was reminded of her injured ankle. Thank God it wasn't broken. But it was badly sprained. She wasn't sure she could walk on it. What was she saying? She had no choice.

She pulled on her shirt and other boot. Dillon. She fought the tears that burned her eyes. She'd gotten him into this.

And if he was still alive, she would get him out. She dug in her saddlebag and found the second gun she always carried, and her knife. Then, as quietly as possible, she cut a slit in the back of the tent and taking the tracking monitor in its case, crawled out. She continued to crawl until she reached the trees before she managed to get painfully to her feet.

Her ankle hurt, but not as much as her heart. She wanted to call to Dillon, except she knew that would only let whoever was out there know exactly where she was. Dillon wouldn't answer, anyway. If he could, he would have returned to the tent for her.

A little voice at the back of her mind taunted that she was wrong about him. That he was the leader of the rustling ring. That he'd gotten her out here for more than a romp in the tent.

She told the voice to shut up, checked the gun and considered her options. They weren't great. Her first instinct was to head in the direction of the horses. She had a pretty good idea that was where whoever had come into camp would be found, given that the horses sounded restless.

That was where she suspected she would find Dillon.

As much as she wanted to find him, she was smart enough to know whoever was out there was counting on her appearing. Waiting down there for her. Figuring she would hear the gunshot and come to investigate.

It would be full light soon. She had to move fast. She worked her way back through the trees, in the opposite direction from the horses. The going was slow and painful, the ground steep.

When she reached the bottom of the bluff, she stopped in a stand of trees. Opening the case, she took out the receiver terminal, listened to make sure she was still alone, and turned it on.

The steady beep of the tracking monitor filled her

with relief even as she reminded herself it didn't mean that Dillon was alive.

But at least now she knew where he was.

CHAPTER FIFTEEN

Dillon came up out of the darkness slowly. His head hurt like hell and for a moment he forgot where he was. He was so used to waking up in a prison cell that at first he thought he was dreaming. Especially when he saw Buford standing over him.

Dillon groaned and, holding his head, sat up. As he felt his skull and found the lump where someone had hit him, his memory gradually started to come back to him.

"What the hell's going on, Buford?" he demanded, taking in the gun in his old friend's hand—and the fact that the barrel was pointed at his chest.

"You should have stayed in prison."

"I'm getting that," Dillon said. "Look, I don't know who else is with you, but don't hurt Wilde, okay?"

"So it's like that," Buford said with a smirk.

"You know, I misjudged you." Dillon's mind was racing. He knew he'd never be able to get to his feet fast enough to jump Buford before he caught a bullet in the chest. But he had to think of something.

"Misjudged me?" Buford kept looking up toward the camp. Dillon was betting that whoever had hit him had gone there looking for Jack.

"I never figured you for the leader of this rustling ring. Frankly, I never thought you were smart enough. I guess I was wrong." The moment the words were out of his mouth, Dillon saw that Buford *wasn't* the man giving the orders. So did that mean whoever had gone up the bluff was?

"Just shut up," Buford snapped. "Too bad he didn't hit you harder."

"Yeah." Dillon reached back again to rub the bump on his head. "You know, I've always wanted to ask you, were you the one who set me up the day Wilde caught me?"

Buford had always been a lousy poker player. Too much showed in his face. Just like right now.

"Well, that solves that mystery." Dillon kept his voice light, but his heart was pounding. It was all he could do not to lunge at his old friend and take his chances.

"You were always such an arrogant bastard," Buford said.

Dillon nodded in agreement, even though it hurt his head, as everything became clear to him. "It's because I wanted to stop rustling cattle, wasn't it."

"You get us involved and then you want to quit just when we're starting to make some money," Buford said, anger in his voice.

Dillon stared at him, a bad feeling settling in his stomach. "You didn't put all the cattle on the W Bar like I told you to."

"What was the point? No one gave a crap about your warped attempt at your so-called justice. Waters bought out my family's ranch just like he did yours. You didn't see me losing sleep over it. The only reason I'd risk rustling cattle was if there was real money in it and not what you paid us to help."

Dillon let that settle in for a moment. It explained a lot. Buford, Pete Barclay and Arlen Dubois had seemed guilty when he'd seen them. Now he understood why. He'd thought it was because they'd set him up. As it turned out, they'd done that, too—and double-crossed him.

"I've gotta know. Halsey's good-luck coin…I'm betting you took it from his pocket at the funeral."

"You'd lose that bet," Buford said.

Then who? "So who do I have to thank for this lump on my head? Pete?" Buford's expression told him it hadn't been Pete. *"Arlen?"*

"I told you to shut up."

Dillon frowned. If it really hadn't been either of them, who did that leave?

"Where's your girlfriend?" a very familiar voice asked, from directly behind him. Dillon felt his skin crawl, and heard Buford chuckle at his obvious surprise.

As JACKLYN WORKED HER WAY around the rock bluff, the sun broke over the horizon. She would have less cover and more chance of being seen before she discovered what she had to fear.

The wind in the trees sounded like ocean waves. Past the trees, she spotted a pond, its surface pitching and rolling, the chop cresting white as it beat against the shoreline. The wind whistled past her, too, tossing her hair into her eyes.

Last night Dillon had taken out her braid…. Just the memory made her weak. His fingers in her hair… The two of them had made love through the night with an intimacy that she'd never experienced before. There was only one way she could explain it. Love.

The wind groaned in the pine boughs, whistling

through the branches, making it impossible to hear if someone was sneaking up on her.

She pushed on through the tall grass. The sky stretched overhead, a pale blue canvas empty of clouds. But the wind had a bite to it.

She stopped to listen, the wind seeming to be her only companion. Ahead was another stand of pines, dark green. She had to be getting near the creek. Near where she believed Dillon had left the horses. She didn't dare check the monitor again.

Angling down the mountain through the pines, she came across a smaller pond nearly hidden in the trees. There, with the dense pines acting as a windbreak, the surface was slick and calm. She stopped to listen, hearing the wind sigh among the treetops.

A track in the soft mud at the edge caught her eye. She stepped closer, crouching down to study the multitude of animal prints. In the middle of the deer and antelope tracks was the clear imprint of a boot heel.

She froze as she heard something other than wind in pine boughs. The water beside her mirrored the sky, the dark green of the trees towering over her. Something moved in the reflection.

She jerked back, her eyes on the pines, the fallen needles a bed at her feet. Even over the wind, she heard the soft rustle. Not of swaying branches, but something advancing through the grass, moving with purpose.

She unsnapped her holster and rested her palm on the butt of the pistol as she moved, just as purposefully, around the pond.

The wind whipped through the pines, sending a

shower of dust over her. She froze, blinded for one ter-
rifying instant.

Her prey had stopped, as well. A strange silence
fell over the landscape. Shadows played at the edge of
the water.

She started to take a step toward the cool shade in
the pines as it burst from the trees. All she saw was the
frantic flutter of wings. She didn't remember pulling
the pistol, her heart lurching, her breath catching. The
thunder of blood in her ears as the grouse flew past was
too much like the heart-stopping buzz of the rattlesnake.

Jacklyn sucked in a breath, then another, her hand
shaking as she slid the pistol back in the holster. But
she kept her hand on the cool, smooth butt, her eyes on
the trees ahead.

He was here. She could feel him. Unconsciously,
she lifted her head and sniffed the air. Crickets began
to chirp again in the grass. Somewhere off to her left
a meadowlark sang a refrain. Closer, the grass rustled
again with movement.

Once in the awning of the trees, she saw the game
trail. It wound through the pines, disappearing in
shadow. She stopped, crouched and touched the soft
damp earth.

Another boot print.

Few people ever knew this kind of eerie silence. Soli-
tude coupled with an acute aloneness. A feeling of being
far from anything and anyone who mattered to her. Entirely on her own. She'd been here before. Fighting not
only a country wrought with dangers, but also men—
the most dangerous adversaries of all.

Tracking required stealth, so as not to warn other animals of her presence. She'd walked up on her share of bears, the worst a grizzly sow with two cubs. The mother grizzly had let out a whoof, but the warning came too late. The sow's hair had stood up on her neck as she rose on her hind legs, even as Jacklyn slowly began to back away. Then the sow had charged.

Jacklyn knew that running was the worst thing she could do, but in that instant it was a primal survival instinct stronger than any she'd ever felt. Fortunately, her training had kicked in. She'd dropped to the ground, curled into a fetal position and covered her head with one arm as she slipped her other hand down to the bear spray clipped to her belt.

The spray had saved her life.

Just as she hoped the gun would today, because whoever, whatever, was after her was nearby now.

MORGAN LANDERS MOVED around to stand in front of Dillon, flashing him one of her smiles. "I lied about hoping I wouldn't see you again."

"It seems that's not the only thing you lied about," Dillon said. He'd always thought he wouldn't put anything past Morgan, but he was having a hard time believing she'd been the one to coldcock him. He had a sizable lump on his head. Morgan must have one hell of a swing. Unless it had been someone else.

He felt a sliver of worry stab into him as he realized that Morgan had just come from the camp on top of the bluff. "See Wilde while you were up there?" he asked, tilting his head toward the camp.

Morgan's gaze said she had guessed how close he was with the stock detective, and didn't like it. Too bad for Morgan. "As a matter of fact, she seems to be missing."

Dillon felt his heart soar. Jack had heard the shot, and being Jack, she'd known what to do.

Buford swore. "So what are you doing here? Go find her."

Morgan sent him a bored look. "It's being taken care of."

Jack was out there somewhere. She would need an advantage, because from what Dillon could see, there were at least three of them, maybe more. And as far as he knew she wasn't armed. But Jack being Jack she'd have a second gun he didn't know about.

What was also clear was that whoever was running this show wasn't going to let them out of this alive.

"Being taken care of by your boss?" Dillon asked Morgan.

"I don't have a boss," she snapped.

"Right. I could believe Buford was running this rustling ring easier than I could you, Morgan."

"You know, Dillon, you always were a bastard," she said, stepping closer.

He grinned at her. "And you, Morgan, were always a greedy, coldhearted bitch."

She lunged at him as if to slap his face. Buford yelled for her to stop, but Dillon was pretty sure she didn't hear him—or didn't care.

He grabbed her arm, using it as leverage as he pulled himself up, then swung her around in front of him for cover as he propelled her into Buford, knocking him off balance.

Buford's gun went off with a loud boom that echoed in the trees as the three of them, locked in a tangle of limbs, went down.

JACKLYN FROZE as the sound of the gun report filled the air. Her heart lodged in her throat. Not knowing if Dillon was alive or dead was killing her.

Worse, that little voice in the back of her head kept taunting her, trying to make her lose faith in him, telling her it was him stalking her through the trees.

As the gunshot blast died away, she heard the rustle of grass, the crack of a limb and knew he'd circled around her and was now right behind her.

Jacklyn took a breath and turned, her weapon coming up and her mind screaming: *Who are you about to kill?*

He stood just a few feet from her. She could see both of his hands. He appeared to be unarmed. He looked confused, almost lost.

"Nate?"

"What happened to you?" Nate asked, having apparently noticed her limp.

"I sprained my ankle." This felt surreal, as if she was dreaming all of it. She held the gun on him, but he didn't seem to care.

"Any luck catching those rustlers?" he asked, his voice sounding strange, almost as if he was trying not to laugh.

She tightened her hold on the gun. "Nate, what are you doing here?"

"Looking for you. Dillon told me to find you and bring you back to camp."

"Why didn't he come himself?"

"He's hurt."

Her breath rushed out of her. "How did he get hurt?"

Nate shrugged.

"Is it bad?" she asked, her heart beating so hard her chest hurt.

"You'd have to be the judge of that," he said. She wondered if he'd been drinking. She'd never seen him like this.

"Nate, what's going on?" she pressed, the way she might ask a mental patient.

He tilted his head as if he heard a voice calling him. She heard nothing. "Are you here alone?"

"Who would be here with me?" he asked, as if amused.

"I thought Shade might have come with you," she said.

"Oh, that's right, you haven't heard. My father was murdered last night in his barn."

DILLON ROLLED OVER, trying to catch his breath. He felt as if he'd been punched in the chest, all the air knocked from his lungs. His hand went there and came away sticky with blood. He'd been hit.

But after a moment, he realized it wasn't his blood. It was Morgan's.

She lay on her back, staring vacantly up at the morning sky. Her shirt was bright red, soaked with blood.

Dillon tried to get up, but Buford was already on

his feet and holding the gun. The cowboy kicked at his head. Dillon managed to evade him, taking only a glancing blow, as he rolled over and came up in a sitting position, his back to a tree.

"You stupid bastard," Buford swore. "You stupid bastard."

Dillon focused on him, hearing the fear in the man's voice. Buford was pacing in front of him, clearly wanting to shoot him. Had whoever Buford took orders from told him not to kill Dillon?

But looking into his old friend's eyes, he saw that change. Buford raised the gun, pointing it into Dillon's face. "You're a dead man."

JACKLYN STARED AT NATE in shock. Shade Waters murdered? "That's horrible. Do they know who—"

"Sheriff McCray has put out an APB. I hate to be the one to tell you this, but I saw Dillon Savage running away from the barn right before I found my father's body."

All the air rushed out of her as if she'd been hit. "Nate, that's not possible. Dillon was with me last night."

He shrugged. "I guess you'll have to sell that to Sheriff McCray, but since Dillon made his getaway in your state truck, the sheriff thinks you might have been an accomplice."

"What? Nate…" She felt fear seize her. "Nate, that's crazy. No one will ever believe it."

"No? Well, the sheriff says the only reason you got Savage out of jail is that you have something for him. And everyone knows he's the one who's been headin' up this gang of rustlers. I'm betting the rustling will stop once he's back in prison."

She stared at Nate Waters as if she'd never seen him before. She'd never seen *this* man, and he frightened her more than if he had been holding a gun on her.

"You must be in shock," she said, realizing that had to be what was going on.

He laughed as if that was the funniest thing he'd ever heard. "You know my father always blamed me for Halsey's death. Dillon thought he blamed him, but he was wrong. I was the one holding the rope on that horse that day. I killed Halsey. His luck had finally run out. So I took his good-luck coin after I saw Dillon put it in my brother's suit jacket at the funeral."

The good-luck coin found near where Tom Robinson was attacked. Nate Waters had just implicated himself. "Nate, why don't you take me to Dillon," she said, trying to keep her voice even.

"Not until you put down your gun, Ms. Wilde."

"I can't do that." Even though Nate didn't appear armed, he was talking crazy. If anything he was saying was true, then he was responsible for the rustling, for the attack on Tom Robinson, the death of Reda Harper and… Jacklyn felt sick. And apparently the death of his father, Shade Waters.

"The thing is, if you don't drop the gun, I'm going to give my men orders to kill Dillon," Nate said. "His blood will be on your hands."

His men? How many were there? "Nate, why would you do that?"

The smile never reached his eyes. "I think you already know the answer to that. The gun, Ms. Wilde. Drop it and step away."

She didn't move. She had to get to Dillon. But without a weapon, she knew they were both dead.

"Buford?" Nate called.

"Yeah." The answer came from the trees behind Nate.

"Everything all right over there?" Nate asked.

"Yeah. Just a little accident, but everything's okay."

Jacklyn recognized Buford Cole's voice and could tell that things were definitely not all right. She hated to think what that last gunshot was about.

"Well?" Nate asked her with an odd tilt of his head. "You want me to give the order?"

"How do I know Dillon isn't already dead?"

"Dillon?" Nate called.

Silence, then a surprised-sounding Dillon said, "Nate?" as if he'd been trying to place the voice, since it had to be the last one he'd expected to hear out here.

"Dillon," Jack called to him.

"Jack!" His response came back at once.

She heard so much in that one word that tears burned her eyes. "Are you all right?"

"He won't be if you say one more word to him," Nate said in that calm, frightening voice.

DILLON TOOK A DEEP BREATH, weak with relief. Jack was alive and Buford seemed to be using every ounce of his self-control not to pull the trigger on the gun he was holding on him.

The overwhelming relief was quickly replaced with

the realization that Jack was with Nate. And Buford seemed to be losing it by the minute.

So Shade Waters was behind the rustling, just as Dillon had thought. He found little satisfaction in being right though. Shade was dangerous enough. But apparently, he'd sent Nate to tie up some loose ends. Nate was unpredictable. Maybe even a little unstable. No way was this going to end well.

"Oh man, I can't believe this," Buford said again as he began to pace back and forth again, always keeping the gun aimed in Dillon's direction. He looked more than nervous; he looked scared to death. Unfortunately, it only made him more dangerous.

"I can't believe she's dead," he said, raking his free hand through his hair. His hat had fallen off during the skirmish, but he didn't seem to have noticed.

"I think you'd better tell me what's going on," Dillon said, trying to keep his voice calm. "What's Nate doing with Jack?"

"You've messed everything up," Buford said, sounding as if he might break down at any minute. "You killed Morgan. What's Nate going to do when he sees that you killed Morgan? Hell, man, he married her. They were going to go on their honeymoon."

"*You* pulled the trigger," Dillon said. "I didn't kill her. You did."

Buford stopped pacing. His eyes had gone wild, and he looked terrified of what Nate Waters was going to do to him. Nate Waters, a kid they'd all teased because he'd been such a big crybaby.

Dillon felt bad about that now. Worse, because he had

a feeling that Nate Waters was going to kill him. He just didn't want the same thing to happen to Jack. He tried to think fast, but his head ached and Buford was standing over him with a gun, acting like a crazy person.

"You'd better let me help you," Dillon said. "Nate's obviously going to be upset about his wife." Dillon avoided looking at Morgan, lying dead on the ground. Even though she was obviously in this up to her sweet little neck, she didn't deserve to die like this.

Buford was right about one thing. Things were messed up big time.

"I'm telling you, Buford, for old times' sake, let me help you."

The man looked as if he might be considering it, so Dillon rushed on. "Come on, old buddy. Things are messed up if you're taking orders from Nate Waters, anyway. Whatever he's gotten you into, Jack and I can help cut you a deal. But if you wait and he kills anyone else—"

"There a problem here, Buford?" Nate asked as he came out of the trees, holding a gun on Jack.

Dillon groaned inwardly. A few more minutes and he might have been able to turn Buford. Now there was no hope of that.

"It was an accident," Buford said. "Man, I'm so sorry. I…"

Nate pushed Jack over by Dillon. She dropped to the ground next to him and he put his arm around her. He could see that she was scared, and her ankle had to be killing her. But he knew Jack, knew she was strong and determined. And with her beside him, he told himself, they had a chance of surviving this. She owed him a dance. Kind of.

Mostly, he couldn't bear the thought that they'd found each other, two people from worlds apart, only to have some jackass like Nate Waters kill them.

Nate walked over to where Morgan lay dead on the ground.

Dillon heard a small wounded sound come out of Jack. He pulled her closer and whispered, "It's going to be okay."

Buford was pacing again, swinging the gun around. "Oh man, Nate, I'm so sorry. It was an accident. Dillon, man, it's his fault. You told me not to shoot him, but he jumped me. Morgan… Oh man."

"Shut up," Nate said, sounding close to tears. "She was just a greedy bitch who slept with anyone and everyone."

"She was your *wife*," Buford said, obviously before he could think.

Nate turned to glare at him. "She tricked me into marrying her. I don't want a woman who's been with Dillon Savage."

Oh, boy, here it comes, Dillon thought, as Nate swung the gun in his hand toward Dillon's head. Next to him, he felt Jack press something hard against his thigh. Apparently she'd taken it from one of her boots.

A knife.

He slipped his arm from around her. "What? This is about Morgan Landers?" He shook his head and sat up a little, dropping his hands to the ground next to him. "Come on. There has to be more to it than that."

Nate stepped closer. "What would you know about it? You have any concept what it's like to grow up with Shade Waters as a father? To live your whole life in the shadow of the great Halsey Waters? You have no idea."

"So all this is to show your father," Dillon said, closing his hand around the knife handle hidden beneath his thigh. If Nate came any closer…

"It was bad enough that he idolized Halsey but when you started rustling cattle to pay back the ranchers who you felt had wronged you…" Nate took a breath and let it out on a sigh. "The bastard actually admired you the way you slipped those stolen cattle in among his." Waters's laugh held no humor. "You were a damn hero. Even the great stock detective here couldn't catch you. I was the one who put up the hundred thousand dollar reward for your capture from the money my mother left me. He never knew."

"Damn, I wish I had known that. I would have had my friend Buford here collect it." He looked past Nate. "But then he already had, huh?" Dillon remembered the truck Buford had been driving when he passed them, headed for the W Bar. It had been an expensive ride— not the kind of vehicle a man who works at the stock-yards could afford. "So it really was you, Buford, who betrayed me."

Buford Cole had looked frightened before. Now he looked petrified. "Kill him. Just get it over. You said nobody knows where they are. We can bury them with the cattle. Morgan, too. No one will ever have to know."

Nate raised his gun, pointed it at Dillon's head. Unfortunately, Dillon wasn't close enough to reach him with the knife. Nor could he launch himself faster than a speeding bullet. He hoped his life didn't pass before his eyes before he died. He wasn't that proud of the things he'd done.

IT HAPPENED SO FAST that Jacklyn never saw it coming.

She'd buried the hand farthest away from Nate's view, grabbing a handful of fine dirt. She was planning to throw it in Nate's face, anything to give Dillon a chance to use the knife.

But as she raised her balled fist holding the dirt, Nate swung around and fired. He couldn't have missed in a million years. Not with Buford standing just feet behind him.

The bullet caught Buford Cole in the face. He went down with a thump.

But before he hit the ground Dillon was on his feet. He drove the knife into Nate's side.

It took Jacklyn a little longer to get to her one good foot. She hit Nate in the face with the dirt and wrestled her weapon from him.

"Nate Waters? You're under arrest for the murders of Buford Cole, Reda Harper, Morgan Landers—"

"Morgan *Waters*," he corrected, holding his side and looking down at the blood leaking between his fingers, as if he'd never seen anything quite so interesting.

"Shade Waters and the attack on Tom Robinson."

Nate looked up at her. "Tom died earlier this morning."

"The murder of Tom Robinson," she said, her voice breaking.

Nate looked up, his head tilted, as if again listening to something she couldn't hear.

After a moment, he smiled. "Halsey said to make sure they spell my name correctly in the paper. Too bad Shade isn't around to see it."

EPILOGUE

JACKLYN HESITATED AT the door. She could hear the band playing. Glancing at her reflection in the window, she ran a hand over her hair, feeling a little self-conscious.

Her hair was out of its braid and floating around her shoulders. She so seldom wore it down that her image in the glass looked like that of a stranger. A stranger with flushed cheeks and bright eyes. A stranger in love.

She felt like a schoolgirl as she pushed open the door to the community center. The dance was in full swing, the place crowded.

For a while there'd been shock, then sadness, then slowly, the community rallied, and pretty soon even the talk had died down. And there had been plenty of talk. The gossips kept the phone lines buzzing for weeks.

The first shock was Shade Waters's murder, followed by the news that his son Nate had confessed not only to killing him and the others, but also to having been behind all the cattle rustling.

Buford had been one of the rustlers Nate had hired but it was suspected that Pete Barclay and Arlen Dubois were also involved. Nate took full responsibility, though, for all the deaths and thefts, posing for reporters.

Jacklyn had wondered if he'd wished his father was

alive to see it. Or had Nate told Shade everything before he killed him? She would never know.

On the heels of all the publicity came word that
Shade Waters had been dying of cancer and had had but
a few months to live, anyway. Everyone loved the irony
of that, since few people had liked either Waters much.

The community had also taken Reda's death fairly
well—especially when it came to light that she'd been
blackmailing nearly half the county, including Shade
Waters. For years, the sinners in the county had lived
in fear of getting one of her letters, letting them know
she knew their secrets and what it would take to keep
her quiet.

But probably the news that had tongues wagging
the most was Shade Waters's will. He'd changed it, un-
known to Nate, about the time that Nate had taken up
with Morgan Landers. In the will, Shade left everything
to the state except for one ranch—the former Savage
Ranch. That he left to a boys' ranch for troubled teens,
in his son Halsey's name.

"I thought you might not come," Dillon said behind
Jacklyn, making her jump as the band broke into another song.

She turned slowly, feeling downright girlie in the
slinky dress and high heels. She'd even put on a little
makeup.

"Wow," he said, his blue eyes warming as he ran his
fingers up her bare arms. "You look beautiful, Jack. But
then I think you always look beautiful."

She smiled, pleased, knowing it was true. Dillon
liked her in jeans and boots as much as he liked her in
a dress. Mostly he liked her naked.

"You know, I didn't exactly win the bet," he said, feigning sheepishness.

"You said Waters was guilty. True, it wasn't the Waters you meant, but I'm not one to haggle over a bet," she said. "I just had to wait until my ankle was healed before I could pay up."

"Well, in that case, I guess you owe me a dance," he said as the band broke into a slow song.

She stepped into his arms, having missed being there even for a few hours. She looked up into his handsome face, wondering how she'd gotten by as long as she had without Dillon Savage in her life. The diamond ring he'd bought her glittered on her finger, his proposal still making her warm to her toes.

He'd bought a ranch up north, near a little town called Whitehorse, Montana. "I'm thinking we'll raise sheep. Nobody rustles sheep," he'd joked when he showed her the deed. "And babies. Lots of babies. I promise you I'm going to make you the happiest woman in northeastern Montana."

She'd laughed. But she was learning that Dillon Savage was good as his word. The man could dance. And he'd already made her happier than any woman in central Montana. She didn't doubt he'd live up to all his promises.

As he spun her around the room, she thought of the babies they would have, hoping they all looked like him. Except maybe the girls.

"You sorry?" he asked, his breath tickling her ear.

"About what?" She couldn't think of a single thing to be sorry for.

"I just thought you might be having second thoughts

about settling down with me instead of chasing rustlers."

She smiled. "Darlin', there's only one rustler I want to be chasing."

"We can both stop running then. Because, Jack, you already caught him. The question now," he said with a grin, "is what you're going to do with him."

* * * * *

YOU HAVE JUST READ A

HARLEQUIN INTRIGUE®

BOOK

If you were **captivated** by the **gripping, page-turning romantic suspense,** be sure to look for all six Harlequin Intrigue® books every month.

HARLEQUIN
INTRIGUE®

HARLEQUIN

INTRIGUE®

BREATHTAKING ROMANTIC SUSPENSE

Use this coupon to save

$1.00

on the purchase of any
Harlequin Intrigue® book!

Available wherever books are sold, including most bookstores,
supermarkets, drugstores and discount stores.

Save $1.00

on the purchase of any Harlequin Intrigue® book.

Coupon expires August 16, 2013. Redeemable at participating retail outlets
in the U.S. and Canada only. Limit one coupon per customer.

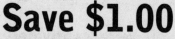

Canadian Retailers: Harlequin Enterprises Limited will pay the face value of this coupon plus 10.25¢ if submitted by customer for this product only. Any other use constitutes fraud. Coupon is nonassignable. Void if taxed, prohibited or restricted by law. Consumer must pay any government taxes. Void if copied. Nielsen Clearing House ("NCH") customers submit coupons and proof of sales to Harlequin Enterprises Limited, P.O. Box 3000, Saint John, NB E2L 4L3, Canada. Non-NCH retailer—for reimbursement submit coupons and proof of sales directly to Harlequin Enterprises Limited, Retail Marketing Department, 225 Duncan Mill Rd., Don Mills, ON M3B 3K9, Canada.

52610790

U.S. Retailers: Harlequin Enterprises Limited will pay the face value of this coupon plus 8¢ if submitted by customer for this product only. Any other use constitutes fraud. Coupon is nonassignable. Void if taxed, prohibited or restricted by law. Consumer must pay any government taxes. Void if copied. For reimbursement submit coupons and proof of sales directly to Harlequin Enterprises Limited, P.O. Box 880478, El Paso, TX 88588-0478, U.S.A. Cash value 1/100 cents.

5 65373 00076 2   (8100)0 11841

® and TM are trademarks owned and used by the trademark owner and/or its licensee.
© 2012 Harlequin Enterprises Limited

HIINC0413COUP

SPECIAL EXCERPT FROM

H HARLEQUIN

INTRIGUE

THE MARSHAL'S HOSTAGE
by USA TODAY *bestselling author*
Delores Fossen

A sexy U.S. marshal and a feisty bride-to-be must go on
the run when danger from their past resurfaces....

"Where the hell do you think you're going?" Dallas demanded.

But he didn't wait for an answer. He hurried to her, hauled her onto his shoulder caveman-style and carried her back into the dressing room.

That's when she saw the dark green Range Rover squeal to a stop in front of the church.

Owen.

Joelle struggled to get out of Dallas's grip, but he held on and turned to see what had captured her attention. Owen, dressed in a tux, stepped from the vehicle and walked toward his men. She had only seconds now to defuse this mess.

"I have to talk to him," she insisted.

"No. You don't," Dallas disagreed.

Joelle groaned because that was the pigheaded tone she'd encountered too many times to count.

"I'll be the one to talk to Owen," Dallas informed her. "I want to find out what's going on."

Joelle managed to slide out of his grip and put her feet on the floor. She latched on to his arm to stop him from going to the door. "You can't. You have no idea how bad things can get if you do that."

He stopped, stared at her. "Does all of this have something to do with your report to the governor?"

She blinked, but Joelle tried to let that be her only reaction. "No."

"Are you going to tell me what this is all about?" Dallas demanded.

"I can't. It's too dangerous." Joelle was ready to start begging him to leave. But she didn't have time to speak.

Dallas hooked his arm around her, lifted her and tossed her back over his shoulder.

"What are you doing?" Joelle tried to get away, tried to get back on her feet, but he held on tight.

Dallas threw open the dressing room door and started down the hall with her. "I'm kidnapping you."

Be sure to pick up
THE MARSHAL'S HOSTAGE
by USA TODAY *bestselling author Delores Fossen,*
on sale April 23 wherever
Harlequin Intrigue books are sold!

REQUEST YOUR FREE BOOKS!
2 FREE NOVELS PLUS 2 FREE GIFTS!

⬥ HARLEQUIN®

INTRIGUE®

BREATHTAKING ROMANTIC SUSPENSE

YES! Please send me 2 FREE Harlequin Intrigue® novels and my 2 FREE gifts (gifts are worth about $10). After receiving them, if I don't wish to receive any more books, I can return the shipping statement marked "cancel." If I don't cancel, I will receive 6 brand-new novels every month and be billed just $4.49 per book in the U.S. or $5.24 per book in Canada. That's a savings of at least 14% off the cover price! It's quite a bargain! Shipping and handling is just 50¢ per book in the U.S. and 75¢ per book in Canada.* I understand that accepting the 2 free books and gifts places me under no obligation to buy anything. I can always return a shipment and cancel at any time. Even if I never buy another book, the two free books and gifts are mine to keep forever.

182/382 HDN FVQV

Name	(PLEASE PRINT)

Address	Apt. #

City	State/Prov.	Zip/Postal Code

Signature (if under 18, a parent or guardian must sign)

Mail to the **Harlequin® Reader Service:**
IN U.S.A.: P.O. Box 1867, Buffalo, NY 14240-1867
IN CANADA: P.O. Box 609, Fort Erie, Ontario L2A 5X3

**Are you a subscriber to Harlequin Intrigue books
and want to receive the larger-print edition?
Call 1-800-873-8635 or visit www.ReaderService.com.**

* Terms and prices subject to change without notice. Prices do not include applicable taxes. Sales tax applicable in N.Y. Canadian residents will be charged applicable taxes. Offer not valid in Quebec. This offer is limited to one order per household. Not valid for current subscribers to Harlequin Intrigue books. All orders subject to credit approval. Credit or debit balances in a customer's account(s) may be offset by any other outstanding balance owed by or to the customer. Please allow 4 to 6 weeks for delivery. Offer available while quantities last.

Your Privacy—The Harlequin® Reader Service is committed to protecting your privacy. Our Privacy Policy is available online at www.ReaderService.com or upon request from the Harlequin Reader Service.

We make a portion of our mailing list available to reputable third parties that offer products we believe may interest you. If you prefer that we not exchange your name with third parties, or if you wish to clarify or modify your communication preferences, please visit us at www.ReaderService.com/consumerschoice or write to us at Harlequin Reader Service Preference Service, P.O. Box 9062, Buffalo, NY 14269. Include your complete name and address.

HI13